Hemlock Flat

Also by the Author

The Broom of God

Exit 8

Hemlock Flat

"This is a story of absence and identity, regrets and redemption, grit and loss and the hard work of love. Atmospheric and tense from the opening page, you won't want to put it down."

Laura Bonazzoli, author of
Consecration Pond: A Novel in Stories

A rich, suspenseful, and layered narrative, with inimitable characters and unexpected plot twists. I was transported to the New Hampshire landscape, which is a character unto itself. The exquisite prose is vivid and crisp.

Celia Johnson, author of
Dancing With Mrs. Dalloway.

"A richly atmospheric, sensual, narrative, with delicious twists and turns. *Hemlock Flat* explores the infinite dimensions of human intrigue—and hunger—that can exist in even the smallest of places."

Robert Klose, author of *Long Live Grover Cleveland,*
Life on Mars, and *Trigger Warning.*

Jonna Bragg, writing as John, is the author of two novels: *The Broom of God,* short listed for the 2017 Banff Mountain Fiction Prize, and *Exit 8,* winner of the 2019 Booklife Prize by Publisher's Weekly and Finalist for the MWPA 2020 Fiction Award. She lives in mid-coast Maine.

Cover Drawing, "The Road," Tony Bragg, tony@tonybragg.com

Hemlock Flat
A Novel

Jonna Bragg

Backroad Press
Camden, Maine
Hemlock Flat
ISBN: 978-0-9964529-5-3
© Backroad Press
All Rights Reserved.

Website: BackroadPress.com
Email: jonna@jkbragg.com

. . .
Then you hold life like a face
between your palms, a plain face,
no charming smile, no violet
eyes,
and you say, yes, I will take you.
I will love you again.

Ellen Bass, "The Thing Is,"
from *Mules of Love*, 2022.

Chapter One

WHEN JIMMY BAKER DROVE over the crest of Penniman Road and saw the arrogant, tapered spire of the Congregational Church silhouetted white against the dark forest and jagged mountains beyond, he realized he'd made a mistake returning. He'd been doing that lately, the mistake part more than the realization. That only came after it was too late.

He pulled over to the side of the road. This approach to the village of Hemlock Flat, New Hampshire, the table-flat expanse of field and meadow spread out at the feet of the Croydon Mountains simmering in the haze, evoked in Jimmy a confusing torrent of emotions. Two ridges reached out from twin summits like arms. A translucent silver quarter-moon—barely visible in the white-hot sky—hovered above the notch between Croydon Peak and Grantham Mountain.

Jet-lagged, disoriented by the long flight from his home in Wyoming and the drive from the Boston airport, he stared at the mountains through the wavering heat of a humid end-of-July afternoon and they seemed to shift and change. If mountains had memories, would these forest-covered crags of ancient granite remember when they were magnificent, snow-blanketed giants, bigger than the Himalaya of today? What did he remember of his time here? Trail-running through hidden dells that time forgot? The sweet summer air and a field of gold and a beautiful girl? Or caged in the back of a sheriff's cruiser, accused of something he didn't do.

He lowered his window and turned off the rental's air conditioning. The humid air, the smell of fresh-cut hay, and the buzzing whine of cicadas in the trees next to the road sent him back to the years he lived here with his aunt and uncle, Paula and George Baker. He was seventeen when he was sent away from Hemlock Flat. He vowed then never to return, and now, seventeen years later, his uncle would be sure to let him know there were still unresolved issues.

New Hampshire folks have long memories.

He drove into the village past old houses with their proud faces and gingerbread scrollwork, most in need of a good scraping and a coat of paint. Chiseled granite posts pock-marked with moss surrounded the village green, and the war memorial at its center was streaked with black mold. He's returned for the funeral of his great-aunt, Altoona 'Tooney' Baker. He owed it to her, but what he really owed her it was too late to deliver: a visit when she was alive.

A tall, dark-haired man in jeans with a deputy sheriff's badge clipped to his belt directed Jimmy to park on Elm Street. There was something oppressive about the place, the trees drooped with humidity, the mountains loomed over the village, dark green pines and near-black hemlocks and slabs of grey rock sucked up the light, and a sense of dread grew stronger as he walked past a long line of cars and pickups to his uncle's house. A cracked stone path led to the front porch. He could hear loud voices through open windows.

In the crowded living room, people stood, red-faced and hot in their good clothes, holding drinks and little plates with small sandwiches. One face, then another, turned to look and it was as though someone, somewhere, turned off the voices with a switch, and the only sound was the soft whir of two window fans.

What the hell?

He'd expected an awkward arrival, but not these sullen, resentful looks. The screen door banged behind him and he turned to see a woman in the tan uniform of the Sullivan County Sheriff's Department rush into the living room. She scanned the crowded room.

"Where's the sheriff?"

She had platinum hair, startling blue eyes. Her uniform fit like he seldom saw a uniform fit a woman, and Jimmy had a thing for women in uniform—didn't matter who, cop, park ranger, soldier—that androgynous hint of masculinity. She was mid-thirties, about his age. Korsak, her name tag read.

His uncle strode toward him through the crowd. He'd put on a few pounds, was turning grey. Why is he in uniform? George Baker put his hand on Jimmy's shoulder, said, "I have to run. We can talk later. Make yourself at home."

With that, his uncle, the Sullivan County Sheriff, followed the deputy out the door. Jimmy looked at the silent living room filled with over-heated, sweaty people, saw two of Paula's grown children, Patricia and Charley. They wouldn't meet his gaze, turned away.

Make myself at home? Yeah, right.

A girl, maybe sixteen, was leaning against the far wall.

Why was she staring at him?

She was tall, fit, with a leggy, coltish look and hair the color of honey pulled back in a ponytail, and was wearing a yellow summer dress and lime-green running shoes, and seemed somehow vaguely familiar.

Next to her was a boy, an inch or two shorter, in hiking shorts, a faded blue polo shirt, and matching running shoes. The girl crossed the room. She had high cheekbones and carried herself with grace and a touch of arrogance, and could well be the model for a Greek goddess, the young Artemis perhaps. There was something of the huntress in her.

"You must be Jimmy." She extended her hand. "Eliza Johnson."

Her grip was surprisingly strong. Her green eyes were flecked with tiny sparks of gold.

"I knew your parents," Jimmy said.

"I know."

"Is your father here?"

"Are you kidding? He never liked Tooney. Anyway, my parents are in New York."

"What about your brother?"

"Will? He's never home," she said with an edge of bitterness.

Jimmy liked to tell people he was six feet tall. He was five-eleven. They stood eye-to-eye in awkward silence. She looked away, surveyed the room. "Seems like you're not real popular around here."

The boy came up next to her, cleared his throat.

"This is my friend Ritchie," Eliza johnson said.

"Richard," the boy said.

"Ritchie, Richard. Whatever."

"Don't you think a person should get to be called by the name they choose?" Jimmy didn't know why he was sparring with the girl, maybe because she was the first person who would talk to him. "What if I decided I wanted to be James, not Jimmy, would you—"

"But you wouldn't, you're the famous Jimmy. Why change? James Baker sounds like some old fart."

Jimmy liked this girl, her flippant attitude, the way she bantered with him. He heard the screen door creak open behind him, saw her flinch, look quickly away. He turned around and saw the deputy who'd been directing traffic scan the room then go back outside, letting the door slap behind him.

"The real James Baker was a big-time political guy," Richard said. "Secretary of State, White House Chief of Staff—"

"Ritchie, sorry, Richard. Why do you know these things?" She punched him lightly on the shoulder. "You're such a geek."

Richard staggered, held his shoulder—a routine they'd done before.

"Not likely to get me confused with him," Jimmy said.

"No," Eliza Johnson said. "You're way cooler." She closed her eyes, opened them on the verge of tears. "I can't believe Tooney's gone. I miss her so much." Richard tried to put his arm around her. She shrugged it away and walked off alone, aware of people watching her.

A sideboard displayed framed photographs from the long life of Altoona Baker. Jimmy saw a picture of Eliza Johnson pushing Tooney in a wheelchair, and another of Tooney in bed, leaning back against white pillows, Eliza sitting close, holding a book, reading to her.

Richard stepped close, said, "It's not right, should be hers," and walked away before Jimmy could speak.

Jimmy found his aunt in the kitchen, her back to him, staring out a bay window. Reflected in the glass, she looked in that moment like a sad little girl.

"Jimmy!" Paula Baker turned, smiled, reached out, pulled him into a hug.

At last, someone who was glad to see him.

"Are you hungry? Can I get you something? A beer?"

Double French doors were open to their screens, and Jimmy stood for a moment gazing out into the gathering darkness, listening to the noises of a teeming New Hampshire summer's evening. He turned back to the room, examined the stainless-steel appliances, polished wide-pine flooring, cherry cabinets, high-tech lighting.

"Quite the kitchen."

"I liked the old one." His aunt seemed nervous. Her hands fluttered over the counter. "Seventeen years, Jimmy. Not a word. Why?" She faced him, reached up, put her hands on his shoulders. "We did miss you. I'm so happy you made it."

He pulled away, walked again to the screen doors.

"Doesn't seem like anyone else is."

"They'll get over it."

He turned back to face her. "Get over what?"

"You haven't heard? Tooney . . . well . . . Tooney left you the house, everything."

"What?"

His aunt returned to the reception. Alone in the kitchen, Jimmy peered through the open door into the living room. People stopped his aunt, talked in hushed tones, looked toward the kitchen. He thought about his great-aunt. She had in her quiet way been important to him during his teenage years, and now she was gone. He didn't know what to feel. Grief? Guilt? He was a washed-up extreme skier who'd never owned anything bigger than a beat-up van. That monster of a Victorian house up Gap Road, near where it dead-ended.

Why on earth would she leave it to him?

Chapter Two

WINDOWS UP, AC ON full-blast, Jimmy Baker peered through the windshield of his car. It was a city house, a classic Victorian with tall windows, ornamental gingerbread, and a steep roof with a round turret-like extension that came to a conical pointy summit, out of place in the middle of overgrown farm fields and acres and acres of forest. A yellowed newspaper article attached to the house's deed reported that it had been moved in pieces from a corner in downtown Lebanon by Mrs. Altoona Baker, an eccentric woman, the article implied, with more money than sense.

He'd planned for a quick, stealth visit. Go the reception to assuage his guilt, then get out of town. He'd brought gear to go hiking in the White Mountains, maybe do a bit of the Appalachian trail. Clearly, that was not happening. Aunt Paula had looked good last night, but not so good this morning. She'd told him to see his uncle at the station, then go to Richards and Ziegler, Attorneys at Law, and barely said another word. Jimmy left her in the kitchen staring out the window. Was she mad at him for staying out all night? Was everyone mad at him?

Certainly his uncle was, yelling at him in front of the entire sheriff's department.

Jimmy, though he'd been ordered to stay away from the place, had driven by Bill Johnson's farm after the reception yesterday, parked on the road, and sat in the car remembering the summer he'd worked there, his last in Hemlock Flat. Big ff'ing deal. What happened back then with the Johnson's nanny was not his fault. Why was his uncle such a hard-ass?

Was it the house? Was that it?

They should be mad at Tooney, but being mad at someone who's dead is nowhere near as satisfying as directing your anger at the living. No way he was keeping the heap. He'd clean it up, sell it. Could use the money. Somebody—a rich doctor from Hanover or a Dartmouth professor—would want it, but when he looked more closely his heart sank: the grey paint was peeling; the wrap-around porch slouched in the middle; the roof needed work.

I should have checked the place out before I signed. Why do I always know what I should have done when it's too late to do it? The sun burned through thin overcast and promised another day of scorching heat. God, I feel like shit. Hungover. Again. Why the hell did I drive up to Killington last night?

He looked at the packet of papers and the big steel ring with six old-fashioned keys lying on the passenger seat, thought about returning to that lawyer, handing him the keys, driving to the airport, and grabbing the first flight back to Wyoming to hie empty apartment. Katrina, his girlfriend, had moved out, but maybe he could find her, patch things up, start over.

Fat chance.

He sighed, killed the engine, grabbed his rucksack out of the back seat, opened the car door, and stepped out into the heat and humidity. Maybe it's not as bad as it looks.

Indeed, it wasn't.

The entrance hall was magnificent. In his years working as a carpenter to support his skiing, before he became famous by almost eating it during filming on a mountain in Alaska and finally got sponsored, Jimmy had never done work like this: raised panel wainscoting, elaborate crown moldings, coffered ceiling.

He dropped his pack, stepped into the middle of the parquet floor, did a little dance step, twirled three-sixty with his arms spread, then stopped, embarrassed, though there was no one there to see. He thought back to the ballet classes he'd done at the University of Utah when he lived in Salt Lake City that were supposed to help his skiing—flexibility, balance—not sure they had, but he'd loved being surrounded by all that femininity, those beautiful, glowing young women.

Exploring the house was like wandering a museum. Murky oil paintings occupied the walls, porcelain figurines filled shelves, and antique stuffed furniture crowded the rooms, and lace doilies graced dark wood tables.

Time warp city.

A spectacular staircase climbed to a landing, then curved left on its way to the second floor. He ran his hand over the polished handrail, admired the twisting, carved balusters, the polished oak treads. A long, open second-floor balcony ran the width of the entrance hall, the entire back wall of which was covered with framed photographs. Even as a young girl growing up in New Hampshire, Tooney had towered over her parents. In Texas with her husband, Herbert Baker, George's uncle, she looked straight ahead and held the camera's gaze, a strong woman, handsome but not beautiful, prominent chin, hair up. Why, Jimmy wondered, had she never re-married after Herbert died? Another series of photos showed Tooney and Eliza Johnson. He saw the girl grow up as Tooney aged.

At one end of the balcony was a hallway with four bedrooms, two on a side. Three looked like they had never been used, but the fourth had been slept in: the bed carelessly put back together, rumpled towels draped over a bar on the wall, a book on a bedside table had a bookmark. A faint hint of lavender drifted in the room.

At the other end was another hall. Across from a large, tiled bathroom was what must have been Tooney's bedroom. Twice the size of the other rooms, it had a big four-poster bed draped with a white lace canopy. An ornate deep-blue oriental carpet covered most of the floor. Jimmy wondered what it was worth. Two large double-hung windows with blue damask curtains filled most of the far wall. He walked to the windows, tied back the curtains, light filled the chamber, and it seemed to him that everything in the room shrank from the intrusion. A large dresser of white-painted wood and a matching dressing table occupied the wall to his left; to his right were double six-panel doors of cherry that led to a deep walk-in closet and dressing room that stretched the entire width of the bedroom. On one wall, a long iron bar was hung with dresses, blouses, skirts. Opposite was a wall of built-in shelves with countless pairs of shoes—high-heels, flats, boots, lined up in perfect order side-by-side—and rows of drawers with fronts of cherry and white porcelain knobs.

He opened a drawer, found carefully folded underwear, in another, pairs of stockings.

A full-length mirror on the end wall was flanked by a comfortable chair in a light blue brocade laced with threads of silver, and an old-fashioned dressmaker's form covered in tan canvas with adjustable bosom and hips. Four crystal light fixtures hung from the ceiling.

Jimmy walked the length of the closet trailing his hand, lightly touching silk, linen, lace, satin, caressing the soft fabrics, entranced by the colors, blues and greens and yellows. And reds, some almost pink, others dark with traces of black. He remembered his mother's closet when he was young, so different, so plain.

He took down a blue dress with a white trimmed neckline. The cloth was light and deliciously soft. He held it up, looked at himself in the tall mirror, returned the dress to its hanger.

He returned to the bedroom, stunned. What was he supposed to do with all this?

At the dressing table, he lifted a heavy sterling-silver hairbrush, the matching hand mirror, held each for a few moments, then returned each to its place. There was a large rosewood jewelry box with intricate veneer inlays. He pulled out each drawer and found carefully arranged jewelry: necklaces in one drawer, bracelets in another. He opened the top to find rings—some silver, others gold. A third drawer held earrings, arrayed in pairs.

Again, how much was all this worth? This time, the thought felt unworthy.

There was a black, lacquered box of cosmetics. He took out a crystal jar, unscrewed the silver top. It was filled with light pink rouge. He looked around as if someone might be watching, then ran his finger across the dry, powdery surface, felt the slippery smoothness of it, brought his finger to his nose to find the faint scent of roses.

He imagined Tooney dressing with care each morning, choosing her clothing, doing her make-up, selecting her jewelry.

He returned to the first floor. The kitchen table was covered with a red and white checked tablecloth, and on the tablecloth was a cream-colored envelope with his name written in his great-aunt's thin, spidery script. Jimmy picked it up, felt reluctant to open it. He held the envelope in his left hand, flicking it against his right when he heard a tapping at the window. A face—moon-like, pale—appeared, then was gone. Jimmy rushed out the door, ran to the back of the house. No one. He scanned the hard ground beneath the window. Nothing. Had he imagined it? Maybe a trick of the sun glancing off the dirty glass? He looked across the empty fields toward the mountains shimmering in the haze, saw an animal flash across the dark wall of the forest. He stuffed the envelope into his back pocket and walked uphill toward the mountains on a narrow game trail trampled in the dry grass. Wildflowers on both sides of the path were parched brown remnants of their once bright yellows and purples and blues.

It had been two years since the accident, though calling what happened an accident was a bit of a stretch, but some days, his legs still hurt deep in the bones. Other days he was good as new.

It was brutally hot. He thought about turning back, but decided to cut over to Gap road, and once on the packed dirt of the road where tall maples arched over his head, he was able to walk more easily in the deep, green shade. Tooney's place was the last house on the road before it became little more than a jeep track. He rounded a corner and stopped, dumbstruck. There in front of him was a chain-link fence fifteen feet high, cutting across the road. He'd almost walked into it.

What the hell? Then, he remembered this road had been blocked off when he was living with his aunt and uncle, but he'd not seen this massive fence before.

There were orange and black signs every twenty feet: KEEP OUT. NO TRESPASSING.

The fence extended into the woods in both directions as far as he could see. Heavy metal posts were sunk into the ground, the bottom of the chain-link buried. He leaned close, peered through the diamond patterned wire at a dense forest that rose steeply uphill. A slight breeze drifted down the rocky mountainside and passed through the fence, bringing to him the cooked smell of granite in the sun, the bitter tang of evergreens, the damp, rich aroma of moss and decaying leaves, and something darker: a rank, animal smell.

All the way back to the house, he wondered, who were they trying to keep out? Or, what were they trying to keep in?

When Jimmy reached the house, the front door was wide open. From the porch, he heard noises inside, doors opening and closing.

Eliza Johnson, in running shoes, pink shorts, and a silver tank top, stood in the middle of the kitchen. Drawers were pulled out, cupboard doors hung open. The poised young goddess from the day before was frantic, frazzled. Her tangled hair hung in damp strands down the back of her neck, and her face dripped with sweat.

"What are you doing?" Jimmy said.

"It has to be here somewhere! She said she would leave it for me in the kitchen. I have to find it."

"Are you in the habit of barging into people's houses?"

"It's not yours, it's Tooney's. This house will always be hers. I don't care who you are." She slumped into one of the metal framed kitchen chairs and looked up at him with pleading eyes. "This was like my real home." A strangled sob.

"Let me get you some water." Jimmy went to the sink, filled a glass, put it front of her.

She looked at it like she didn't know what it was, then picked it up and drained half of it in a single pull, said, "This house always had the sweetest, coldest water."

Jimmy filled a glass for himself, sat across from her, and was struck by a memory, a dream perhaps? She seemed so lost that he felt a sharp pain in his chest.

"What are you looking for?"

"None of your business."

She rallied and became again the self-possessed child-star she had been at the reception. She stood, walked out into the grand entrance hall, looked around.

"So, this is yours now. What are you going to do with it? She was my aunt, not really yours. She should have left it to me."

"You're a kid."

She danced across the floor, did an arabesque, a jeté. She was somehow both graceful and clumsy at the same time.

"I love this place . . . I'm going to miss it. You better take care of it."

"You can visit if you want."

Why he said that he wasn't sure, since he was certain he'd be out of here as soon as he got his shit together. What's to miss, this big, drafty thing in the middle of nowhere?

"Yeah, right."

She walked quickly to the front door, scanned the driveway as if expecting someone, then darted into the living room. She plopped down on a vast, maroon velvet sofa with carved wooden arms shaped like lion's claws. A cloud of dust swirled up into the pale, yellow sunlight slanting in through the tall windows, and she sat as if floating in a golden cloud.

"It was in this room, you know."

"What?"

"Hospice. They brought in all this hospital stuff. I was here when she died. She talked about you near the end. Why weren't you here?"

She looked at him, waited for him to say something, but his throat squeezed so tight he couldn't speak. Still, she waited, her look almost pleading. Still, he was silent.

She stood, turned away, went to the front hall and returned with a photo from a past where a handsome older woman stood next to a beautiful younger woman holding a baby. The women wore white summer dresses with bright yellow ribbons in their hair, and the baby a little knit cap of the same yellow. Tooney was tall, striking; Harriet Johnson, gorgeous, radiant; Eliza, cute and lovable.

A hand grabbed his stomach and squeezed.

"You remind me of your mother," he said when he could finally speak.

"I was four when she died." Eliza held the frame in both hands, as if it contained some great secret. "I kind of remember someone holding me and this feeling that everything would be okay . . . I've never felt that way since . . ." She placed the framed photo on the table next to the couch, said, "Can you miss someone you barely knew?" She lifted her hair off her neck, said, "It's so hot."

She held a delicate silver chain from which dangled a teardrop pendant of silver and pale blue stone. Her hands fluttered like birds in a cage, the necklace swinging back and forth.

"Can I have this?"

"Of course. Is that what you were looking for?"

She seemed nervous; her eyes darted this way and that as though she worried someone might come into the room at any moment. Jimmy had never known anyone who could change so quickly: sad, despondent; in an instant angry; then alight with a childish glee; then jumpy, almost frightened.

"How did you get here?"

"I ran. Bet I could beat even you, the great Jimmy Baker." She pulled a curtain aside, peered out the window. "I have to go." It was as if she was in motion, standing still.

"It's too hot. I should give you a ride."

"No. I want to finish my run."

Jimmy walked onto the front porch where poorly tended rose bushes and honeysuckle vines withered in the heat. Eliza ran her fingers through her hair, tied it back in a ponytail. She surveyed the front yard as if to make sure it was safe to go, then turned to look at him.

What was in that gaze, so innocent yet frank, so shielded yet open?

Then she was off, striding down the driveway. She seemed to flow inches above the ground, effortless; her ponytail lifted and bounced behind her. She slowed at the end of the driveway, looked back, gave a little wave, then, to his surprise, turned uphill toward the mountains, not down toward the village and the shortest way home.

Jimmy continued to look at the end of the driveway, and it was as if she'd left behind some vaporous hologram of herself hovering there.

The sun had settled behind the Penniman hills to the west. Where had the day gone? The clinging humidity and the sounds of a New Hampshire summer evening—so familiar—made him feel, despite himself, that he was in some way home. He watched the last light leach from the sky, and then realized he was about to spend his first night in his house. He started to laugh. His house. How fucking weird was that?

A hot, still night. Jimmy pulled the lace canopy off the four-poster and pried the windows open, but the air didn't move. The sheets were damp with sweat. He couldn't get to sleep.

In the station this morning, he had watched a bead of sweat leave Deputy Korsak's hairline and wander slowly down her neck, and had waited to see if she would wipe it away. Though not quite beautiful in the classic sense, she had something special that made her so. In the midst of attraction, a strange, brief pang of envy. The deputy Jimmy had seen outside his uncle's house—Gaetz by his name tag—had come up to him, and said, "Don't get your hopes up, kid," then leaned close. His breath stank of cigarettes and stale coffee. He whispered a single word in Jimmy's ear, then stepped back, shook his head, said, "Shame though, what a waste."

A mosquito whined somewhere in the room. He could hear it, that horrible whinging noise, coming closer. He waved his hand, it disappeared. Then it was back. His slap left a ringing in his left ear.

Questions circled like the mosquito. Why was he here? What was he doing with his life? He realized that he had still not, even after seventeen years, moved past the heartbreak of his last summer in Hemlock Flat, the summer he'd worked for the Johnsons. They say that your first love never leaves you, and if that's true, then it must also be true that your first heartbreak never goes away.

He untangled himself from hot, sweaty sheets, and went downstairs to the kitchen. He looked in the refrigerator for something to drink even though he knew it was empty. He carried a glass of water to the back steps, and looked across the meadow as mist filtered through the tall weeds and an owl called somewhere in the woods, and clouds drifted in the dark, silvered sky. He heard tapping on the kitchen window. He put down the glass, slipped silently around the corner of the house, and saw a hunched figure standing on a block of wood, peering in the window, tapping on the glass.

Jimmy crept up and dragged them away from the window. "What are you doing?"

The figure crumpled to the ground, and as the clouds moved away from the moon, Jimmy could see it was a man in ragged clothes.

"Get up," Jimmy said.

The man sat on the block of wood. He was big, bulky, but somehow child-like. He smelled of stale sweat, urine.

"Where's Tooney? She talks to me. She's nice to me." He had a small voice that didn't match his size.

"What's your name? It's okay. I'm not going to hurt you."

"Lonnie."

"She's dead, Lonnie. I'm sorry."

"No. She can't be. She's my friend."

Lonnie looked away, wouldn't meet Jimmy's gaze.

"Off you go, Lonnie."

He scampered away, hunched over, partially sideways, crab-like. Jimmy heard him laughing as he disappeared into the mist drifting over the field.

It was too hot to go back inside. He got the ultralight screen tent he'd brought from Wyoming out of the car and pitched it on the front lawn.

He lay on his back wearing a silk nightie that he'd taken from Tooney's closet; the distant smell of her perfume lingered like a vision from a dream that fades after waking.

The black sky was stippled with high cirrus and the waxing quarter moon lit the mesh canopy of the tent above him with a chalky luminescence, and the night was cluttered and somehow sentient: owls hooted, frogs croaked, creatures rustled in the weeds, and he felt himself close to the loneliness that was the truth of things.

The world went silent in a heartbeat.

He heard something rustle in the overgrown garden, rasp through the dead tomato plants that hung from rotted stakes, then a sough, like a slow wind through the leaves of a parched tree. A hot, pungent animal smell moved across the lawn toward him. Moist breathing, low rumbling in a throat came closer. He held his breath, lay absolutely still as padded footfalls circled the tent, though for reasons he did not understand, he was not afraid.

An animal brushed against the mesh of the tent. The footsteps stopped. A grumbling sigh brought the smell of blood and meat. Silence, then soft steps moved away, and after some moments he heard in the distance a deep, resonant growl, and the small noises of the New Hampshire night returned and he breathed again.

Tonight, he wouldn't sleep and the lustral moon would set and the sky return to star-studded black and he would lie on his back and listen to the sounds of night and above him the Big Dipper would circle the North Star, and then, just before dawn, dive for the horizon trailing its tail behind it.

Chapter Three

Never had Anna Korsak thought when she'd taken the job as Deputy Detective in the Sullivan County Sheriff's Department that she'd be required to supervise the removal of the mangled, decaying body of a calf from a field, but that's what she did last night, and now as she pulled into the sheriff's department, despite a late shower and another this morning, and a perhaps overly enthusiastic application of Santal 33, the smell of rotting flesh still lingered on her skin, hidden behind the scents of cardamom and sandalwood.

She couldn't get the image of that dead animal out of her mind, the belly ripped open, pink and grey intestines looped over the ground crawling with maggots. What could do that? George Baker had muttered something about farm dogs.

Cars and pickups filled the parking lot of the station in Newport and spilled out onto Route 10. Near the front door, Deputy Dick Gaetz, head of the Enforcement Division of the Sheriff's Department, leaned against a dark green truck with the shield of New Hampshire Fish and Game on the door, smoking a cigarette.

"What's with all the cars? What's going on?"

"Korsak. About time. Don't you smell nice."

Another day, another wisecrack from Gaetz.

He took a drag, dropped the butt, crushed it with his foot. She felt his eyes as she brushed past.

The station was in chaos, phones rang, deputies ran in and out of the side door.

"What's going on?" Anna asked Lorraine in Dispatch, hoping for an answer this time.

"The Johnson girl is missing."

Through the glass partition, Anna could see the sheriff in his office gesturing to her.

"Eliza Johnson went running Sunday after the reception," George Baker said. "You must have seen her there. Tall girl in a yellow dress? That was day before yesterday. Hasn't been seen since. Fish and Game is organizing a search based at the elementary school parking lot."

"Want me to head over?" The village of Hemlock Flat was on the other side of the Croydon Mountains.

"No. I need you to man the fort here for the morning. I'm taking Gaetz. I've sent Paul Arnold to interview the neighbors. I'll leave Dennison and Jenkins in case something else comes up. McCarthy and Nathan are on road patrol. Fish and Game has volunteers coming in from all over. Bringing in a couple of choppers. We're setting up a temporary headquarters in the school. Meet me there this afternoon. We'll decide how to proceed. You need me, I'll be on my cell."

Why, she wondered, was she always being asked to man something?

Anna settled at her desk as the station emptied. She could hear Connie Armstrong, the station manager, on the phone telling someone where to volunteer for the search.

Eliza Johnson. Who the hell is Eliza Johnson? Anna often felt that she was expected to know the name of every kid in the county. She'd been here barely a year, and face it, she didn't.

So, ask Google.

Eliza was the daughter of Bill Johnson—some sort of local big-shot—and his first wife, Harriet Lindsay Johnson, now deceased. There was a step-mother, Eva, and a brother, Will, four years older, currently enrolled at the University of Vermont. As she scrolled through the online archive of the Valley News, Anna realized the girl was something of a local sports star. Field hockey: scored the winning goal in the state semi-finals. Anna remembered playing field hockey when she was in high school—the chance to smack all those snotty girls with a stick almost made up for having to wear the silly skirt and knee socks. Cross-country skiing: Eliza was first in the state. Anna didn't get the point of skiing, and worried that if she lived in New Hampshire long enough, she'd end up trying it, landing on her butt, and making a fool of herself. Running: Eliza was captain of the Lebanon High School Cross-country Running Team, and tried to enter the Boston Marathon, but wasn't old enough. And if those weren't enough accomplishments to make Anna dislike her, there was her volunteer work. The kid was practically a freaking saint. The old folks home in Lebanon, kids groups, 4-H, whatever the hell that was.

There was a photo from last fall's New Hampshire Cross-Country Running Championships of Eliza with two other girls on a three-tiered podium. She was a good four to five inches taller than either of them. The girl had a striking physical presence. She stood straight, proud, unlike many tall girls who slumped as if apologizing for their height. The photo triggered a memory. She accessed the Manchester Union Leader archive, searched, "missing girl runner," and found a series of articles. Sally Hopkins, star on the Manchester High School Cross-Country Team, had disappeared while on an evening training run three days before Thanksgiving, barelt two weeks after her victory in the championships. Her body was found in the woods near Pawtuckaway State Park three days later. Raped. Strangled. No one was ever charged.

Why is it the perfect ones, Anna wondered, the stars, the beautiful young women, who go running at dusk, end up in danger? Is it that they're so good at everything they think they're invulnerable? That nothing bad could ever happen to them?

She went back to the photo from the state championships, zoomed in on the caption: Eliza had placed second to the same Sally Hopkins, and now Eliza was missing. Anna felt air move on the back of her neck. Her email dinged, a report from Paul Arnold asking her to follow up on his interview with one of the Johnson family's neighbors. She picked up the phone, confirmed Eliza's father was home.

Why wasn't he out searching?

George had told her to stay put, but no way was she going to sit around doing nothing.

Tall, evenly spaced poplars lined both sides of the drive leading to the Johnson farm. What was the point, Anna wondered, of a paved driveway when you lived on a dirt road? The house, a white, two-story colonial with add-ons added to add-ons, looked more like a small college than a residence. A long, low building with a columned porch led to a bigger structure that was painted red like a barn, but judging by the tall, elaborate windows, was clearly more house.

She parked in front of the main entrance. A maid answered the door.

"He's in the barn," she said, and closed the door before Anna could ask, "Which barn?"

There were three, arranged in a U shape. She followed a crushed stone walkway past plantings of rhododendron, azalea, and beds of roses, saw someone working in a vegetable garden off to the side of the house. The first barn was filled with stacks of large, shrink-wrapped rounds of hay. The center barn, the largest, had four stalls on each side, wood planked with black metal bars above. She peered into the first. A magnificent black horse looked at her, snorted, kicked the wall. She jumped back.

"Watch out," an older man, dressed in overalls and a short-sleeve plaid shirt, said. "He's a mean one."

"Mr. Johnson?"

"Nope. He's out by the breeding pens." He looked her up and down. "He's kinda busy."

"So am I. I'll try not to take up too much of his time."

She found Bill Johnson wearing jeans, a faded polo shirt, and tall rubber barn boots standing with his arms draped over the top rail of a four-bar, steel-pipe fence watching two rust-colored, hairy creatures with wide-spread horns. The larger one paced, pawed the ground sending up pale dust that swirled in the hot sun.

"Scottish Highland cattle," Johnson said as if he'd read her mind. "Best meat you can find."

"Mr. Johnson, I'm Deputy Korsak. Mind if I ask you a few questions?"

His hair was classic salt and pepper. He was two or three inches shorter than she was, maybe five-six max, a little soft around the middle. Where did Eliza get her height?

"You have news?"

"The search is ongoing. We're doing everything we can to find your daughter."

"I'm sure you are and we appreciate your efforts." He kept his attention on the two animals.

Anna was impressed by how insulting Johnson could seem even when he was being polite.

"Did you talk with Eliza when she got home after the reception?"

"My wife and I were away."

"Any idea where Eliza went on her run?"

"She left a note. Dick has it."

One of the cows slammed against the fence, startling her. It was so hot, the air so thick with animal stench, that she found it hard to breathe, hard to focus. Finally, she said, "When did you realize she didn't come home?"

"Not till this morning."

"Two days went by before you noticed she was missing?"

"I came back from New York early because two cows are about to give birth. I've been busy with them. Eliza comes and goes as she pleases."

"Why did you finally report it?"

"My wife became worried."

Anna couldn't shake the feeling she'd missed something, but could sense his impatience, as if he was much too busy for all these questions, though leaning against a fence like some cowboy in some lame western watching shaggy-assed beasts run around in the dirt did not seem all that important. The bigger animal was circling faster, kicking up more dust. She felt it coat her face, clog her throat.

"Deputy Arnold talked with Otis Thrasher."

"Of course he did. What did my fine neighbor have to say?"

"He said he heard a very loud argument coming from the vicinity of your barn Wednesday of last week."

Johnson shifted, put a foot on the lower paddock bar, turned to face her, his elbow on the top rail. "It was a family matter, Ms. Korsak. None of your business. Are you offering family counseling services now?"

"It's Deputy Detective Korsak, sir." He smirked and Anna was sorry she'd taken the bait. "Your daughter is missing, that makes everything to do with your family my business. Mr. Thrasher recognized your voice, said you were arguing with a female, but wasn't sure who. Was it Eliza?"

"Otis, Otis. I wouldn't put too much stock in anything that old man has to say." He shifted his position again, waited before continuing. "My wife and I were leaving that afternoon, and Eliza and I had a disagreement about her plans while we were gone."

"What plans?"

"That was the problem. She wouldn't tell me. Do you have children, Deputy? Teenagers?"

She didn't answer.

"I thought not. Everything is a disagreement with teenagers, especially this one."

It came to her, what she'd missed. "Who did you give Eliza's note to?"

"Deputy Gaetz. Shouldn't you know that?" Johnson stared at her. "Dick's a good friend, comes by during breeding season, happened to be here early this morning, likes to watch the action." He turned back to the scene in the corral. The bull had a huge erection. It snorted, pawed the ground. The cow turned away.

"Come on, big boy."

"What?"

"You should see this. Look at that equipment."

The bull cornered the cow, placed his forelocks on her back, mounted, and began thrusting violently. Johnson watched intently, breathing hard. His face was flushed, sweat-sheened.

Jesus, Anna thought, he's getting turned on. She turned to leave.

"One thing, Deputy."

"Yes?"

"Thrasher recognized my voice, but not the female's? That's strange don't you think?"

"Why's that?"

"Since he knew Eliza quite well. She was over there all the time. Too much for my liking."

Anna couldn't understand his lack of concern for his daughter. As she walked toward her car, there was a distant rumble of thunder, felt through the ground more than heard in the over-heated gunmetal sky.

Jimmy Baker descended the grand staircase and stopped in front of the full-length mirror at its base. Gold-plated ivy grew around the silvered glass. He felt a fluttery, timorous excitement looking at himself in his great-aunt's clothing: mid-length blue dress, embroidered scoop neckline, silver and blue necklace, and above it all his wide-eyed, surprised face. It was strange how Tooney's clothing seemed to fit him perfectly.

The front door opened and there was Aunt Paula holding a bag of groceries staring at him with her mouth open.

"Oh! . . . Oh dear!" She put her hand to her chest, struggled to draw breath, turned to go.

Jimmy wanted to run back upstairs, instead he said, "You might as well come in."

She marched into the kitchen. he followed, high-heeled shoes clacking on the hardwood floor.

"I need to sit down," Paula said. "You look so much like her, I thought Tooney was still alive, that the funeral … all of it … hadn't happened, and the last few days were just a bad dream. Why would you—"

"I'm sorry, I didn't mean to upset you. I was thinking how I never really knew her, and now it's too late, and I was looking through her things, and all her clothing is so beautiful, then . . . I don't know . . ."

There was a long, awkward silence. Finally, Paula said, "Clothing was so important to her."

Jimmy watched his aunt struggle to regain her composure until she seemed to somehow accept him as this strange reincarnation of a woman who'd died just days ago. They sat at the kitchen table looking at each other with a startled how-did-we-get-here look.

He became aware of himself in the dress, heels. Looked away.

"Don't worry about it, dear. You look quite nice. Better looking than Tooney ever was . . . but you must do something about your hair."

They looked at each other, started giggling, then laughed so hard they couldn't speak.

Had he ever laughed with his aunt like this? Who was this woman?

"I thought you might need some food." Paula stood, started putting things away, then stopped, and turned back to him with an expression he couldn't read. "You were family, Jimmy, only twelve when your mother dropped you off, and I remember you changing Patricia's diapers when she was a baby, then playing with her when she was older. I can almost see the two of you there, sprawled on the floor with that old dollhouse George's mother gave her, moving the little pieces of furniture around, laughing and giggling . . . Did you ever think of her? That she would miss you? We took you in, cared for you. What happened? You didn't write. You didn't call. You never answered my emails. No one knew where you were. When Tooney died, we had to hire a lawyer to find—"

She stopped mid-sentence as if out of breath, and stood there looking at him. The air in the kitchen seemed to thicken, and he regretted, again, returning to this place where everyone seemed to blame him for something, and every place was filled with heartache.

"I ..." Jimmy thought back to the pain, the rejection when he was sent away. How could he explain? "At first, I was pissed off, then the longer it went, the harder it was to break the silence."

"I don't know whether to smack you or hug you. Do you have any idea why Tooney left you all this?"

"No. She was a mystery to me."

"Are you going to stay?"

"Why would I?"

Paula flinched as if she'd been slapped, and Jimmy regretted his flippant remark. But really, why would he stay?

"I don't suppose you have tea?" Paula said after a moment.

"I found some instant coffee."

He put water on to boil, found two coffee cups. He could feel his aunt's eyes on him. Her amused acceptance felt like a challenge.

"When you were a teenager, it seemed like you were always mad at something, at someone. Certainly you had reasons . . . you worked so hard to be this tough guy. I should have tried harder to understand. I never knew what to do to help you. I—"

"Aunt Paula—"

"Call me Paula. I mean, really . . . It's just us girls." She struggled to contain more laughter.

"Paula—"

"Oh, Jimmy, relax. I don't care if you want to wear a dress. With all that's going on in the world, how could it possibly matter? You seem quite nice. Not so angry. Gentle. Don't lose that when you go back." She took a sip of her coffee. Made a face. "My god, that is dreadful."

Jimmy was proud of his appreciation of bad coffee, but his aunt was right, it really was awful.

"I have to go. My wifely duties, you know."

"You won't tell . . ."

"George? Goodness no. This'll be our little secret."

She turned at the door, gave him a little wiggle-fingered wave.

He went slowly back upstairs carrying the shoes, reluctant for what seemed a special moment to end. He lifted the necklace off, unclipped the heavy earrings, placed them gently on the dressing table. The lobes of his ears throbbed. He watched in the mirror as he pulled the dress slowly over his head, took off the lace underwear, put on his baggy shorts and t-shirt. He felt a lingering sense of loss, as if he'd found something small and precious, but then misplaced it, as if he was less than he had been, there in the kitchen, talking with his aunt in a way he never had when he lived with her and her young family all those years ago.

A helicopter flew past, low; the bedroom windows rattled in their frames.

Paula Baker started her car, but couldn't bring herself to drive away. She looked through the windshield at Tooney's house, tall and grey against the pale sky, and thought back to when Tooney had moved to Hemlock Flat after the death of her husband. The air conditioning was slow to kick in and Paula felt sweat trickle down her cheek, then realized it wasn't sweat but tears, and she was crying and soon she was racked with sobs, tears and snot streaking her face.

Where did this devastating wave of sorrow come from? Was it seeing Jimmy and the shock of thinking, for just one moment, that Tooney wasn't dead and gone, and that there was still time to get to know her better? Were these tears for Tooney, or for herself, for her failure to be a better friend to an old woman who lived alone?

She pulled herself together and managed to drive home, but couldn't stop thinking about Tooney. What could have possessed her to leave the house to Jimmy, George's sister Sandra's only child? He wasn't really a Baker—he'd changed his last name after his parents divorced. Tooney had no children, there were whispers that after suffering a terrible miscarriage she couldn't, but nothing was certain, nothing actually spoken. So much about Altoona Baker was a mystery, but she never did anything without a reason. And, when the will was unsealed at the memorial reception, and all her worldly possessions and the house and twenty-six acres of land had been left to Jimmy, and him not even there yet, there had been a loud gasp.

"Who?" someone shouted.

Paula looked around her beautiful, modern kitchen, but could think only of the old kitchen and what was gone: scratches on the cabinets, dents in the floor, drawings on the refrigerator, dated marks on the door jamb, signs that three children had lived and grown, safe and happy, in this house. It had been good to see Charlie and Patricia yesterday, but why did they visit so infrequently, and why had they been so cold to Jimmy? Tracy, her youngest, had stayed in New Mexico after finishing college, and Paula was still not used to this emptiness, and found it hard to remember how the noise and chatter of her children had echoed off these walls, and their clutter had filled these rooms, and she had been busy and needed.

Why do they have to grow up and leave?

With those memories, her eyes filled, and she was crying again.

What is happening to me?

The refrigerator clicked on and the faint hum of its motor only made the silence seem deeper, somehow ominous. The air in the kitchen was heavy and thick and her damp blouse clung to her back.

She stood at the sink, but couldn't bring herself to wash the last dishes from George's breakfast, and went out the back door to the deck and down into the garden. She gasped as the sun hit her. Everything was wilted, the soil baked dry even though she'd watered yesterday. She couldn't remember the last time it rained, couldn't remember the way the air became dense and the leaves on the trees lifted their faces to the clouds before the first few drops fell and hit the ground with little slaps, raising first the odor of burnt dust and then the rich green smells of trees and grass, and couldn't recall how her garden came to life and seemed to grow right before her eyes.

Across the flats, the Penniman hills, brown and barren and criss-crossed with dirt paths worn into the hillsides by Randy Emerson's livestock, hovered in the haze, and looked to her unreal, like something out of Africa in one of those nature shows, open savannah, sere grasslands, widely scattered trees, and the dairy cattle arrayed across the hills became indistinct shapes that could be elephants or wildebeest on the vast Serengeti. In this unrelenting heat, the world had become unreliable to her, and could no longer be counted on to be what it was, what it should be, and the Croydon Mountains were no longer what she had known them to be all these years, and seemed now to her unfathomably deep, to descend into depths rather than ascend to heights. Over the years George had dealt with accidents in those mountains: deaths, lost hikers, rescues, body recoveries. And she had been a bystander to it all.

She moved the soaker hose, turned it on to a trickle, and stood looking at the rows of vegetables and flowers, lost in thought. A deep sound, felt in her chest, seemed to come from far underground.

Had Tooney been the last of the Lindsays? Harriet Lindsay Johnson, Tooney's niece, had been gone for years. She had been Paula's best friend despite the difference in age, Harriet trying for her first child while Paula was dealing with the chaos of three. Harriett was smart, educated, and they talked about books, life. She introduced Paula to yoga and got her to start eating better. Paula turned to look back at the deck where they once sat on summer afternoons sipping lemonade as Paula's children played on the grass. How could someone so alive, so healthy, get suddenly sick and die at such a young age?

Oh, Harriet—

That Harriet in her absence could disturb her thoughts this way gave Paula the feeling that it was dangerous to remember one to whom you had been close, that the past could reach out and grab your heart and squeeze it the way the super-heated air over the garden squeezed her chest and made it hard to breathe.

Her phone pinged. A text from George asking her to meet him at the elementary school. What? George never texted. She didn't think he knew how.

The sun was a fiery ember above the western horizon by the time Paula reached the school parking lot. Over-heated men and women straggled in from the nearby woods, climbed out of dirt-spattered pickups, grabbed bottles of water from shrink-wrapped bundles, then stood near big misting fans. She spotted George's empty cruiser parked next to a dark green truck with the New Hampshire Fish and Game Department shield on its door.

What's going on?

Eva Johnson, wearing white cropped pants and a pale-blue sleeveless blouse that rippled like moving water, walked toward her. She was a beautiful woman, exotic for the small-town world of Hemlock Flat. She'd married Bill Johnson not a year after Harriett's death, and her return from Sweden to the Johnson family, and the speed of that courtship had sent small-town tongues wagging.

"Eva, what are you doing here?"

"She went for a run. I told her it was too hot. She never listens to me." She shook her head slowly, said, "Have you seen my husband?" Then walked away without waiting for an answer.

Paula wondered again, what was going on?

Deputy Dick Gaetz came up to her. "Mrs. Baker, how nice to see you. Can I help you?"

None of the other deputies called her Mrs. Baker, and she sometimes wondered if he was making fun of her, and felt somehow uncomfortable around him.

"I'm looking for my husband."

A Fish and Game pickup pulled into the parking lot, skidded to a stop. George got out. Paula pushed her way through the crowd of deputies and rangers toward her husband. His face was pale and splotched with red, his shirt sodden with sweat.

"George, what's going on?"

"Eliza Johnson has disappeared."

"What? When?"

"Hasn't been seen since the day of the reception."

Why, Paula thought, am I the last to know?

She looked through the haze at the gnarled mountains glowering above the edge of the village. They were getting closer, it seemed to her, creeping up on them all. She felt again that low, distant sound. She watched Anna Korsak talking to another deputy. Anna seemed to sense her gaze, turned away. George strode off toward the cooling fans. Paula followed in his wake. The fan's mist on her face almost made her believe that the weather was going to change, that this parched season would end, but as she walked back toward her car all she could feel was the suffocating heat and a growing sense of impending disaster.

❖

Anna Korsak had thought she would escape this kind of heat and humidity when she left Boston, that it would be cool up here in New Hampshire with refreshing breezes wafting down from beautiful mountains.

It's never this hot, the locals said. Yeah, right. It was and had been for days.

She didn't have AC—her second-floor apartment in Lebanon was like an oven—she had fans, one in the living room window, one in the kitchen, and a funky looking ceiling fan in the bedroom. She'd thought the thing was decoration, some cultural reference to an old Humphrey Bogart movie, but when it moved air down over her naked body at night, she realized she couldn't sleep without it.

She draped her uniform over the old couch she'd found on Craigslist and stood in front of the living room fan in her underwear. She pictured the searchers out scouring the woods and hills for the girl, and they would, these good country folk, slog and sweat in the heat for days looking for one of their own. You had to admire the way an entire community would come together in a crisis, but when the crisis passed and the search was done, would they disappear back into their big, white houses, their nice, private lives? And when a family had problems simmering just below the surface who would take the time to notice?

Eliza Johnson. Nobody was that perfect. Something about the girl annoyed Anna. The privilege. The success. The good works. It was too much, and in photos she seemed posed, stiff, her bright, cover-girl smile not quite matching her eyes, which were clouded and troubled. It seemed obvious to Anna that the Johnsons were not the picture-perfect family that everyone thought, and Anna knew about troubled families, about secrets, growing up with them, living with them, and how they can torment you from the inside.

What was Eliza Johnson's secret?

It was too hot to stay in the apartment. Crystal's, her favorite hangout, was air conditioned.

She peeled off her damp underwear, took a cold shower.

What to wear?

Anna sometimes missed the city, the anonymity, the freedom. Before she moved in with Jess, her girlfriend of a year, she'd lived in Allston in an apartment even worse than this one, and on a humid, restless night like this she could put on leather shorts, a black bra and see-through top, and spike her hair and be this bad-ass chick and go out and tear it up. But here, everywhere she went, Anna felt eyes on her; here, everything she did reflected on the department.

She loved clothes, but deciding what to wear had always been a struggle. Mornings had been hard when she lived with her family in a working-class neighborhood in Dorchester. Who was she that day? She'd been a tomboy growing up, but when the talk during her first year in high school made it back to her parents, she went totally girly, did her hair in waves, wore make-up, heels to school. Dresses. Short skirts. She might have overdone it, because after one year her parents sent her to St. Mary's Catholic School, and she became another nice Catholic girl in a white blouse, plaid skirt, and knee socks, getting ready to go to a good Catholic college, and then marry a handsome Catholic boy. It had been a relief, though she never admitted it, to know each school morning what to wear, to not have to think about it. She still had trouble. What was her style? Femme? Butch? She had things from Tomboy, a great pair of Wildfang cropped pants in an outrageous black and white check, but she also liked to wear skirts, dresses (Ann Colson, Michael Kors, thrift shop finds), liked feminine things, jewelry, a little make-up.

She put on a black bra. No. Then a neutral. Better. She pulled on jeans—too hot—took them off, tossed them on the bed, put on a pair of red shorts, looked in the mirror, took those off.

What is wrong with me?

Tried a short, patterned skirt—better—a plaid blouse, no, then an off-white Yayoi Kusama scoop-necked T, a present from Jess. She loved this shirt, had loved it almost to death. The screen-print was faded, the fabric threadbare.

Why do all good things come to an end?

She stopped at the small mirror near her front door, tied her hair back, grabbed her shoulder bag, and headed down the stairs into the heat.

Chapter Four

PEOPLE FILLED THE DARK interior of the church in two parallel lines, and as Jimmy Baker walked between those two lines toward the open casket at the far end of the weirdly elongated nave he wondered why they were staring at him, and then he realized he was wearing the blue dress with the white trim and his face was made-up, and he felt his breath being stolen from him as he walked up to the casket and looked down at Great-Aunt Tooney in the same blue dress. And then he was lying in the casket looking up at Tooney, and she was looking down at him, and Lonnie was next to her, looming over him, laughing. The lid of the casket closed, and Jimmy was in the dark, and he heard tap-tap-tapping on the lid of the casket, and he woke, slick with sweat, in the big bed.

He lay on his back as the ghost of a feminine fragrance drifted in the room. The old house creaked and groaned, and something scurried in the ceiling over his head. Raccoons squabbled in the trees nearby, a bobcat screeched somewhere in the forest behind the house, and from the mountains came a distant, high-pitched howl, like a baby crying, and bugling, like elk, which was impossible because there were no elk in New Hampshire.

He picked up a t-shirt from the floor, pulled it over his head, went downstairs and out onto the back porch. The mountains were a black void in a silver world of faint starlight. He heard tree frogs call to each other and small animals rustle in the tall weeds, and then it all went silent so abruptly it was like going deaf. A shadow moved in and out of the pools of mist that hung over the meadow, its long, curving tail twitching as it crept slowly through the weeds. It pounced, something squealed, there was a brief struggle, then it bounded forward and was gone, as if it had never been there at all. The earth breathed again, the night noises returned, and birds near the house began waking before dawn.

In the kitchen, four-thirty in the morning, Jimmy knew he would never get back to sleep. He picked up the letter from his great-aunt, and read it for the third time.

> Dearest Jimmy,
>
> It may surprise you that I address you in such an intimate fashion, but though you visited me here at Mountain Manor only a few times, each of those encounters left a vivid impression upon me, and I came to feel that we are, in many ways, kindred spirits.
>
> It also, I have no doubt, must have surprised you that after all these years I have left the Manor and all my possessions to you. I hope that you will come to love this house and this place as much as I have, and that it will become an anchor for your life. Please take care of Eliza Johnson. She has been a good friend to me.
>
> I have followed your skiing exploits (yes, even this old lady has learned how to use the internet at the library), and have been aware of some of the trials and tribulations in your personal life.
>
> Keep your courage up! We have all faced such difficulties.
>
> This place has, through its unique qualities, helped me through the most difficult times of my life and will, I am

sure, do the same for you.

Please don't think me forward or presumptuous, but it is time for you to settle down.

As you read this, you know I am gone, but I have always believed that our spirit never leaves the place we love most. I will be with you in the times to come.

With love,

Altoona Lindsay Baker

He put the letter, wrinkled from being jammed in his back pocket, down on the kitchen table, and tried to smooth it out. Mountain Manor. Seemed to be a New Hampshire thing, buy a place, give it a name. He'd always thought it pretentious. Bill Johnson called his place Running Acre Farms. What the hell is a running acre? And, how did this place get to be a manor? And, why should he take care of a girl who had parents and seemed more than capable of taking care of herself? He kept working on the thick sheet of stationery, smoothing it left, then right, but the thing wouldn't lie flat. It was a sweet, loving letter, but who was she to tell him it was time to settle down? He kept flattening the letter as if smoothing out the wrinkles would somehow squeeze the weirdness out of it.

He returned to the back porch. A single light in the village of Hemlock Flat refracted up through the humid air. Another lonely soul who can't sleep?

Again, that dark silhouette moved across the field. It stopped, seemed to stand up on two legs. Jimmy shook his head, rubbed his eyes, blinked; it was still there, a tall, dark profile. The mist closed in, obscuring the figure, then drifted away. It was gone.

What the hell was that? God, I'm losing it.

Above the mountains, hints of the coming dawn. He stood there bare-assed in his t-shirt, sweating.

Damn, it's going to be another scorcher.

The morning simmered, and Jimmy festered in the kitchen until he couldn't stand the inactivity. He was restless, needed exercise, and was burning to know what was inside that chain-link fence, so dressed in climbing shorts, tank top, approach shoes, and carrying a daypack with two water bottles and a couple of power-bars, he walked up Gap Road to where it was blocked by the fence. He squeezed his hands into the diamond shaped openings of the chain-link, felt the wire crusted with thick galvanizing, and wished he'd brought gloves. He pushed the toe of his right shoe into one of the openings—his feet would not get much purchase.

He craned his neck and looked up. Doable, but not as easy as he'd thought.

Jimmy was prone to obsessions. Once an idea got into his head, he had to see it through. Sometimes that was good: it took him to the top of the extreme skiing world. Sometimes, it was not so good: he broke both legs three years ago going off the Olympic Ski Jump in Park City, Utah in his alpine skis. It wasn't the going off that was the problem, it was the landing, and that was only a problem because he'd been going so fast he flew past the landing slope and came down hard on the flat runout area. Got himself arrested for trespassing in the bargain. They let him off with a warning. Seemed the judge felt him being in a wheelchair with both legs in casts was punishment enough. All because, standing there in the near dark in the venue's parking lot with a couple of friends, he had wondered, wondered is all, if he could do it.

He pulled up onto the fence, trying to keep his weight on his feet, moved his hands, slick with sweat, up, then his feet, then again, and again. He reached the top, hands throbbing, half-blinded by sweat, thought about climbing down, being smart for once, but then thought that as long as he had to climb down, he might as well climb down on the other side, which had been the point all along. He wrapped his left hand around the top of a post, worked his feet up, swung a leg over. The fence wobbled, his foot slipped, and he found himself perched with the top of the fence working its way up his butt-crack. There was no time to ponder how stupid the whole idea had been as he was in danger of getting a full-on rectal exam by the damn thing.

He swung his other leg over, felt one of the sharp wire ends tear across his thigh, then he was on the other side, backing down. The wire tore at his hands. Blood streaked his forearms. He got about halfway down before he couldn't hold on any longer and dropped to the ground.

He heard something crack, felt a twinge in his ankle. Fell on his ass.

He sat there for a while, saw that he'd landed on a stick, flexed his feet, stood. Everything seemed to work, but his hands were raw meat, blisters on the pads torn open and bleeding. Blood trickled down his left leg.

Okay, smart guy, now what?

The forest was darker and wilder on this side of the fence. He came on a narrow game trail and followed it up and away from the fence toward the summit of Grantham Mountain. Tendrils of mist drifted down the mountainside and humidity dripped off the needles of hemlock and spruce. Jimmy felt the touch of eyes, the hair on his neck stood. He heard something crashing through the undergrowth, coming closer. He froze, held his breath, then heard it moving away. He clambered over jumbled rocks covered with moss, scrambled alongside a rounded ridge of rock the looked like the humped back of some giant prehistoric beast buried long ago. Huge boulders leaned, ready, it seemed, to tumble down on him. He came to a ragged, low cliff line. The open mouth of a cave breathed out a dark, rancid smell.

After about two hours, he stopped, finished one liter of water, started on the second.

The trees became smaller as he climbed higher. He bush-whacked through grasping balsam fir up steep talus, his feet on branches and twisted, gnarled trunks, stepping from one to the next without touching solid ground, until at last the trees thinned and he climbed onto an open slab of granite that rolled up toward the sky. Even here, high on the mountain, it was deathly hot.

❖

Day two of the search for Eliza Johnson. More than one hundred volunteer firefighters, rangers, sheriff's deputies, and townspeople scoured almost fifty square miles of forest. Two helicopters from the state's Search and Rescue Department flew back and forth along the foothills of the Croydon Mountains. One flew close, the pulsing of its rotors shaking the walls of the school classroom George Baker had chosen for a temporary office. He figured it was just for the PR, those helicopters, the forest canopy was so thick they could be of little help.

Another brutal, hot, humid day. Folks had been searching for hours, pushing themselves to the edge of exhaustion as concern for the fate of one of the village's favorite daughters rose. I'm gonna need to call some of them in, George thought, or we'll be looking for them as well.

Lieutenant Joe Colson of New Hampshire Fish and Game's Search and Rescue Team rapped on the doorframe. He was tall, rugged, with the weathered face of a man who spent a lot of time outdoors in all kinds of weather. His dark green uniform was patterned with sweat. He went to the window where an ancient air conditioner struggled to keep up with the broiling day outside and stood in front of the vent.

"Sending the choppers back to Concord," Colson said. "Can't see anything. Waste of time." He stepped away from the AC unit. "Mind if I sit?"

"Help yourself."

"Tell me about the girl."

"She's sixteen, a cross-country runner. Last seen wearing pink shorts, a silver top, and green running shoes. According to her coach at the high school, she's one of the best in the state. Trains on the trails around here. Seven, eight miles is nothing to her."

"What the hell is she doing running in this heat?" Colson said.

"She's always been a bit reckless, pushes things too far. I figure she got injured, a leg or something, can't walk."

"She didn't call on her cell? Teenagers never go anywhere without their phone."

"Not this one. She leaves it at home."

"I've got two more K-9 teams coming. Labs. If she's out there, they'll find her." Colson stood, turned to leave. He stopped in the doorway, forcing Anna Korsak, on her way in, to squeeze past him. She faced him as she slid past.

"Close the door, will you?" George said.

"You wanted to see me?"

"Sit. What the hell were you thinking?"

"What?"

"Hassling Bill Johnson."

"I didn't hassle—"

"Goddammit!" He slapped the teacher's desk, splashing coffee over the map spread out in front of him. "He said you insinuated he had something to do with his daughter's disappearance."

"I didn't insinuate anything. What the hell's his problem? All I did was ask a few questions. You'd think he'd welcome me trying to find his daughter. All he seemed to care about was those cows of his, and what's up with those weird looking things anyway?"

"You should have checked with me."

"Okay, okay." Anna held up her hands in surrender. "You're right, but what did you want me to do? Sit around with my thumb up my ass? Maybe she hurt herself and is out there somewhere, but maybe she ran away. We need to look at the family."

"I've known the Johnsons for a long time. I'm not going to start digging into their lives when they're suffering like this."

"Didn't seem like Bill Johnson is suffering. Why isn't he more concerned? At least let me make some discreet inquiries. Who knew Eliza well? Who might Eliza confide in?"

"Talk to my wife. She's spent a lot of time with the girl."

"You remember the case down in Manchester? Sally Hopkins? Runner. Found raped, strangled." Anna produced a printed copy of the photo from the internet. "That's her . . . and that's Eliza Johnson. Coincidence?" Anna slid the photo closer to George, pointed at a man standing off to the side staring intently at the girls in their skimpy shorts and tight racing crop-tops. "Look at this guy. He gives me the creeps. Know who he is?"

"No idea."

"I'll ask around. Also, I was thinking a follow-up with Manchester PD might be in order. They never charged anyone."

"Can't hurt," George said. "I know the chief. I'll give him a call."

"Monday in the station, that nephew of yours. What was that about?"

"He was seen parked near the Johnson farm after the reception, the day Eliza went missing."

"So?"

"Years ago, he was working there when their nanny disappeared. Jimmy was a wild kid, in and out of trouble. We thought he had something to do with it. Turns out she went back to Sweden without telling anyone, but a lot of folks still think Jimmy was why she ran back home. I don't care how long ago it was, he was ordered to stay away from the place and he should damn well stay away."

"Did you have to ream him a new one in front of everybody?"

"First day back and he stays out all night, upsets Paula, comes back stinking of booze, tells her he went up to Killington to see old friends, was there all night. You have no idea the trouble that kid caused us."

"Hardly a kid now."

"Then he should stop acting like one. I can't believe Tooney left him the house. He's bound to screw it up."

"You don't actually suspect him?"

"No— Christ, I don't know. Gaetz is going to check out his Killington story, just to be sure."

The door swung open, Dick Gaetz appeared as if summoned. There was a dark edge to the man's good looks: near black hair, tanned angular face, perfectly pressed uniform.

Anna stood, glared at Gaetz, who returned her look with equal disdain. She turned her back, walked to the plate glass windows that formed one wall of the classroom, and craned her neck to look up at the sky.

"Christ, Gaetz, will you ever learn to knock?" George said.

"Sorry, boss, but I thought you'd want to know right away. Just got off the phone with the Rutland County Sheriff's department." Gaetz sprawled in the chair facing the desk.

"And?"

"They talked to Grace Kimball, who tends bar at the Red Parka Pub where Jimmy claimed he went Sunday night. She said he got loaded, crashed on her couch, but the deputy I talked to said Kimball is not particularly reliable, has been busted for DUI twice."

"Okay, thanks."

"What'd Fish and Game have to say?" Gaetz said.

"No sign of her."

Gaetz didn't move.

"Something else?"

Gaetz glanced at Anna by the window, lowered his voice. "Don't you think it's a strange coincidence? Your nephew returns, talks to the girl at the reception, parks in front of the Johnson farm, she goes missing."

"Any way to confirm Kimball's story?"

"Jimmy claimed he drank with an old friend, Bob Stark, but Rutland PD hasn't been able to track Stark down."

"Let me know what he says when they find him."

Gaetz, with another glower in Anna's direction, pulled the door closed behind him. Anna turned and faced the room.

"What is it with you and Gaetz?" George said.

"He reminds me of a guy I had problems with in Boston."

"Gaetz is a good cop, came highly recommended by Manchester PD. Keep it professional. Any serious problems with him, you come to me."

"Understood, but there's something about him. He's too smooth. I don't trust him."

"Just do your job, let him do his. I'll ask around about the Johnsons."

"You've known the family for years. You're too close."

"Okay," George said after a long pause. "See what you can find out, but be discrete."

Another helicopter went past, shaking the building.

"Are you listening to me? Bill Johnson is an important man in this community. Be. Careful."

"Got it, Chief."

"Don't call me chief. Now get out of here."

George had always thought the Johnsons to be a perfect family, but he had to admit Korsak could be right. The woman had been a detective with the Boston Police Department, was over-qualified to be a deputy in rural New Hampshire, and had a way of looking at him with her ice-blue eyes that made him feel she knew what he was thinking and somehow distracted him from those very thoughts. But he was the sheriff, damn it, not her, and it'd be nice if she acknowledged that once in a while.

He sometimes missed the old days, before the department re-org encouraged by the state and supported by the New Hampshire Sheriff's Association. Things had been simpler then. He could focus on being a cop. Now the department had twelve deputies and three divisions: Law Enforcement, headed by Gaetz;

Traffic, headed by Mac McCarthy; and Investigations, headed by Korsak, and he'd become like a referee trying to keep everyone on track.

It'd be nice, George thought, if Korsak and Gaetz would stop feuding for a change. He picked up his cell, hit speed-dial for the station, got Connie Armstrong, the office manager, on the line.

"Connie, can you pull a couple of files for me? . . . Gaetz and Korsak . . . No rush. Put them on my desk when you get a chance . . . Thanks." He ended the call.

Of course he remembered the Hopkins case. It had been in the news for weeks, statewide searches, a couple of suspects—an uncle, if he remembered right, and her coach—but no arrests.

He googled Manchester PD, called the station. "This is Sheriff Baker, Captain Richards available?" He waited.

"Not in," the operator reported.

"Have him call me when he gets back."

The rumble of a large diesel engine pulling into the parking lot brought George out of the school building to see a Mobile Command Unit being backed into position by a green tractor trailer cab, the beep-beep-beep of its back-up warning boring a hole into his brain.

Early afternoon. Blistering sun. Cumulus clouds massed over the mountains. Search teams—red-faced, drenched with sweat—stood in front of the cooling fans drinking from plastic jugs of water. George saw Lieutenant Colson holding a walkie-talkie to his ear.

"We got something!" Colson shouted. "Dogs picked it up off Gleeson Road."

George crossed to his SUV, the pavement so soft his feet seemed to stick with each step. "Hop in," he said. "I'll drive." He threw the cruiser into gear, tires squealing as he drove onto the highway.

"Strong scent," Colson said. "Not good."

George pulled in behind a line of pickups parked along the

gravel road. As soon as he got out of the car, he caught a whiff of rotting flesh. He charged up the path.

"Sheriff!" Paul Arnold yelled. "Wait."

The smell got stronger as he headed up the narrow trail. God, he thought, how will I tell the Johnsons? He came to a small clearing. There was a buzzing in his ears. Two Fish and Game rangers stood off to one side.

"What the hell?" George pulled out a handkerchief, held it against his nose. It was one of Bill Johnson's cows, all torn up, one side ripped open. grey coils of intestine spilled out, covered in flies.

"I tried to warn you," Arnold said.

Lieutenant Colson pulled on blue latex gloves and a medical mask, knelt by the carcass, and pulled up a flap of skin. A swarming mass of maggots spilled out onto the ground. Colson lifted the head. It had been almost completely ripped away from the body. There were dark holes where eyes had been. Crows in a nearby tree screamed. Colson dropped the head. It made a sickening plop as it hit the ground.

"It's those goddamn farm dogs," George said. "They run in a pack around here. I try to get the farmers to keep 'em chained up, but—"

"You got a problem, sheriff," Colson said. "No dogs could have done this."

"Then what?"

"Bear maybe? But it doesn't look like any bear attack I've ever seen. Cougar? But there haven't been big cats around here for more than seventy years."

"People say they've seen 'em."

"People say a lot of things aren't true. I'll have the remains sent to the lab in Concord, see what they think."

"That'll be fun," George said. "I'll drop you off at the school, meet you there."

❖

Why, Anna Korsak wondered, did George take Gaetz's side? It was obvious the man was a jerk. He'd been hired a few months after she'd joined the department as chief deputy detective. She knew what Gaetz, in his efforts to ingratiate himself with some of the other deputies, said about her. It undermined her, but after the blow-up in Boston and her resignation from the police department, she tried to keep her anger in check. She pulled the file on Eliza Johnson, but couldn't find the note she'd left about her run. She shot a text to Gaetz. Got an immediate reply, "should be there."

George wanted her to talk to his wife for background on the Johnson girl. Anna thought back to when she'd first met Paula Baker. How had such a smart, independent woman ended up married to good-old-boy George? Anna had been in the area only a week when Paula had called and invited her to lunch. Anna, a little apprehensive about meeting the boss's wife, had walked from her apartment into the center of Lebanon on a glorious spring day while children played near a white bandstand, their voices drifting on the fragrant breeze that ruffled the newly-green leaves of the oaks and maples that shaded the town square.

From an outside table at Sweet Tomatoes, Anna had watched a slender, attractive woman walk toward her. She had wavy auburn hair that lifted in the breeze and wore a simple skirt that swung about her knees and a pretty yellow and white blouse, and was so clearly enjoying the fabulous spring weather that she had brought a smile to Anna's face. When she walked up to the table, and said, "You must be Anna Korsak," Anna had felt a jolt—as of recognition, though they had never met—and surprise: this was not the middle-aged, slightly (at least) overweight, frumpy woman she had thought would be married to George Baker.

"Mrs. Baker?"

"Call me Paula, please. It's so good to meet you. How are you settling in?" She pulled out a chair, sat, straightened her skirt, and crossed her suntanned legs. "I am kind of shocked."

"Oh?" Anna wondered if she'd done something to offend.

"Shocked that George finally had the sense to hire a woman. What's it like, being the only female deputy? I can't imagine it, all those men with their trucks and toys and guns. Do you have to wear that dreadful uniform?"

"I don't mind, though I think I'm going to have to get it tailored."

Paula laughed and Anna felt herself relax.

"Let's get something to eat," Paula said. "Will you join me in a glass of wine? I never do during the day, but this is a special occasion, a milestone. The Sullivan County Sheriff's Department is at last entering the twenty-first century."

The wine arrived and then two plates of fresh pasta. Anna had the carbonara, Paula the primavera, and as they enjoyed a leisurely lunch, Paula spun tales of the characters in the sheriff's department. She had a wonderful sense of humor, not unkind, but with just that bit of an edge.

They talked and gossiped until, reluctantly, Anna had to go. "Thank you for this."

Paula flashed a little-girl smile. "We have to make it a regular thing, don't you think?"

Back in the present, Anna, hesitant to call Paula after barely speaking to her for months, stared at the contact screen on her cell phone. PB. No picture. Would Paula even talk to her?

Paula Baker had been working in the garden when Anna had called for the first time since their friendship, which Paula had come to cherish, had ended without explanation. Paula still wondered what she'd done wrong. Anna wanted to stop by, and Paula had no doubt what it was about: two days with no sign of Eliza, Anna would start digging into the Johnson family, the neighbors, the friends. George wouldn't be able to stop it. Everybody would be questioned, probed.

Paula showered and changed into clean shorts and a dark pink sleeveless top. She examined her reflection in the front hall mirror. She'd kept herself in shape with long walks, a weekly spinning class, and twice weekly yoga in Lebanon which she had been going to for more than fifteen years despite George's jokes. Maybe I should use more sunscreen, she thought, looking at her freckled nose, the small creases around her eyes. Wear a hat. She almost never wore makeup, but sometimes when she was meeting friends in town, she'd do a little around the eyes, add a touch of lipstick, and George would make some crack about her getting all gussied up.

A knock on the front door pulled Paula from her thoughts, and through the screen door she saw Anna, fuzzy like one of those old-time movies she had loved as a teenager where the heroine was always in soft focus, looking up dewy-eyed.

"Paula?"

"Oh . . . I'm sorry . . . come in. Don't wait for me."

Anna stepped into the front hall wearing the khaki, everyday sheriff's uniform, shirt buttoned up tight, tie, shoulder patch, metal badge pinned over her left breast, carrying a shoulder bag of light blue leather. Her face was flushed; little beads of perspiration hung in the edges of her platinum hair. An awkward silence took possession of the hall and the two women stood as though they were guests meeting for the first time, waiting for their hostess to introduce them.

"It's been too long," Anna said finally. "I've missed our little get-togethers."

You have? Paula thought. Then why did you stop returning my messages?

"Can I get you something cold to drink?"

"Please."

"Come into the kitchen. I made some iced tea this morning."

"That would be great. This heat. These pants are wool, for god's sake."

Paula took down tall tumblers, filled them with ice, poured tea from a large glass pitcher, and added a slice of lemon. They sat across from each other at the breakfast counter as gauzy, white light, filtered by curtains drawn against the heat, filled the kitchen, robbing the room of color, and the air sat heavy with not a hint of a breeze, and the buzzing whine of cicadas rose and fell outside. Paula had put her book aside after breakfast, and she could see Anna trying to read the upside-down title.

"Terms of Endearment?" Anna said.

"Have you read it?"

"No."

"You can borrow it after I'm done. It's wonderful, sensitive. Hard to believe a man wrote it."

"Hard to believe a lot of things men do."

Paula laughed, and remembered how she had liked this woman, her sharp humor.

"Your kitchen is so nice. I remember it from the Christmas reception."

Nice? Paula thought. What did that comment mean? She looks at everything like she's evaluating it.

"How's yoga?" Anna said.

"Still going to the community center twice a week."

"I love your top. Lululemon isn't it?"

Paula felt her face flush. It's the sun, she thought. I got too much sun this morning.

"I've started at Power Yoga in Hanover," Anna said. "You should try it. You're strong."

Paula had visited Power Yoga once; it was chic and modern and filled with super-fit twenty-somethings. Was Anna implying that her version of yoga was better than some middle-aged house-wife's? What does she think of me? Paula held the tall glass of iced tea in both hands, trying to absorb the cold.

"How long have you known the Johnsons?" Anna said.

Good, Paula thought, let's get on with it.

"Forever," Paula said.

"Mrs. Johnson's much younger."

"Harriett was William's first wife. She died twelve years ago. Eliza was four. Her brother Will was eight. At the funeral that little girl cried and cried. It was so awful."

"Was she tall, Harriett?

"What? No, not really . . . I'm not sure. Isn't that terrible? She was such a good friend, and I can't remember."

"Bill Johnson re-married pretty quickly. That must have been hard."

"Oh, I got over it. Men don't do very well on their own."

"George said you know Eliza well."

Do I? Paula thought. Do you ever really know anyone?

"George never liked her."

"Why?"

"She and George butted heads. He felt she was arrogant, spoiled. I think losing her mother scarred her somehow. She's amazing, incredible, but driven, has to be perfect at everything, and she can be aloof, private. It seems like she never opens up to anyone, really trusts anyone. Except Tooney. Eliza worshipped Tooney."

"What about her family? Was she happy at home?"

Paula shifted on her stool, played with a lock of her hair.

"She rarely talks about her home. Her father enrolled her in a boarding school a couple of years ago without telling her. Can you imagine? Without even talking to her? She refused to go. I don't think she's ever forgiven him."

"What about the brother?"

"Will has been away at school and college for years. From what I hear, he stays away, never comes home."

"Any idea why?"

Paula thought about her youngest daughter, Tracy, who hadn't been home in what seemed forever, said, "Kids grow up, leave, want to be on their own," as if that was just fine with her, as if she didn't miss them every day, but was unable to tell them for fear of seeming needy, clingy.

"Paula?"

"Sorry."

"What about friends? Any that Eliza is especially close with?"

"I can only think of two. Ritchie Kelley. Jessica Williams."

"I saw her with Kelley at the reception. Are they a couple?"

"I don't know . . . they seemed more like brother and sister to me, always kidding, teasing each other."

"Can you think of any reason she would run away?"

Paula picked up her glass, took a long sip of iced tea. Every movement felt forced, artificial under Anna's gaze. Paula did not like to gossip. Living in a small village you heard things, but you also learned to live your life and let others live theirs.

It had become a regular thing. Eliza would arrive at the Baker house Saturday morning at nine, always exactly nine, to help Paula with her garden. She was usually cheerful, upbeat, but last Saturday Eliza had been troubled, had not been her usual self. I should have seen she had something on her mind, Paula thought, that she needed to talk, but then she stepped into a bed of flowers that I had been working so hard on, and I snapped at her, and her face closed up and she didn't say another word. What had been bothering her?

"Paula? Anything at all?"

"No. Nothing."

Anna leaned back, loosened her tie, pulled at the stiff collar of her shirt. "Stupid things, ties."

"How can you stand that uniform in this heat?" Paula said.

"Do you ever wake up and can't decide what to wear? In the morning, I don't have to think. Could be worse, I could be a UPS driver. God, that is an ugly brown."

Paula thought for a moment and realized she pretty much wore the same thing every day. Her uniform?

"Would it be all right if I used your bathroom?" Anna grabbed her bag from the back of her stool.

"Of course."

When she returned, Anna had changed into tan shorts and a

white sleeveless blouse, and had put her hair up. Her badge and gun were clipped to her belt.

"Please," Anna said. "Don't say anything to George. You look so comfortable, it made me realize I was about to melt."

"Phalaenopsis," Paula said.

"What?"

"The tattoo on your shoulder. It's a phalaenopsis orchid, a moth orchid. Why an orchid?"

"I had a girlfriend who told me that the Japanese name for this orchid means, 'happiness flies to you.' I liked that."

Alone, Paula sat in the shade of a backyard maple. The air moved, the tiny breeze a hot caress on her neck. Summer days like this, when it was too hot to do anything, reminded her of those summers of youth when to be lazy was not the lack of activity, but an activity in and of itself, a kind of accomplishment, and memories came back of high school and her best friend Abby O'Neal. They had been inseparable, were going to be together forever, and those memories—staying up late, sharing dreams, secrets—came as a pang of loneliness. Abby went away to college and Paula stayed here. Had she ever felt as close to anyone since?

I wonder where she is?

Again, that deep sound on the edge of hearing, as though the earth shifted beneath her feet.

The session with Anna had left Paula feeling unsettled. Months ago when Anna had stopped returning her calls, she had felt Anna had used her for information and moved on, and despite a niggling resentment at having, in a sense, been dumped by Anna (dumped? what an odd choice of words), Paula couldn't help but remember their times together, and how much she respected Anna's ability to make her way in this man's world.

She hadn't appreciated Anna asking her to keep the clothing change from her husband (how had she not noticed that tattoo before?) and wondered if the wardrobe switch had been an act to put her at ease, to keep her talking. If so, it had worked, and as Anna continued questioning her, it became like they were friends again, talking, chatting about kids, families, marriages.

Paula felt a wave of regret. She'd said too much, shared too much.

The branches of the maple above her whispered to each other in the hot, restless air.

Before Paula's family moved to Lebanon, when it was this hot, the village kids, Paula, George, Paul Arnold, Bea Marsden, used to go to the swimming hole where the Blow-Me-Down Brook cascaded over layers of granite before plummeting into a deep, cold pool of crystal-clear water. Paula wondered if the swimming hole was still there (of course it was), then she wondered if kids still went there, but was pretty sure they didn't. Hemlock Flat had a swimming pool now with lifeguards, and parents today did not let their children run wild the way we did. And then she had the crazy notion that she should go to that swimming hole, cool off the way they used to, but forty-seven-year old women did not go jumping into backwoods swimming holes. Then she thought, why not?

George will have a fit if he finds out, but why should he? Why would he?

She left the house, crossed Route 120, and walked up Leavitt Hill Road past a white SUV parked alongside the road, sweat bursting from her skin, running down her back, between her breasts, soaking the waistband of her shorts.

The sandy pullout where folks used to park was empty, speckled with weeds burned brown by the sun, and the path was overgrown with vines and low bushes. She felt a moment of sadness that this place had been forgotten, but as she pushed the vegetation aside, a delicious shiver of anticipation ran up her back. She kicked off her sandals and stepped onto a flat slab of rock that projected out over the deepest part of the pool, ten feet below. The waterfall roared in her ears. She remembered the first time she'd worked up the courage to jump, kids teasing her, urging her on (she'd been so scared), but she had jumped then, and still in her shorts and top, she jumped now.

It seemed to last forever, that glorious flight, that rush of wind, and then water crashed and bubbled around her, and it was just as cold as she remembered, and she felt her whole body come alive. She spiked down into the water until her feet almost touched the rocky bottom, then holding her breath as long as she could, drifted slowly up, wishing she could stay there forever, the current singing in her ears, but broke through the surface gasping, and saw Anna Korsak standing on the opposite bank in her underwear, dripping wet.

Chapter Five

THIS BEING NEW HAMPSHIRE, George Baker had to drive north from Concord so that he could drive south to Hemlock Flat. He cruised Interstate 89 with the AC on high. The cold air from the dashboard vents dried his skin, but did little to cool his thoughts. He'd hoped to have heard something from the search by now, but there was still no sign of Eliza Johnson. If she was stranded somewhere, tonight would be her fourth night.

His mind drifted. He still hadn't talked to Jimmy to smooth things over, and wondered why he had been so hard on him, so insistent on verifying his Killington story. Was it because he'd been such a pain in the ass when he'd lived with them? Cutting school, shoplifting, trespassing. Then there was the time he went camping by himself for three days without telling anyone.

In the last twenty years they'd had only two instances of a local girl disappearing—first, the Johnson's nanny; now, their daughter—and in the first case his nephew was, at least in some way, involved. It must be a coincidence that Eliza Johnson disappeared the day Jimmy returned for the first time in god knows how many years. What could be the possible connection?

His thoughts bounced back and forth from the search for Eliza Johnson to the examination of the grisly remains of Bill Johnson's Highland cow in Fish and Game's lab. He could still smell it on his clothes. It was almost enough to turn a man into a vegetarian.

He drove on autopilot.

The carcass had been spread out on a large, stainless steel table in the center of the frigid lab. Lieutenant Colson was there, and a lab tech, a pretty young woman.

"Virginia Cho is our chief forensic biologist," Colson said.

"What's a forensic biologist?" George said.

"I test for and study the diseases that affect our wildlife. Right now we've got an epidemic of brain worm in the moose population that we're trying to understand."

"So," George said. "My cow."

"Your cow," Virginia Cho said, "is a bit of a puzzle."

They walked over to the table.

"The carcass is such a mess that it will be tricky to get clean samples to analyze. It was torn apart, and a good chunk of it had been eaten. Probably by the original predator, possibly by scavengers that came along later. But, here"—she gestured with a slim metal baton—"we can see claw marks. By measuring the spacing, we can get an idea of the size of the predator."

"Lieutenant Colson thought it might be a bear."

"Do you have cats at home, Sheriff Baker?"

"We used to."

"Then you know their claws are thin and curved. A bear's are flatter, coarser." She pointed to four thin, parallel cuts in the cow's hide. "Notice the way the edges are pulled up. A bear would tend to gouge, the edges would be pushed in. This was done by a cat."

"Bobcat?"

"Bigger. Look at these bite marks. The spacing would suggest an animal on the large side of a full-grown mountain lion."

"Or a cougar?"

"Different names for basically the same animal."

"I thought the eastern cougar was declared long gone by the feds."

"It was, but some claim there is a population in northern New England and the Canadian Maritimes, and there have been instances of a western mountain lion wandering all the way to New England. One was killed by a car in Connecticut in 2011. There's no doubt you've got a very big cat in your woods."

She walked around the table, not at all disturbed by the gruesome carcass. "This could be a major discovery. I need to isolate DNA for the predator to determine what species we're dealing with. It might take a while. The lab is backed up."

"We need to keep this quiet," George said.

"We'll do our best," Virginia Cho said.

"Just give us time to find the girl," Lieutenant Colson said.

George started, as if waking from a nap, and realized he had no idea where the miles had gone. If he wasn't careful, he'd miss his exit and end up in Vermont.

I've got a missing sixteen-year-old girl and a goddamn mountain lion? When word gets out—and it will—it'll be chaos, panic. If this cat got Eliza . . . Christ . . . but, maybe somebody she knows picked her up and she's off in Manchester or Boston pretending to be a big girl, or . . . and at that moment George finally allowed himself to think the worst, and wondered if it was time to talk to Dick Gaetz about issuing an Amber Alert.

When George arrived back at the mobile command trailer, he found Dick Gaetz, Paul Arnold, and Sergeant Bob Dawson of Fish and Game's K-9 Unit waiting for him in the meeting room sitting behind narrow tables facing a whiteboard.

George moved to the front of the room. "Day's almost done, just a quick review."

"Where's Korsak?" Gaetz said.

"I sent her to talk to my nephew," George said. "Paul, update everyone on what you got from the neighbors."

They'd grown up together, George and Paul Arnold, and even after all these years in the department, Paul was still, to George, the shy awkward kid he'd been all through their school years.

"May Turnbull … she's on the uphill side of the farm … saw her running, but when pressed wasn't sure what day. Otis Thrasher lives on the downhill side, didn't see Eliza, but he sure had a lot to say about the Johnsons. We know about the loud argument Saturday, but he also tried to say, without really saying, that Bill Johnson was violent with his family."

"That's bullshit," Gaetz said.

Paul Arnold flinched, almost as if struck.

"You can't trust anything Thrasher has to say about Bill Johnson," Gaetz continued. "They've been at each other forever. Thrasher still claims Johnson screwed him when he bought the farm from him and it's been more than twenty years."

George turned to Sergeant Dawson. "Bob?"

"The dogs were able to track her scent up Turnpike Road." He pointed to the map on the wall. "Until right about here, where a trail crosses the road. She's obviously been on that trail many times in the past so the dogs couldn't tell which way she went. It's also possible she got picked up by a car."

"Any chance we could identify the vehicle?" George said.

"No. Road's hard-pack," Paul Arnold said. "There's been cars going up and down every day, trucks, a couple of four-wheelers."

"I don't know why we're going to all this trouble," Gaetz said. "When I interviewed him, Johnson told me the girl's done this before, snuck off somewhere, come back all innocent and apologetic. Waste of time, you ask me—"

Sergeant Dawson interrupted. "We'll expand the search area five miles north and south, but we're getting stretched thin."

"Dick," George said. "Is it time to contact the state about an Amber Alert?"

"Doesn't meet the criteria," Gaetz said. "There's no indication she was abducted."

"Is there anything else on the enforcement side we should know about?" George said.

"There was a break-in at the Rite-Aid in West Lebanon. Looks like they tried, but couldn't get at the meds, had to settle for a couple of six-packs of beer. Probably just kids."

"Okay," George said. "Keep me posted. Paul, go back to the neighbors, see if anyone saw a vehicle they didn't recognize Sunday around the time Eliza went for her run. Dick, follow up on that break-in. Bob, get going on the expansion of the search area."

The roof of the abandoned fire tower on the summit of Grantham Mountain was mostly gone, there were holes in the wood floor, and a slat of wood creaked and groaned in the hot wind that blew from the valley. Looking west from where he'd come, Jimmy Baker could see, far below, the roofs of the village and the tall, white tower of the Congregational Church. He turned to the east. At the foot of the mountains, just visible through the murky haze, was a group of buildings in a cleared area. A paved drive left the buildings and headed east, downhill, to where the Sugar River Valley sweltered in the thick, yellow air. Somewhere to the south, behind the mountain's shoulder, was the city of Newport.

The sun was a nasty orange ball in the western sky.

Time to get moving if he didn't want to be out here in the dark. What to do? Go back the way he came? Or go down the eastern slopes, continue exploring? But then, he'd end up on the opposite side of the mountains from Hemlock Flat.

He looked west, then east, shrugged, started down. Below the summit crags, the terrain descending the east side was gentler, and soon Jimmy was able to move quickly downhill through farm fields overgrown with forest and crisscrossed with ancient stone walls covered with vines until he came, after about two hours, to where the woods ended at a broad cleared area of weeds and scrub grass.

Across the clearing he could see a massive log structure with a steep, gabled roof and tall, mullioned windows facing the mountains, and thought about going to the building to see if he could get a ride into town, but wasn't sure how these people, whoever they were, would take to his trespassing. He skirted the cleared area, staying hidden in the trees, until he came to a group of aluminum-sided buildings with attached stock pens, like a cattle farm or horse ranch. Next to the largest building, there were two pickups and a panel truck parked near a closed metal garage door and loading dock. The lodge and all the buildings were connected to the fence or inside the perimeter, and it was then that he remembered so was he.

Damn.

He looked at the raw blisters on his bloody hands. He did not want to climb the fence again, even though it was lower here, maybe only six or seven feet.

Someone had left a ladder leaning against the largest metal building like they had been working on the roof, and planning on coming back the next day, hadn't bothered taking the thing down.

When he was ten, Jimmy, a lonely kid from an unhappy home, had started sneaking around his Hanover neighborhood at night, peering at the glowing windows with their tableaus of other people's lives, families sitting together at dinner, talking, watching TV. One time, Mrs. Robertson, alone in her living room, had turned and stared at the big picture window with a sad expression on her face, and Jimmy had been terrified that she had seen him until back in his own bedroom looking at his window, he realized she had been looking at her reflection in the dark glass.

He felt now that same fear of being caught, that same illicit thrill.

He lifted the ladder away from the building, moved it to the fence, and leaned it back as quietly as he could. He climbed the ladder, swung a leg over the fence, and dropped to the ground with a dull thud. He ran, crouched, along the outside of the fence until he could duck back into the woods, his heart pounding.

The front of the log building had a large overhang supported by tall pillars of raw tree trunks that reminded him of the new base lodge at the Jackson Hole Ski Resort. Two large black SUVs were parked near the entrance. He moved a few yards deeper into the woods, then headed east. When he was out of sight, he angled over to the paved driveway. It was in better shape than most of the roads in the area, but after about a mile downhill it turned to dirt before coming out on Route 10 as just another unremarkable dirt road with a padlocked, rusted metal gate. No sign. Nothing.

The sun, setting on the other side of the mountains, turned the sky lurid shades of red, as Jimmy—hot, tired, thirsty, hungry— walked the highway through beat-down scrub-land that had been logged and forgotten He passed abandoned car repair shops, a rusting metal silo, used up gravel pits, empty mobile homes, with not a vehicle in sight, wondering what the hell was that place, and wondering if he was ever going to get a frigging ride.

 Heat so intense he thought the road might melt radiated up from the blacktop in waves, creating mirages of small lakes on the road ahead of him. Strange vertical shapes wavered on the edges of his vision. He was running on empty.

He heard the sound of an engine, turned to see an old flat-bed farm truck coming toward him, stuck out his thumb. The truck rattled past, then slowed, stopped. He hustled up to it, climbed into the cab. The driver was old with a scraggly beard, wearing jeans and a flannel shirt despite the heat. The cab smelled of oil, cigarettes, and manure.

"Thanks."

"Where you headed?"

"Hemlock Flat."

"Zeke." He held out a gnarled and calloused hand.

"Jimmy."

"Reckon I can get you past Claremont. Got to pick up a tractor part at Richardson's." He struggled with the gearshift, finally wrestled it into gear. The truck stuttered into motion. "How the hell you end up all the way over here? You weren't messin' with that place, were you?"

"What place?"

Zeke looked at Jimmy like he knew bullshit when he heard it.

"If you were, good thing you got out to the road. They don't take kindly to folks trespassing."

They stopped for gas. Jimmy bought a Mountain Dew.

An insect hit the windshield splattering yellow goo in front of Zeke.

"How the hell do the goddamn bugs know to kill themselves right in front of my goddamn eyes?"

Jimmy drank the Mountain Dew. It was sickly sweet and he wondered why he'd picked it. He'd never liked the stuff. It was gross and did little to cure his desperate thirst. There must have been something better.

"God, I hate this," Zeke said. "Driving all the way around these damn mountains just because a bunch of rich big-shots own 'em and closed the old road through. Don't seem right ... Way back, the son-of-a-bitch who started the place took my great-great-grand-dad's farm, stole a hundred acres."

"How could he do that?"

"Got enough money, you can do whatever you damn well please."

It was almost dark. Jimmy had the window open, felt the hot air on his face as they drove the Claremont strip. The lights from the stores were fuzzy and vague in the humidity.

Paula Baker put nail clippers, an emery board, and a bottle of nail polish next to her glass of white wine on the breakfast counter. She hadn't done her nails in years, working in the garden had made it seem pointless, but had decided that it would be fun for a change. She started on her left hand, heard the front door open, George's heavy steps in the hall. He went into the den to lock away his gun, then there he was filling the entrance to the kitchen, somehow bigger than he had been this morning.

"What are you doing?"

No hello, no how was your day, no hug, no kiss.

"My nails."

"I can see that."

"It's called Fearless Pink." Paula held up her hand, blew on the nails. "Any news?"

She watched him go to the refrigerator, open the door, then stand there for a moment like he'd forgotten what he was doing. He grabbed a beer and fell into a chair by the kitchen table.

"Nothing." George picked up a magazine from the table, fanned himself. "Christ, this heat. If she's out there, she won't last much longer." He twisted the cap off the beer bottle. "We got another dead cow. Concord says it's a mountain lion."

"A what?" Her hand twitched; polish dripped on the counter.

He drained half the bottle.

"The editor of the Valley News, Bob Gilman. Remember him?"

She didn't, but no matter.

"He asked me today about Eliza, wanted to know if we suspected foul play." He snorted. "Foul play. Like it was a goddamn baseball game." He tilted the bottle, took another drink.

After almost thirty years of marriage, Paula still found this quiet, taciturn man a mystery, but she could see when he was troubled: his brows tightened, he slumped a bit more than usual, sighed, though unaware of having done so. He wouldn't say anything sitting there with his beer, but he was, it seemed to her, waiting for something from her, some gesture, a word of encouragement. She looked at the bottle of polish, the pink drops on the counter.

"Korsak's been asking a lot of questions," George said. "Seems like the Johnsons are not the perfect family they appear to be. I told her to talk to you about Eliza. She contacted you?"

"I talked to her earlier. How does she survive in that good-old-boys club of yours?"

"That woman can take care of herself."

"There's food in the fridge. I'd make you a sandwich, but I need to finish this." She held up her hand. "It'll look silly half done."

"Looks kinda silly anyways, woman your age."

"You sure know how to make a woman feel good. Can't a girl have a little fun?"

Later, polish dry, George upstairs in the shower, Paula was alone in the kitchen. Somehow fitting this last bowl into the dishwasher had become an insoluble problem, and the longer she stood there holding the dish, the more absurd the situation became. She gave up, put the bowl in the sink, closed the heavy door, and started the dishwasher. She wiped sweat from her eyes, looked at the breakfast counter and thought of Anna perched there on a stool this morning, and it was as though time folded in on itself, and the past months of no contact vanished, and it was last Christmas and they were here in the kitchen, the two of them.

It had been an annual event for years, hosting deputies and staff and their families for a Christmas open house. Unmarried deputies were encouraged to bring a date, and Paula had wondered who Anna would bring. She came alone. Holiday attire was encouraged. Most of the men made do with ugly sweaters or ridiculous red and green ties, but Anna had worn a reindeer-themed tunic so garish it was beautiful, red and green plaid leggings, and Santa Claus earrings.

Anna looked at the decorations, said, "I feel like I'm in a Christmas Tree Shop."

"The Bakers have always gone over the top for Christmas. Don't you think it's a bit much?"

They were drinking champagne.

"My parents didn't observe Christmas," Paula said. "What about your family when you were growing up?"

"I like your dress," Anna said.

Paula was wearing red leggings and a green dress embroidered with multi-colored ornaments.

"Isn't it the silliest thing? I wear it every year."

Anna raised her glass, said, "Merry Christmas."

"I got you something," Paula said. She handed Anna a small box wrapped in silver paper with a bright gold bow. "Open it."

Anna carefully removed the wrapping, folded it, put it aside, and slowly lifted the lid as if afraid to see what was inside, then held up a delicate pendant necklace that, from the first moment Paula had seen it in the jewelry store window, had made her think of Anna: the white gold would shine with her hair, the lapis would bring out her eyes.

"Oh . . . Paula. I can't accept—"

"You have to. You can't turn down a Christmas gift. In the Baker family it's absolutely not allowed."

Anna went to a mirror near the door into the dining room, held it up to her chest, and looked at herself for what seemed a long time, then sighed so deeply Paula could hear her across the room.

Anna put it back in the box, replaced the lid.

"It's beautiful."

Anna took Paula's hands in hers, leaned close, and said in a husky voice, "Thank you."

Paula felt the warmth of her and was enveloped by her scent, and Anna kissed her on the cheek, a lingering touch of soft lips, and before Paula could think of what to say, the door banged open, and Tooney in her wheelchair rolled into the kitchen, pushed by Eliza. Anna pulled away, dodged the wheels, and returned to the party.

The sound of George stomping down the stairs dragged Paula from her memories. She heard him go to his den, the TV come on. She opened her book but couldn't concentrate. She didn't know what was going on in the world, what was happening in her life.

Her husband seemed a stranger to her. And wherever could Eliza be? Paula walked to the French doors feeling as if her legs were not her own, and stood at the screen staring out into the darkness. She couldn't seem to catch her breath, and felt as if she teetered on the edge of a bottomless abyss.

❖

The evening was humid and grey and the fading light was flat and things seemed, to Anna Korsak, not to be positioned in the world as they should be, but suspended like cardboard cutouts in a museum diorama. Cicadas clattered in the trees near the porch of Jimmy's house where she had been waiting for more than an hour, but quieted as light bled from the sky and night approached. From the edge of the forest came the hammering of a woodpecker. Something snuffled in the overgrown garden next to the house, coyotes yapped in the distance. The indifference, the immediacy, the there-ness of nature, brought to Anna a nameless anxiety, and the feeling that she didn't belong.

A shadow moved up the driveway toward her, faded, then materialized into Jimmy walking slowly, favoring his left leg. He limped up to the porch steps. He looked terrible. His face was dirt-covered, haggard.

"Where have you been?"

"Exploring."

"In the dark? I brought dinner . . . and a bottle of wine."

"You what?"

"Takeout from the Chinese place in Lebanon."

He looked puzzled, like he couldn't believe that she had come all the way here to bring him dinner. George had told her to talk to Jimmy, smooth things over. She wasn't sure why she'd gone to the trouble to put on nice clothes and get dinner, but there was something still of the boy he'd once been that seemed in need of someone to take care of him. A local legend, she'd heard, Jimmy Baker had been both good: champion skier in an area that loved its ski racers, and bad: a total screw-up all through his school years. He was, the local wags said, a classic, "I could have been great if I wasn't such a jerk," type of guy.

Jimmy walked ahead of her into the house, dropped his pack next to the kitchen table, took down a tall glass, filled it from the sink, leaned his head back, and drained it without stopping. He collapsed into a chair. He looked even worse in the harsh kitchen light. His face had scratches down the left side, there were streaks of blood on his forearms, and his legs were covered with dried mud and more blood. He slowly flexed his hands, looked at the raw palms, the open blisters.

"God, that was awesome. I thought I was gonna drop walking up the road."

"And that's good?"

"Oh, yeah." He seemed immensely pleased with himself, then stared at her like he only now realized who she actually was. "Why would you do that? Get food and stuff. I mean, thanks and all, but I'm a mess. I need to take a shower."

"Go ahead. I'll set the table."

Pipes clanked in the ceiling. Anna heard water rushing some-where. She put the food in the oven to warm, found dishes, glasses, set the table, and opened the large bottle of white wine she'd brought. Restless, she carried her glass into the hall. She glanced at the framed photographs hung there, then walked through the formal dining room with its long oak table and eight matching chairs into a living room crowded with stuffed chairs and couches and glass-front cabinets with porcelain figurines.

God, she thought, if I had to live surrounded by all this old crap, I'd shoot myself.

Back in the kitchen, Anna turned on a floor lamp, cut the overhead lights, finished her glass of wine and was about to pour another when Jimmy came through the door, clean, wet hair, his shaved face free of blood, wearing a sleeveless apricot dress that came to just above his knees.

"Holy shit," Anna said. "Give a girl some warning."

"What?" He looked surprised she was still there.

"What do you mean what? The dress, for god's sake."

Anna poured, handed Jimmy his glass, and watched him lower himself slowly into a chair. He drank the wine like it was beer, and ate like he hadn't seen food in days.

"A little advice?" she said.

"Yeah, sure."

"You want to wear a dress, fine, but do us all a favor . . . shave your legs."

He leaned back from the remains of his mandarin chicken, looked at his hairy legs and laughed, then turned serious. "Really, why are you here?"

"Okay, no bullshit. Three reasons. One, I felt bad about the scene in the station. Why does your uncle treat you that way? Didn't you live with them?"

"Yeah. Five years. My mother dropped me off, never came back." Anna watched Jimmy do that thing guys do when they're trying to pretend they could care less. "He never wanted me there. Sometimes I think he hates me ..."

Jimmy started to fidget, wouldn't look at her.

"Two," she continued. "I want to talk with you, learn what you know about the Johnsons, and three, I get tired of eating alone." The first parts were true. Actually it was all true, but she felt embarrassed admitting it.

"I do appreciate you coming all the way out here. The food saved my life. I'll try to answer any questions you have, but remember I haven't lived here for a long time." He sipped his wine, looked down, then up at her. "Oh, and three? I'd be happy to have dinner with you anytime."

Oh dear, he was starting to flirt. "Jimmy—"

"Just looking for company."

They looked at each other, letting their eyes connect, until they both, at the same time, looked away, Anna not sure if he was thinking what she was thinking, but thought he probably was. A good-looking guy—if one were into that sort of thing—sandy hair, boyish face, great shoulders, ripped arms. And, he was kind of cute in that dress.

Jimmy crossed his legs, uncrossed them, crossed them again, then tugged at the hem of the dress.

"I saw you with Gaetz at the station," Anna said.

"What an asshole. What's his story?"

"He's head of the enforcement division. Only been here a year. What'd he say?"

"Called you a dyke. I should've slugged him."

"Aren't you in enough trouble? Don't worry about it. I can take care of myself. The sheriff had Gaetz talk to people in Killington."

"Typical. My fucking uncle should mind his own business."

"This is his business. Eliza Johnson is missing."

"What?"

"Hasn't been seen since Sunday."

He opened his mouth, stopped, held up his glass for more wine, but wouldn't meet her gaze. She filled his glass, then her own. He seemed lost in some internal debate.

"You were going to say something?"

"I met her at the reception." Again, that hesitation. " And, I saw her Monday. My first day here."

"What did you say?"

"She was here Monday."

"Why the hell didn't you report this right away?"

"Why would I? I didn't know she was missing. Didn't seem like a big deal at the time. She talked like she spent a lot of time here, like it was her home, and how she was going to miss it."

"What time Monday?"

"Five, maybe six? There's something you should see."

Jimmy led her upstairs. Anna stood in the doorway to the bedroom.

"You think she spent the night here?"

"Looks like it, but how the hell would I know? I checked out the place when I first got here, didn't see her, went for a walk, wasn't gone more than an hour, and when I got back she was in the kitchen looking for something."

"Any idea what?"

"She found a necklace, but I'm not sure it was what she was really after."

"You need to come to the station, make a formal report."

"No way. My uncle will make a federal case of it. You saw how he treats me. Been there, done that. I wasn't going to say anything at first. I knew you'd make a big deal out of it."

"This is a big deal. Write down everything she said, did. Leave nothing out. If she slept here, it changes everything. And it's damn good you didn't keep quiet. You could have been in deep shit."

She gestured toward the bedside table. "Can you look in the kitchen for a baggie big enough for that book? I'll come back in the morning, get your statement, and go over it with you. Keep this door closed and stay out of this room."

Descending the stairs, Jimmy Baker couldn't escape the wish that he'd kept his mouth shut, that he wasn't involved. Back in the kitchen, dinner finished, take-out containers in the trash, wine bottle empty, Jimmy looked across the table at Anna. He needed something to drink, something to do with his hands as an awkward silence settled between them. This happened to him, even on dates with Katrina. He would run out of things to say, and the longer the silence lasted, the more uncomfortable he felt, and the harder it became for him to break it.

"How'd you get to be so famous?" Anna interrupted his thoughts.

His ascent to stardom in the extreme skiing world seemed so far in the past, it was as if it had been someone else.

"I was support for a film shoot in Alaska. This hotshot was going to do the first ski descent of Bleak Mountain. The helicopters, two of them, were hovering. You have any idea how much it costs to keep a bird in the air? Anyway, he wouldn't do it, didn't like the snow, said it was too dangerous, chickened out, and I said fuck it, I'll do it, and I did, and I survived, and the rest, as they say, is history."

"Why would you do that if it was so dangerous?"

"Why not? What's the worst that could happen?"

"You could die?"

Silence again took possession of the room.

"What happened between you and Bill Johnson?"

"I worked for him the summer I was sixteen. My uncle thought that hard work would straighten me out. Every summer, he'd make me get some miserable job, each one worse than the one before."

"Johnson."

"Sorry. They had this beautiful nanny. She loved to flirt. Near the end of the summer, after weeks of teasing me, she came on to me, pulled me to her, kissed me just as Johnson came into the barn, then started crying, said I'd forced her. It was almost like she'd set me up. Then she disappeared. They hauled me in like I was a fucking criminal. She turned up in Sweden a week later. Even so, that was the last straw. My aunt and uncle packed me off to the Killington Ski Academy."

"Any idea why Johnson got so angry when he saw you kissing her?" She looked at a little notepad. "He went after you with an axe handle."

"There was some disagreement whether it was an axe handle or a shovel handle."

"How old was the nanny?"

His mind drifted, and lost in memory he didn't hear the question.

"Jimmy?"

"What?"

"The nanny, how old?"

"Eva? Older than me. Twenty-two, twenty-three?"

"You're a kid, she's an adult, and he goes after you."

"Said it was his church, taking a stand against sin and all that crap."

"Seems more like jealousy to me . . . Wait— Eva? The same?"

"Yep."

"Huh," Anna said, then quietly, to herself, "Why didn't I know this?"

"Can I ask you a question?" Jimmy said.

"Of course."

"Why are you here?" More to the point, he thought, why am I here? Why don't I just sell this dump, go back where I belong?

"I thought we covered that."

"No. I mean why are you here in this two-bit county working for a guy who isn't half as smart as you? I checked the department website. You were a detective in Boston, you've got a bachelor's in criminal justice from Boston College and a master's in psychology."

"Yeah," Anna said. "And a PhD in pissing people off."

They stood, walked to the front hall. Anna, carrying the book in a ziplock bag, stopped at a framed photo. "Who's this?"

"That's Tooney and Harriet and Eliza," Jimmy said. "Tooney was a Lindsay. She had a younger sister, Felicity. Harriet Johnson was Felicity's daughter."

"What's your relation to Tooney?"

"Tooney was married to Herbert Baker, George's uncle."

"Is everybody around here related?"

"Pretty much."

"I come from a big family, and grew up in a neighborhood filled with cousins and aunts and uncles, and uncles who weren't uncles but were called that anyway, and I've never been able to keep it straight." She continued to study the photo. "So, that makes Eliza your cousin?"

"Second cousin-in-law once-removed."

"Is that even a thing?" Anna said.

Jimmy watched her walk to her car. He felt trapped. He'd been suspected of the worst when Eva disappeared to Sweden, and now they'll be on him again. He returned to the photo in the front hall and stood staring at it for a long time wondering again why he came back to this place that held so many painful memories.

Chapter Six

NIGHT LINGERED AS PAULA Baker stepped out of her door. The world was still and the air smelled of flowers and cut grass, and in the darkness she could almost believe that the sun would not rise, that the valley would not again bake and suffer. The houses of the village were dark except Mark Wilson's, whose kitchen windows shone bright yellow. He was up before dawn, as always, for the early shift at McKesson Manufacturing in Claremont.

Paula crossed the village green on troubled and wilted grass, came to Penniman Road, turned right, and walked toward the western horizon. The road rose gradually. She passed the house where she had lived with the Marsdens so long ago, then the house that nice young couple (what were their names?) had recently moved into, and came to Randy Emerson's dairy farm. Past the long, low milking barn was the fenced pen where, every year, Randy raised fifty turkeys to sell come Thanksgiving. In the dimness, she could see the young turkeys huddled at one end, and at the other, the torn bodies of two or three birds, victims of a nighttime predator. White feathers, splattered with blood, blanketed the ground like an early season snowfall.

The road continued to climb. Wooded hills rose on her left, but on her right the ground dropped away and she could look out over the flats to the Penniman Hills, grey silhouettes in the pre-dawn light. It was hard to remember the long, harsh winter, and how deep snow had covered that ground, scoured into strange feathery shapes by winds that blew from the north, and Randy's cows had been confined to the low metal barn, and the world had been ice-hard and uncaring.

She came to the Blow-Me-Down Brook where it slowed and meandered in sinuous curves through a marshy area. Tall cattails lined the brook and small willows grew on its banks. A dragonfly skittered over the shimmering surface, occasionally dipping down to touch the water, leaving a small, expanding circle.

The sky was a frothy grey with a faint pink underside, and she could sense the earth turn toward the sun and anticipate the coming heat, but now, at this moment, the pre-dawn morning was soft and pleasant and all around her the birds of the marsh, redwings, wrens, hermit thrush, were awake and busy and their songs filled the air, and she could breathe and feel some goodness in this life of hers.

Looking back at the mountains, still in shadow, she wondered if Eliza was there, somewhere, injured, perhaps dying, and in that moment she felt separate from everything that mattered.

Light took the sky. She walked back toward the village, faster, broke into the hint of a run, and by the time she reached the village green, sweat soaked her shorts and tank top and dripped on the road. She stopped to look at the mold-marked war memorial and felt a vague sadness that no one had bothered to clean it, and stood, hands on her hips, breathing hard, wondering what to do with the coming day that seemed somehow already lost.

Paula showered, but even after standing under water so cold it gave her a headache, she still felt hot and a little queasy and hadn't been able to eat, but George liked his breakfast—eggs, bacon, toast—so she'd cooked and now here she was scrubbing the bacon grease out of the cast iron skillet that had been in the Baker family for decades. She heard George in his den, getting ready for work, and as she looked out the window a single tear slid down her cheek and realized she was crying again. It had been happening like this ever since the funeral. She would be going about her everyday life, and for no apparent reason the tears would start. It was almost as if she was someone else. Paula couldn't understand where these waves of sadness, of abject misery came from. Tooney had lived a long, good life (she was 92 when she died), why this overwhelming grief? A good life. But, had it been? Or, had she died lonely and almost forgotten up there in the woods, wondering why she had left her life in Texas?

She heard heavy footsteps in the hall, turned to see George standing in the doorway. He could see that she had been crying.

"What's wrong? What is it?"

"Tooney,"—Paula choked back a sob—"I can't believe she's gone."

"Christ. I thought it was one of the kids. You're crying over that old biddy? She lived longer than the rest of us have any hope to."

"But don't you see? She was the last . . . and . . . I feel so bad . . ."

"I have to get to the station. We'll talk later."

She heard the front door close, tires crunch on the gravel drive, then squeal as George pulled out onto the main road, and silence settled around her, and she was alone in her house, in this place that she loved so much, with nothing to do. She listened as the whine of George's SUV faded into the distance and thought: Talk later? That's all you can say? What about now? You can't spare ten minutes—five minutes?—to talk to your wife of almost thirty years when she is so clearly upset? But, then she wondered, why didn't I ask him to stay, to wait? Am I afraid he would say no, and I would feel even more alone?

We'll talk later ... but she knew they wouldn't.

❖

When Jimmy Baker woke, his entire body was stiff: he could barely open and close his hands, the gash on his leg was angry and red, and his right knee was a little swollen. His clothes from the day before, encrusted with dirt and stained with blood, were still in a pile in the bathroom. He scoured Tooney's closet, found a pale yellow blouse, pulled on shorts, and stumbled downstairs to find Anna Korsak waiting for him in the kitchen. She was all business while they worked on his statement, but as the afterglow of the day before faded, he couldn't stop wondering what she thought of him.

Last night, after his shower, Anna downstairs, the cuts on his legs still stinging from the hot water, he'd gone into the bedroom looking for something clean to wear, and had wandered into Tooney's closet, and had looked at the long line of clothes and wondered what did his great-aunt see when she stood in this place. What had they meant to her?

He took down a sleeveless dress, and held it up and so wanted to wear it, the feeling was like an ache in his gut, and he wanted Anna Korsak—why her?—to see him in it.

To be seen, for once.

He put it on, did a little twirl, the flared skirt lifting as if on an invisible breeze, and felt himself swept forward, like before a big descent in Alaska. But now, this morning, as he watched her drive away with his written statement and the day came on harsh and bright and he struggled to get his ass in gear, he was filled with a mixture of embarrassment and regret.

Hunger and the need to check his email finally motivated Jimmy to head to town. He settled at a corner table at the Filling Station Cafe, a converted gas station on the green in Lebanon, with a bottle of water, a double Americano, and a ham and cheese croissant. He opened his laptop. Logged in. There were several emails from work. He decided to ignore those for a day or two. Nothing from Katrina.

Where was she? He clicked on new message, but what could he write, what could he say that might get her to come back?

He closed email. On a whim, he googled, "land preserve, Croydon, NH," and was led to a website about Corbin Park. A half-hour later, his coffee had grown cold and he was still reading. It was not like the place was a secret, it was just that people in the area seemed to have chosen to ignore the existence of the largest private hunting preserve in the United States right in their midst.

Founded by Austin Corbin in the late 1800s, a man the New Hampshire Historical Society called, "the most loathsome blight the state had ever produced," which was saying something when you thought of the crooks and politicians who got their start in New Hampshire. Corbin, a robber baron of the classic nineteenth-century mold, purchased land from farmers in the area; some sold willingly, others were forced to sell when they became surrounded by Corbin's holdings and could no longer access their homes.

It was now owned by a secretive group of extremely wealthy men, nobody was sure how many, maybe ten, fifteen. They stocked it with elk, wild boar, deer—possibly other game—and then these brave hunters would go out and shoot the fenced-in beasts and go back to their penthouses or mansions, mount the stuffed head on a wall, and declare themselves real men.

Jimmy found an article in the Manchester Union Leader about a local man, Robert Langdon, who had been shot dead while hunting without permission in the park in 2003. The shooter, an ex-cop named William Laroux, was reputed to be employed by the park as security, but that claim was denied, and all charges were dropped. The owners beefed up the fence, closed off the park, and the place had faded from public view.

He thought about the lodge he'd seen, the big SUVs, and was glad he'd kept out of sight.

A state law, written in 1894, exempted the park from all hunting and fishing restrictions, and from any and all laws or regulations that New Hampshire Fish and Game might enact. It was like a separate country. Twenty-six-thousand acres. Private. Walled off.

The first night in the house, it had been elk he'd heard. But what was that howling screech, like a baby crying in the woods?

❖

Before leaving the village of Hemlock Flat to drive to the station, Anna Korsak stopped to talk with Jessica Williams, a classmate of Eliza's and according to Paula Baker, one of her few close friends. Anna waited in silence with Jessica's mother, who sat at one end of a big couch tucked up against the arm as if she wanted to get far away from something.

"This is so awful," Mrs. Williams said. "I can't imagine how Eva Johnson must be feeling."

"Do you know her well?"

"No. The Johnsons keep to themselves."

When Jessica finally came in wearing plaid pajama bottoms and a short-sleeve hoody and the surly attitude of a teenager forced to get up before noon on a summer day, and plopped herself down on the other end of the couch in the mirror image of her mother, Anna realized that it was Jessica that Mrs. Williams was trying to keep away from. Jessica had the hood pulled low over her forehead. She twisted a long strand of hair in her fingers, held it in front of her, looked at it as if expecting to see something other than her own light-brown hair, then released it, running her fingers through to un-twist it, and then repeated the process.

"Why haven't they found her?" Jessica said.

"We're doing everything we can. I'm trying to get a better feel for Eliza, where she might be. I understand that you and she were close."

"We used to hang out all the time . . ." Jessica looked at her mother, uncrossed her legs, then re-crossed them, stared at her bare feet, then looked at her mother again.

"Mrs. Williams, do you think I could talk to Jessica alone?"

"Why? I mean—"

"Please. She's not in any trouble."

Mrs. Williams rose slowly, and after a long look at Jessica, left the room. Anna couldn't tell if Jessica was relieved, or scared to be alone with a uniformed sheriff's deputy.

"When was the last time you saw Eliza?"

"Last Saturday? At the swimming pool. We were going into Hanover after to hang out? But she changed her mind, said she had to train. She's such a jock. She even lifts weights with the boys?"

Jessica fiddled with her hair again, pushed it back behind her ear.

"What did you talk about?"

"You know, stuff . . . boys . . . school? We're going to be juniors, and I was talking about the classes I want to take, and how it would be our next to last year and all, but she didn't seem interested, like she could care less? I mean, Eliza loved school. She's such a star. I couldn't understand why she wasn't more excited."

"Does she have a boyfriend? Girlfriend?"

"Not that I know of."

"Did she seem worried about anything? Troubled?"

There was a long silence.

"She . . . I don't know . . . started to say something . . ." Jessica shifted on the couch. "But . . ."

"But?"

"It was nothing ..." She drifted off, and Anna felt herself losing patience.

"Jessica, what?"

"I think she's scared?"

"Of what?"

"She never said, I mean, not in so many words, but Saturday she was jumpy, kept looking around, and she had these bruises? Said she fell, which she could have, I guess. She runs up and down mountains and stuff."

Don't jump to conclusions, Anna told herself, thinking about Paul Arnold's reports of his conversation with Otis Thrasher.

"Can you remember what the bruises looked like? Where they were?"

"They were bruises, you know, blue, purple? It's not like they were big or anything. On her back. Behind her shoulders?"

"Anywhere else? What was she wearing?"

"She has this bikini. She's so hot. Sometimes I hate her . . . I mean, not really . . ."

There was a long pause during which Jessica returned to examining her hair, and fidgeting on the couch.

"Which of Eliza's friends have their own cars?"

"Why? I mean, what has that got to do with anything?"

"Just answer the question."

"Mary borrows her mother's car any time she wants, and . . . "

"And?"

"Ritchie Kelley? I don't know why Eliza hangs out with him. He's such a dweeb and even he has his own car."

Anna, back in her SUV, AC blasting, wondered why do girls talk like that? As if everything they say is a question.

At the station, Anna filed Jimmy's statement, wrote a report on her interview with Jessica Williams, made a note to herself to contact Ritchie Kelley, and tried to write a summary of last night's conversation with Jimmy, but didn't know where to start. The entire evening had been strange, a little off in ways she couldn't identify. Had she been too friendly? Had dinner been a mistake?

More importantly, what had she learned? Eliza had spent the night at the house. This meant that the last sighting of her was one day later and miles from where originally thought, but equally of interest to Anna was what was the girl up to? Why had she spent the night in an empty house? What was she searching for when Jimmy interrupted her? And, why had she run uphill, toward the fence instead of downhill toward the village? Where as she going? Had something happened to her on the way?

She wrote a quick summary focusing on Eliza, downplaying the dinner, the wine, the flirting, and completely omitting Jimmy in a dress, then sat staring into space wondering about Jimmy Baker. Who was he? What had possessed him to wear that dress?

She had pinned the newspaper photo of Eliza and Sally Hopkins at the race awards ceremony on the wall next to her desk. She picked up her phone, tracked down Eliza's high school coach, who led her to the New England Running Association where she learned that the man she thought creepy was Marty Gleeson, a Manchester businessman and the chair of the race organizing committee. She called the Manchester Police Department, spoke to a Lieutenant Torneau who confirmed that Gleeson had been questioned during the Hopkins investigation, but had been in Colorado interviewing for a position with a Denver company at the time Hopkins was killed, and had since relocated to the Denver area.

The man still looked sketchy to her—but not her problem—she took the photo from the wall crumpled it into a ball and tossed it at the wastebasket. She missed, as usual.

By late-morning it was well into the nineties, but inside the mobile command unit it was frigid. George Baker had the AC, one of those new split units, turned all the way up. Anna had called late last night, and he had called Bill Johnson first thing, who had confirmed that Eliza spent a lot of time at her great-aunt's, too much for his liking, and had occasionally spent the night there. It was clear, even over the phone, that he hadn't cared for Altoona Baker.

Thinking of the old woman got George wondering what had come over his wife this morning, crying over nothing. It wasn't like her.

The grey melamine wall of the conference room was covered with a taped-together topographic map of the eastern side of the

Croydon Mountains, over-written with eight red squares, each further divided into nine areas. The search area comprised more than twenty -thousand acres of hills and woods, crisscrossed with narrow valleys, gorges, dotted with rock outcroppings and small cliffs. They'd marked her usual trail runs based on interviews with her coach at school. There two red Xs, one for each dead cow. One was north of the Johnson Farm on Maple Hill Road, the other just south of the farm.

There was a blue X on Turnpike Road about a mile and a half uphill from the Johnson farm marking where the dogs had lost Eliza, and new marks, one at Tooney's house, the other where that trail crossed Gap Road. Sergeant Dawson had taken his dogs, but once again her scent went both directions. They knew her movements up to that point, three days ago, but after? Nothing. She could be anywhere.

Lieutenant Colson entered, interrupting his thoughts.

"I'm losing guys every day to the heat," Colson said. "If she's out there, well . . ."

He didn't have to complete the sentence. George knew what he was thinking, and knew that he was probably right, but he also knew that Colson didn't have to deal with the community and Bill Johnson.

"We need to keep at it."

"I understand your situation, sheriff, but three searchers went down yesterday. Two ended up in the hospital hooked up to an IV. You have to admit, everything points to her having run away."

Sergeant Ray Marchand of Fish and Game came up to them. "We're done with quadrant four—"

The radio on Colson's hip squawked to life.

"Lieutenant," a hoarse, breathless voice said. "We got a problem. Bridger collapsed. Might be his heart. We need to evacuate him immediately."

"Where are you?"

"Q-3, area 7."

"Got it."

Colson turned to Marchand. "March, you good to go? There's a jeep trail, here"—he pointed at the map—"off East Notch Road that gets close to where they are. Grab everyone you can find. Take the two trucks."

The door slammed as Marchand ran from the room.

"I don't know how much longer we can keep at it," Colson said. "She's probably at a friend's place or on her way home, but if she's actually stranded in this heat with no water, there's little chance she's alive."

"Understood."

George shooed everyone out of the office and closed the door. He hadn't wanted to call Corbin Park, expecting they would stonewall him as they had in the past, but after the two dead cows and the results of Concord's analysis, he knew he had to.

"It is not ours, I can assure you sheriff."

The spokesman for the hunting preserve gave his name as Jones, Robert Jones. George thought the name phony.

"We've got two mangled and half-eaten cows from a very important farm, and New Hampshire Fish and Game says it's a western cougar, and I need to be sure that—"

"We have no animals of that kind, keep accurate counts of all our animals, and are fully aware that raising certain species is tightly controlled if not illegal. Our arrangement with the state does not require providing more detailed information."

"The preserve used to be more open with the community."

"I'm aware of that, sheriff, but this is the way the owners want it, so that's the way it will be."

"Who are these owners?"

"You know I'm not going to answer that."

"Look, a young girl is missing, and two cows have been killed. I need to know that nothing has escaped. It happened in the past, and the girl was last seen near your fence. And, I need to be certain she hasn't ended up in the preserve somehow, and I want you to organize a search of—"

"The new fence is totally secure. There is no way she could be in the preserve. I understand your situation, and my sympathies go out to the girl and her family, but this is private property. I'll have to speak to the owners."

"But, if an animal got loose that was a danger to the community, you would, I trust, contact me. Am I right on that at least?"

"Of course, sheriff. We want to be nothing if not good neighbors."

George put the phone back in its cradle. Not very forthcoming was Mr. Jones.

If that call to Corbin Park was disturbing in its lack of information, the call he'd taken with Virginia Cho just prior had been disturbing in the information it had provided: DNA confirmed it was a cougar, and judging by the bite size, probably Canadian.

Maybe, he thought, the damn thing will wander off? Go somewhere else? We should be so lucky. Eliza Johnson, that was what he should be thinking about. Where the hell is she?

There was a knock on the door. Paul Arnold peered in.

"Sheriff? Got a moment?"

"Don't stand there, come in."

"I was talking with May. She wants to know if we're going to cancel."

May was Paul Arnold's wife. She was leading the volunteers organizing the Sheriff's Department Summer Picnic for the county's families to be held at Lebanon High's football field in two days.

"We're going ahead with it."

"But—"

"I understand her concerns, but it's been an annual event for longer than I've been sheriff—every year, not one missed—and I am not going to be the first to cancel the damn thing no matter how hot it is."

❖

"I'm sorry Mrs. Baker, Mrs. Johnson is resting," the maid who answered the front door of the Johnson residence said. "I'll see if she wants to come down. Why don't you wait in the living room?"

It was eleven-thirty in the morning, and although Paula Baker, in her entire life, had never been able to lie down during the day, she supposed Eva Johnson deserved all the rest she could get. Paula wondered how she would have felt if Patricia or Tracy had gone missing when they were sixteen, the worry, the struggle to not envision the worst, but she couldn't imagine it, and couldn't put herself in Eva Johnson's place.

The maid (since when did anyone around here have a maid?) directed her to a bright and spacious living room with a beamed ceiling, blond wood floor, white walls with carefully hung art, and tall arch-topped windows that looked out to a perfect flower garden. There was no sign that children had ever lived in the house, no clutter, no family photographs. She thought to sit, but the couch and matching chairs in white and blue did not seem like they wanted to be sat on. Paula grew impatient as minutes ticked past. She picked up a copy of Architectural Digest from the coffee table, and paged through lavish color photographs of houses even more formal than this, but she grew bored and decided to look around. They were friends, weren't they? She walked through a wide doorway into a formal dining room with a long, glass-topped table, and modern chrome and leather chairs for eight.

A memory came to her: she, George, and their children here for dinner. A family with two younger children, she couldn't remember who, had also been the Johnson's guests. Kids everywhere. The dining room then had been homey and comfortable, not cold and empty like this, and Harriett had been healthy and happy, with Eliza, three years old, underfoot. Paula had almost tripped over her as she carried a platter of food from the kitchen, and Bill John-son shouted at Eliza, grabbed her by the arm, and dragged her away. Later, Eliza took Paula's hand and led her up the back stairs to show Paula her room filled with stuffed animals, dolls, and posters of Disney characters. Paula had thought the girl was upset, needed comforting, but she acted as if nothing had happened.

The dining room this morning was empty and the house was silent, and the hiss of Paula's sandals on the polished floor as she walked through to the kitchen was the only sound. Where was everyone? The back stairs were as she remembered them, narrow and twisting. At the top, what might once have been a servant's room, was still Eliza's. Why didn't she have a nicer room in this giant house?

On a shelf were a few stuffed animals, but now the posters were of sports stars and pop singers. A built-in desk occupied one wall. On it was a charger but no computer. Above the desk was a bulletin board covered with photographs: Eliza in a group of kids at the town pool; Eliza with Tooney; Eliza with her arm around the shoulders of an older man that Paula recognized as Eliza's neighbor, Otis Thrasher. Her head was turned to look at him with an expression of love and care. Eliza: so good, caring for Tooney, caring for Otis Thrasher. Paula felt a stab of guilt. Otis had lost his wife several months ago. Paula had visited regularly for a few weeks, but hadn't been back in quite some time.

She heard rustling in the kitchen below. How would she explain this intrusion? She went through a door into the main house, descended the front stairs, and walked quickly back to the living room where she picked up a magazine and tried to look as if she had been there all along, but no one came and she became restless again.

An open archway led to a long hall, on the left side of which were two pairs of French doors that opened onto a columned porch overlooking another fabulous garden. At the far end of the hall, a door of polished cherry was open partway.

"Hello?" she called. No answer.

She pushed gently against the door, it swung open, and she found herself in what must be Bill Johnson's study: dark wood wainscoting, a massive desk, and matching shelves filled with books. A large stone fireplace dominated the far wall, and on the oak floor in front of it was a tiger skin rug with claws reaching out as if to attack whoever came through the door. Its red mouth gaped open, showing huge white fangs.

That can't be real, can it?

Animal heads stared at her from the walls: deer, a bobcat, a wild boar. A huge bear stood in the corner. The room smelled of dust and old fur. She lived in a farming community where hunting in the fall was a part of life, but that was for food, venison for the winter. This was obscene.

"Paula, what a pleasant surprise." Bill Johnson appeared next to her.

"Oh my god, you about scared me to death!"

"Do you like my trophies?"

"I was hoping to visit your wife. The maid said she was resting. I started wandering, I didn't mean to—"

"Yes, she's not feeling well."

"I'm sorry to hear that. Completely understandable. I'm so worried for Eliza, we all are, of course, but I'm sure she'll turn up." Paula knew she talked too much when she was nervous, and something about Johnson's presence—the way he stood too close, the way he stared at the dead animals adorning his study—was making her very nervous. "George and everyone are working around the clock to find her."

"I should hope so. Now this one"—he pointed to the bear—"I got in the Klondike. It's not easy taking a grizzly with bow and arrow."

"Where do you think she is?"

"Eliza will turn up when she feels like it."

Paula walked to a wall of photographs, as much to get away from Johnson's looming presence as to look at the photos. She pointed to a shot of Johnson and a dark-haired man kneeling with long rifles pointed at the sky, posed in front of a spectacular hunting lodge, the body of a huge wild boar between them.

"Isn't that Deputy Gaetz?" she said.

"We hunt together once in awhile. Good man."

"What does Eliza think of all this?"

"Eliza, I'm afraid, does not approve." He gestured at a wooden pedestal on which a stuffed bobcat had been posed as if ready to attack. The animal was missing much of its fur and one leg had been broken off. "She did that when she was twelve. She's not allowed in this room, and I've long since stopped concerning myself with what that girl thinks."

Paula looked at the tiger skin rug, the red, lolling tongue, said, "That can't be real, can it?" before she could stop herself.

"Oh, yes," Johnson said, turning and looking directly at her. "I'll tell my wife you stopped by."

She walked to her car. She had come to visit someone in a time of need, why did she feel so guilty? It was those dead animals. She felt dirty having been in that room.

Her hands trembled as she reached for the door of her car.

A gust of wind came as out of nowhere and pushed Paula's hair across her face. She brushed it away from her eyes, and with that gesture somehow came the awareness that there was something at work that she did not understand. The maples above her lifted their branches to the sky, and the poplars lining the drive swayed in unison in the hot breeze.

Chapter Seven

It was seven minutes after twelve when Anna Korsak stepped out of her SUV. The sun poured down its fury on the elementary school parking lot. By the time she reached the command trailer's metal steps, she was sweating. How could it be this hot already? Inside, she breathed a sigh of relief as cool air washed over her.

Connie Armstrong had installed herself at the desk in the outer office. She was a big woman somewhere in her mid-forties with a substantial bosom. She wore a skirt, blouse, and light cardigan sweater every day, and seemed, to Anna, from a different era, and to be constantly disappointed that others didn't meet her standards of dress and decorum.

"I told you, Ritchie, he's in a meeting," she told a slender, sandy-haired boy who was standing at her desk.

"But it's important!"

"You'll have to wait."

He saw Anna in uniform, came up to her, said, "I need to talk to the sheriff."

She led him to the corner where there were two chairs and a small, round table. He couldn't sit still.

"What's your name?"

"Richard Kelley."

"Okay, Richard Kelley, what's so important?"

"I saw her."

Anna had, this morning, when tying and re-tying the stupid uniform tie, decided to hell with it and instituted a new personal uniform policy of no freaking tie when it was this freaking hot, and was distracted by Connie giving her the look that meant she was going to hear about it. Anna returned her stare. Connie turned away and busied herself with a stack of papers.

"Who?" Anna said.

The door opened and Dick Gaetz entered, bringing with him a blast of hot air and the smell of sun-baked asphalt.

"Eliza!" Ritchard said. "Listen to me. I didn't know she was missing until this morning. I came as soon as I heard." His words started to run together.

Anna reached across, put her hand on the boy's arm. "Slow down. Tell me what happened."

"I was driving, saw her walking along the road. It was so hot and she was red and sweating like crazy, so I gave her a ride to the old swimming hole." He stopped, took a quick breath. "Eliza's my friend. We have to find her!"

"She say anything?" Gaetz interrupted, stepped closer. Richard looked up at him, then back at Anna.

"When was this?" Anna said.

"The day before yesterday!"

"Take it easy. You did the right thing. It's good you came." She turned to Connie. "Who's the sheriff with?"

"Colson."

"Do we have a bottle of water for Richard?" She turned back to him. "Are your parents home? We need to ask you some questions, get more detail. It would be good if one of them was there."

"Mom's at work. Dad should be home soon. He has to pack to go to Boston."

The Kelley family lived near the high point of East Road in some architect's re-creation of a Victorian mansion with large gables on three sides and a wall of glass facing north past the Croydon Mountains toward the Meriden hills.

"Wow," Anna said. "Quite the view."

"Wouldn't want to heat the place," George said.

They found Martin Kelley loading a black roller bag and matching briefcase into the trunk of a red BMW parked in a wide, newly paved driveway.

"Sheriff, what brings you up here?"

Kelley had short brown hair with a touch of grey at the temple, and the lean, healthy appearance of a runner. He was some kind of financial wizard with an office in Hanover, and looked, to Anna, to be about forty.

"This is Deputy Korsak," George said. Anna nodded. "Is Ritchie here?" George continued.

"What has that boy done now?" Martin Kelley shook his head.

"Nothing," George said. "We just need to talk to him."

Kelley stopped as they walked past the front of the house and pointed at wide boards forming a column on either side of the front door. "Look at this. Replaced the architectural trim not five years ago, and it's already rotting."

"Wood'll do that," George said. "Your son?"

"In the garage, working on that car of his."

Ritchie was waxing a silver Honda Civic with a look on his face that might be mistaken for true love.

"Ritchie?" George said. "Have you thought of anything else? Anything Eliza said, did?"

"Hold on," Martin Kelley said. He turned to his son. "What's this all about?"

"Your son came to the station earlier with important information about Eliza Johnson," Anna said.

"I would of told you first, Dad, but you weren't home. I was driving on Clark Camp Road, saw Eliza, and gave her a ride to the swimming hole."

His father looked, to Anna, worried, maybe upset. Why? The kid did the right thing, coming forward as soon as he heard.

"I have to leave for an important conference in Boston. I'm not comfortable with you interrogating my son without me. Can't this wait?"

"We're not interrogating him, Martin, relax," George said. "He's helping us. And no, it can't wait. We just want to know if he's remembered anything she said or did, that might give us a hint as to where she was going after her swim."

"I offered to hang around, give her a ride home. She said she was going to walk home when things cooled off. I asked if she wanted to come over, play video games. She looked at me like I was joking or something. I mean, she used to come over all the time. I asked again and she got, like, angry with me. I gave her a ride, and she's mad at me. What did I do?"

"What was she wearing?" Anna said.

"Her usual running stuff. Pink top, silver shorts?"

Somebody's confused, Anna thought, hadn't Jimmy described Eliza wearing a silver top and pink shorts?

"Did she have anything with her?" George said.

"Just a waist pack that holds a water bottle."

"Did she say anything at all unusual? How did she seem?" Anna said.

Ritchie put down the polishing rag, leaned against the fender of the car.

"When I pulled up next to her, she started to run off, like she was scared, then saw it was me. She seemed, I don't know, jumpy or something, and it was weird the way she waved and shouted good-bye as I drove off. I mean, we hang out all the time."

"Wait," Anna said. "You picked her up on Clark Camp Road yesterday?"

"Yes."

"And, you're positive it was Clark Camp."

"I know where I was."

George and Anna left Ritchie standing by his car.

"Something doesn't make sense," Anna said. "Eliza was at Jimmy's Monday afternoon. Ritchie picks her up Tuesday miles away on Clark Camp Road. Where was she Monday night? What the hell is going on?"

Anna looked to where Martin Kelley stood by the garage. When he saw her looking at him, he turned away and busied himself with his luggage.

"I'll talk to Colson," George said. "You know where the swimming hole is? Off Leavitt Hill? Go there. Keep everyone away. I got a bad feeling about this. We pulled a dead kid out of there years ago, before the town came to its senses and built the pool."

Ritchie caught up with them as they walked back to the cruiser.

"Let me come with you"—he grabbed Anna's arm—"she's my friend."

"You've done enough." She pried his fingers loose.

Anna sat on a moss-covered stump near the top of the waterfall in the shade of a big maple to wait for the others to arrive.

The circular pool at the base of the falls was about twenty feet across before it narrowed back to a stream and continued downhill toward the village. The water was crystal clear but very deep: she'd not touched bottom when she dove from the cliff above. Could Eliza's body have been there, trapped under a rock, or pinned by the force of the waterfall? Anna remembered opening her eyes underwater, seeing the polished boulders covering the bottom, and imagined coming face-to-face with Eliza's body, seeing cold, blue skin, white, empty eyes, hair drifting in the current. She shuddered, it was too horrible.

The thick moss and bright green ferns that draped the rock walls on both sides of the waterfall dripped with moisture. Spray and mist cooled the air. A breeze came up from the valley, lifted the branches of the maple that reached out over the pool, and caused a tattered rope that hung from the largest branch to sway back and forth.

Anna imagined kids swinging from that rope, rising up into the air then plunging, screaming and laughing, into the cold water, and wondered if Paula had been one of those kids. What was it like, she wondered, knowing people your entire life? Growing up together, marrying, working together, living in the same small village, seeing each other day after day. She couldn't imagine it. She hadn't been back to her neighborhood in Dorchester for years, hadn't seen her parents, hadn't talked to her brothers.

In her imagination, those country kids—George and Paula, May and Paul Arnold, who else?—were laughing and smiling, playing together, and in that fantasy they were happy and safe and felt like they belonged, and she searched her memories for a time when her life had been that carefree, when she had played and laughed with the other kids in the neighborhood, but all she found was an image of those kids splashing in the spray from an open fire hydrant while she watched from the side encased in a bubble of fear and loneliness.

The memory came back of Paula jumping from the ledge yesterday, her face alive with joy. Anna had watched her drop through the air, hair flying up, and heard her girlish shriek just before she hit the water, and when Paula surfaced and their eyes met, it had hit Anna hard: she was crushing on the boss's wife. She'd felt it the moment they first met, and despite months of trying to avoid Paula, she felt it still, and didn't know what to do.

She sighed, forced herself to stand, and went to scan the upper parking area for tire tracks.

❖

George Baker pulled in behind a brand new blue pickup parked on the side of the road with a DIVERS DO IT BETTER bumper sticker and saw Dr. Reginald Phillips unloading a tanks and a huge black duffle bag. George had never understood why Phillips would live in the hills of New Hampshire when he was obsessed with scuba diving. An orthopedist at the hospital in Lebanon, Phillips went on vacation at least twice a year to where the water was warm and clear, and would spend as much of his time as possible under that water while his wife, Jocelyn, would spend an equal amount of time at one spa or another, and if you had the misfortune to run into him at the Corner Store after he returned, he would talk your ear off about his underwater adventures.

"Sure you got enough gear there, Reg?" George said.

"Give me a hand, will you?" Phillips said.

Maude Richards, who lived up in the hills, came down the road in her fancy Prius, stopped, rolled down her window.

"What the hell's going on, Sheriff?" She was a crusty old thing, a notorious busy-body.

"Lookin' for something." George waved at the smoke from her cigarette.

"I can see that"—she took a drag—"Let me know if you find it." She laughed then started coughing and wheezing and slapping the steering wheel with the palm of her hand. She finally drove off.

George stood at the edge of the pool. The swinging rope his father had put up was frayed and rotted. He found it hard to believe that he had been young once, that he had swung on that rope showing off for the girls, and he remembered the time he held on too long and landed flat on his back in the water just feet from the rocks that lined the edge. Damn near killed himself. While the other kids were laughing so hard they couldn't move, Paula had rushed over to make sure he was okay.

Ever since they'd talked to the Kelley boy and learned that Eliza had been last seen at the swimming hole, the feeling had been growing of what they would find, until George couldn't escape the horrible image of a girl's wet, naked body, hair plastered to her face, being pulled from the water. He watched Phillips struggle into a blue wetsuit, strap on a tank and weight belt, and lower himself into the water. Moments passed, Phillips surfaced, stood in the water near the edge, took out the mouthpiece, tilted up his mask.

"Anything?" George said.

"Not so far. This thing's almost twenty feet deep. There's a cave goes back under the falls." He staggered up onto land, rummaged in the open duffle bag, pulled out a bright yellow rubber flashlight, slipped the lanyard over his wrist. "Couldn't see."

Again, George waited.

Anna stumbled down the narrow path, holding onto bushes and tree branches. She stood next to him beside the pool, stretching and twisting her back, her shirt mapped with sweat.

"You done with the pullout?" George said.

"At least five different vehicles have been there. Looks like two cars, two SUVs and a four-wheeler. The road's dry, the pullout's loose sand. I don't think Crime Scene Services could determine make and model of the tires." She held up her phone. "I took the best pics I could. I'll send them, see what they say, but I doubt it's worth bringing them in."

Phillips surfaced, hauled himself out of the water, shouted, "Found something!"

"What have you got?" George said.

Phillips held up a silver teardrop-shaped earring with a small emerald at its center.

George slipped it into a clear plastic envelope, handed it to Anna. "Check with the Johnsons, see if it was Eliza's."

He watched her stare at the gemstone shimmering bright green in the hot sun. She turned it over, looked at it from the other side.

Back at her house, Paula Baker was still unsettled by the image of those animal heads staring at her as if the rest of their bodies were on the other side of the wall, and they were about to break through and attack. She opened her laptop and skimmed the first page of The New York Times. The headline was the heat wave, warnings to stay inside.

She logged onto Facebook and discovered a friend request from Eliza sent the day before the funeral. Why would the girl want to connect on Facebook when they saw each other in person almost weekly? Of course she accepted, and was taken to Eliza's homepage. Paula followed Eliza's posts back through time—she was a wonderful photographer—and stopped at a picture of Eliza in Paula's garden with the 4-H chapter. There was her beautiful, young face staring at her.

I do love that girl. A small sob escaped her lips.

Her daughter, Patricia, had texted a reminder that Jennie's eighth birthday was coming up (my granddaughter, eight, where did the time go?). Jennie was quite the reader, and especially loved paranormal mystery stories, so Paula went to Amazon to search for a book. She scrolled through books about spirits, books about ghosts, books about hauntings, and stopped at The Haunting of Madame Cherie's Castle, set in New Hampshire. Perfect. Her mouth fell open. The author was Abby O'Neal. Could it be?

She rose from the desk, went to her bookshelves, and there, on the top shelf, she found her high school yearbook with its once white, now yellow, soft vinyl cover. She remembered how her kids had loved looking at it when they were young, laughing at the hairstyles and clothing. She'd come close to throwing it away several times. She turned to her page, looked at her school picture and wondered had she ever really been that young? Her classmates had voted Paula most likely to succeed. Shows how much they knew. She paged through the book, and there was Abby, serious, brooding. Voted most likely to: nothing. Goal: move to California, become a writer.

Paula put the yearbook aside, and went back to her computer, and clicked to this Abby O'Neal's author website. Her breath caught in her throat. It was her. A portrait showed Abby, beautiful, as she had been when young, wearing dangling earrings, a tailored shirt unbuttoned just enough, light make-up, and an enigmatic smile. She had published seven books, some for young readers, others for adults, made The New York Times bestseller list, won the Lambda Award, been shortlisted for something else. Her biography made a single, brief mention of growing up in New Hampshire.

One sentence? Was that all she had been to Abby?

Paula stared at the portrait trying to see the girl she'd been so close to so long ago. There was a "Contact Me" button, with the entry, "I love to hear from my readers." Paula hovered over it, clicked. A screen came up with a space to write a message. Her fingers hesitated. What could she say after all these years? She closed the window and there was Abby with that mysterious smile.

Paula rose, went to the kitchen and poured herself another cup of coffee. She returned to the computer, sat lost in memory staring at the picture until the computer went to sleep, but Abby and their past together, was still there, hidden behind the black screen, as it was in Paula's life, hidden behind everything around her.

Her coffee had gone cold, bitter. How can something so good, turn bad so quickly?

There was no answer when Anna Korsak knocked on the screen door, but she heard Paula's voice coming from the backyard. She followed a flagstone path around the left side of the house and stopped next to a large bush with pink and white flowers. Paula's voice was soft, intimate, but Anna couldn't make out the words. Who was she talking to?

She felt a flutter in the air, and saw a tiny hummingbird, its wings moving so fast they were no more than a blur. She held her breath and watched as it probed a blossom with its long, sharp-pointed bill, then moved to another in an eye-blink, so tiny, so delicate, then in another blink was gone.

The backyard was amazing. A grey wood fence planted with a border of tall sunflowers surrounded a carefully ordered vegetable garden. There were clumps of flowering bushes, banks of flowers, their colors faded, and in the center of it all an old car, painted royal blue, had rose bushes growing where its hood and trunk should be. Anna stepped forward slowly until she could see Paula kneeling in her garden talking to herself. Paula stood, put her hands on her lower back, and arched toward the sky. She wiped her face with her arm, then went back to work pulling up plants and tossing them into a pile near her feet. She was wearing faded cut-off jeans and a pale blue tank top that was sweat-plastered to her back. Her bare legs were streaked with dirt. There was a tear in the seat of her shorts, a flash of red underwear as she moved.

Paula turned, saw her there. "Anna."

"I heard voices. I hope I'm not disturbing you."

"That's just me, talking to the plants."

"Seriously?"

"Oh yes. I was apologizing for the drought."

There was something endearing, almost child-like about Paula, her freckled nose, her dirt-smudged face. Anna saw herself reaching out, gently wiping the dirt from Paula's cheek, but didn't.

"Your garden is incredible," Anna said.

"It's a disaster. There are aphids on everything. There's cutworms. The tomatoes have sun-scald. Look"—she pointed—"What do you see?"

It looked like the thick, fuzzy green stem of a tomato plant. Paula poked it with a stick, it moved, and Anna could see a fat green caterpillar almost three inches long with two horns at its front.

"Oh my god, what is it?"

"Hornworm. They'll kill the whole crop if I don't keep after them." She flicked it to the ground, picked it up, and dumped it into a bucket that smelled of gasoline.

"Love the car," Anna said.

"It's George's old car from when he was in high school. He keeps threatening to have it towed away, but I like it. Adds a certain touch, don't you think?"

"I have a question or two."

"Of course. Let's go inside, get out of the sun."

A tentative smile crossed Paula's face as she pushed the screen door open. Anna followed her into the shadowed interior. Paula went to the sink. Her hair, darkened by sweat but showing touches of auburn, was up off her neck in a lop-sided top-knot secured by a red bandana. She washed her hands, rinsed her face, then brought out glasses of lemonade.

"Your garden must be an incredible amount of work."

"When you love something, it doesn't seem like work. Wouldn't you agree? And I have help. Eliza and some of the 4-H kids are here once a week."

Anna took the evidence envelope out of her bag and showed it to Paula. "A diver found this in the swimming hole."

"I wondered where I lost it. Why were you—"

"Eliza got a ride there the day before you and I were there."

"Oh . . . you thought she might have . . ." Paula hesitated. A look of worry crossed her face. "Did you tell George it's mine?"

Anna shook her head. "Not yet."

"I'd rather you didn't."

"Why?"

"It's hard to explain." A flicker of a smile faded to a frown. "Don't you have to? I mean . . . I don't want to get you in trouble."

"We know she was there. Proving she actually went in the water isn't important, but given that it was ninety-five degrees, we can be pretty sure she did. If you don't want to acknowledge it as yours, I will have to follow through, show it to the Johnsons."

"Thanks." Again, that uncertain little smile.

Why, Anna wondered, was Paula so worried that George would find out she went swimming?

"You said you had questions." Paula said.

"I talked to Jessica Williams. She said that Eliza was afraid, almost implied that her father abused her, was violent."

"She never said anything to me."

"Did you ever suspect? Think that—"

"No." Paula stood, walked to the sink.

Anna let the silence settle around them.

"Why did you join the police?" Paula said.

It was a question Anna sometimes asked herself. Ever since she was a young girl, she had wanted to be a detective, to dig into people's lives, find out their secrets. Was it growing up hiding her true self that made her so interested in finding out what other people were hiding? What did that smile of Paula's that came and left so quickly, as if it took too much effort to hold, hide?

"It's funny you never asked me that before."

"Are you going to answer?"

No, Anna thought, not really. Instead, she said, "It seems so trite now, all that wanting to do good, protect people stuff. Maybe, I just thought it would be interesting, would be fun."

"Fun. What an odd thing to say … Why did you leave Boston?"

"Aren't we the inquisitive one today?"

Another question Anna didn't want to answer. Her sergeant, Evan Morrisey, harassed her from day one, called her a dyke whenever no one could hear. She filed a complaint, it went nowhere. He cornered her in the station gym, grabbed her crotch. She headbutted him, broke his nose. He claimed she assaulted him. The bras—all me—sided with him. A settlement kept all that out of her employment record if she agreed to leave quietly. She couldn't tell Paula the truth, then ask her to keep it from her husband.

"I'm sorry," Paula said. "Was that rude?"

"I needed a change."

"I didn't mean to pry."

Anna stood. "I have to go. Thanks for the lemonade."

❖

George Baker stared at the topographic map on the conference room wall: the Johnson farm on Turnpike Road, the Kelleys' house above the village on East Road, the swimming hole on Leavitt Hill, Tooney's house on Gap Road. All of these roads headed east from Route 120, the only north-south road, and were connected by a network of trails, some known and marked, others faint animal tracks in what was almost wilderness, and all had one other thing in common: they dead-ended at the Croydon Mountains, at the fence for Corbin Park.

He'd added a mark where Ritchie picked Eliza up on Clark Camp, and another where he dropped her off at the swimming hole.

Lieutenant Colson stormed into the room.

"What the hell is going on?"

"You heard."

"Damn right I heard." Colson was fuming. "Let me get this straight. She leaves her house for a run, spends the night at the house on Gap Road, disappears for a day, then turns up miles from where we thought she was, gets a ride, and goes swimming while my people are almost dying in this fucking heat, then vanishes again."

"That's about it."

"She's up to something. You know it and I know it. She's playing some goddamn game of catch me if you can."

"Maybe you're right, but maybe you're wrong," George said. "We have indications that she's frightened of something or someone. She could be in trouble. The one thing we know for sure is she was alive yesterday, but we have no idea where she is today. We have to keep looking."

"Okay, but I'm not going to put people out there forever. Volunteers are giving up right and left. I'll give you another day, two max. We find her, you should lock her up."

"What's the charge?"

"How about wasting tens of thousands of dollars of taxpayer money, risking people's lives? Maybe just being a spoiled little-girl royal pain-in-the-ass?"

George followed Colson to the outer office, watched as he stormed out the door, found Connie Armstrong at her desk.

"You seen Gaetz?"

"Right here." The man appeared behind him as if out of nowhere.

"Christ! Don't sneak up on me like that."

"You wanted to see me?"

In the conference room, George returned to his desk, Gaetz walked up to the map and stood with his back to George, then finally turned to face the sheriff. "Any news?"

"Sit," George said.

Gaetz lowered himself into a chair facing George, but couldn't sit still. His right foot twitched and bounced up and down.

"What's going on between you and Deputy Korsak?"

"Nothing."

"Don't bullshit me. I've noticed the sniping, heard about what you say to some of the other deputies. I can't have it."

"I try to be nice. She takes everything I say the wrong way. The woman's got a giant chip on her shoulder."

There was some truth to that, George thought. Korsak often did seem ready for a fight.

"Well, keep trying. We need to work together."

"Understood."

"Any leads on the Rite-Aid break-in?"

"Yeah. A couple of geniuses from the high school couldn't keep their mouths shut with their friends. The County Attorney is working on it."

Gaetz stood, turned toward the door.

"Hold on. One more thing. How long have you known Bill Johnson?"

Gaetz seemed caught off guard by the change of subject, lowered himself back into the chair reluctantly, hesitated as if gathering his thoughts.

"I don't, really. We've hunted together a couple of times."

"How well do you know the family?"

"What's this about, sheriff?"

Anna had reported Bill Johnson's statement that Gaetz visited the farm frequently. Why was he was being so cagey? It was a simple question. George had planned to ask about Eliza's relationship with her father, but something about Gaetz's attitude changed his mind.

"Nothing special. Just hoping to learn a bit more about the family. Anything that might help us find the girl."

"Look, I barely know them."

"Another thing," George said. "We can't find Eliza Johnson's note that she left with the maid."

"I put it in the file." Gaetz stood, walked back to the map on the wall, said, "What's got Colson so worked up?"

"He just heard that Ritchie Kelley gave Eliza a ride to the swimming hole on Leavitt Hill the day before yesterday, and was upset they've been searching the wrong area."

"Hard to blame him." Gaetz continued to study the map. "I saw the Kelley boy here earlier. What's his story?"

"Good kid. Maybe the girl's best friend."

Gaetz turned back to the map, touched his finger to a spot in the foothills of the mountains, muttered under his breath.

"You say something?" George said.

"Just talking to myself."

Chapter Eight

Curiosity is like an itch. The more you scratch, the more it itches, and the more it itches, the more impossible it becomes to resist scratching, and what Jimmy Baker had learned about Corbin Park had made him very, very curious. He stepped onto the front porch and gazed over the valley percolating in its haze of humidity and sulfur-tinged pollution drifting up from the south. He looked at his blistered hands—he wouldn't be climbing anything today—but he could stretch his legs, follow the fence to the south, check out this side of it.

The chain-link marched ahead. The image of a prison returned and Jimmy wondered was he inside or outside? He traversed across a steep sidehill for about an hour and a half, and given his slow pace and the number of times he'd stopped to peer through the fence at the thick forest on the other side, he figured he'd covered two, maybe three miles.

Most New Hampshire forest has been logged and logged again, and second and third growth trees—trash pines, hemlock—come in scraggly and thick. Jimmy pushed his way through tangled bushes, then looked up in astonishment when he emerged into a hidden grove of ancient old-growth forest. Tall pines and oaks soared one hundred feet to a broad canopy that shadowed a forest floor devoid of undergrowth.

The ground was soft with decades of duff and leaves, and he walked in a primeval quiet, as if the air itself, dense and heavy with the smells of damp and decay, impeded the passage of sound. He came to a pile of huge boulders, stacked one against another that reminded him of a bouldering area in the Sierras called the giant's workshop. The fence ran directly into the first boulder and was secured to its sheer face. A fang-shaped rock, twelve, fifteen feet high, leaned against a boulder as big as a large house, creating a tunnel-like opening into which a well-worn dirt path disappeared. He followed the path into a narrow crevice, inching forward until he emerged into a small courtyard surrounded by walls of granite, open to the sky. Heat radiated off the rocks. Animal skins hung from a drying rack: deer, fox, bobcat. Body parts lay in piles: skulls, ears, paws. The ground of hard-packed sand and crushed stone underneath the drying rack was stained with dried blood.

What was this place?

A primitive structure of rough timbers and rusted metal roofing had been constructed against an overhanging wall on the opposite side of the space. Inside the shelter he found a hand-made bed of interlocked and lashed branches, a table of similar construction, a fire pit of stones, the rock wall above blackened, a few soot-stained pots.

The smell was hideous. He turned to go. A shaft of light shot through a gap in the boulders that towered around him, and he saw three figures standing in a shallow crescent, facing him.

His heart almost stopped.

What were they? Manikins? Sculptures? Offerings to some demented god? Each was made from animal parts on a framework of tree branches attached to a post set in the ground. One had a deer skull with round, dark red stones fitted into the eye sockets, an open ribcage scabbed with tatters of dried flesh, and arms of bone with deer hooves for hands. Another had a small bobcat skull with five-point deer antlers and a body of layered bronze turkey feathers that shimmered in the sunlight. In the center, the tallest figure had a torso of animal pelts crudely stitched together with thin rope, the skull of a wild boar, and stick arms with bear-claw hands.

A few unused parts—bones, a small skull—were arranged in front of the largest figure.

There was a horrible, perverted artistry to the things.

A buzzing, faint at first, grew louder. The figures seemed to be moving. Millions upon millions of flies covered them, the bottle-blue bodies teeming in the sun. He backed slowly away, on the edge of panic, as if any quick movement could bring these nightmares to life. The figures seemed to turn, to watch him leave. He stole his way out the passage, fighting the fear that the boulders would move, seal shut, and trap him inside forever.

He emerged from the rocks dripping with sweat, heart racing.

The smell coated his mouth, his skin, had seeped into his clothes. The silence was unnatural—no birdsong, no rustling of small creatures along the ground.

The path led downhill away from the boulders. It was well-used, and worn into the soft forest floor. After following it for an hour or so, Jimmy stepped out of the forest into an overgrown field that sloped down towards the back of an old farmhouse flanked by a crooked barn missing most of its back wall. The house looked abandoned, siding hung loose in places, several window panes were broken. The field was burned dry by the relentless sun. What had once been hay disintegrated into dust beneath his feet. The brittle stalks made a rasping sound as he walked. The buzzing whine of cicadas ebbed and flowed in waves of sound. He back-tracked into the forest, skirted the fields, came out on a dirt road, and walked downhill past the front of the farm. The yard was littered with junk: an old boxy TV set, broken farm machines.

Just past the farmyard was a stand of evenly spaced pines about fifteen feet high. Hadn't they come here, he wondered, back when his family was still a family, to buy a cut-your-own Christmas tree? He still remembered going into the house with his mother to pay when he was eight or nine. The place had been filthy—half-eaten breakfast on the table, trash everywhere. An old woman, bent double with a deformed spine, had taken their money while her strange son leered at him through thick coke-bottle eyeglasses. For days afterward, he'd had nightmares filled with people he knew contorted into strange shapes, looking at him with huge, distorted eyes.

He walked slowly on. A feeling that he was being watched came over him, then faded. He came out onto Leavitt Hill Road, turned right, and followed it downhill. He was lost in thought, when a sheriff's department cruiser came up next to him, slowed, and crept along at his pace. The passenger-side window slid soundlessly down, and Deputy Dick Gaetz leaned over, one hand on the steering wheel.

"Need a lift?"

"No, I'm good."

Gaetz drove ahead a few yards, pulled over, got out, stood by the cruiser. There was no way to avoid him without looking ridiculous, so Jimmy walked slowly up to him.

"So, the famous Jimmy Baker. What're you doing way out here?"

"Walking."

"Kinda hot isn't it?" Gaetz waited for a response, but getting none, continued. "Got a question for you."

Jimmy wondered why Gaetz was hassling him.

"What's going on between you and the Johnsons?"

"As little as possible."

"You shack up with the Johnson girl Sunday night?"

"You know damn well I was forty miles away."

Gaetz lowered his voice, leaned closer, like they were two friends sharing gossip about their Friday night dates. "How about Korsak? How're you doing there? Manage to convert her yet?"

Gaetz was about Jimmy's height, around forty, and had the look of a man who was once an athlete but had let himself go. Jimmy wondered if he could take him, thought maybe, maybe not. If the guy wasn't a cop in uniform with a gun and billy club and can of mace strapped to his waist, he'd be sorely tempted to find out. Instead, Jimmy said, "Have a nice day, Officer Gaetz," and walked around the cruiser and continued down the road. He heard tires squeal as Gaetz did a three-point turn and drove back up into the hills.

Jimmy saw recent tire tracks near the pullout for the swimming hole, thought about stopping, taking a dip, but decided a cold beer (or two or three) sounded better.

No one was sure why they called it the Corner Store because the long, low building wasn't on a corner. Pools of black tar pulled up by the heat spotted the recently paved parking lot. Jimmy walked around a sheriff department's SUV, stepped up onto the front porch that ran the width of the building, pushed open the big screen door, and let it slap closed behind him. It was almost as hot inside as out, though two big floor fans at least moved the air around. He saw his uncle standing at the counter paying for a cup of coffee.

"Sheriff," Bob Olsen, the store owner, said, almost shouting to be heard over the fans. "You talk to Betty Clarkson? She's been trying to get ahold of you."

"Been kinda busy, Bob. You know what about?"

"Her dog Mitzy. The poodle? You know how she loves that dog. Well, the dog's disappeared." In addition to being the only local outlet for such essentials as coffee, stale donuts, beer, and toilet paper, Olsen's Corner Store was—at least in Bob Olsen's mind—an essential communication hub for the village.

"What am I, the dog catcher?"

"Course not, but this sounded like something you might want to look into. You see, she, Betty that is, had the dog tied up in the backyard while she went to do her shopping in Leb. When she got back, dog's gone, but the collar's lying there still hooked to the tie-out. Betty says there's blood all over the lawn."

"The dog just ran off. Cut itself somehow. Probably nothing."

Jimmy, who could tell, looking at his uncle, that it was definitely not nothing, said, "How can you drink hot coffee in weather like this?" Changing the subject.

"Jimmy." His uncle turned to him. "I've been meaning to come up and check on you." He looked him over. "Jesus, what have you been up to? You look like hell."

"Hey, look," Jimmy said, pointing at the big antique clock on the wall. It had Roman numerals and looked like it belonged in a train station. "It's almost five o'clock. You want to go get a beer? I heard there's a new place up in Meriden, across from the Academy."

His uncle laughed. That old clock hadn't kept time since Bob Olsen put it there, and it was always almost five o'clock, and in Bob Olsen's philosophy, it was always time for a beer.

"We'll take the cruiser," his uncle said.

"Okay if I sit up front?" Jimmy said, as he squeezed himself in next to a built-in hardened computer. He turned around, looked through the wire grate at the back seat. How many times, he wondered, had he ridden in the back of a cop car of one sort or another? Picked up after another escapade: trying to buy beer with a false ID, caught peeping in a neighbor's window, hauled in after a fight at the town swimming pool, arrested trying to climb the tower of the Congregational Church.

Each time, bailed out by his uncle the sheriff.

The earring in its plastic sleeve glistened in the sheriff's department ceiling light and Anna Korsak remembered Paula in her kitchen, the silver against her suntanned neck, the green emerald. Why was Paula so insistent on keeping a swim on a hot day from her husband? What's the big deal? She would have to show the earring to Eva Johnson—George was sure to ask at some point—though she knew it was a waste of time.

That was the trouble with secrets. They get more and more complicated to keep, and Anna knew a lot about secrets.

Growing up in Dorchester with her plumber father and housewife mother in a nice ethnic neighborhood of Poles and Italians, her whole life had been a secret. They were good people, her parents, but conservative—to say the least—and as Catholic as the Pope. She had to be careful. It was almost a new century, for crying out loud, but in her family and neighborhood, gay liberation was a multi-cultural plot to destroy America. Her father would sit with his Boston Herald and rail at the fags and dykes that were ruining his country, and Anna had kept her real self hidden deep.

Eva Johnson took afternoon Pilates at the Fitness Spa—the same place where Anna had a morning yoga class three times a week—and should be finished in half an hour. Anna drove to her apartment, changed out of her uniform, grabbed some workout gear, and headed for Hanover.

The locker room was tastefully done in shades of mauve and pale grey: the lockers were fronted with fake wood laminate, and the changing stalls had dividers made to look like Japanese shoji walls with perfectly proportioned lattices of honey-colored wood.

Eva Johnson was two or three inches taller than Anna and almost model thin. Her pure black hair, tied in a pony tail, gleamed. She peeled off her long-sleeve top and stood there in a sports bra and tights, and Anna found herself wondering if they were natural, those gorgeous breasts. Eva seemed to sense her stare, turned away and quickly pulled a baggy sweatshirt over her head. Anna saw bruises on her right midriff and upper arm, and thought back to what Jessica Williams had said about bruises on Eliza's back.

What was it like, she wondered, for such an arrogant man to have the women in his life tower over him? It was a cliché, smaller men being pushy and aggressive, but clichés are clichés for a reason, right?

Once she had covered up, Eva Johnson turned back to her and said, "Have we met?"

"Deputy Anna Korsak." She held up her badge.

Eva Johnson removed a scrunchie, shook out her hair. "You have news?"

"I'm afraid not, but I do have a couple of questions I'd like to ask you."

"This is hardly the place, Deputy. Can't it wait until I finish changing? Perhaps we can talk out by the juice bar."

Eva Johnson emerged from the locker room in a pale grey skirt and cream-colored silk top carrying a silver sports bag and small purse. She'd put her hair up, a few strands strategically curled beside her face. The contrast between her black hair and crystal-blue eyes was striking. She'd applied discreet make-up and wore a thin string of pearls. Truly a beautiful woman. She'd been blonde when younger, according to Jimmy. Why, Anna wondered, the change? She joined Anna at a high table, and placed a bottle of kombucha on the silver tabletop.

"How can you drink that stuff?" Anna said.

"You have questions?"

Anna held up the earring in its plastic bag, handed it to her. "Do you recognize this? Could it have been Eliza's?"

Eva held the plastic bag delicately, her fingertips with their perfect lavender nails touching it as if it might somehow contaminate her.

"Where did you get this?"

"I can't say."

"It doesn't strike me as the sort of thing Eliza would wear." She handed it back to Anna. "I remember when she got her ears pierced. Her father did not approve."

"So, an argument."

"Eliza is a very strong-willed girl. They argue frequently. Sometimes, I think the girl was born angry. When she was five years old, she wanted nothing to do with me. She cried and screamed whenever I held her. But, in the last couple of years we've managed to become something like friends, not close, but at least friendly. We've gone shopping together, even went to a spa once."

All the way here in the cruiser, Anna had gone over and over in her mind how to ask about possible abuse at home, but had been unable to decide how to broach the subject. Seeing the bruises on Eva's torso and arms had made the approach seem even trickier. What would her response be? Would she rush to defend him? Many women did. Anna decided to wait, to see if she could gather more evidence, though that decision, as wise as it might be, felt like a cop-out.

"How had Eliza been lately? Has anything changed? Anything at all?"

Eva took a long drink of her kombucha, scowled at the bottle. "It's supposed to be good for you." She put the bottle back on the table carefully, positioning it just so. "Yes . . . recently there has been a difference. She started to withdraw, barely answered when spoken to."

"When did that start?"

"I'm not sure, perhaps a week ago."

"We're trying to access her phone. You don't happen to have any idea what the passcode might be?"

"Are you kidding? Eliza wouldn't tell me her name if I didn't already know it." She spoke with the barest trace of an accent. She looked impatient.

"What happened between you and Jimmy all those years ago?"

"Who?"

"Jimmy Baker, Sheriff Baker's nephew."

"That boy? Nothing happened, as you put it, between us."

"Can I ask you a personal question?" Anna couldn't resist.

"Do I have to answer?"

"Why did you change your hair to black?"

"Really, is that any of your business?" She smiled. "Considering a change? Blonde is so trite, don't you think? Are we done?"

She stood, gathered her things, tossed the half-full kombucha bottle into the trash, and headed for the door without a glance in Anna's direction, trailing a disturbance in the air behind her, like the wake a boat would leave in calm waters.

Anna slipped the earring in its plastic sleeve into her bag: mission accomplished.

She remained at the table writing up her notes on the conversation with Eva Johnson, then went to the Community Center in Lebanon to pump some iron, work out her frustrations. She lifted in a near frenzy, cranked her final bench presses as if she was pissed off at the weights.

Anna was dripping with sweat as she walked toward the locker room to shower and change. She loved the pump, the blood coursing through her veins, the pleasant throbbing of her arms, but was embarrassed to have been such an asshole, crashing the weights to the floor, as if it was the barbell's fault she had kept the truth about the earring from the sheriff. Thoughts of the earring brought memories of the waterfall, the smell of the ferns, the cool shade from the trees leaning out over the deep pool with its crystalline water, and how when that water hit you, you shivered and felt alive again.

And Paula rising like Venus herself, her wet top like a second skin, nipples hard from the cold.

Anna stopped at the spinning studio to watch a class pedaling away, going nowhere. The glass wall vibrated with some dreadful bass-heavy techno thing, and there she was, Paula Baker, dressed in pink and black bike shorts and matching skin-tight sleeveless top, cranking away furiously. The music dropped in volume and the riders slowed, warming down. Paula tossed her head back and forth, spraying sweat from her hair.

Paula bent over to extricate her water bottle from the bike's cage. Her neck and shoulders glistened with sweat, and her bike outfit was slick and shiny with moisture. She turned, their eyes met, she smiled, and gave a little wave.

Later, in the lobby, they stopped, made small talk, and Anna, basking in the post-workout glow she loved so much, heard herself ask Paula if she wanted to go somewhere for a drink. Paula hesitated, then said yes. Anna asked if she needed to call home and Paula said no, George could take care of himself.

The William Tell Pub had been open about a year. Nice building, Jimmy Baker thought, as he pushed open the massive front door: cedar shake siding, big windows, the cool interior done in plaster and pine wainscoting. Two couples occupied separate tables in the restaurant. The bar was empty, Red Sox pre-game on the widescreen with the sound off.

"William, how're you doing?" George said. "You change your name yet?"

The joke around town was that he should change his last name to Tell and then nobody would get confused.

"Very funny."

"You ever meet my nephew, Jimmy?"

"The skier? It's a pleasure." They shook hands across the polished bar. William pulled a couple of draft beers.

Jimmy perched, his uncle slouched, side-by-side, on sturdy stools with turned legs of maple, looking at the TV, drinking.

"Any sign of Eliza Johnson?" Jimmy said.

"Nothing. Fish and Game's running the search, they're close to calling it off." George took a long pull of beer, wiped the foam off his lip. "Look, I'm sorry I came down on you so hard, but you hadn't even been here a day and you go by the Johnson place? What the hell were you doing there?"

"Remembering,"

"You couldn't have done that somewhere else?"

Jimmy waited for the inevitable tongue lashing, but his uncle said, "What are you going to do? You going to stick around?"

"No. I'm going to sell the place. Head back to Jackson."

"To see that girl of yours Paula told me about?"

He had told his aunt that he and Katrina were still a couple, had wanted her to think he'd settled down, got his shit together, and he didn't want to have to answer questions about why Katrina left, and he also didn't want to admit how confused he was, how he had no ff'ing idea what he wanted to do. He decided to pretend he hadn't heard the question.

"Remember that farm where people used to buy Christmas trees? The cut-your-own place?"

His uncle took a while to catch up to the change of subject. "Yeah, sure."

"What was the family name?"

"You must mean the old Pierson place. Why do you ask?" His uncle turned to him with his what-the-hell-are-you-up-to-now look that Jimmy knew well.

"I walked by the place coming down from a hike. Just curious." Jimmy thought to mention his encounter with Gaetz, but decided best not.

"Used to be a fine farm. My grandfather and Malcolm Pierson were friends. Malcolm died, his son, Caleb, married a gal from Claremont. They had two kids if I remember right. One day Caleb was driving the tractor, their little one, a girl, couldn't've been more than five, on his lap. Wheel came off on a side-hill, tractor rolled and crushed 'em both. Horrible …" He shook his head slowly. "His wife, Maxine, had the worst back you ever saw. Spent most of her life staring at the ground. Tough old bird. Worked that place with her son."

"I still remember. It scared me half to death seeing her bent that way. Whatever happened to them?"

"She died years back. The son was put in care, hasn't been seen since."

Jimmy drained his glass, turned to his uncle. "Another?"

"One'll do me," George said.

"You need to get home?"

"No, I'm good. Paula's in town. Another fool exercise class." He turned to look at Jimmy. "What did Eliza say when she was at the house?"

"I went over everything with Deputy Korsak."

"I know. Humor me. We're starting to think Eliza planned this. You talked to her at the reception, then at the house. Did she say anything, anything at all that might give even a hint what she was up to?"

"She was amped, skittish, talked about Tooney, about the house, then said she was going to finish her run. That was it."

"Didn't it strike you as odd that she headed uphill?"

"Kind of, but I figured she knew a trail home."

Jimmy ordered another Long Trail, kept his attention on the TV. The game was about to start, a young woman was singing the national anthem, her mouth open wide, her lips easy to read. Jimmy had never felt comfortable around his uncle, but when he thought about it, he realized he never felt at ease with other men in general, had always preferred the company of women. He searched for something to say that might begin to bridge the gap between the two of them, but couldn't find the words. Finally, he said, "What was that about the dog?"

"Maybe I will have another." George gestured to the bartender, waited while he pulled the draft, said, "I read you're having trouble with cats out west."

"What?"

"Mountain lions."

"They're coming back. Mostly keep to themselves, though a big male was seen in Colorado walking through downtown Boulder around dawn one time, right down the middle of the pedestrian mall like he owned the place. Some people are freaking out, carry 45s just to go hiking. Won't let their kids out in the evening. People don't like not being the top of the food chain." A light goes on. "You have one here?"

"Keep this quiet. Two of Johnson's cows have been found, torn to pieces, half eaten. Fish and Game thinks it's a western cougar. Probably Canadian. This dog, taken out of the back yard. Could that have been the cougar?"

"Same thing happened in Jackson last year. Malamute killed in someone's yard."

"Have people been attacked?"

"A trail runner was mauled near Flagstaff Mountain in Colorado. And I read how a woman was killed in California, just outside LA." Jimmy sipped his beer, frowned. It had gone flat.

"Christ." George finished his beer, sat scowling at the empty glass.

His uncle seemed distracted, lost in thought, and their conversation withered. They watched the first inning in silence. George stood, put two twenties on the bar.

They stepped outside into a sweltering evening.

When Anna had asked if she wanted to have a drink, Paula Baker had assumed they'd pop over to Sweet Tomatoes, have a glass of wine, and then head home. Apparently not. They left Paula's car in the parking lot of the Community Center and were off in Anna's massive SUV. It was early evening and the sun had dropped behind the hills to the west, but the heat of the day lingered when they exited Anna's car. White River Junction, Vermont had once been a prosperous railroad town, but by the time Paula was growing up in Lebanon it had acquired a seedy reputation. She'd heard recently that the place with its period brick buildings was on the rebound.

Anna was wearing a silky, patterned skirt that hugged her hips and swung about her knees as she walked up Railroad Row. Paula, in her old shorts and blouse, felt underdressed. How was she to have known she would be going out?

Crystal's was down a half-flight of stairs to a polished steel door, then down another half-flight to the bar itself. Paula hesitated on the landing, looked down over the interior where couples leaned toward each other as if sharing secrets: two men, two women, a man and a woman. She saw Anna observing her, waiting for her reaction. She should turn around, Paula thought, go home to George and their house and the framed photos of her children and grandchildren, but instead she followed as Anna walked the floor from darkness into a circle of light and back into darkness, her hair flashing in the bar's spotlights as if under closely spaced street-lights on some dark, mysterious lane. The other couples (what did she mean other? they weren't a couple) looked up from gazing into each other's eyes and watched Anna cross the floor of the club.

It was arctic in the bar. A shiver ran up and down Paula's back.

They perched side-by-side on tall bar stools, their legs almost touching, facing a backlit wall of glowing many-colored bottles, the light warbled, as if they were deep underwater, drifting along looking up at the shimmering surface. The bar-top was frosted glass, lit from underneath by a pale blue light which cast strange shadows on Anna's face. She seemed, to Paula, somehow different, more herself.

"Anna, how are you?" The bartender, a tall, thin man in black, wiped down the bar-top. "Haven't seen you in ages! Who's your friend?"

"This is Paula."

"Hi, Paula." He reached out a slender, manicured hand; his skin was cool, soft to the touch. "I'm Jerome. What'll you have?"

The music got louder and the lights dimmed and at the other end of the bar two women were kissing. Anna looked worried. Probably, Paula thought, wondering if she had not made a terri-ble mistake bringing the boss's wife here. Paula didn't want her to worry, didn't want this to be a mistake, so she turned to Jerome and said, "I'll have what Anna has."

"Two Manhattans, coming up."

The drinks arrived in tall, stemmed glasses, the red-brown bourbon glowed and swirled in the conical bowl.

"Isn't this fun?" Paula said. "I haven't had a Manhattan in ages."

"So." Anna turned on her stool to face Paula. "What do you think of Crystal's?"

Paula's hand trembled slightly as she lifted her glass. A little bit sloshed over the edge, dripped down the side of the glass to the stem, then formed glowing brown beads on the bar top.

"I didn't know this place was here. George and I never go out."

"I like the nails," Anna said.

"George thinks I'm crazy."

"I think they look nice."

"Me too," Jerome appeared out of nowhere. "Good color. Very sexy."

Paula shifted on her stool and looked at her calloused hand that seemed anything but sexy holding the graceful stem of her glass, and at her painted nails that now seemed to her more red than pink. She wasn't used to being the center of attention, to being called sexy.

"I hope we can be friends again," Anna said.

And, it seemed, they could, and soon they were chatting, gossiping, and laughing.

It was so nice, Paula thought, to be talking like this, two women, friends, but she couldn't stop thinking, how can we just sit here gabbing away?

"Why haven't they found her?" Paula said, then, "I'm sorry, I didn't mean to blurt it out like that, but I can't stop worrying about Eliza. I feel wrong being here, being anywhere."

"Another round, ladies?" Jerome said before Anna could respond.

Why not, Paula thought, why not.

Anna looked at Paula, nodded. Jerome went to make the drinks.

"Honestly? We don't know where she is, what might have happened to her, but we're doing everything we can."

Anna reached over, touched Paula's hand as she talked, like friends do, and Paula was okay with that. She was okay with everything.

"What is up with your nephew?" Anna said. "I went to the house to let him know his Killington story checked out, and he comes staggering up the drive covered in dirt and cuts and blood."

"He loves doing that to himself."

"But then mister hard-ass himself comes downstairs cleaned up, wearing this beautiful apricot colored dress. I about died!"

Paula wanted to show that she wasn't shocked, so despite Jimmy making her promise not to tell anyone, told Anna about finding Jimmy dressed as Altoona Lindsay Baker and how she thought Tooney had come back to life.

Anna started laughing.

"You shouldn't laugh," Paula said.

"He was kind of cute," Anna said.

Paula twisted her glass by the stem, one way, then back, and thought about Jimmy in that dress looking so vulnerable, looking as if he needed something from her, some care, some understanding. He'd lived in her house, but had she ever really known him? Known what he thought, what he felt? She wasn't his mother. Shouldn't that have been her job, to understand him, to help him grow up knowing who he was? How could she abandon him like that?

Then came thoughts of Tooney, and Paula felt that devastating sadness hovering close, threatening to overwhelm her. She sipped her drink and looked across the bar at the wall of beautiful bottles and glasses and told herself everything's okay, it is all okay, even though she knew it wasn't, and told herself she would not cry.

"You alright?" Anna said.

"Are you going to tell George?" Paula said.

"About Jimmy?"

Ever since the day before, when Anna had shown her the earring, Paula had not been able to stop worrying that George would find out she had gone swimming with Anna. Of course she hadn't really gone with Anna, but that wouldn't matter to George. She knew what he would think.

"God, no. The earring. I still can't believe George didn't recognize it. He gave them to me for Christmas two years ago."

"I showed it to the Johnsons. Don't worry about it," Anna said.

She reached over and gently lifted a beaded earring away from Paula's hair. Her fingers brushed Paula's cheek. "These are beautiful." She pulled back as if she'd gone too far.

Paula touched her cheek where Anna's fingers had been. She was suddenly aware of her heart beating in her chest, of the cold air of the bar filling her lungs. She looked at her half-full glass, took a sip, and felt herself glowing. Two women were dancing to trance-like electronic music, and the light seemed to shift and change around them, and it was as if all else, save the two women on the dance floor, save her and Anna, was in darkness.

"They're Indian. I mean Native American. Tracy bought them for me in New Mexico. I remember when Tracy was still in high school. Eliza must have been seven or eight. She used to come over to the house and follow Tracy around like a puppy dog."

A sharp inhalation, almost a gasp, gripped Paula. "What has happened to her?"

Anna turned to look at her.

"Otis Thrasher reported a loud argument between Eliza and her father. Maybe it caused her to run away. She vanished, re-appeared, then vanished again. Nothing makes sense, but we're starting to think she's left town or is hiding out somewhere, but we don't know why."

Otis Thrasher. Paula thought about the photograph of Eliza and Otis in Eliza's room. It was so obvious Eliza cared for the old man, and Paula felt again the guilt at not having been to see him. Tomorrow, she told herself, tomorrow.

"Did I ever tell you that I wanted to name Patricia, my oldest, Anna?"

"Really?"

"It's such a beautiful name. I spent half that pregnancy reading Anna Karenina, but George insisted on naming her after his grandmother. The Bakers are big on family names."

Paula waited. Is she going to say something? Will we spend this entire evening together and not talk about it? Isn't that why she asked me to have a drink? To explain why she pulled away all those months ago?

Paula raised her glass to her lips, realized it was empty, and returned it to the bar top.

The two women were dancing slower, holding each other, swaying gently. They must have sensed her stare because as they turned slowly, one of them, a woman with killer red hair, stared back and smiled and looked so happy a longing hit Paula and she felt as though she had been punched in the stomach.

It was almost dark when they stepped outside. The brick buildings gave back the day's heat and the summer evening's humidity wrapped itself around her and it felt good at first after the chill of the bar, but soon Paula started to sweat and felt her clothes cling to her skin. She stumbled on the uneven sidewalk. Anna took her arm, and Paula was lost in her own thoughts as they walked to the car, occasionally glancing over to wonder what Anna's were.

Chapter Nine

Friday morning the valley lay comatose under a dense, pewter sky as Paula Baker sat in her car in front of the Corner Store, motor running. The chilled air from the dashboard vents reminded her of Crystal's, and how, when you were there, it seemed the only things that mattered were that moment and the person next to you, and how the complications and obligations of your life, for that short time, didn't matter at all.

Paula turned the car off, rolled her window down, and felt a blast of hot air on her face.

But of course, they did.

She put the car in gear and drove toward Turnpike Road.

Otis Thrasher's house was plastic-sided with fake green shutters. The expansive lawn was clipped as close as a golf course (not that Paula had ever set foot on a golf course), the flower beds were trimmed and symmetrical, and there were young trees planted at regular intervals. It looked like one of those computer renderings of a planned development available for pre-sale.

"Paula," Otis said as he opened the door. "Haven't seen you in some time." There was an edge of bitterness in his voice.

"How've you been, Otis?"

He produced an exaggerated sigh. "You might as well come in."

They stood in the front hall.

"Have you heard about Eliza Johnson?" Paula said.

"Of course. My wife loved that girl. After Deborah died, Eliza visited here regularly." His look made it clear that Paula had not. "Forty-two years, we were married. Do you have any idea what it was like to lose someone after forty-two years? Without Eliza, I don't know what I would have done."

The implicit criticism stung Paula.

"I wish you people would stop bothering me. Arnold was here, and that woman deputy, then another deputy yesterday. He needs to learn some manners, that one. Anyway—"

"Aren't you worried about Eliza?"

"She made me promise—"

"Promise?"

"She came to say goodbye, said she had a place to go. Told me not to worry."

"What?"

"She was scared. Didn't want anyone to be able to find her."

"Scared of what?"

"Didn't say."

"Do you realize what you've done?"

"She said a friend was coming to get her, made me promise not to say a thing for five days. That's all I know. She wouldn't tell me more. I offered to help. She said no. Five days, that's all she needed, and now it's been five, and I figure she's safe."

"Are you hearing me? There have been people out in these woods in this heat. A man had a heart attack. He's in the hospital."

"She made me promise."

❖

George Baker slumped at his desk trying to shake a hangover and figure out what the hell to do next. Too many beers last night: first with Jimmy at the Tavern, then at home, and then a nip from the bottle of Irish whiskey that his son, Charley, gave him for his forty-seventh birthday. He had watched the end of the Sox game, or rather the game had been on and he'd sipped his whiskey and brooded and fallen asleep. He woke with the post-game commentators yelling at him, lumbered into the kitchen, and saw Paula sitting outside on the deck. When had she come home? What was she thinking, sitting there, staring into the darkness?

He thought back to when they were first married. She would be waiting when he returned from his day on highway patrol, and he would talk about his day, and she would listen, take his hand.

Last night, she had been lovely alone like that on the deck, and he had wanted to speak to her, and it had bothered him that she could be so distant and that he felt he could not reach her. He'd let her be last night, though he'd wanted a word from her, of encouragement or support, and now he could see her coming through the outer office toward him, and all he could think was, what is she doing here?

"Paula."

"I need to tell you something."

He watched Paula walk through the outer office without pausing, then sat in stunned silence. Five days wasted. Five days of a hundred people suffering in this heat, scouring these woods when the damn kid is off somewhere gallivanting around, enjoying herself. Five goddamn days. I'll kill him, swear to god, if I get my hands on Thrasher …

George saw Anna by the coffee machine, leaned out of his office door. "Bring me a cup, will you?"

She walked into the office, handed George his mug, stood in front of the AC unit with her arms up. He filled her in.

"Can you please tell me why it took my wife to find out that Thrasher knew what Eliza was up to all along? Arnold interviewed him. You interviewed him. What the hell? One of you couldn't have found this out?" He sipped his coffee, made a face. "Jesus, you think we could figure out how to make a decent cup of coffee."

Anna held her shirt away from her skin, let the blast from the AC cool her back.

"Think you could let some of that head this way?" George said.

"Sorry." Anna stepped away from the vent.

"Thrasher said Eliza was scared," George said.

"I told you that Jessica Williams saw bruises that, the way she described them, could be from someone slamming Eliza against a wall, and Eva Johnson had a nasty looking bruise on her torso when I saw her in the changing room at the Fitness Spa."

George scowled, as if the coffee had somehow gotten worse.

"Be careful, don't start accusing Bill Johnson of something you can't prove. Let's get the girl back, see what she has to say. Maybe then, and only then, we'll dig into Bill Johnson."

"You seen the report from the Grafton County Cyber Forensics Lab? They can't get into her computer or her phone. They're so heavily protected we'd need the FBI, and even they might not be able to. Don't you find that interesting? What was she so paranoid about?"

"Why'd she leave the computer behind?" George said. "It was right there when we searched her room. I get the phone, she knows it can be tracked. She was last seen in her running outfit. She must have stashed things somewhere. Why not the computer?"

"Maybe she planned to come back for it, but something prevented her?"

"What about this friend who was coming to pick her up?"

"It's clear from Facebook that Eliza knows people all over New England. She could be anywhere. We should get a formal Missing Person report to State Police right away."

"I talked to Colson," George said. "Fish and Game is calling off the search."

"Yeah, about time." Dick Gaetz appeared in the open door. He had a long scratch down the right side of his face, looked tired, like he'd been up all night.

"What'd you do to your face?" George said.

"I was out with Fish and Game, got tangled up in the pucker brush."

"That looks nasty," Anna said. "You should get it looked at."

"I'm fine."

"Almost forgot," George said after Gaetz left. "What'd you find out about the earring? Not sure it matters."

"Bill Johnson had no clue. Eva didn't think it was Eliza's, but she wasn't sure. The only thing the earring would do is confirm Ritchie Kelley's story. I called and left a message that I wanted to talk to him. Haven't heard back."

Lorraine leaned in the open door. "Claremont Police on the line. You might want to take this."

"Who is it?"

"Sergeant Flanagan."

"Thanks." He turned to Anna. "Weekend coming. Get that report to the state, then take off. Big day tomorrow."

"Oh?"

"You haven't forgotten the picnic?"

"Of course not, chief. Just kidding."

George waved her away, picked up the handset, said, "Mike."

❖

Paula Baker laid a section of newspaper on the kitchen counter, and on the paper put a bottle of nail polish remover and a small pile of cotton balls. She looked at her nails. Fearless Pink. She'd liked the name and the bit of rebellion it implied, but maybe she wasn't so fearless after all.

When the heat and humidity built like this, day after day, the village seemed to sink deeper into the valley, and the hills move closer, and the trees get heavier and hang over everything, trapping the damp and the smells of old wood and forgotten dreams. Paula wondered what her kids were doing. Charley was probably at his office. Patricia was devoted to her family, but what was she going to do when her kids were grown? Would she find herself like this, sitting in an empty house wondering what to do with her life? And Tracy. Who even knew where she was?

A knock on the front door roused her, and gave her an excuse to put off deciding about her nails.

"It's open!"

Jimmy strolled into the kitchen in a red sleeveless top, shorts, and a silver and turquoise necklace, and at that moment, in the sun's light filtered by the white curtains, he did not look a day older than when he'd lived with them. His hair was damp and disheveled.

He pushed his sunglasses to the top of his head, looked at the table. "What're you doing?"

"Getting this stuff off."

"Why?"

"Your uncle didn't like it."

"Don't listen to him."

Paula screwed the cap back on the bottle of remover. Jimmy pulled out a stool and sat across from her. He seemed distant, distracted. She wanted to ask about his cross-dressing, but was afraid he would think she was criticizing, judging.

"Paula?" A voice at the screen door. They heard it creak open, then clap shut, footsteps in the hall.

The woody aromas of cedarwood and sandalwood announced Anna's presence, and it was as though Paula had been transported to somewhere in the vast American west, and for one brief moment she felt as if cool winds swept down from distant mountains, but then she was back in the sweltering kitchen with Anna standing over her in full police regalia—gun, taser, walkie-talkie.

"Oooh, a nail party," Anna said. "Don't think the color suits you, Jimmy." She noticed the remover. "You're taking it off? Why?"

"George."

"Don't listen to him," Anna said.

"That's what I said." Jimmy came back from wherever he'd been. Paula jumped up and started puttering around the kitchen.

"How did you get Thrasher to open up?" Anna said to Paula. "Both Arnold and I talked to him, got nothing. George let us hear about it, that's for sure."

"I didn't do anything, the five days were up. I think he was tired of holding it in."

Paula took down three handmade glasses that had little air bubbles in the translucent pale blue glass, filled them with ice, poured tea, heard Anna sit, her duty belt bang against the edge of the counter. She took a lemon from the refrigerator, sliced it, and put a slice carefully on the rim of each glass. Keeping busy allowed her to not look at Anna, to not think about last night at the bar, their knees touching, and Anna's hand on her arm as they walked through the sultry night.

All three of them sat perspiring in damp clothing. An undercurrent of exhaustion filled the room. How desperate we all are, Paula thought, for the slightest breath of air, the barest hint of coolness, the smallest moment of relief.

Jimmy looked at Paula, then at Anna, then at Paula, said, "I should go."

"Stay," Anna said. She took a long drink of iced tea, stared at the glass. She seemed distracted, as if she didn't know where to start.

"We've got Missing Person reports out to five states. What we don't know is why she would run away. How well do you know Bill Johnson?" She looked at Paula. "You didn't answer my question before. Was Eliza afraid of him?"

"She never said anything to me," Paula said, but again remembered Eliza in the garden that Saturday. What had been bothering her?

"That's what you said before," Anna said. "I want to know, do you think he abused her?"

"I wouldn't be surprised," Jimmy said. He walked to the screen doors, stood looking out over the backyard, his back to the two women, then turned around. "But then I'm not exactly an objective source when it comes to good old Bill Johnson. I hate the guy. He's a mean fucker."

"Jimmy!" Paula did her best to look shocked, but then remembered that tiger skin rug, the look on Johnson's face, and found it hard to disagree.

"What's got you so worked up?" Anna said to Jimmy.

"I don't know, life maybe?"

Paula watched Anna and Jimmy and wondered at their relationship. They'd known each other less than a week, yet already seemed close, to have some special connection, an understanding, like brother and sister.

"What about Eva? She came back and raised Eliza." Anna turned away from Jimmy to look at Paula.

"You could call it that," Paula said, surprised by the bitterness in her voice.

"What would you call it?" Anna said.

Paula paused.

"Neglect."

Anna, wearing a department baseball cap instead of that ridiculous Smokey the Bear thing, drove with an intense concentration totally unnecessary for the road on which she and Jimmy Baker travelled. Her ash-pale hair emerged from the back of the cap in a tangled ponytail. Again, Jimmy felt that seductive stab of envy. He searched for the beginnings of conversations, heard in his mind each veer into some potentially embarrassing area, and abandoned each, one after the other. Paula's body language had been different with Anna in the room, she walked with more grace, was some-how lighter, and Anna had followed her with her eyes as Paula moved through the kitchen, and for one moment it had seemed to Jimmy he was not there at all, and the two women were alone in the world.

Dust from the powder-dry road swirled behind them, gravel pattered against the rocker panel beneath his feet. Soon, there it was, the house. Every time he returned to it, he was struck with a moment of despair, and the nagging question of what the hell was he going to do?

She stopped the car, turned to him. "Can I come in? I need to talk to you."

"It's nicer in the cruiser, unless you like hanging out in an oven."

"You told me you didn't know Eliza before last week. Did you get together when she was in Jackson?"

"What?"

"She posted that she spent winter vacation last year skiing at Jackson Hole."

"So did a few thousand other people." Jimmy adjusted a vent to blow directly on his face.

"And, she followed you on Facebook. Has been for almost four years."

"Did you look at my page? It's bullshit. A publicist did all that."

Jimmy exited the vehicle, and watched her drive away; dust kicked up by her SUV settled around him on the overgrown front lawn. He walked to the front porch and found Lonnie slumped on the steps in the hammering sun. He looked ill and was struggling to breathe. Jimmy helped him to his feet. He smelled of wood smoke and sweat and grease and some unidentifiable odor behind it all.

"Are you thirsty? Come inside, get out of the sun. I'll get you a glass of water."

Lonnie came into the kitchen and sat at the kitchen table in a chair that seemed to groan under his weight.

"I sit here and Tooney sits there and we talk." He looked around. "Where is she?"

Lonnie did not seem able to accept the fact that Tooney was dead. Maybe he doesn't understand the concept? One moment, Jimmy would feel he was talking with a seven-year old, but then a shrewd expression would come to Lonnie's face, and he would look at Jimmy out of the corner of his eyes.

"She's upstairs, resting. She's not feeling well."

Why was he lying to him? Because it was easier?

"People get sick. They shouldn't, but they do," Lonnie said. Jimmy handed him a glass of water. "She's sick . . . I should go."

They walked outside. Lonnie, carrying his glass, sat on the edge of the porch in the shade of the porch roof. Jimmy sat in the rocking chair.

"That's Tooney's chair," Lonnie said.

"Where do you live?" Jimmy said.

"Here."

"Where's your family?"

That seemed to be enough conversation for Lonnie. He finished his water, put the glass down on the top step of the porch. A large spider emerged from a gap between two porch planks and walked toward Lonnie. Lonnie picked up his glass and smashed it down on top of the spider, squashing it flat.

"Don't like bugs." Lonnie got up and walked away.

He would, no doubt, be back. It seemed to Jimmy that along with the house and everything in it, he had inherited some vague obligation to Lonnie. To his surprise, the thought didn't bother him.

In the kitchen, Lonnie forgotten, Jimmy thought back to what Anna had said. That Eliza Johnson followed him on Facebook didn't seem like a big deal—the New Hampshire skiing community wasn't all that big—and that she had spent a week skiing at Jackson Hole not unusual. It was, after all, the best ski mountain in the country. A forgotten moment from last winter came to him. As he walked in his ski patrol uniform past the morning tram-line, he noticed a tall girl wearing silver pants and a yellow jacket. Her helmet was decorated with stickers, one of which had the letters, NH. She had her goggles up on her helmet. Their eyes met, but he had to rush to get on the tram. Could it have been her?

A feeling came over him that everything was somehow connected—Tooney dying, his return, Eliza vanishing, the western cougar, the apocalyptic heat—all of it emanating from some nodal point, and that if only the heat would break and he could think again, he would be able to see what that point was.

Driving into Claremont was depressing, George Baker thought: boarded up stores, car dealerships, even the Staples was out of business. Ever since, back in the late sixties, the interstate highway had been routed north to Lebanon, the town had declined, and now it was yet another once prosperous New Hampshire mill town on hard times. George followed Sergeant Flanagan's directions through downtown on pot-holed roads past abandoned buildings that had once been a shoe factory, a paper mill, a machine shop. Their brick walls were stained by time, windows covered with plywood. He drove down Sullivan Street past the Claremont Soup Kitchen to a neighborhood of tightly packed, run-down clapboard row houses built for long-gone mill workers. He parked behind a grey and blue police car, stepped out of his vehicle into heat and damp and the cloying smell of rot and neglect.

The relationship between city police departments and county sheriff's departments was complicated: city police had primary responsibility for all crimes within city limits, but the county sheriff had overarching jurisdiction for everything within the county. Often, rivalries developed, but George had always had good relations with the Claremont Police and in particular Sergeant Mike Flanagan, a tall, shock-haired Irishman, central casting's idea of a big city policeman from 1930.

Flanagan stood on the sagging porch of a house pockmarked by missing chunks of siding and scarred by windows shattered into gaping fangs of glass. George stepped through a low chain-link fence missing its gate, and crossed a yard filled with trash.

"George, thanks for coming."

Inside, plaster hung off the walls, trash and feces littered the front hall. The smell of urine and rotten food and shit. Flanagan stopped at the door to what had once been some family's living room. A torn, rotting rug spotted with cigarette burns covered the floor; decaying mattresses in front of a wall streaked with black mold spewed stuffing from open wounds. Clothing, food, trash was piled against the opposite wall.

The room was unbearably hot, suffocating.

"What happened?"

"Two kids OD'd. Heroin, fentanyl? Won't know till the post-mortem. We identified the guy, Robbie Marks. He's local, known about him a long time, but the girl had no ID. Two other kids who crashed here said she showed up a couple of days ago. They were too stoned to be sure when. Called herself Zee. That's it, Zee."

"Where are the bodies?"

"Morgue."

"Why am I—"

"Thought you should see this first."

Flanagan walked to a pile of moldy and half-rotted clothing—jeans, work shirts—but off to the side was a brightly colored pink top, and nearby, a single running shoe. George felt his heart sink into his stomach.

"I don't believe it," he said. "This girl was an all-star runner, great student, the best family. How could she have ended up here?"

"How does any kid end up in a place like this?"

"Morgue?"

"Follow me."

He followed Flanagan's cruiser past the emergency entrance of Valley Regional Hospital to the back of the building, then down a hill to where the basement level was above ground. They exited their vehicles, entered through a single door to the right of a grey steel overhead door.

The metallic, frigid air, and the smells of cleaning fluid and disinfectant were all too familiar. They walked down a long, sickly green corridor under harsh fluorescent light. Sweat on his back cooled, dried to a sticky salt-crust. The memory of Fish and Game's lab in Concord came back to him as they stepped into the morgue itself. It was painted pale grey and had a stainless-steel floor and two steel examination tables. A white coated attendant, Derrick by his badge, handed the two of them surgical masks.

George looked at the wall of stainless steel drawer fronts, four wide, three high, and was hit with the realization that no matter who you were, no matter the life you'd lived, if you died in suspicious circumstances you could end up here, in a three-foot by seven-foot steel drawer waiting for someone to cut you open and determine exactly how you'd died.

Derrick pulled out the first drawer. It was a skinny boy of impossible-to-guess age.

"Seen him up your way?" Flanagan said.

George leaned closer and studied a face ravaged by acne and long-term drug use.

"Nope."

Derrick gently closed the drawer, moved one bank over, double-checked the label, paused, slowly pulled it out, and stepped aside.

George moved to the side of the shrouded figure, delicately pulled back the sheet, felt sadness overwhelm him as he stared at the sweet, innocent face of a young girl, maybe fifteen, sixteen. It wasn't Eliza, but it was someone's daughter. He thought of his own when they were that age, and felt gut-punched, enraged, and wanted to hit someone, anyone.

"Well?" Flanagan said.

"It's not her."

They stood in the parking lot. Even the oppressive heat and humidity at the end of another blistered day was preferable to the hopeless cold of that room.

"Goddamn," George said. "I wonder who she was."

Flanagan shook his head slowly.

George sat in the cruiser for a long time, unable to get himself to put the car in gear. That house. The morgue. That young girl. He couldn't understand it. What is happening to our young people? Where have we gone wrong? How have we failed them?

Jimmy Baker picked up the business card from Karen Armstrong, Realtor. He'd left it on the kitchen table since their first conversation, but hadn't called her back to schedule an appointment, and he couldn't understand his reluctance, his hesitation. It should be easy, sell the place, pocket the cash, get the hell out of here. What was the hold this place had on him? It was as if the house was somehow alive, that this house that should be what it had been yesterday, and should be tomorrow what it was today, had become somehow fickle, changeable. Wandering the rooms, he sometimes felt that behind each wall there was an alternate wall and that when he left a room the walls flipped—moved by mysterious machines somewhere in the basement—changing dining room to kitchen, parlor to living room. How else to explain the time he walked into the dining room when had he not just left the dining room to walk into the parlor? No, it seemed he had left the parlor—having no memory of having entered or been in the parlor—to walk into the dining room.

In those moments he realized that it was his life that had slipped, that no longer made sense, that it was he who had become unreliable, and that this vast and incongruous house had become a manifestation of his confusion.

Who was he? Why was he here? Who had Tooney been? Why had she chosen to hide herself here?

He should go back to Jackson. There was nothing for him here, and he felt a sense of panic that if he didn't get in the car right now, and leave at this moment, he would be trapped, and he would end up old, alone in this house, and die here.

He went out the front door, down the steps, into a dense, sweltering evening that seemed alive. Bugs swarmed, creatures scrabbled in the undergrowth. Everywhere, life. The calls of tree frogs and peepers. The buzzing of mosquitoes. Somewhere an owl.

He looked down toward where the lights of the village were coming on. He imagined the good folks of the village in their houses, sitting by an open window, in front of a fan, or out on the back lawn, drained after another sweltering day. He wondered where Anna was.

There was something at the edge of the world, just beyond his reach. He could sense it there, hiding, taunting, coming closer, then pulling away, teasing, and he felt an ache that caused him to lose his breath and double over in anguish for something lost that he hadn't known he had.

He hadn't asked Tooney to give him the house, and if she'd asked him, did he want it? He would have said, no thanks. He didn't belong here. He would leave. With the decision made, he felt a bit of peace. Decided to get up early, go for a run, call the realtor, pack up his shit, say his good-byes, and get his ass back to where it belonged.

Friday night, Crystal's was loud with frenzied happy-hour conversation, but Anna Korsak was drinking alone in the cool after another overcooked day. She watched Jerome work, admired his efficiency and grace. Drink tickets were lined up in front of him, but he never rushed, was never frazzled. He mixed two drinks at the same time, one her second Manhattan, swirling the brown liquids in a tall tumbler of ice, while the inverted cone of her glass chilled with ice water, all the while keeping up a running conversation with a couple to her left.

This afternoon, Paula had looked somehow out of place in the station waiting to talk to George, Anna thought, like a nervous little girl at the door of her father's private study. Shouldn't she be comfortable there? Feel she belonged? Paula had glanced at her as she left, but hadn't stopped to talk. Was she thinking about last night here? Had it been a mistake? Anna hadn't planned to ask her out, the words were out of her mouth before she could stop them. Hadn't I promised myself to stay away?

Why, she wondered, do I so often vow one thing, and then do the exact opposite?

Jerome placed the drink, so full it domed above the lip of the glass, in front of her without spilling a drop. She felt as if loneliness bulged above her own rim and wondered what would prevent it from spilling onto the floor. She leaned over the bar for the first sip—not daring to pick up the glass—then swiveled on the stool to survey the room.

Couples everywhere—straight, gay—was she the only one flying solo?

Nights like this it seemed to Anna that she was always alone, had always been alone, that there was something in her that kept her separate from everyone around her . . . even when she'd been with Jess.

The memory of her made Anna sigh.

Jeshika Abe was her full name. She had beautiful smooth skin, glorious black hair, dark bottomless eyes, and a sharp intelligence that made every conversation an interesting adventure. Jess owned a condo in Brookline near Cleveland Square. They had been happy living together. Jess had been loving and affectionate, and her place became Anna's refuge from her cop days on the Boston streets. They stayed in, cooked together, watched movies, cuddled on the couch, and Anna had felt for the first time in her life that she had a home where she truly belonged, and had hoped that it would last forever.

But, of course, it didn't.

She wished Paula was here, and thought back to last night. A night when she had not felt alone.

At first, it had seemed to her that Paula had led a sheltered, shallow life, but Anna now realized that Paula knew things about life that she did not, what it was to be a mother, to love and care for a family, things that she had never experienced, and that she had, with her circle of queer friends in Boston, often disparaged. How rare to find one's familiar and what a cruel joke for her to be married, straight.

Jerome was on a Van Morrison kick, and as Van the Man sang, "When will I ever learn?" Anna wondered the same.

"Where's your friend?" Jerome stood across the bar from her.

"Who?"

"Paula. Who else? I liked her."

"She's married, Jerome . . . to my boss."

"Ooh, exciting."

"Besides, she's not interested."

"Don't be so sure. I saw the way she looked at you."

Van was now singing, "Precious time keeps slipping away," and it was as if shuffle on Jerome's tablet knew what she was feeling. She saw a man at the far end of the bar tapping his wallet on the frosted glass.

"Don't you have work to do?"

"Touchy, touchy."

Anna wished she had someone to talk to. Jerome was busy, and Paula wasn't here and anyway it was becoming, for Anna, more and more difficult to be relaxed in Paula's company as the specter of desire loomed larger every day. Was that why she'd, almost despite herself, come to like Jimmy so much? She felt, when she was with him, that he understood this aching loneliness.

There was a couple at a high-top, a man and a woman in their forties in all black, staring at their phones, faces pale yellow from the glow of the screens.

C'mon people, talk to each other!

When Anna climbed the half-flight of stairs to the sidewalk, she was hit with a hot, wavering breeze carrying the dark-green smell of the river. The air was thick, and the glow of the street-lights was furred in the sweltering humidity. The night seemed to her full of unspoken hopes, and she felt a restlessness that meant sleep would not come easily, and she wanted to drive to Hemlock Flat and walk to Paula's house and go to her window and call up to her to come down, come down into the night. Instead, she drove slowly, carefully across the bridge to Lebanon.

It was late, and Paula Baker was tired, but knew it was pointless to go to bed before George returned. She would wake when the bed shifted and settled under his weight, and would not be able to get back to sleep. She turned off the reading light by the bed, went to the tall window that looked out over the lawn, and waited for her vision to adjust to the dark. Mosquitos whined and buzzed against the screen.

They say that bad things come in threes.

Tooney died, Jimmy returned, Eliza ran away.

Paula wondered if the saying meant that Jimmy returning after all these years was a bad thing. He had been a part of their family and despite his teenage wildness had brought a bit of fun and joy to them those years. Tracy had adored him, and he had been wonderful with her and Patricia, kicking a soccer ball in the back-yard, buying them ice cream at the town pool. Looking back, Paula could see in Jimmy what she had not seen then, a neediness, a desperate longing to belong that he worked so hard to conceal.

Tomorrow was the annual sheriff's department picnic and George was not home yet.

The houses surrounding the village green were silent and dark. Was she the only person awake? Coyotes yapped in the distance.

Tree frogs called. An owl. The soft whir of the window fan. These sounds of night comforted her, though she felt wrong to be comforted with Eliza gone.

What could have caused her to run off, to leave us all?

Fireflies traced tangled ribbons of light over the lawn. She imagined Anna there on the grass, looking up in the light of the gibbous moon, throwing tiny pebbles up against the house to call to her, waiting for her the way Abby O'Neal had done when she and Paula had snuck away from their homes, and gone out into the night to wander the streets of their Lebanon neighborhood, holding hands, whispering to each other.

"It's like that scene from Romeo and Juliet," Abby had said.

"Why do you get to be Romeo?"

"Because I am."

Memories.

Paula saw a young deer step tentatively out of moon shadow. It nosed about in the freshly watered lawn, head down, bracing itself with thin, delicate legs spread wide as if it might fall over at any moment. It looked up, tense, ready to flee, returned to the grass.

The moonlit sky reached in through the tall windows and filled the room with a darkness like silvered velvet. Paula turned away from the fan and the air caressed her back, raising tiny hairs on her neck. She turned again, faced the fan, lifted the hem of her nightie and felt the air between her thighs, like warm breath, the softest of touches.

Twin shafts of light swept the lawn. The fawn vanished. A car pulled into the drive. George. At last.

Chapter Ten

Premonitions of dawn peeked in through the open window, and as Jimmy Baker woke a vision at the edge of a dream—a tall woman wearing a yellow dress, hair blowing in a dark wind—faded. Had she been about to speak? What was she going to say? He reached for the memory, but the harder he tried to find her, the further away she moved, leaving behind the feeling that whoever she was, was important. He lay naked on sheets clammy from the steamy night.

He padded downstairs in shorts and t-shirt carrying his trail running shoes. He needed exercise before he hit the road, and if he didn't go now it would soon be too hot. To a sensible person, it was already too hot, but about the most sensible Jimmy felt capable of being was to go early and cut it short: head up Gap Road, run the trail that paralleled the fence south until he hit Leavitt Hill Road, jog down the hill, jump in the swimming hole before he completely melted, and then walk back to the house before the sun was too high. Maybe, he thought, he should just go for a swim. That would probably be smarter, but since when did he do the smart thing?

The run would be five, six miles. Piece of cake.

Anna Korsak couldn't do it, could not wear wool to the picnic on a day that promised to be in the upper-nineties. She took off the uniform pants with their shiny stripe down the side, threw them on the bed, and pulled on khaki shorts. They worked with the uniform shirt, looked good with her tactical boots. Maybe she'd start a new summer uniform protocol. Fat chance. She knew she would hear about it, but it would be worth a little grief to be comfortable.

She stopped at the Filling Station, got the largest iced coffee they had, black, no sugar. The hills south of downtown Lebanon were barely visible in the haze of humidity. She stepped out of the shade of the Mascoma Savings Bank building, and the sun hit her back and sweat burst from her skin like she was leaking.

The bank had installed a new sign the past spring which featured a large digital display of the temperature alternating with a display of the time and date. It was 6:26 AM on Saturday, August 5 when the sign flipped to show the temperature as 90° Fahrenheit, well on the way to a new record.

They should have cancelled the picnic. Why was George Baker so damn stubborn?

George had barely touched his breakfast and had left early to get ready for the picnic. After cleaning up, Paula Baker stood under a cold shower and watched swirls of water disappear into the drain. She walked naked into the bedroom. She lifted her breasts with her hands, turned sideways, looked over her shoulder at herself in the full length mirror. What did she see? Who was she?

The long, hot day stretched out before her. What to wear?

She remembered how Anna said we all have our uniforms, but she was tired of wearing a uniform, today something different, something cool, a sun dress, a summer frock. There was something light-hearted about the word frock, old-fashioned, as if she would spend her day playing lawn croquet, or relaxing in the shade of a colorful umbrella sipping a tall, cold drink.

A frock. Did she even own a such a thing? She did, once.

She opened the doors to her closet. Clothes were crammed on hangers, some had fallen to the floor and lay there in sad, crumpled piles. There must be something here that matched how she felt. She pulled out a black dress. No, not in this heat. She remembered when she bought that dress. George was to receive an award from the Sheriff's Association at a banquet in Concord. She'd gone shopping with Tracy, home from college, and Paula had been looking at a navy blue pant suit when Tracy bounced up holding the proverbial little black dress.

"Oh, no. I couldn't—"

"Mom! Dress like a girl for a change. Dad'll love it."

But he hadn't, had he? She had loved the way that dress made her feel. When did she ever get a chance to dress up? She'd put her hair up, wore jewelry, heels, a little make-up. She got so many compliments, but George had acted like he was uncomfortable to be with her.

She rummaged deeper into the closet. Here was the blue and white candy-stripe sun dress she'd worn almost every day that summer with Abby thirty years ago. Did she never throw anything out? She held the dress up in front of her, felt a pang of sadness for the years that had fled away, for the way, looking back, her life seemed to her to have been so short.

With a little tremble of anticipation, she slipped it over her head. It fit, a little snug, but it fit.

❖

George watched the final preparations. Banners drooped from the Lebanon High School football goalposts, red, white, and blue helium balloons wobbled in the thick air above the fence where they had been tied. A big red-and-white striped tent had been set up by Brown's Catering with tables and chairs underneath so folks could eat out of the sun. There were booths—face painting, fortune telling, and the favorite, Dunk-a-Deputy. And games—three legged races, watermelon seed spitting contests, corn-hole.

Dick Gaetz, the day before, had tried to convince George to have Anna be the deputy dunkee, saying she could wear one of the department's extra-small t-shirts, but Paul Arnold had volunteered, said he wouldn't mind getting dunked as hot as it was.

George called Anna over. "I need someone to man the barbecue."

"Don't look at me. Where's Gaetz?"

"McCarthy's out sick, Gaetz volunteered to cover for him."

"Since when does he volunteer for anything? How about Bobby Jenkins? He strikes me as a grill kind of guy."

George often complained about the political part of being sheriff, but as he fiddled with the hand-held megaphone and silently rehearsed his speech, he admitted to himself that he loved the attention. When else did he get to be the center of everything?

Jimmy jogged near the fence line, warming up. Harsh sunlight poured down, hurting his eyes. He'd dithered too long, started later than he'd intended, but as he wove through the trees like the gates on a slalom run, his blood started to flow, and his heart settled into a rhythm. He cranked it up, the fence now a blur, the trees staccato punctuation on the edges of his vision. He felt alive, things made sense. This was when he was himself, hitting it, proving that he still had it.

Already, his t-shirt was a heavy wet rag plastered against his back.

The giant's workshop loomed ahead. He slowed, then was past, but the smell of the grotto followed him and with it the image of those strange figures.

He accelerated, pushed harder. He was in the zone. He ran without thinking, without care, barely seeing where he was going, carried forward by the anticipation of the swimming hole and its cold, silver water.

❖

Anna saw Paula at one of the food tables, arranging paper plates, cups, plastic forks and knives. Not yet eight o'clock and already her uniform shirt was soaked through and the heat was still growing. Paula was wearing a pretty blue striped dress that brushed above her knees, had a lighter blue scarf in her hair. She looked young and fresh despite the heat, but moved slowly, as if each action required tremendous effort, as if the stacks of paper plates were almost too heavy to lift.

Volunteers had worked most of yesterday, setting up the booths, the decorations; there was nothing for Anna to do. The point of the day, George had made clear, was to show folks that the sheriff's department worked for them, that the deputies were part of the community.

She watched helpers come up to Paula, who would point, direct them.

❖

She looks like she's sixteen, thought Paula, there in her shorts and uniform shirt with the collar open and sleeves rolled up, and her almost-white pony tail coming out of the back of the department baseball cap.

The air was thick and heavy and everyone was standing around looking bedraggled and wrung out. The trees drooped, the people drooped, even the kids, normally wild and crazy with excitement, were subdued, and looked like they didn't know if it was okay to have fun. Paula watched Anna walk to where kids sprawled on the grass in front of misting fans. She was instantly surrounded by a gaggle of young girls. Anna knelt, showed the girls her badge, her walkie-talkie, her black leather duty belt.

It was as if Paula could hear her from where she stood on the far side of the field: Anna telling the young girls, that, yes, she was a sheriff's deputy, and yes, they could be one when they grew up if that's what they wanted to be. They could be, Anna would tell them, whatever, whomever they wanted to be.

Paul Arnold walked toward one of the game booths, his head down as though he had to watch his feet to walk. Paula remembered him as a shy, quiet boy growing up, and watching the slow, tentative way he moved, she realized he was still that awkward boy. Do we ever really change?

Smoke drifted across the field from the barbecue carrying the smells of grilling chicken and burgers. Tables were laid out with potato salad and watermelon.

Jimmy's vision narrowed. The heat was so intense it seemed that at any moment the forest might burst into flames. He slowed. Stopped. Put the water bottle to his lips. It was empty. How could he be out of water already? Where was the road? Shouldn't he be there?

He smelled it first, then saw the mangled, shredded body. His eyes stung as sweat poured off his forehead. Things were blurred. He couldn't grasp what he was seeing. Greenish skin. The face was torn away, leaving empty eye sockets and a congealed mass of blood and sickly white lumps of something, and the smell hit him and a crow screamed at him and the buzzing of flies was in his head and the carcass seethed with swarming insects and he staggered off into the bushes and puked.

He wiped vomit from his lips. The edges of things quivered in the merciless sunlight. He was dizzy. His legs wobbled.

He staggered back to the body. There was black-red dried blood everywhere: on the ground, splattered on the trees. He bent over, gasped, puked again, dry heaves, stomach cramps. Bile burned the back of his throat. There was no shade. Why was the sun so high?

And then he saw the lime-green running shoes.

❖

A hint of a breeze, the air came to life. Banners on the goalpost lifted and fluttered, balloons danced as if surprised that the air, so thick and dense, could actually move. Paula turned toward it, felt the sweat cool on her skin, felt a rumble in her chest. Heard thunder in the distance. Then closer. Clouds swept in from the west and gathered above the field.

Please, she thought, let it finally rain.

Several of the balloons broke loose and were swept away in the swirling winds.

A department cruiser, lights flashing, skidded to a stop in the parking lot. A uniformed deputy jumped out and ran to where George was getting ready for his speech, pulled him aside. She saw George put down the megaphone, shout something to Anna, and then the three started running toward the parking lot.

She caught up to them by the fence.

"George, what is it?"

"Jimmy found her body."

It can't be, she told herself over and over. It just can't!

She watched them drive off, tires spinning, gravel flying, The first fat drops of rain hit the parking lot making small craters in the dirt, and then the heavens opened up and it was pouring and thunder rolled across the fields and lightning cracked the sky and everyone was running for shelter, men and women shouting, kids screaming. A rapier of wind swept across the parking lot and knocked the grill over scattering smoldering charcoal and burned pieces of chicken over the grass. The face painting booth disintegrated sending shards of wood and particle board in all directions. One of the posts on the big tent snapped in two. The tent came loose and the people who had taken shelter there ran for their cars.

Paula stood in the downpour, water streaming down her face.

❖

George stepped out of his SUV onto the sizzling pavement of Clark Camp Road. A hot wind blew up the road, raising little devils of dust from the powder dry roadside. It was like standing in front of a blast furnace. He gasped for air. In the distance, he could hear thunder as the storm cell moved off to the northeast without touching where he stood.

"You ever seen such heat?" Bob Wilson said. A local electrician and one of Hemlock Flat's most active volunteer firemen, he leaned against a shiny aluminum toolbox on the side of his truck drinking from a gallon jug of water. His face was red and blotchy.

"Got here as fast as I could," George said. "Needed to talk to him."

"EMTs took him to the hospital. He was in rough shape. The heat got to him bad. I made him take some water, but he vomited it back up. Said he found a body back in the woods, along the fence somewhere. I told him what Lorraine in Dispatch said about a calf. He shook his head, said cows don't wear running shoes. He was almost incoherent, kept going on about a woman. He could see her. She was trying to tell him something."

"Who's there?"

"A couple of deputies, volunteer firemen is all."

"How is it?"

"Bad."

This is the third time, George thought as he walked up the trail, that he had come to a place expecting to find Eliza Johnson dead: first, Johnson's cow; second, the swimming hole, convinced her cold body would float up to meet him; third, the Claremont morgue as he slowly pulled the shroud back to reveal the chalky grey face of a different, young girl.

Cicadas buzzed and whined in the trees, the heat was a heavy weight on his shoulders. He was the last to arrive at the scene.

Anna and two volunteer fireman were standing well away from the body when George got to the clearing in the forest. He held his breath as the smell rose up to greet him. Dick Gaetz was walking around the body, bent over, peering down.

"What're you doing?" George said, "Step back."

"What difference can it make?" Gaetz said. "The scene's a complete disaster."

George saw bloated skin black with decay and crawling with maggots, hair in dark, blood-stained clumps above a bare toothed eyeless face, green shoes, a bit of gold jewelry that glittered in the sun. It had to be her. He turned away, staggered into the trees, vomited, not at all ashamed. There was something wrong with you if this didn't make you sick.

He left the crime scene and walked slowly through a bleached forest toward his vehicle. Volunteer firemen had already marked the trail with bits of orange tape to guide Crime Scene Services to the body. Something squeezed his chest, his breath came in short, harsh gasps. He stumbled. Anna came up beside him.

"You okay, chief?" She took hold of his arm

"I'm too old for this shit."

"It's not much further to the car. Hang in there."

To the west, clouds piled up over Vermont. They reached the department cruiser. Anna helped George into the passenger seat, handed him a bottle of water, then walked around to the driver's side. They sat in silence, the AC on high. George slumped in his seat. He felt muddled, confused, couldn't think straight.

"We have to tell the Johnsons," he said finally.

"We should wait, be sure."

"You know this won't stay quiet, better they hear it from us."

"I've contacted the state police," Anna said. "They're sending someone, a Captain Wagner. Know him?"

"No."

George covered his face with his hands, and for one of the few times in his twenty-year career in the Sullivan County Sheriff's Department, regretted his career choices, regretted everything in his life that had brought him to this point where he would have to tell a father his daughter had been killed by a mountain lion.

It was his fault they hadn't found her.

He felt the cool air on his face, took a long drink of water, tossed the empty plastic bottle into the back seat. His mind began to clear. Something didn't make sense.

"How the hell she end up here? Where has she been?"

It was past seven in the evening. Paula had been sitting with George in a quiet corner in the waiting room of Alice Peck Day Hospital since five. Jimmy, pale and drawn, walked slowly over to them in shorts and a t-shirt Paula had brought from the house, purple hospital socks on his feet, tape from an IV on his left forearm.

"They're not going to keep you overnight?" Paula said.

"The nurse said to take it easy is all," Jimmy said.

"Jesus, Jimmy, how do you do it?" George said.

"What?"

"Manage to find trouble."

"Seems like it's trouble that finds me," Jimmy said. "I just went for a run."

"In this heat?" Paula said. "What were you thinking?"

They sat in hard plastic chairs, Jimmy slouched over his knees, looking, to Paula, young and weak and vulnerable. Captain Hugh Wagner of the New Hampshire State Police walked up carrying Jimmy's shoes in a plastic bag, handed them to a uniformed officer. George stood quickly.

"What's happening?" Wagner said.

"CSS just got to the site," George said. "They brought in lights, will be there most of the night. Korsak is there. She'll keep me posted."

Paula put her hand on Jimmy's shoulder, said, "I've reserved a room at a hotel in Hanover. They assured me their AC is working. You need to stay out of the heat, take a cool shower."

"I'm fine," Jimmy said.

But he wasn't. Paula could see that, anyone could, but he would never admit it. A tidal wave of fatigue swept over her and she slumped in her chair and an involuntary cry, small, like a kitten's whimper, escaped her lips and she looked at Jimmy and felt tears come to her eyes and knew that there was something she should tell him, something important, but she couldn't, at that moment, think what it was.

Chapter Eleven

IN HER DREAM THAT night, Paula Baker was standing in a field and golden hay rippled in a breeze that blew her hair across her face. A woman came walking toward her, golden like the hay, and was about to speak when a loud noise came from somewhere, and Paula couldn't hear what she said.

She jolted awake to the theme song from Rocky. George's cell.

Paula lay there, jarred into a reality where young girls were killed by raging wild animals. Would he never wake and turn off that ridiculous music? The world could end and George would sleep on. It's one of the kids, she thought. Something terrible has happened. Why else would someone call in the middle of the night? Finally, she felt him stir. The light on his side of the bed clicked on. She heard him fumbling to find the phone; it rattled across the bedside table, fell to the floor. He groaned. The bed shifted as he leaned over to pick it up.

"Do you know what time it is?" His voice was thick with sleep. "What? I'll hold . . . Yes, this is he . . . What? You're sure? Jesus H. Christ. Yes . . . Okay. In the morning."

"George. What is it?"

"It wasn't her."

"What?"

"The body. It's a boy."

What was he saying? She couldn't understand. A boy? What about Eliza?

❖

George Baker scanned the briefing room of Fish and Game's mobile command unit. Seven o'clock in the morning, and the faces looking back at him were drawn, haggard. The room smelled of burned coffee and stale sweat, and a pervasive undercurrent of exhaustion. Paul Arnold looked devastated, Joe Colson like he hadn't slept in days, and Anna Korsak like anger was the only thing keeping her going.

"Give me a moment," George said.

Even Captain Wagner, normally fresh and crisp, was rumpled, disheveled. He walked to the front of the room. "As you all know, State Police's role in local investigations is support and assistance as needed. Crime Scene Services is done at the locus, the body has been sent to the Medical Examiner. Your team should work the investigation with Fish and Game. We're treating it as suspicious until the ME can determine the exact cause of death. My money's on the damn cougar."

George couldn't concentrate. Hiking out of the woods the day before had damn near killed him, or maybe it was the weight of what he saw—that poor kid, all torn apart—or maybe it was the tongue lashing he got from Bill Johnson this morning. Why the hell did I call him last night, tell him his daughter's been killed, when it turns out it isn't her? Why didn't I wait? And, what the hell is a locus anyway? Speak English, for crying out loud.

"What has CSS come up with?" Anna said.

"We're lucky the storm missed the area," Wagner said. "We've got clothing, a gold pin, footprints—the cougar's, other animal's,

Jimmy's, the kid's, other unidentified prints, some from emergency personnel"—a pointed look at the assembled deputies—"and you know as well as I do that CSS does not like to speculate. Full report, scene diagram are in the works."

"That's it?" Anna said. "They must know more than that. It'd be nice if you guys communicated with the locals once in awhile. I mean, who the hell was he?"

"You need to work the local angle," Wagner said. "The lab is backed up. They'll run DNA as soon as they can, but that won't mean anything until we have something to compare it to."

"What about time of death?" Anna said.

"The heat increased the speed of decomposition, so time of death is going to be hard to nail down. Best guess is approximately thirty-six to forty hours before the body was found. That damn cat and whatever fucking scavengers chowed down on the body did a hell of a job. I've never seen anything like it."

"Ff'ing state. You must have more than that," Anna said.

Wagner made his way toward the door, stopped, said, "When I know more, you'll know." He gestured to George, led him away from the others. "I'm not going to make a big deal of this, but you need to teach your deputies how to respect a crime scene. There's duty boot prints all over the place."

After Wagner left, Anna moved close to George, said, "You talk to Bill Johnson?" quietly into his ear.

"First thing—"

The phone rang. George grabbed it, put it to his ear, shouted, "What?" Listened. Slammed the phone down. "Goddammit. The crazies are out."

The community softball field, pickups everywhere, men holding rifles, drinking coffee, sun burning down, reflecting off the chrome of the trucks. George blipped the siren, screeched to a stop, jumped out of the cruiser, staggered when the scorching air, dense with exhaust fumes, hit him full on.

"What the hell is going on?" he shouted.

He knew most of the men: locals, farmers, construction guys.

Bill Johnson stepped up, red-faced, glared at him. "You've got no standing with me, Sheriff, after what you put us through. We're going after it. Think I'm going to do nothing while that animal is out there?"

Twenty-four hours, George thought. We couldn't keep this quiet for twenty-four goddamn hours.

Johnson held a hunting rifle pointed at the ground, fanciest looking thing George had ever seen. There was something odd about the way he held the gun, close to his body, the way he moved his hands over the polished wood stock, gentle, like it wasn't a weapon.

"Put the guns away, boys," George said. "Nobody's hunting anything today."

"We got a right to defend our families," Larry Walters said. He was dressed in weird, angular camo. The rest of the men, awash in sweat and testosterone and caffeine and who knew what else, muttered agreement.

"Look," George said. "I know you all want to do something, but if you run off half-cocked, the only thing'll get shot is one of you knuckleheads."

"Heard it was a mountain lion!" Walters shouted, held up an assault rifle.

"Put that thing down before you hurt yourself." George smelled alcohol. "You been drinking Larry? Anybody else had a couple? How about I get out the breathalyzer, test you all. Reckon you drove here. You blow more than point oh eight, it'll be DUI for sure."

Heat radiated off the cracked dirt of the parking lot in waves.

Bob Wellman, dressed in hunting clothes that looked like he'd just bought them at Walmart, walked up. "George, you know New Hampshire has a Bounty Law? Passed in 1878. You know what else? Never bothered to repeal the darn thing. Cougar's got a two-dollar bounty on its head, and any citizen is authorized to go after it."

Christ, George thought, there's always a damn lawyer. "Bob, you look ridiculous. Go home."

Dick Gaetz walked up wearing jeans and a camo t-shirt, carrying a hunting rifle, badge clipped to his belt.

"Dick," Johnson said. "Glad you you could make it."

"What the hell are you doing here?" George said.

"Trying to keep things under control. You can't stop them, boss, Wellman's right."

"What're you going to do, sheriff?" Johnson said. "Arrest us all? Eliza might be out there. I'm going after it." He looked at the others. "You with me?"

The men jumped in their trucks, roared out of the parking lot. Some headed north on Route 120, others south. George had lost control. All he could do was hope nobody was out in the woods. It was going to be a war zone. He sat in his cruiser, and stared at the now vacant parking lot. It seemed to him that the world had gone off the rails. A dead kid. A missing girl. The woods full of armed hysteria. The more he thought about it, the more he felt that this was all about Eliza Johnson. She's up to something, Lieutenant Colson had said, playing a game with us. What if he was right? And that game turned deadly.

When Eliza was younger, she had been almost a member of their family. Paula had often taken in strays: dogs, cats, Jimmy, Eliza. The girl had been stubborn, uncooperative, and despite being several years younger than Patricia and Tracy, Eliza became the ringleader, got his otherwise well-behaved daughters in trouble. George had tried to be understanding—she'd lost her mother after all—but he'd never taken to her.

His radio squawked. They were waiting for him back at the command unit.

❖

A warm breeze filtered across the shaded porch, dried the sweat on Jimmy Baker's neck as he drank from a tall glass of water. He felt weak, wobbly. His uncle had made it clear he needed to be available if there were more questions, so his plan to leave would have to wait. Besides, he didn't feel strong enough to travel, and he could use the time to get the house on the market.

A gun shot in the woods to the north of the house shattered the quiet.

How did I get mixed up in the death of a girl I barely knew? Couldn't somebody else have found the body?

He waited for confirmation, but it had to be her.

Why does this shit happen to me?

He walked into the house, went upstairs, sat at Tooney's dressing table. The room had become a sanctuary for him. Maybe that was it, this wearing her clothes, her jewelry, sleeping in her bed, a chance to be someone else, to escape his train-wreck of a life, but it was more than that, he had come to like himself in women's clothing, and had felt a new comfort from the first time he put on that blue dress, had felt somehow more alive.

He opened a drawer and took out a long, slim box covered in black leather, lifted a string of pearls off the vermillion velvet lining, and reached the ends behind his neck. He fumbled with the clasp. He imagined Tooney here. Did she struggle with the clasp? Or, had there been a man standing behind her, his hands on her shoulders before placing the pearls around her neck, gently, like a caress, fastening them for her. Were pearls like this the sort of thing a woman bought for herself? Or would they have been a gift from a husband, a lover?

Perhaps, he thought, it was a woman standing behind her.

At last he got the clasp to work, and he felt the pearls, smooth and cool against his neck.

He wandered downstairs into Tooney's office, and looked at the shelves filled with scrapbooks and papers and decided to go through them. Anything to keep busy, distracted, to help him escape the memory of what he saw yesterday. He loaded two boxes and carried them into the dining room. He tied the red velvet curtains back from the floor-to-ceiling windows, dust swirled in the invading daylight. He emptied records, statements, letters, loose photos from the first box onto the big table.

In the second box he'd put two thick scrapbooks, memory-books, the kind you buy in a craft store, one blue, one red, with thin gold stripes on the padded covers.

One of the scrapbooks was about him.

Here was his school picture from when he was twelve. He looked at the camera with a scared, timid expression, as if he knew what was to come. It was that year that his mother took him to live with his aunt and uncle. He remembered her packing his things, explaining it would only be for a short while, until she got on her feet, but of course it hadn't been, had it? She'd sold the family house, moved away, left him behind, as if the collapse of her marriage was somehow his fault. He'd worked so hard to erase her from his memory, and now this stupid photo threatened to bring her back. He turned the scrapbook page, but had never been able to turn the page on the festering pain of that abandonment.

Here were clippings from the Valley News about his local ski racing victories; the Jackson Hole News about extreme ski comps out west; articles from Ski Magazine; the Outside Magazine cover that screamed, "The Best Skier in the World?" He'd never lived that one down. Here was the press coverage of his escapade and arrest in Utah, and another article from a more recent Outside that asked, "Can the Party Boy Still Ski?"

Why had Tooney collected all this?

On that first Outside cover he was grizzled, sun-burned, gazing off into the distance looking rugged and heroic, the mountains of Alaska in the background.

He didn't recognize himself in that face.

The other scrapbook was about Eliza Johnson. There were articles from the local sports pages about her running, cross-country skiing. By the end of the winter of her fifteenth year, she had been ranked fifth on the Junior National Nordic Team. And so many photographs. Paging through them was like a stop-motion movie of Eliza's life, but each photo triggered a flashback of what he had seen, and could not forget, yesterday. A little girl played on Tooney's porch dressed in tomboy clothes with two short braids sticking out like antenna—empty eye sockets stared at him. Eliza running—a green shoe covered in blood. Eliza in a red dress—blood splatters on plants and trees.

It was too much. He stood, tried to walk away, but returned.

There was a professional portrait of her smiling at the camera, perhaps for her high school yearbook. Jimmy stared at that photo for a long time, and the longer he looked the more he could see behind that smile a sadness in her eyes, in the slight furrow of her forehead, in the tightness at the corners of her mouth. It was an expression he recognized, an expression he saw every time he looked in the mirror. He tore the school photo of himself from the other scrapbook, held the two side-by-side.

They could be brother and sister.

A puff of air touched the back of his neck and the pearls were cool against his skin and he felt his great-aunt there in the room with him. He turned back to the picture of newborn Eliza in a fluffy pink knit cap, dated May 25, 20__. She had turned sixteen two and a half months ago. He counted back. He felt as if the floor opened up beneath him and his stomach fell out of his body, down through that hole in the floor. He should have known. When and how had he become so good at not seeing, not knowing?

He pushed the scrapbook away, staggered out to the porch, letting the screen door slam behind him.

The humidity, the sheen of sweat on his skin, the sound of cicadas in the hot sun, and the fragrant breezes from the wetlands and meadows, all, since he had arrived in Hemlock Flat, triggered his memories of Harriett Johnson. How could parents name a baby girl Harriett? It was an old lady's name, and Harriett Johnson was most decidedly not an old lady. She was gorgeous.

Jimmy had been trimming trees near the house with his shirt off when he turned and saw Harriett watching him. He'd never forgotten that moment. She had asked if he wanted some lemonade. In the kitchen she stood close as he drank, took the empty glass from him, put it in the sink, touched his bare chest, took his hand, and led him further into the empty house, and there, in a guest room, Jimmy had sex for the first time and fell in love. They met those last weeks of summer—which for him seemed to last forever—when the house was empty, at a motel, at George and Paula's when they were out, always, Harriet guiding him, Harriet in charge. And then, one last time.

The Sunset Motel was tucked into a grove of trees on the banks of the Connecticut River south of West Lebanon. Jimmy was lying on his back in the rumpled bed, the cool draft of the AC unit drifting over him. He watched her adjust her bra, pull on panties, slip a pale yellow cotton dress over her head. She turned to face him, brushed her hair away from her eyes, looked down as if suddenly shy, and as he wondered at the different meanings that could reside in a woman's gesture, she said, "We have to end this, Jimmy."

"Why?"

"I'm sorry. It's been fun, but we have to stop."

She looked back at him from the doorway, then softly closed the door behind her. He lay staring up at the ceiling, stunned. He brought his hand to his face and smelled her on his fingers and couldn't believe it was over. In the days that followed when Jimmy was working at the farm, she avoided him, wouldn't look at him, and he was devastated. He had been abandoned, again. And then Eva came on to him, Bill Johnson attacked him, Eva disappeared, everything went to hell, and he was sent away.

Here on the porch, he could look down Gap Road toward the village and feel himself safe from the troubles of life. Was that why Tooney had moved the house here, to feel herself apart? He remembered sitting here just days before he was shipped off to board at the Killington Ski Academy. End-of-summer fireflies darted across the meadow, crickets called in the gathering dusk as the humid evening settled around them. Faint flickers of heat lightning, distant trembles of thunder. Mist rising up from the damp grass. It was like they were the only people in the world.

"What happened, Jimmy?" his great-aunt said.

They rocked in their chairs and sipped their iced tea and he told her about Harriett and his broken heart.

When had Tooney realized that he was Eliza's father? Was that why she left the house to him? For Eliza? Why did she wait until she was dying to summon him back, to leave a trail of clues? Why not come right the fuck out and tell him? Had she been mad at him for cutting off all contact? He didn't know that Harriett had died, didn't know when Tooney took sick, didn't know and thought he didn't care, but he realized now that no matter how hard-ass you think you are, no matter how many times you tell yourself they don't matter, the people that you've known and loved stay a part of you whether you like it or not.

He had a daughter. The idea stunned him. He thought back to when he and Katrina had talked about marriage, kids, and he'd been adamant: he did not, and would never want, kids. But. He had a daughter.

He was torn. What did it matter who's genes the girl carried? She was dead. Who else knew? Could he pretend he didn't know, put everything back, and leave? Walk away? He stumbled down the steps and stood in the middle of the front yard and looked up at the mountains and the flat-white sky, and felt the urge to run, run as far as he could, but isn't that what he'd been doing all his life?

It hit him, the horror of the way Eliza—his daughter!— had died. What had been her last thoughts as the cougar attacked?

After George had gone to work, Paula Baker had spent most of the morning sitting in the kitchen trying to understand what was going on. It was so like him, she thought, to dump something on her and then refuse to explain. After the middle-of-the-night phone call he'd gone back to sleep, risen early, and left for the station without another word. What was she supposed to do, what was she supposed to think? A boy has been killed? And Eliza is still missing?

She hadn't been able to get back to sleep, and had lain there in the dark listening to George snore next to her, and now she was tired, but it was not the kind of fatigue that can be helped by rest. Rest only brought more time to think, to worry, and left her more exhausted than before.

She finally roused herself, and cleaned the kitchen, then found herself in the middle of the bedroom, lost, unaware of how she came to be standing there, unable to recall why she had come upstairs, what she had meant to do. The night before she had stood at the open window and watched the fawn on the grass, so beautiful and delicate, so timid and ready to flee, and felt, now, that she was like that fawn, and didn't understand why she was so anxious, so sure there was danger somewhere, just out of sight, on the edge of her life, waiting for her, and she was hit by the sense that nothing is real—her, this house, this life—and that everything around her was fake, and that she spent her time pretending, pretending to be someone she was not, pretending that what she did mattered, and that if she stopped pretending, everything would crumble and fall away and there would be nothing left. Nothing.

She made the bed, then returned downstairs. She paced the kitchen, the dining room, the living room, and looked at the shelves filled with books she'd read, but couldn't for the life of her remember what any of them had been about. She stood at the door to George's den. There were papers strewn on the floor, an empty beer bottle on the table next to his chair. His big TV sat blank, mute. She thought to clean the room, then thought no. He didn't like her moving his things, and with that her thoughts went back to George. Why did everything in her life revolve around him?

She'd often thought about getting a job, but the one time she brought it up George became angry, and had acted like it was a criticism of him, like it meant she thought he didn't make enough money. They'd argued and then George had gone silent, and she didn't have the energy to try again.

This is what I do, Anna Korsak thought, sit in meetings. Paul Arnold, Bob Lester, and Ralph Nevins, two deputies newly brought into the case, were across the table from her in the briefing room. The team. Looking at them and thinking about her own distracted state of mind did not inspire a lot of confidence.

George came into the room, red-faced and hot and clearly exasperated.

"Where's Gaetz?" Anna said. "Shouldn't head of Enforcement be here?"

"I'm covering for him," Bob Lester said, glared at her. "You gotta problem with that?"

Why, Anna wondered, are the enforcement guys such jerks?

"CSS emailed their preliminary report. Here's what we've got so far," Anna said. "The victim is a white male, estimated to be somewhere between fifteen and seventeen years old. He was not killed by the cougar. He was struck violently from behind with a round, smooth object, probably a rock. The skull was crushed. Death would have been almost instantaneous."

"That's it?" Paul Arnold said.

"The rest of it was post-mortem. Apparently the cat played with the body very soon after the kid was killed, batted it around, tossed it up in the air. All kinds of fun. Think house cat with a catnip mouse was the tech's idea of being helpful. Then scavengers—crows, coyotes, maybe farm dogs—joined the party." Paul

Arnold stood quickly and left the room. Even Bob Lester seemed at a loss for words.

"Are you having fun?" George said.

Sometimes, Anna thought, I hate myself, but if I stop joking . . .

Paul Arnold returned looking a little pale.

"Sorry," Anna said.

"What about the scene diagram, the footprint analysis? Something that might actually be useful," George said.

"It's coming, so they say," Anna said.

"We need to identify the vic," Bob Lester said.

Vic? Anna thought. What is this, a cop show on TV?

"He was wearing nylon shorts, Adidas tank top, and Adidas running shoes," Anna said. "The clothes almost match the description of what Eliza was last seen wearing, and the shoes match hers, same color, same size. It's got to be Ritchie Kelley, he and Eliza were often seen dressed alike."

"We need to wait until we're certain," George said.

"I know we jumped the gun with the Johnsons, but we can't wait," Anna said. "We need to talk to them."

"Okay, okay," George said. He paused, looked lost, like he didn't know what to say, what they should do. She was about to speak when he rallied, continued.

"Nevins, see if you can track down the ski team list, find out who else might have one of those ski pins. Paul, start looking at Eliza's friends again, see who she might have given hers to. Anna, contact the Kelleys, but don't alarm them until we know more. Then talk to Jimmy. See if he can show you where that trail goes. He was running on the damn thing, he ought to be able to tell you something. That's it, get going. Hopefully, we'll have more from the state soon."

"What about Eliza Johnson?" Anna said. "There must be a connection."

Everyone cleared out, leaving Anna alone.

Her cell chirped. Jimmy. He had to talk to her. It was important.

Did he want to come to the command unit? No. Should I drive up? No, I'll meet you somewhere. She told him to meet her after work at Crystal's.

Anna spent much of the rest of the day catching up on paperwork and trying to get in touch with the Kelleys. She called Martin's office, learned he was in still in Boston at his conference. She tried his cell, got voicemail, left a message. She talked to the neighbors, learned that Theresa Kelley was visiting friends in Vermont, tried her cell. Another voicemail. The neighbors also said that they hadn't seen Ritchie in a couple of days. She looked up from her desk at the station clock. It was almost five. Where had the day gone? How can time collapse like that?

She drove to her apartment, changed out of her uniform, then drove to White River Junction to meet Jimmy.

"Alone again," Jerome said as he started to work on her drink without a word from her.

"Waiting for someone."

"Why so down?"

Jerome walked to the end of the empty bar, fiddled with a tablet, and Melissa Etheridge blasted out of the speakers. He stood across from her.

"Really?" she said. "Are you trying to make me feel worse? You know what that woman's music does to me."

"Sometimes you have to feel worse to feel better."

Jerome, like all great bartenders, had an uncanny ability of sensing when you needed to talk, and she needed to talk, but she couldn't talk about what was really bothering her. She'd held it together at the scene, played funny-tough during the meeting with Arnold and the others, but she was haunted now by the vision of that mangled body. It was Ritchie Kelley, she was certain, and she remembered him washing his car, how young he'd seemed, his smile when he said Eliza's name, and how concerned he had been about her.

"Damn, this music reminds me of college—"

The door opened, and there was Jimmy on the landing wearing shorts and a top that glowed in the ultraviolet black-lights. She saw him notice two men dancing slowly in the far corner of the dance floor.

Jerome placed the drink in front of her. "You were saying?"

"Another time."

"Cool place," Jimmy said when he arrived next to her. He looked at her glass. "Manhattan?"

Anna did the intros, watched Jerome check Jimmy out.

"Baker?" Jerome said. "Any relation to Paula?"

"My aunt," Jimmy said, looking puzzled. "How's your Manhattan?"

"The best," Jerome said. "Right, Anna?" Anna glared at him.

"I'll be the judge of that," Jimmy said, then smiled. "Do you have Four Roses?"

Is he flirting with Jerome? Jimmy Baker was one surprise after another.

They sat while Jerome mixed the drink with more than his usual flair, conscious, it was obvious, of Jimmy watching. Jerome hovered. Jimmy's hand trembled slightly when he raised the glass. The happy hour crowd started to file in, Jerome got busy, and soon there were people sitting on either side of them.

Jimmy looked right, left, said, "Let's find a table."

"Before you start, Jerome is a good friend of mine. Don't lead him on."

"I was just trying to be friendly."

They carried their drinks to a far corner. She realized he was wearing another thing of Tooney's. It was sleeveless, the thin fabric somewhere between ivory and ecru with tiny pearl buttons and delicate embroidery. She wondered if it would fit her.

"Cute blouse," Anna said. "Very pretty."

"What? It's a shirt."

"Yeah, right."

"How does Jerome know Paula?"

"I ran into her at the fitness center. We came for a drink."

The idea of his aunt here seemed to require serious consideration.

"You wanted to talk?" Anna said. "So, talk."

"That summer I worked for the Johnsons? It wasn't Eva I had a thing with, it was Harriet Johnson."

"This is very interesting, Jimmy, but kind of ancient history."

"It was seventeen years ago." Jimmy said.

Anna saw Jimmy staring at her like she was an idiot, did the math in her head.

"Holy shit— Are you sure?"

"Yes. Harriet ended it and I was broken-hearted, and then the shit with Eva hit the fan, and they sent me away, and I was so pissed off and miserable that I vowed to never have anything to do with this fucking place." He clenched his hands, hunched forward. "And, now Eliza's dead before I ever knew her. I can't get the image of those shoes caked with blood out of my mind. Isn't that weird? It's the shoes . . ."

She saw him shudder, heard a little strangled cry. He drained his glass like it was water, said, "I need another."

"I'll get it. Stay here."

Anna stood at the bar while Jerome mixed two Manhattans. No sense letting Jimmy drink alone. What does this mean? Does Bill Johnson know? Suspect? Did Eliza? Who else would care? She looked back across the room at Jimmy in that beautiful blouse. Who was he really? He. Was Jimmy really a he? Or a they? But, Anna still couldn't get used to they, though she knew she should, and if she thought about it, maybe Jimmy was really a she, but didn't know it. How could he not? Acting as if the dress, the blouse, were just a bit of fun.

Jerome saw her glowering at him. "I have a big mouth."

"No shit."

He slid the drinks across the bar. "Sorry."

"Jimmy's okay, but be more careful." The music changed to a slow house beat, the bass line throbbed in her chest. "Not sure the sheriff's wife wants it known she hangs out in a gay bar." Saying that made her realize how hopeless it was, this crush.

She returned to their table, handed Jimmy his drink.

"What did Paula think of this place?" he said, then looked at her like he wanted something from her, needed her to tell him it was going to be okay. George had told her to tell no one until they identified the body, but how could she leave him like this?

"If I tell you something, can I count on you to keep it to yourself? Not a word."

He nodded.

"It wasn't Eliza. The body was a boy. And, he wasn't killed by the cougar. State says he was murdered."

Jimmy stared at his hands that looked, to Anna, too big to be holding the delicate stem glass.

"Who do you think knows?" Anna said.

"About Paula?"

Why would he think she was asking about Paula?

"No. You. Eliza."

"Where is she?" he said.

They left their cars in White River Junction. They'd had another round, and Jimmy was almost drunk, and he was pretty certain Anna was more than a little tipsy. Jimmy was going have the driver take him all the way to Hemlock Flat until he realized he was basicaslly broke and asked if he could crash on her couch. They stumbled up the stairs to Anna's second-floor apartment. There was a beat-up couch and a yoga mat in the middle of what was essentially an empty living room.

"You got anything to drink?"

"Tea?"

They sat at the bare formica table, two mis-matched mugs of tea on the scratched table top.

"I have to ask." Anna broke the silence. "What's with the women's clothing?"

"I came with one backpack, thought I'd be here for a day, maybe two, max. I need something to wear."

"Don't bullshit me."

"That first time, it was … I don't know . . . almost like the dress put itself on me. I was holding it and the cloth was smooth and soft and the next thing I know I'm wearing it, and it felt … good, and I remembered things . . . then Paula showed up, and I felt different with her. We actually talked. And that time with you? I . . . It's like the world is brighter . . ."

"You certainly are prettier as a girl than as a man."

"It's not like I'm going to go total femme or anything."

"Why not?"

Why not, he thought, looking at her, beautiful even in the harsh light of the ceiling fixture. If there was a magic button which, when pushed, would turn him into Anna Korsak—not she, herself, he's not some soul-sucking zombie—but into a duplicate of her, would he push it? Two Anna Korsaks. Wouldn't the world be better with two of her?

"I still like being a guy. It's easier."

"You have no idea . . . so, be both."

"I love what you've done with the place," Jimmy said, changing the subject.

"Nice. I should make you sleep on the floor."

"Fine with me."

"Don't be ridiculous. I've got a big bed, but there's a line down the middle. You stay on your side, and I'll stay on mine. Keep your hands to yourself."

"That shouldn't be hard for you."

She punched him on the shoulder.

He lay with his back to her and felt the warmth of her body radiate across the space between them. Her scent—woody, musky—drifted in the breeze from the ceiling fan, and he couldn't sleep and he missed Katrina and remembered how empty his life in Jackson had been after she left. There'd been no word since she walked out his door. Katrina Gieger was German Swiss. She was a good looking woman in a tightly controlled sort of way, and lived her life in a carefully controlled sort of way, and that was one of the things Jimmy had loved about her. Five years together, and then something changed, he still didn't know what, maybe it was that he lived his life in anything but a controlled way, and the chaos that seemed to follow him everywhere drove her away.

Where had she gone? Was she ever coming back?

"Jimmy?" Anna said. "You awake?"

"Yes."

"Would you hold me? Just hold me."

She had her back to him. He rolled over, moved to her, put his arm around her waist, and felt her settle into him, and it felt good to be able to offer comfort, and he wondered if he had ever felt as close to someone as he did at that moment, and they slept at last.

Chapter Twelve

ANNA KORSAK STOPPED AT the Filling Station for her morning coffee and saw Paula sitting with two women at a round table under a huge umbrella plastered with the logo for LaVazza coffee. At first, she hesitated to even say hello, but when she saw the way the woman with the butch hairdo was looking at Paula, she couldn't resist. She intended a quick peck on the cheek, but her lips lingered and she felt Paula stiffen.

I hope I didn't embarrass her.

She left the cafe and drove to Jimmy's. She pulled into the driveway, sat in the cruiser listening to the engine tick as it cooled, and leaned forward in her seat to look up at the big house, tall and solid against a turbid sky.

After an awkward early morning, each a little hungover, Anna and Jimmy had shared a silent ride to White River Junction to pick up their cars and then had gone their separate ways. Last night had been her first good sleep in a week, and the fact that it had taken Jimmy Baker with his arm around her was more than a little confusing. And now there he was, sitting on the porch, staring off into space.

"Long time no see," Jimmy said.

"Very funny."

She worried that he might say something about last night, wondered if he thought her weak. He was wearing a blue skirt with little orange and yellow flowers, and a wrinkled grey t-shirt that had "Fight Gravity" written across the chest in bold, red letters.

Good luck with that, she thought.

grey clouds roiled out from the mountain ridge; the air was thick and humid.

"Think it'll rain?" Anna said.

"God, I hope so. Have you told my uncle about Eliza, me?"

He seemed older. The boyish enthusiasm was gone, replaced by a somber reticence.

"Not yet, but I will. I don't know what it means, what it changes, but it could be important."

"If it wasn't her, then, who?"

"Pretty sure it was Ritchie Kelley, a friend of Eliza's, but it's not confirmed."

"Shit. He was at the reception. Seemed like a nice kid, funny, into political history. What teenager is into political history?"

"You saw them together."

"For a few minutes."

"And?"

"Eliza liked him, thought he was cute. Ritchie probably thought he was in love."

"I want to figure out what he was doing on that trail. Could use your help."

Anna followed Jimmy into the dining room. The table was covered with stacks of paper, photo albums, loose photos in boxes, framed photos, and letters in envelopes that had been slit open. There were two school photos next to each other, Jimmy and Eliza. It was obvious when you really looked.

"Where had he been?" Anna said. "How did he end up where you found him? I'm told you know these mountains."

Jimmy pushed the books and photos to the side, unrolled a large topographic map, and weighted the corners. The foothills of the Croydon Mountains were crisscrossed with trails: narrow twisting paths through thick undergrowth, gentle footpaths beneath park-like forest, jeep tracks rutted by the passage of ATVs, rocky scrambles, and sinuous single-tracks through stands of pine and hemlock.

"I'm not sure anyone really knows them. I was running to Leavitt Hill Road but ended up on Clark Camp Road miles to the south without crossing Leavitt Hill. How is that possible? I was wiped out, had no clue where I was, but I'm telling you, these hills and mountains are fucking weird. Things are often not what I remember, are not where they were supposed to be. The years I was here, I practically lived on these trails, and I still get lost. " Jimmy pointed. "Here's Clark Camp Road. This dotted line must be the trail."

"Can I borrow this map?"

"Sure, I have another."

He was sitting on the porch as she drove away.

The command unit had been withdrawn and everything had been moved back to the sheriff's department. Driving around the mountains to Newport, Anna's mind raced. Ritchie Kelley. Eliza Johnson. Two friends, one murdered, the other missing. What was the connection? She pulled into the parking lot. The station was teeming. DNA had confirmed what Anna already knew: the body was Ritchie Kelley.

"How'd we get results so quickly?" Anna said.

"I guess you scared them," Paul Arnold said.

Anna unrolled the map on George's desk.

"I talked to Jimmy. He said that trail runs north-south, paralleling the park boundary fence, all the way from Plainfield to close to Claremont, and there's all these connecting trails.

"Six days ago," Anna said. "Ritchie gave Eliza a ride to the swimming hole, then a day or two later he's killed a few miles away in the middle of nowhere"—she tapped her finger on the map— "What was he doing, where was he going, coming from? Was he looking for Eliza? If so, why there?"

She looked at George. He didn't seem to be paying attention. "Sheriff?"

George looked at his watch. "I have to talk with the Kelleys . . . Christ."

She stood, said, "I'll get the cruiser.".

"No," George said. "You stay here, talk to Fish and Game. See if you can learn more about that trail, what's out there, any reason Kelly would have been there."

George Baker gazed through tall windows past the dark ridge of the Croydon Mountains toward Lebanon while behind him on a dark leather couch in the middle of an enormous living room, Martin and Theresa Kelley dealt with the worst news parents could face. He knew Martin from town meetings, but had never met his wife, an executive at the big hospital in Lebanon. He did remember seeing her at some village affair, a good looking woman in a sharp-tailored business suit. Today, she was wearing elegant pants, a pressed blouse, a bit of make-up, but Martin was a mess: he hadn't shaved, his clothes looked like he'd slept in them.

This was not the first time George had notified parents of the death of their child, there'd been car accidents, drownings, but it was the first time the death was a murder. He'd seen parents collapse to the floor in hysterical sobs, or go numb and unresponsive.

"I am so sorry for your loss." George didn't do sympathy very well. He tried, but he came from a long line of yankee men who, from birth, were raised to be uncomfortable with emotion. "I know this is difficult, but I need to ask you some questions." He unrolled the map on the coffee table. "Can you look at this?"

Theresa Kelley had her arms crossed tightly in front of her, trying to hold herself together, but looked like she might shatter into a thousand pieces. Martin had a vacant look to him, like he wasn't really there, like it still hadn't registered that his son was dead.

"We've marked where Ritchie was found. What was he doing on that trail in this heat? Can you think of any reason?"

Martin seemed unable to speak. He flinched as if expecting a blow every time George spoke

"Theresa," George said. "Can you think of any connection Ritchie might have to that area?"

She leaned forward slowly, looked at the map, said, "Where is this?" She shook her head. "Ritchie's idea of adventure was playing video games in the air conditioned rec-room downstairs. He hated hiking. I always wished he would spend more time outside, tear himself away from that computer of his. I can begin toi understand why he would be there."

"Martin?"

He glanced at his wife, nodded.

George lowered himself into a matching chair set at a right angle to the couch, leaned forward, his elbows on his knees.

"What can you tell me about his friends?"

"There's the guys he played computer games with, and those weird card games, Dungeons and Dragons, that kind of stuff," Theresa said.

"Names?"

Martin looked away as if by staring into space he could be somewhere else and what was happening wouldn't be happening to him.

"Bob Tyson, Timmy Marks … Kyle Hernandez," Theresa said.

"You didn't mention Eliza Johnson," George said.

"I never liked that girl."

"Oh?"

"She never looked me in the eye. I often felt she was hiding something. She took advantage of Ritchie, treated him like a pet.

I kept hoping he'd get over her, but he was totally infatuated. If he was off in the woods, it's because of her. You find her, you'll find who killed my boy." She shuddered, started to cry, stood, and abrubtley left the room.

George looked at Martin, but Martin wouldn't meet his gaze.

"Did you ever see Eliza rough with him?"

"What? No!— She liked him …"

George sensed he was about to lose him, tried one last time.

"You're certain you can think of no reason your son would have been on that trail?"

Martin said, "I can't believe it. I can't believe it," over and over.

"Humor me. If you had to take a guess, what would it be?"

"Sheriff—"

"Would it have something to do with Eliza Johnson?"

"Why?" He said, then again, "Why?"

Anna Korsak heard the side door of the station creak open, saw George enter, scan the room as if he'd never seen it before, then walk slowly to his office. She followed Paul Arnold into the office.

"How'd it go?" Anna said.

George shook his head slowly. He'd always seemed, to Anna, easy to read, and she could tell he was struggling with something. He started to say something, but stopped. She'd been debating with herself when to tell him about Jimmy and Eliza, and was about to speak when Bill Johnson entered the office without knocking, and it became as if he had been there all along, and it was she and Paul Arnold and George Baker who had entered, and were there at his request. Arnold stood, glared at Johnson, left without saying a word.

What, Anna wondered, is the history behind that look?

Bill Johnson pulled out a chair, sat facing George across the desk. He crossed his legs, affected a polished, almost genteel manner that Anna was sure hid a raging ego and a ruthless determination. You don't make a zillion dollars in New York finance by being a nice guy, no matter how hard you pretend otherwise.

"You wanted to talk to me?" Johnson said, as smooth and controlled as ever.

"We now believe Eliza has run away," George said. "Do you have any idea why?"

"I know what Thrasher said. You can't believe that old man. He still claims I cheated him, and that I built the barns too close to his property. No way would Eliza run away. She has everything a girl could want."

Yeah, right, Anna thought. Johnson, in a way, reminded her of her father—was that why she'd disliked him from the first?—not because they were alike, but because the way he treated Eliza was so much like the way her father had treated her. Her father had been a violent man, and Anna had often wondered if that was where the anger she had to work to repress came from. She thought back to the Williams girl's description of the bruises on Eliza's back. Anna had endured more than a few of those growing up.

Maybe it was simply Johnson's attitude she didn't like. She could see why he and Gaetz were buddies. Both were arrogant pricks.

She looked at Bill Johnson and George Baker, both sitting in that smug way men did, as if they had all the time in the world. What was the point of this meeting? Why had George brought Johnson in? What does this have to do with Ritchie's murder? She was tempted to drop the bombshell about Eliza's parentage just to see Johnson's reaction, but she felt a certain sense of power knowing something they didn't, and decided she'd hold on to the information a bit longer.

"Where do you think she would go?" Anna said. "If she did?"

"Isn't that your job?"

What if he already knew? Was playing the same game she was? Was his seeming lack of concern for Eliza because he knows that she is in fact not his? Were the arguments, the difficulties the neighbors and friends reported, because he knows? Or, as he claimed, merely the struggles of dealing with a headstrong teenager.

"I heard the news," Bill Johnson interrupted her thoughts. "How are Martin and Theresa?"

There was nothing in his voice that made her think he was sincerely interested in their state of mind.

"What do you know of Eliza's relationship with Ritchie Kelley?" Anna said.

"Richard was at the house frequently, seemed a fine a young man, respectful, polite. He worshipped Eliza, but I never understood why. She treated him like he was her mascot."

"I'm sorry to have to ask this, but was she ever rough or violent with him? With anyone else?" George said.

"What?" Anna said before she could stop herself. Where did that question come from? Did I miss something? When had the sheriff started wondering if Eliza was violent? She saw Johnson tense. He tried to hide it, but it was there in the way he re-crossed his legs, sat up a little straighter, stared intently at her out of the corner of his eyes. She could feel him thinking, calculating.

"Violent? You know her, certainly your wife does. Eliza is an intense young woman, has a bit of a temper. She's very strong, and capable of being quite fierce if threatened."

"Fierce? Threatened?" Anna said. "What do you mean?"

"Perhaps that is a bad choice of words. How do I put this? What I meant was that if faced with losing something that was important to her, she would fight to prevent that from happening."

He left without saying another word.

"What is wrong with that man?" Anna said. "Throw Eliza under the bus like that?Shouldn't he defend her?" She moved to the recently vacated chair, studied George. What was he thinking?

"Yes?" He said.

"There's something you should know."

Why, George Baker wondered when Anna finished, is it that my goddamn nephew is always at the center of things when the shit hits the fan? He shook his head, said, "You have got to be kidding me." He looked across the desk at her. "You couldn't have told me this before Johnson got here? Didn't think maybe I should know?"

"Sorry chief, I only found out last night."

"What's going on with you and Jimmy?"

"What?"

"You're too close. Why'd he go to you about this?"

There was a surprised look on her face. He watched as she tried to control her anger. She stood, her gun in its holster caught on the arm of the chair almost tipping it over. It clattered back upright.

"Two things. One, there's nothing, as you put it 'going on' between me and Jimmy, we're friendly, that's it, and two, even if there was, it's none of your business."

"Everything about this investigation is my business, and, I don't—"

"Do you ever think about him as a person? Not that teenage thorn in your side? He's a good guy. Got anybody else who knows these hills like he does? Fish and Game doesn't have a clue."

"Alright . . . alright." George held his hands up. "Settle down, but it's become too personal, keep him out of it from now on, and remember one thing, he doesn't have limits like normal folks, he gets riled up, no telling what he'll do."

She turned to leave.

"Hold on," George said. He thought to tell her what Theresa Kelly had said, how she essentially accused Eliza of killing Ritchie, but something about these new connections between Eliza and Jimmy made him stop. Instead, he handed her a sheet of paper. "I've put together a list of Ritchie's friends. Talk to Arnold, divide it up. I want them all interviewed as soon as possible."

"Got it."

Alone in his office, George tried to make sense of this latest twist. Harriett had been a helluva good-looking woman. Why would she hook up with a punk like Jimmy? What connection could it have to the murder of Ritchie Kelley? It was revelations like this that made him realize how little he really understood people. He wondered if Paula knew. They'd drifted away from each other, didn't talk, didn't share things the way they used to. That Paula might keep a secret like this didn't surprise him, but that he had not seen the truth, did. *Jimmy was living in my house, how could I not have known?* George understood now why he had never liked Eliza. She was just like Jimmy—cocky, selfish, wild—one of those people whose talent and looks make them think they can get away with anything. He couldn't escape the growing suspicion that Eliza Johnson might not be who everyone thought she was.

And, Korsak. Why did she withhold this information? Why didn't she call him right away? What was she up to? And, why were she and Gaetz still so at odds?

He looked at the two employment files that Connie Armstrong had pulled for him, opened Anna's.

Here was her application, college transcripts, and her record as a District Detective with Boston PD. He paged through the papers: she'd aced the civil service exam, passed the physical exams with flying colors, graduated at the top of her class from the Boston Police Academy. He came to the recommendation from her commanding officer. At first reading, it was a glowing endorsement, but when he re-read it more carefully, what it didn't say—that she was a valued member of the squad, respected by her colleagues— became more evident. She'd resigned, it reported, for "personal reasons." No further explanation.

He moved on to Gaetz. He had been a Sergeant in the Special Enforcement Division of the Manchester Police Department for two years. Excellent record, strong recommendation. Prior to that he'd been a sheriff's deputy in Maricopa County, Arizona, also for two years. George wondered why Gaetz had decided to leave Manchester, couldn't remember if he'd asked during the job interview twelve months ago, or if he had, what Gaetz's answer had been. He had also moonlighted for Allied Services, a private security firm—another strong reference—and did volunteer work with a couple of local youth organizations.

George realized Gaetz had been in Manchester during the Sally Hopkins case. Why had he never mentioned it?

Nothing in either file really explained the difficulties the two had working together, and nothing in Korsak's, the deep visceral dislike she displayed toward Gaetz. George had heard second-hand faint grumblings about Gaetz from some of the younger deputies, but no one had come to him with anything specific. When this case was done and he had more time, he would look into this deeper, but for now he had other things on his mind.

He closed the files.

Anna was right about one thing, Bill Johnson did not seem to care about the girl who grew up in his house and lived under his roof for sixteen years. Maybe if he'd taken the time to be a parent to Eliza, this whole goddamn mess wouldn't have happened. But, if he was going to assign blame where would he start? Harriet? Jimmy? Seemed to him there was enough to go around.

❖

Paula Baker put the phone down and sat in stunned silence. Jimmy and Harriet. How could she? Paula didn't know what to think, what to feel. Betrayed? Deceived? She couldn't sit still, couldn't stay inside.

The village green, usually deep in shade, was mottled with harsh light, as if the big maples had given up fighting the relentless sun, and the grass, usually thick and verdant, was brown and wilted. There was nobody outside, the village was deserted. She crossed the street, felt the hot blacktop through the soles of her sandals. The screen door of the Corner Store creaked open. A man brushed past her as if she wasn't there, then looked around furtively as though not sure he was allowed to be on the store's porch.

It didn't seem possible, but it was hotter inside than out. She walked up to the counter. Bob Olsen was alone.

"Who was that?"

"Alonzo Pierson."

"I didn't know he was around."

"Comes in once in awhile. Always buys the same thing. Coke. Hostess cupcakes."

Paula walked to the cooler. She stood staring through the condensation streaked glass lost in the weird, multi-colored cans of energy drinks, and thoughts of Jimmy and Harriet. She took a Coke out of the cooler, though she knew knew it wasn't good for her.

Back outside on the porch she pressed the cold skin of the can against her forehead.

She should have known.

Paula had known that Harriet had been unhappy in her marriage. What had it been like? The affair with Jimmy? Had Harriet felt guilty, cheating on her husband with a boy of seventeen? She certainly had not seemed to. Harriet, that summer, had a sparkle in her eyes. Looking back, Paula felt hurt that Harriett had not confided in her. Or, was she envious that Harriet had broken free, and for that one summer had lived the way she wanted to? Those summer days when they lounged on the back deck, drinking iced tea, talking. How could Harriett have kept that secret? When did we all become so good at keeping secrets?

And Jimmy that summer had seemed to grow before her eyes, his face tan and freckled, his hair burned blond, and he had smiled in a way Paula had never seen before, had seemed for that short while to lose his bitter teenage attitude, to enjoy life, but then at the end of summer had turned angry, sullen, withdrawn. How could Harriet have been that selfish, seduce a young boy like that? Had she somehow damaged Jimmy? And now, it seemed to Paula that he was, in many ways, still that wounded teenager.

This past spring, Eliza had been working in the garden, weeding in the sun. She stopped, straightened her back, and looked at

Paula and smiled. It was the smile; it was her tan, freckled face, her sun-streaked hair, and that smile, Jimmy's smile.

Yes, Paula thought, I should have known.

Again that deep sound felt in her chest, and she looked across the road toward the mountains, where a boy had been murdered, and the mountains seemed bigger and darker and steeper, like they were leaning out over her, and she had, again, that sense that the world was not as she had thought it was.

She heard a distant rifle shot, then another.

Jimmy Baker hung up the kitchen wall phone after listening to his uncle confirm that the body was Ritchie Kelley. He'd asked about the search for Eliza, and his uncle's tone of voice had puzzled him. Something was going on. He heard someone at the door, found his aunt. He barely had the door open when she said, "How could you have sex with my best friend, a married woman?" in an angry voice.

He didn't answer. He could see she was upset, couldn't look her in the eye. He walked away. She followed him into the kitchen. Jimmy lowered himself into a chair. She sat across from him.

"She was so beautiful that when I started working there I was afraid to even talk to her, but then she came on to me. I was a kid. I'd never had sex … and she took my hand, and … I don't know how to describe that moment. She led me, told me when we would meet, she knew when you and George were out, and—"

"You were at our house?" Paula said, clearly outraged.

"And when we were together, it was like I was alive for the first time in my life, and I thought it would be forever, and every moment … I saw myself in her eyes, the self I wanted to be, but then those eyes turned hard.

"I loved her. I still do. I think about her so much, but she's dead, and I can never talk to her again, can never know if I meant anything to her? Anything at all."

Jimmy stood, walked to the kitchen counter, braced himself with his hands, and stared out the window.

"I haven't felt that way since, and I don't think I ever will. It's like I measure every woman I get close to against my memories of her. Remember how I told you Katrina and I are together? That was a lie. She left me. It ended just like every relationship I've ever had . . ."

"Why didn't you ever come back to us?"

"How could I? When every place would remind me of her, of those few moments. Can you understand what it's like to have what you thought was everything, what you thought would be forever, taken away in an instant? Can you?"

He turned, looked at her her hoping for understanding, reassurance, but she was hunched over into herself, and the agonized expression on her face stopped him. She was so miserable, so shaken she couldn't speak, and he wondered why has this hurt her so?

Paula said, quietly, almost to herself, "Yes . . . yes, I can . . ."

"How long have you known?" Jimmy said.

She gathered herself, said, "I started to wonder a few weeks ago. Eliza looks so much like you . . . but really known? Not until George called me earlier."

"Why didn't somebody tell me?"

"Tell you what? No one knew about you and Harriet."

"Did she ever talk about me?

"Not in so many words, but near the end all she could talk about was how she wanted me to take care of Eliza, how she should be with the Bakers, and then one time, she said, 'He doesn't know.' She was so sick, on serious meds, wasn't making a lot of sense.

"I was there when she died. Tooney was there. Bill wasn't. Can you imagine? His wife is dying and he's in New York? She was comfortable, but totally out of it. I was holding Eliza. Harriet woke up, called me over, whispered, 'I didn't mean to hurt him.' She reached out to Eliza—it was so awful—then drifted off to sleep. She never woke up.

"I didn't know what she meant at the time, but now I think she meant you, Jimmy." Paula gasped, a single hiccup of breath. "She was my best friend. I miss her. Twelve years and I still miss her." A silence came between them, finally Paula said, "What are you going to do?"

"I was ready to get out of here, but now I ..."

Jimmy felt himself unraveling, his eyes sting, realized he might start crying, but instead turned away, walked into the dining room. The map was spread out on the table.

"What's this?" Paula appeared at his side.

"I was trying to see where I found Ritchie's body."

"Show me."

He pointed to the trail he'd taken. Paula followed the thin dashed line with her pink fingernail to Croydon Pass Road, then traced that road toward the mountains until it turned into a jeep track marked with a faint double-dotted line, followed that to where, at its end, not far downhill from the fence, was a tiny black square.

"Must be a cabin," Jimmy said.

"Pierson's," she said. "George used to hunt with Caleb."

And then he remembered. It was a hunting shack. He had been there once.

He drove the jeep road, little more than two ruts in a narrow gap through scrub forest. Weeds scraped the bottom of the car. The grass in the ruts was pressed flat, and in places, freshly disturbed. He came to a weathered, shed-roofed building set on tall pilings in the middle of an acre or two of meadow that had been recently mowed. He climbed the steps to the deck that cantilevered out from the front of the cabin, stooped to examine some footprints on the dirty boards. Tried the door. Locked.

The memory of that awful weekend long ago was like a bad dream. His father and mother and he were still doing their imitation of a happy family, and Uncle George had invited Jimmy's father down for a weekend's hunting. Matthew Spenser ran a small private equity firm, wore a suit and tie every day in his office on the second floor of the Wheelock building in Hanover. On the weekend, when he donned casual clothes and was outside in their backyard, he never looked comfortable, and the idea that he would go hunting, sleep in a rustic cabin, tromp around in the cold, damp November woods was, to eleven-year-old Jimmy, a joke. His father got an L.L. Bean catalog and ordered what he must have thought was the requisite apparel needed for a manly weekend in the New Hampshire woods: camouflage pants, jacket, blaze orange vest, hat, waterproof boots. The works. Two days before the big weekend, Jimmy's mother announced she was going to spend a few days with friends in Boston, and the woman who stayed with Jimmy when both parents were away was sick, so Matthew would have to take Jimmy along.

"A little father-son quality time," his mother said. "It'll be fun."

Jimmy had no doubt this was the same cabin. He wondered who owned the place. He went to the nearby barn. The big sliding door was chained with a new padlock, but Jimmy was able to squeeze between the door and its frame. The barn was built with hand-hewn timbers, thick rough-cut planks, and was filled with the overheated smell of old wood and dry-rot. He found a screwdriver and a pry-bar, and went back to the cabin. He jiggled the door, but hesitated before attacking with the pry bar. What was he doing? Was he so curious to see inside that he was going to break and enter? He noticed a large flower pot off to the side of the porch that had been moved recently, found a key under it, and all thoughts of not checking the place out vanished.

The interior had been completely re-modeled: oak flooring, bright pine wainscoting, a modern kitchenette, and a new propane heater that looked like a wood stove. There were dishes in a bamboo drying rack on a polished maple counter-top, porcelain plates, wine glasses. Off the main room was a bedroom with a platform double bed covered by a wood-print camo bedspread.

I could live here, he thought. It would be perfect.

The bathroom was small, he had to close the door behind him to use the toilet. When he turned around after relieving himself, there, hanging from the back of the bathroom door, was a girl's running outfit: pink shorts, silver tank-top.

He went back to the bedroom, found girl's clothing in the back of the closet, a dress, a pair of jeans, cute sandals with pale blue trim. He found condoms in a small drawer in a bedside table; there was a photo lying face down on the dresser, he turned it over to see Eliza in a smaller version of her school portrait. He opened the refrigerator, found leftovers from a simple meal, a half-empty bottle of white wine.

Jimmy sat in one of the Adirondack chairs facing the fake wood stove. You never know, he thought. You never fucking know anything about anybody. He felt … what? Shock? Disapproval? But, who was he to feel anything about what this girl did with her life?

Again, he wondered who owned the place and who Eliza met here.

His mind went back. The cabin was bare studs with a rough wood floor, a few camp chairs, and he was sitting in the corner while the men drank whiskey, told jokes, and got drunk. That's all they did, drink. No one did any hunting, and his father, who'd forgotten Jimmy was there, was talking about moving his business to California where the real money was.

Ten months later Matthew Spenser was gone, leaving Jimmy and his mother behind.

Chapter Thirteen

Anna Korsak leaned back in her desk chair, felt a wayward spring in the cracked, green seat poke her in the butt, and wondered, not for the first time, why she didn't go find a better chair. She couldn't stop thinking about George insisting on interviewing the Kelleys alone. What had they talked about that caused him to return to the station wondering if Eliza was violent? Did he actually suspect her?

She saw him leaning into the Dispatch window, talking with Lorraine. She walked over, said, "What's going on?"

"More Bigfoot calls."

"What?"

"Lorraine, can you show Deputy Korsak 'the book'?"

Anna paged through the red logbook. There were entries dating back several years: car break-ins, huge footprints, sightings, damaged outbuildings, all attributed by the callers to Bigfoot. There was an article from the Concord Monitor about a man who had a money raising scam called, "Searching for Bigfoot," and had come to New Hampshire to investigate the reported sightings. There were copies of letters to the editor from some nut-job in Conway claiming that instances of recent bear mischief were actually Bigfoot.

"You have got to be kidding me." She looked from George to Lorraine.

"Nope," Lorraine said.

"What do you say?"

"I thank them for calling and assure them we'll look into it."

"Don't we have more important things to do?" Anna said.

"What could be more important than Bigfoot?" George said, holding back laughter.

"But, these most recent calls are different," Lorraine said. "Food, cooking pots, and clothing have been taken."

"Where?" Anna said.

"Spread along the hills above Hemlock Flat."

"Eliza?"

"That's what I'm wondering," George said. "Why don't you look into a few of these incidents. Start with Maude Richards. She's called me twice. Get her off my back."

Anna's cell phone pinged. A text from Jimmy. "CALL ME!!!"

She walked off, figured it was better if George didn't hear her talking to Jimmy. He answered after the first ring.

"What's up?" Anna said. She listened, then almost shouted into the phone, "You what?" She scanned the squad room, saw George leaning against the wall, watching her closely.

She ended the call.

Anna contacted the county attorney—neglecting to mention Jimmy's illegal entry—to see if the footprints on the front deck matching the make and size of either Eliza Johnson's or Ritchie Kelley's running shoes were enough to get a search warrant, also not mentioning that she hadn't actually seen those footprints, then set about trying to find out who owned the property. A call to the town office got her the name KWB Enterprises, LLC which led her to a New Hampshire database of corporations in which she found that KWB had been incorporated seven years ago, and the incorporation form listed Martin Kelley as principal shareholder, which brought Anna and George to the conference room of Kelley's office in Hanover.

Why was he at work? Shouldn't he be home comforting his wife?

With Kelley was his attorney, a Mr. James Whittenden, Esquire, from the firm of Whittenden, Goldfarb, and Reynolds. Located in Manchester, it was one of New Hampshire's largest law firms. She flicked his gold embossed business card with her thumb. How, she wondered, does one get to be an Esquire? And, what the hell is an Esquire anyway? Isn't that like a knights-in-shining-armor thing?

"Can't this wait?" Whittenden said. "My client has just lost his son."

"We understand this is a difficult time," George said. "But I'm sure Martin wants to do everything he can to help us catch his son's killer and find Eliza Johnson. There is clear evidence that she was at the cabin, and that his son was there as well."

Maybe it was being in his office protected by the vast expanse of a massive conference table that Anna assumed was mahogany from some endangered rain forest, Martin Kelley seemed to her to be strangely composed considering his son had been murdered.

Whittenden nodded at him, and Kelley denied any knowledge of the cabin. KWB was a holding company. He couldn't possibly—being as important as he is, Anna thought—be expected to know every property it owned.

George sighed the deep sigh of a tired man, a man who in the next few moments would be looking up at the sky mouthing, "Why me?" to the gods, instead, he said, "You know Bobby Porter?"

Martin Kelley leaned over, whispered something to Whittenden who whispered back.

"Well?"

"In what context?" Whittenden said.

Anna felt she would explode with all the prevarication and posturing. She leaned forward in her chair and was about to say something when George spoke.

"In the context that your client hired Porter to renovate the cabin eleven months ago."

"That was supposed to be confidential. I paid him under—"

"That's enough, Martin." Whittenden put his hand on Kelley's arm.

"Martin, how long have you lived here?" George said.

"Eighteen years."

"Long enough to know that nothing stays quiet in a village like this."

"I had no idea Ritchie was meeting Eliza there."

George smacked his hand on the table. "Martin, can we please cut the crap?"

"Sheriff," Whittenden said. "That is hardly necessary. A little respect might be in order. He has made it clear that he can't remember the last time he was there, and that he had no idea his son was meeting the girl there."

Anna couldn't keep quiet any longer.

"It was Ritchie who was meeting Eliza there? How stupid do you think we are? Can you explain why we found Eliza's fingerprints and yours inside, but not Ritchie's. He was outside the cabin, but there's no evidence that he was ever inside. None. Do I need to list the places we found your prints?"

Kelley seemed to collapse. "Okay . . . I had a relationship with Eliza Johnson. Can we keep this quiet? It'll kill my wife."

"Relationship? She's a kid," Anna said. "Give me a break."

"Spare me your judgment, deputy. You're hardly one to criticize. Like the sheriff said, nothing stays quiet in a village like—"

"What's that supposed to mean?" Anna seethed. What the hell was he trying to imply? This wasn't about her. Calm down, she told herself. He's trying to distract you.

"Did Ritchie know of this relationship?" George said.

"Absolutely not," Kelley said.

"Then why was he at the cabin?"

Once again, Whittenden stopped Kelley from speaking, and said, "My client will have a complete, signed statement on your desk this afternoon, but for now, we're done. He'll have nothing more to say, and I suggest that you might want to spend more time finding who killed my client's son and less prying into his private life."

Later that afternoon, Whittenden delivered the promised statement. Martin Kelley and Eliza had been, "seeing each other," Kelley's words, for four months. Just over a week ago they had agreed to end things. There were no hard feelings. Eliza had asked if she could stay in the cabin for a few days, claimed her parents were out of town, no one would know.

"What did I tell you about Jimmy?" George Baker wanted to be angry, but couldn't seem to summon the energy. "If anyone finds out he broke into that cabin—"

"He didn't break into anything, and without him," Anna said. "We'd still be sitting here with our thumbs up our asses."

"What did you think of Kelley?"

"Can't we bust him for having sex with a minor?" Anna said.

"The age of consent is sixteen. Eliza turned sixteen last May."

"He knew where she was when we talked to him in his driveway. What about withholding evidence?"

In his statement, Kelley made it clear he didn't believe Eliza could have had anything to do with Ritchie's death.

"It does seem like he actually cares for her," Anna said. "He defends her in no uncertain terms."

"Of course he does," George said. "He thinks that by denying the obvious, that his little fling may have led to his son's death, he can make it not be true. We know that Eliza spent time at the cabin, and that Ritchie was there, likely the day he was killed.

Think about it. Ritchie finds out about his father's love nest, has a big-time crush on Eliza that was not reciprocated. What if he confronted her, threatened to reveal everything? Eliza loses her temper, kills him, then runs off."

"You can't be serious. She's a teenager, people find out she's having sex, big deal."

"Theresa Kelley as good as accused Eliza of killing Ritchie, and remember what Bill Johnson said about her if she feels threatened."

"I don't believe a single word out of that man's mouth."

"Maybe she's terrified of what Bill Johnson would do?" George paused. "Who the hell else would have a reason to kill Ritchie?"

"Kelley had a lot more to lose than Eliza," Anna said.

"You think he'd kill his own son?"

"Who knows what he would do to protect his reputation. He will face a shitstorm when this comes out, lose clients, maybe his marriage, everything. What if it was dark and he thought Ritchie was Eliza?"

George leaned back in his chair, sighed. "Go ahead, check Kelley's alibi."

After Anna had returned to her desk, George stared at the wall. Why did he find it so easy to believe that a sixteen-year-old girl could be a killer? Was it her connection to Jimmy? He still remembered all the trouble Jimmy caused when he lived with them, and realized he had never stopped wondering if Jimmy had done something that made the Johnson's nanny run back home to Sweden.

And now, Jimmy's daughter was, to him, suspect number one.

Anna put Martin Kelley's statement next to a timeline. According to him, he last saw Eliza Johnson the morning of August 3rd. After visiting her at the cabin, he returned to his house, packed a suitcase, talked with Anna and George in the driveway, and left for Boston immediately thereafter. Ritchie had most likely been killed the night of the 3rd, the exact time of death still in question, when Kelley, according to his statement, was a prominent participant in a conference called, "Protecting your Wealth for Generations to Come," sponsored by Billings Capital Group. It occurred to her that with his money Kelley could have hired somebody to do his dirty work, but the idea of a contract killer wandering the woods of New Hampshire seemed absurd, and wouldn't a professional have used something a little more subtle? Made the body disappear?

Ritchie was coming from or going to the cabin on a trail that runs north-south in the foothills of the Croydon Mountains and was hit from behind with great force with the proverbial blunt object. Eliza was at the cabin the night of August 2nd, and possibly the night of the 3rd, and was still missing.

Didn't look good, she had to admit.

Anna grabbed her shoulder bag and left the office to get some fresh air—though calling the stagnant blanket of humidity that had settled over the state for the last few days fresh was at best a stretch. She decided to go talk to Jimmy about their suspicions. At least her SUV's AC worked. The road up the Sugar River Valley was smooth with new pavement, the curves gentle, her SUV swooped one way, then the other, the forces pulling her left, then right, as she sped north. She had thought things would be simple in a tiny town like Hemlock Flat, but was starting to realize how wrong she'd been: all the connections, the family relationships, all the shit everyone knew but never said, all the crap they kept hidden.

She tried to imagine what it had been like for Eliza: losing her mother at four, growing up in a small village with a step-mother who had little time for her, and a father who wasn't really her father but tried to control her life. People had such varying impressions of her, as if they were talking about a different person. To Paula she was sweet, caring; to George, wild, a pain in the ass; to Bill Johnson a difficult, intense teenager; to Otis Thrasher, a helpful, caring neighbor. What could a young girl like her have seen in a man like Kelley? What did this affair say about her? Who really knew her? Jimmy had no part in raising her, yet Anna now saw Eliza as his daughter, so much like him—smart, talented, good looking, superb athlete—yet somehow not able to be at home in the world. Is everything that we are due to genes?

Anna found Jimmy sitting on the porch, wearing a dark red, almost burgundy, tank top, and a pale grey skirt, facing off to the left, gazing uphill toward the mountains.

"Eliza is now considered a suspect in Ritchie Kelley's murder," she said. "This changes everything. The state's waiting to take over if we don't get some results."

She couldn't see his face.

"I don't believe it."

"Of course you don't. The thinking is Ritchie found out about her thing with his father and was either so pissed off that he threatened to go public, or so jealous that he tried to get a piece of the action, and she killed him in a struggle."

"She would never do that."

"You think you know her, but do you? You met her twice. Would you have thought she would get it on with a man like Martin Kelley?"

"What about him?"

"He's got an alibi. I'm going to follow up, but it looks solid."

Jimmy uncrossed his legs, turned to face her, and leaned forward. Anna wondered, she couldn't help it, what he'd used for breasts. He had managed to create a fairly convincing pair of boobs. She brought her eyes up and saw Jimmy looking at her, and she had a strange flash of reverse deja vu of men looking at her chest, then forcing themselves to look up.

"I saw them together at Tooney's wake," Jimmy said. "They were good friends. Ritchie worshipped Eliza, you could see it a mile away, and Eliza treated him like a little brother. She liked him."

"That's exactly the point. Ritchie was in love, she kept him around like a pet. It was not an equal relationship."

"Fuck. What do you think?"

"I don't know what to think, but this is where the investigation is headed."

"There has to be something else going on. What if someone killed Ritchie because he got in the way?"

"You got some idea who? Something you're not telling me?"

Jimmy wouldn't look at her, as if he was hiding something, or maybe he was suddenly aware of himself and felt self-conscious.

"No."

"What's with the boobs? I thought you weren't going to go total femme."

"Oh, god, I don't know." An edge of hysteria crept into his voice. He started to say something, stopped.

She watched him walk across the porch. There was a difference in the way he moved, a grace she'd not seen before. This was a person who did not know who they are, but was it her job to tell them?

He turned back and looked at her, said, "What are you going to do now?"

"It's been a long day. I'm going to go home, try to get some rest. You should do the same."

George Baker stopped at the entrance to his driveway and admired the house that his parents had given him and Paula a few years after their marriage. Needed paint, but otherwise it was a damn fine house. Built in the late 1800s, it had the pleasing proportions of Victorian architecture without being overloaded with the usual scrollwork, gingerbread and the like, that rotted and had to be repaired. The house was white with white trim. Across the town green, Bea Marsden's place was a bluish grey with purple trim. He liked the grey, the purple not so much.

Their house was boring, Paula said, but to George it was a proud, sensible house. His father had grown up in that house, and

George had grown up in that house, and he had never understood how his parents could have traded it for a small house outside of Claremont.

"Too big to keep up," his mother had said. "Besides, we got wall-to-wall and central AC."

Ten years his father had lasted in that depressing raised ranch. Ten years. George often thought it was moving out of the house that had been in the Baker family for generations that had started his father's decline, not the man's prodigious consumption of alcohol and cigarettes.

Thinking about his father got George thinking about fathers and sons, and Martin and Ritchie Kelley. He couldn't believe that Kelley would kill his son to keep his fling with Eliza Johnson quiet. Sure, his own father had been pretty rough with him at times, a smack upside the head when he got out of line, that kind of thing, but that? No way. And, that got George thinking about his son Charley, and how they'd drifted apart the last couple of years. When things calmed down, he told himself, he'd do something about that.

He parked the cruiser, walked around to the backyard to see if it needed mowing, decided it could wait a few days, and entered the kitchen through the back door, expecting to smell dinner cooking. Nothing. Disappointed, he went to the front hall, hung up his duty belt, stopped by the den to lock his gun in the safe, returned to the kitchen.

"Paula?" he called.

"Upstairs! Be right down."

Rapid steps on the stairs. She rushed into the kitchen wearing a flowery dress. She'd done something with her hair.

"What—"

"I'm going to the Hood Museum, see some art, then grabbing dinner in town with Helen Lambert and Sarah Chase. There's a plate in the fridge. Two minutes in the microwave. You do remember how to use the microwave, don't you?"

"Lambert? Chase? Since when are you three friends?"

"I had coffee with them the other morning. I know you remember Sarah from school, blond, beautiful. Helen teaches art at Dartmouth. She invited us both to the opening of this new exhibit."

"But—"

"Got to go. I'm late." She swept past him trailing the scent of flowers. "You didn't block me in, did you?"

It had always seemed to him that Paula had the perfect life, the life she wanted—home, garden, her volunteer work—but something had changed, and he didn't know what. She'd been different since Tooney's death. There was that morning when he'd found her weeping at the kitchen sink, and since then he'd come upon her at her desk wiping her reddened eyes, but she'd not said anything and he'd not asked, and now she was off for an evening with two women who, in George's memory, she had never been friends with in the past.

Jimmy Baker stood on the front porch of what he had come to think of as Casa Tooney watching the gibbous moon, a strange, disturbing shade of dark reddish-orange, rise. Red skies at night, sailor's delight; red skies in the morning, sailor take warning. What about red moons? He was no sailor but he felt this moon, this overfed, bulbous moon, as a warning. This night was one to beware.

But, since when did he, Jimmy Baker, heed warnings?

He changed into a pair of jeans and a sleeveless black top with little silver buttons and headed to town. The Maple Leaf Tavern was what might euphemistically be called a dive bar; somewhere else it might be considered downscale cool, but here, in Lebanon, New Hampshire, it was just plain a dump.

His kind of place.

Jimmy, propped up on both elbows, was staring across the sticky bar top at bottles. He was trying to classify them, to count and compute the percentages of how many were square and how many were round, but the flashing multi-colored lights intertwined around the bottles kept distracting him. The bar's lighting was lurid, red-tinged, the ceiling jazzed up by small dangling objects—pulsing red hearts, white stars, crystal teardrops—and twinkie lights everywhere. A pulsing, blue neon martini glass invited him to try Sipsmith's London Gin.

It was that kind of place.

Exactly how, or when, it had become important to calculate the breakdown between round and square bottles and to understand what the possible implications of said percentages were to the bigger questions of life he couldn't remember. Perhaps after the third shot of tequila, or maybe the fourth.

Then it occurred to him—how could he not have noticed before?— that some of the bottles, some of the fucking bottles, were neither round nor square.

 Shit! How can they do that to me?

He felt whiplashed. First, a girl he'd just met disappears, then he stumbles on what he thinks is her body, then he discovers the girl is his daughter and tries to deal with the fact that she is dead before he even knew her, then he finds out she's not dead, it's another kid, and she's been shacking up with some asshole thirty years older, and now they think she's a murderer.

No wonder he was going nuts.

There were squat bottles and tall, skinny bottles, and bottles that were neither square nor round but somewhere in between, and with that came the question: where was the line between round and square anyway? And how did you know when you'd crossed from one to the other?

He had almost been out of here—free—but he knew now, though he didn't want to admit it, that he couldn't leave until Eliza was found.

When did a place become a home? When was that line crossed? And, did that mean he would remain in that museum of the life of

Altoona Lindsay Baker at the end of that dead-end road where the only neighbors were bears and fisher cats and coyotes and other unnamed creatures and spooks that screamed in the night?

Next to the bottles was a metal sign that proclaimed: Even a Toilet Can Serve Only One Asshole at a Time. He thought about that for awhile.

But, again, where was the line between round and square?

How the hell should he know?

And, where was the line between man and woman and how do you know which side of that line you were on? Why did he feel better in her clothes than his own? Why was the world brighter?

Back to the bottles.

He now had five categories: round, square, squat, tall, and something-in-between. And then he noticed bottles of a seductive, curving, feminine shape that defied classification.

Meltdown.

The bartender, Marcie, materialized across from him. A short, dark haired girl, pretty in her way, with cleavage that made him want to lean in and flow up and over the bartop like one of those rubber cartoon characters on TV and lose himself into the sweet, warm embrace of possibly the most beautiful pair of tits he had ever seen. He pushed the wrinkled stack of bills in front of him toward her and turned away before he made a complete fool of himself. Just looking at her made his heart ache.

God, to be held again, to feel that warmth and softness, to be loved again.

Outside, he felt the night squeeze him in a damp embrace. He looked up at a streetlight, fuzzy in the humid air, and watched insects circle and swarm and batter themselves against the globe of light. Then there were two lights, next to each other, and two swarms of suicidal bugs, and he felt dizzy and disoriented. He closed his right eye and there was one light. He opened it. There were two. He closed his left eye and there was one.

But, it had moved!

He walked to the rental car and stood looking at it, and all the times he'd driven wasted and gotten away with it came back to him, but tonight, for once, he turned away. The streets were empty. No one. Not a car. Nothing. Houses, white and tall with darkened windows, seemed to move away from him, as if trying to say, don't bother us, we're fine respectable citizens tucked up safe in our homes. Where could he go? He wandered through the dead town. The only sounds were the whirr of window air conditioners on this hot, muggy night, and the distant tinny voices of someone's TV.

He came to a street and realized through the fog that was gradually engulfing his brain that he was outside Anna's building. He climbed the stairs, knocked on the door. He sat down to wait, thinking dimly that it could be pretty awkward if Anna and a lover came back from a romantic dinner, and as he realized he should leave, he slumped over, curled into a ball, and fell asleep.

Walking back toward her car, Paula Baker was relieved that her time alone with Helen Lambert was almost over. (Sarah had cancelled at the last minute, and now, thinking back to Sarah's expression when Paula had accepted Helen's invite, she wondered had Sarah ever really intended to come?)

Paula had loved the paintings of Cape Cod, the sun-bleached colors, the whites of the old-fashioned dresses, the pale yellow sand, the soft, lazy clouds, and the liquid light of the sun, but Helen had barely seemed to notice them. When they went for a drink and dinner at the sleek One Seven Seven restaurant in Hanover, Paula had felt completely out of place in her Laura Ashley dress surrounded by the black leather and chrome of the restaurant, and Helen, in tight red-leather pants and black t-shirt and an enigmatic smile on her face, had made Paula feel herself studied and observed, and she had been so uncomfortable it was all she could do to not rush from the restaurant.

It was late when they said goodnight in the parking lot. Helen put her hand on Paula's shoulder, leaned in, kissed her on the cheek.

"This was fun, Paula. I hope I see you again."

In her car, Paula touched the spot with her fingers and remembered Anna kissing her there, and as she was remembering the touch of those lips, softer than Helen's, her cell phone chimed and it was Anna, and when Paula heard her voice it was like Anna was there in the car, and for a brief moment Paula thought she caught a whiff of Anna's scent.

"Paula? I'm sorry to bother you, but your nephew just barfed all over my rug."

"What?"

"I called George first. He said you went to the Hood, might still be in town."

Paula followed Anna's directions through the back streets of the Park Heights neighborhood of Lebanon. She'd never known how it got the name. There was no park and certainly no heights. She was surprised by how modest Anna's place was, had thought it would be trendy and decorated in some hip way, but it was plain and simple: mismatched chairs, battered sofa, and had few personal touches. There was a wet stain in the middle of the faded carpeting that smelled terrible. She could see a kitchen off to her right. There was a closed door to the left, probably the bedroom, and an open door to a bathroom in which she could hear Jimmy retching into the toilet.

"I found him asleep in front of my door," Anna said.

Seeing Anna here, at home, made Paula want to look around, learn how she lived, but Anna seemed nervous, uncomfortable.

"How was the museum?" Anna said.

Paula didn't want to talk about her evening with Helen Lambert.

Jimmy walked unsteadily to the couch, wiping his face with his forearm.

"Are there more towels?" Paula said.

Anna went to the bedroom door, opened it part way, slipped through the narrow opening, closing it behind her, then re-appeared with two towels. She handed one to Jimmy. He wiped his face, handed it back to her. He was pale, looked exhausted, and reeked of booze, and it was as if the last seventeen years had vanished and here she was again, Aunt Paula, taking care of her juvenile delinquent of a nephew, but she felt something shift, a change in herself, and she saw Jimmy's desperation, how he hovered on the edge of despair.

"Come on, Jimmy. I'll take you to our house."

"No. Take me back to my place . . . just need to sleep it off."

Chapter Fourteen

AFTER HER USUAL MORNING stop at the Filling Station, Anna Korsak drove to Hemlock Flat, turned onto Leavitt Hill Road, slowed briefly as she passed the pullout for the swimming hole, then followed the road up into the hills a few miles until she came to Maude Richards's overgrown driveway. She parked next to a relatively new Toyota Prius, and sat in the cruiser looking at a mobile home tucked in front of an ancient farmhouse that was half caved-in around a jagged, blackened hole in the roof. Vines crawled up the side of the house trying to pull it to the ground. The entire yard was an overgrown garden hacked out of the forest that encroached from all sides. She tried to reconcile the car with the place, but finally just filed the incongruity of it with all the other oddities of rural New Hampshire she'd encountered. She found Maude in her garden wearing loose jeans and a plaid shirt, her grey hair in a tight bun.

"Let's go inside," Maude said in a gravelly voice.

They moved back outside to talk after Anna explained that if they didn't she was going to pass out from lack of oxygen for all the cigarette smoke.

"You're a feisty one, aren't you?" Maude said as they sat at a round table of cast concrete near the garden.

"So I've been told." The breeze shifted, and Anna caught a whiff of charred timbers, melted plastic, burned fabric. "When was the fire?"

"About ten years ago. It was my father's place. I moved here to take care of him. Happened a few years after he passed. You ever see a chimney fire? Damn exciting, let me tell you."—she extricated a cigarette from a crumpled packet, lit it—"I had insurance, but the place was such a wreck, didn't seem worth re-building. Bought the trailer, all new furniture, moved in. I like it, things are simple. Got all I need."

"So, the break-ins."

"Not really break-ins, just stuff taken, food, clothes off the line, a shirt, a blanket, and a couple of pots from the kitchen."

"Then why did you call the sheriff twice?"

"I didn't appreciate the way that deputy who called wouldn't take me seriously, couldn't even be bothered to drive up here. He wanted to know if I saw anyone, if there were footprints or anything. When I told him I knew it was the hermit, he hung up on me. Just like that. So, I went back to George, and he sent me you, and I must say you're a big improvement over that moron."

"Hermit?

"Lives up in the hills somewhere. Folks see him sometimes, usually at night."

"Do you remember the deputy's name?"

"Gets or something. Why bother? There ought to be more women deputies. We're better at most things, get the chance ..." She exhaled a plume of smoke, stubbed out the cigarette in a half full ashtray. "Now, what's going on with this tiger that's out there? Everyone's talking about it, why Bob over at the store told me—"

"Did you ever marry? Have children?"

"Nope. Never had the time, but I'm not ... you know ..."

"Gay?" Anna paused. "I am."

"Figured." Maude took another cigarette from the pack on the table, lit it, sucked the smoke in like it was oxygen itself. "I like men well enough, it just seems most of 'em aren't worth the effort. Consider yourself lucky. Bunch of babies, you ask me." She held the cigarette away between two fingers like an old-time movie star, the smoke trailing up into the air in a lazy blue spiral, smirked, batted her eyes. "Don't go getting any ideas."

Anna laughed, said, "Talk about feisty."

Maude tried not to laugh, but couldn't hold it in, then couldn't stop, finally did, but was hit by a hacking cough.

"You should quit."

"Tried, haven't I? More than once. By now, I think it's the nicotine keeps me alive."

Could be, Anna thought, the woman had a yellowish tinge to her.

At the station, Anna spent the rest of the morning on the phone talking to the organizers of the conference in Boston, and Martin Kelley had, indeed, been there, prominently visible. After arriving late afternoon of the 3rd, he had been a panelist in the opening night's presentation, spent the rest of that evening schmoozing at the hotel bar until almost midnight, and then had an early morning breakfast meeting the next day. It almost seemed to her that he had made a particular effort to be seen, ensuring that there was no doubt that he was there and never left. But, Anna thought, isn't that why people go to these things? To network?

Her idea of networking was a Manhattan at Crystal's.

She phoned a few of the other reported break-ins and discovered that Gaetz had talked to them as well. She had been assigned to follow up on these. Was he trying to make her look bad?

Things taken from houses scattered in the hills. What the hell was going on? If she set aside Eliza as a suspect in Ritchie's murder, who was left? As far as they knew, no one, but what if this thief, who Maude called the hermit, but who Anna had already nick-named Bigfoot, had been caught in the act by Ritchie, and killed him. Wasn't that more plausible than Eliza killing her close friend?

There's something going on that no one talks about. What? That no one wants to think about. Why?

She felt at a loss. Her experience was in the city where there were witnesses to be interviewed, CCTV to review, crime scene data to be analyzed. Here, Ritchie had been killed in the middle of nowhere, and the scene totally trashed by a giant freaking cat, and the only witnesses were a bunch of trees. Martin Kelley was off the hook, but to her he was responsible for his son's death. And, the question remained: why was Ritchie on that trail, at that time? And, who the hell is my Bigfoot?

Then came thoughts of Jimmy. His drinking. Why did he do that to himself?

She tossed her notes aside, and turned to see Captain Wagner looking anything but his usual crisp self: rumpled grey pants, suit coat over his shoulder, tie pulled loose, damp white shirt clinging to his body.

"Christ, you guys ever think about getting air conditioning that worked?" He fanned himself with a copy of the Concord Monitor. "You seen the paper this morning?"

"Can't say I have."

"There's an editorial pushing hard for the state to take over the investigation. Says there's too many personal connections." He gestured at a chair. She nodded. He pulled it over, draped his jacket on the back, sat across from her. "What do you think?"

"I think it'd be nice."

"What?"

"AC that worked."

"Cute. I'm serious. There's a lot of concern in Concord that George Baker is too close to the principals in this situation to effectively run the investigation. I want to know what you think."

"What would you suggest we do? Got any bright ideas?"

"How long have you been in the department?"

She had no doubt that Wagner knew exactly how long she'd worked here, but what she didn't know was where was this conversation going. Was he trying to turn her against George? Why? State Police have no supervisory role over a county sheriff. What was Wagner fishing for?

"Just over a year," He answered his own question. "There may be changes coming. The state is considering creating a major crimes unit to handle cases too difficult or sensitive for local forces. Could be a good opportunity for you. It'd be a shame if this case goes south and tarnishes everyone involved."

"I see," said Anna, who didn't.

"We're going to be looking for talent," Wagner said.

"Talent? What am I, a hooker?" Anna said before she could stop herself.

Wagner laughed. "Sorry, bad choice of words. But, I'm serious. It would be better than working in this backwater. What's it like, being the only"—he paused, as if searching for the right word—"woman? Dealing with these guys?"

"You mean gay woman."

"That too."

Anna realized she was starting to like Wagner.

"Look. Can I say something, just between you and me?" Wagner said.

"Of course."

"I'm aware of your record in Boston. All of it. You were a good detective. I also know you got a raw deal. If this new unit comes to pass, I will be in touch."

How could he know everything? Those records were sealed. Clearly, there was more to Wagner than she had thought.

"I am, however, concerned about the current investigation."

"Don't underestimate the sheriff, but we could use a little help."

"What do you need?"

"The full CSS report would be a good place to start."

"It's coming." He stood. "The sheriff around?"

"On his way to Vermont to talk to Eliza Johnson's brother."

"Tell him I stopped by."

George Baker had arranged to meet William Johnson Jr. at a coffee shop on Main Street in downtown Burlington. What was it about some men, he wondered, that think they're so goddamn special they name their son after themselves. He'd often wished he'd grown up with a name all his own, and wondered if Bill Johnson's son felt the same. William had finished his sophomore year at the University of Vermont, but was staying in Burlington for the summer.

The interior of Muddy Waters was an overdone mix of exposed brick, salvaged hand-hewn posts and beams, and a slate-shingled overhang above the coffee bar. The young woman behind the counter had red-streaked hair, almost shaved on one side and long on the other, and so many piercings it hurt to look at her.

"I'm Kendra," she said. "What'll you have?"

George stood lost in a blackboard that read like a handwritten list of half the countries in Africa and Central America.

"Isn't there plain coffee anymore?"

"Have the Bolivian," Kendra said. "You'll like it."

William approached the table carrying an insulated purple coffee mug, a messenger bag with a huge red and chrome buckle slung across his back. He pulled the strap over his head, set the bag down—the buckle hit the floor with a metallic clunk—and lowered himself into the chair opposite George.

"Thanks for meeting me, William," George said. "How are you holding up?"

In addition to carrying his father's name, William shared his looks as well: slender, dark hair, dark brown eyes set a little too close together, sharp nose. Not quite handsome, George thought, the parts were good, but there was something a little bit off. He couldn't put his finger on it.

"People call me Will. I don't see why you wanted to talk to me."

"We're trying to learn more about Eliza and I figured you'd know her as well as anyone."

"Me? Not really. I hardly ever go back there. I mean, like, never. I go to school, do summer programs."

"What about growing up?"

"I was sent to boarding school when I was eleven." Will went on about the different schools he'd attended.

How can you send an eleven-year-old away to school? George wondered. And, what could cause that boy to never go home?

"How old were you when your mother died?"

"Eight."

"That must have been tough."

Will shrugged.

"And Eliza?"

"Four. That's when she started acting crazy."

"Crazy? How?" George leaned forward.

"I don't mean like crazy, crazy, just out of control. She was seven the last time I lived at home. Eliza was never normal, she was special and she knew it, and when she was little, Eva let her run wild, do whatever she wanted."

"What about your father?"

"Dad?" Again, Will shrugged. "He's fine with me, formal, shakes my hand, says 'welcome home son' when I see him. Which is, like I said, almost never. The few times I've been home, he and Eliza argued constantly. I can't stand it. It's like they hate each other."

"We've been told she was afraid of him."

"Afraid? I don't think Eliza is afraid of anything."

"Was he violent? Did he ever hit her?" George said.

"Not when I was there. I blame myself. When she was little, she used to cry when I left for school, hold on to me as if she could keep me from leaving. I was her big brother and I abandoned her."

"How about Eliza, was she ever violent?"

He picked up his coffee, looked at it, put it back down.

"Not really. I mean, she's intense, can be a little scary. You don't want her mad at you."

Will turned the mug left, then right, then back. Stared at the damp ring it made on the table. "I was home for two days last spring. Late that night, I was reading. She came in through the back door, snuck up to her room, returned carrying some clothes. I asked where she was going, trying to be friendly, and she got mad, grabbed me, pushed me against the wall. Made me swear not to say anything. She didn't mean to hurt me, and, like, she apologized and all, so it was okay. She's bigger than me. How weird is that? My little sister bigger and stronger."

After talking with Will, George had lunch at a sub shop on the Burlington pedestrian mall, then drove out of town, merged onto Interstate 89, and headed south. The department's newest cruiser, a Ford Expedition, had all the latest: hardened laptop, GPS, riot gear, shotgun. The works. He didn't need all that equipment, but the grant from Homeland Security had requirements. It was all or nothing, so George had said what the hell. He loved the sense of control driving this great beast—a good solid car, Ford—gave him, especially now when everything else seemed so out of control.

Somehow, in the days she had been missing, George thought as he drove, Eliza Johnson had changed from everyone's golden girl to an intense, scary bully. Her father—but he wasn't really her father, was he?—called her fierce. Theresa Kelley, called her dangerous, troubled, and now her brother said she was scary, had attacked him. Who was she? These three seemed to be saying she was violent without actually saying it.

There was something weird about Ritchie's and Eliza's friendship, the way Ritchie wore the same shoes, the same clothes. The state lab was definite that he was struck from behind hard enough to crush his skull and kill him almost instantly. No way could that have been accidental. Eliza killed Ritchie because he got in the way of her plans, and was hiding out somewhere, on the run.

George looked up and saw the sign for New Hampshire. Where had the last thirty miles gone? He drove the bridge, and looked past the railing at the shrunken Connecticut River flanked by banks of dark mud.

It often surprised him how different Vermont and New Hampshire were. The Vermont countryside was a mix of farms and woods, gentle, pastoral, but as he drove past the Lebanon exits, he saw the dark, jagged peaks of the Croydon Mountains, the ragged woods, the beat-up landscape, and realized he preferred the rawness of New Hampshire to the prettiness of Vermont. He thought about exiting, going home, but tonight was the monthly Lions Club Leadership Team get-together in Manchester, and he was looking forward to the chance to connect with friends from around the state, drink a few beers, tell stories.

Maybe the time away would give him a new perspective on things.

As he drove, he tried to put the case out of his mind, but it nagged and niggled at him. There was something he was missing, wasn't seeing.

Jimmy Baker felt empty and it wasn't only that he had spent much of the night divesting himself of everything he'd eaten in the prior twenty-four hours, he was mentally hollowed out, scraped clean. Rock bottom. Isn't that what they say? You have to hit bottom before you can climb back up, make things better. He'd ubered into town to retrieve his car, and twenty-three dollars later he wanted to be mad at someone, but the only person he could think of was himself, and he was tired of being mad at himself. And now, at the house, he was thinking about obsession and possession, and which was this thing with his great-aunt and her clothes and jewelry?

The wall of the second floor landing was covered with photographs of his great-aunt's life: her childhood in Lebanon, a skinny girl with pigtails in a blue pinafore; her time as a WAC in World War II, standing with her husband-to-be, Herbert Baker, both of them in uniform, she in her whites, he in his lieutenant's khakis, the flat, billed cap with its gold-braid insignia too big on his head; their life in Texas, where Herbert made money in the oil business; Tooney at a charity ball for the Boys and Girls Clubs of Dallas, gorgeous in a long, silver evening gown, hair up, sparkling jewelry, tall, elegant.

Paula had said that Tooney went to New York twice a year and came back loaded down with packages. There were clothes in the dressing room from Macy's, Bergdorf's, some with hangtags still attached. Chiffon print dresses from Hilfiger, Vince Camuto, a short sun-dress from Michael Kors. There were soft floral prints in pastel shades of blue and pink, a little green, and bright solids in apricot, emerald, royal blue. There were bright geometrics. Elegant greys and blacks. Armani. The fabrics, silk, linen, fine-thread cotton, rayon were soft and sensuous. Irresistible.

There it was, the silver evening gown. On the landing, a life remembered in photographs; in this room, a life lived in clothing.

He held the silver dress up in front of him and looked in the mirror. He'd never worn anything so feminine, so beautiful. He shed his shorts, t-shirt, put on a bra, panties, slipped the dress over his head and felt it slide down his body. Found matching heels, strode into the bedroom marveling at how this new way of walking felt, how the perspective of everything around him changed with just these few extra inches of height. At the dressing table, he fastened a crystal necklace around his neck, clipped on matching earrings. He turned slowly in front of the mirror—who was that in the reflection?—and for one moment he lost the self he understood himself to be, and that lost feeling was as exhilarating as anything he'd ever felt on a ski descent where if you fell you would not stop for thousands of feet and would die broken-bodied.

He returned to the dressing room, pulled the dress over his head, replaced the heels in their slot on the shelf, and returned the silver gown to its place.

Later, Jimmy rocked on the porch wearing a floral print dress, the fabric so light it's touch on his skin was the barest of sensations. A warm breeze gentled his bare neck and shoulders as he watched the sun flatten against the western horizon, and the first hints of dusk creep up the hillside from the valley.

Just three days ago he had been certain, had known what he would do, but now he felt entangled in things beyond his control. He couldn't escape the wish that he had stayed in Jackson, could go back to before, before this house, things were simpler then. And, that he had not gone for that run, not found that body, not learned about Eliza. He would be free, back home in Wyoming. But, the thought occurred, was it? Home?

"Tooney?" He heard a quiet voice. Lonnie. "Tooney? I see you, why don't you answer me?"

"What is it, Lonnie?" Jimmy tried to remember his great-aunt's voice.

Lonnie lowered himself to sit awkwardly on the edge of the porch with his feet on the top step.

"What's the matter? You don't sound right, are you still sick?" he said. "I like it when you rock in your chair, the creak, creak, creak." He did his best to imitate the sound of the chair, then started giggling, then said, "Everyone's sick."

Jimmy was sorry he'd spoken, didn't feel up to dealing with Lonnie's non-sensical ramblings, wanted to be left in peace to watch night envelop the mountains, to wait for that one brief instant of alpenglow on their summits.

"I'm fine. Don't worry."

"I used to be lonely, but now I'm not." Lonnie paused. "Did you know that there are monsters in the woods? I saw them."

"Don't be silly, Lonnie. You should go home."

"Don't you believe me? Not nice to call me silly."

"I'm sorry. I believe you."

"You don't sound like you mean it . . . You have to mean it, when you say sorry . . . I'm thirsty."

Jimmy, staying in the shadows, went into the house to get him a glass of water. He noticed, with a shock, that he didn't feel strange in the dress with Lonnie there. He saw him now as a child, and felt a twinge of compassion for him. He returned to the porch, the glass of water cool in his hand, but Lonnie was gone, and Jimmy tried to remember what he had said.

He returned the glass to the kitchen. Two photos that he had walked past many times without stopping to look were hung near the door to the dining room. In the first, Tooney and Lonnie sat side by side on the front porch, Tooney in her rocking chair, Lonnie in a straight backed chair. Lonnie's hair was combed, his clothes relatively clean. He looked like a over-grown boy in the third grade forced to sit for his school picture. In the other, Eliza and Lonnie were walking along Gap Road in the fall, the leaves of the trees arching out over the road were red and orange, and the entire photo was suffused with an otherworldly glow, as if the air was light itself. Eliza was gazing off to the side, laughing, while Lonnie stared at her. Jimmy felt as if he could see the scene in real time: the girl, thin and light, walking easily up the road, Lonnie, heavy and bulky, lumbering beside her.

What was she doing? Paula Baker asked herself: tending her garden, keeping house, staring out the window in her nice, neat little world while her coffee cooled. In other words, nothing. She often wondered about the choices she made: getting married, having kids so young, being a housewife (she so hated being called a housewife), but there was no point. You can't go back. Can't change what is. She was still discomfited by the evening before, and not just Jimmy and how awful he'd looked and how lost he'd seemed, but the more she thought about it, the time with Helen Lambert, and the way Helen had looked at her as if she was about to say something but changed her mind, and how she had felt so intimidated by Helen.

Why am I so timid? Always so afraid?

She remembered Helen from school, and with those memories came a sense of despair that she, a grown woman, couldn't stop dwelling on things that happened almost thirty years ago, still lived so much in the past. "Are you pregnant?" the guidance counselor at Lebanon High School, Mrs. Tillson, had asked (even now Paula remembered her name, and could still see the disappointment on her face when Paula had told her she was getting married after graduation). Of course, that's what everyone thought. She wasn't, but no one believed her because no one could believe the valedictorian of her class, who had been accepted by three colleges, would choose to stay in Hemlock Flat with the unremarkable George Baker.

George.

How, she wondered, had he come to so dominate her life? He was almost certainly unaware of how he occupied her thoughts, of how she heard his voice in her head, of how, though not an especially big man, he filled the space around her, and how, when he was home, the house seemed smaller. He had become a reference point against which she, despite herself, measured everything she did, everything she thought. But, this night he was away, and in his absence Paula felt herself, at least for this night, untethered, free.

She stepped onto the back deck. It was one of those summer evenings when rather than cooling off, it seemed to get hotter as dusk turned to dark, and the warmth grew and wrapped around her, and she remembered those summers when to be alive was a blessing, and it was as if she was back there, young and tan and lazy, lying iin the grass with Abby O'Neal, imagining the bright future that lay before them: dreams fulfilled, worlds conquered. She could see Abby's face as if she was standing in front of her. They had been inseparable that summer: Abby lying topless in the sun; Abby sneaking a cigarette behind the Methodist Church; Abby riding her bike through their neighborhood, hair streaming behind her, Paula trying to keep up, the bright summer air on her face.

On this hot, humid night when the air was thick with the smells of plowed earth, cut grass, and weeping oak trees, and the dark was alive with the sound of frogs and buzzing mosquitos, and the rays of the rising moon slanted like cracks on the glass surface of the night, she remembered a kiss at dusk while crickets sang in the grass, and a walk through a meadow holding hands that so clearly promised more. Later that night, Abby had kissed her again, gently then firmer, her lips sweet with the taste of berries, and had slipped her tongue in between Paula's lips, and had whispered in her ear, her breath warm and moist, and had placed her hand on Paula's hip and pulled her close. Paula felt Abby's body mold itself to her, their breasts touch, and a sudden hot rush filled her. They parted, stood looking at each other in the aniline dark. Abby took her hand, led her to the back door of her house.

Now, Paula knew that was the moment. Imagining what might have been, she realized that there is nothing, perhaps, that can equal having been young and in love.

The bushy tailed silhouette of a fox flashed across the lawn. Bats, small stuttering shadows, flitted back and forth feasting on insects that swarmed around the tall post-lights at the edge of the deck. A moth beat itself against the lamp on the kitchen wall behind where she sat looking out across the grazed fields of Emerson's farm. Thin snakes of mist wove in and out of tall clumps of weeds. She could hear the herd out there in the dark, snuffling about.

The breeze turned; their animal warmth drifted toward her.

None of this would be happening to her: car keys would not be jingling in her hand, she would not be about to get up from her chair and go to her car and drive into Lebanon after drinking two glasses of wine if she did not now know exactly where Anna Korsak lived.

She got in the car; she drove to Lebanon; she parked on Elm

Street; she climbed the stairs; she knocked on the door, heard quiet steps coming toward her, the door opened and there Anna was. Before Anna could speak, Paula moved to her, reached up, held her face in her hands and kissed her with the passion of thirty years of memories and regrets, and then stepped back to gaze at the face that had haunted her thoughts, filled her dreams for months. Her heart raced. Blood pounded in her ears and she felt herself encased in a throbbing silence.

A look flashed across Anna's face—surprise? shock?—and then Anna turned, and walked away, toward the kitchen. Paula followed, stopped at the door to the kitchen, and realized she had made a terrible mistake.

Paula drove through the dark green night; trees heavy with moisture leaned out over the damp pavement; insects swirled and swarmed in the arrows of her headlights, splattered against the windshield. It was a straight drive on this road back to Hemlock Flat, but Paula felt as if she did not know the way. She struggled to see through the streaked windshield. Thin ghost-like tatters of mist laced the surface of the pavement. She felt as if someone was chasing her. Her hands gripped the steering wheel as if she could squeeze away the anguish.

Why am I here driving home through the dark? Why did Anna flirt with me? Why did she kiss me in front of my friends? Tonight, when I kissed her, why did she pull away?

"You have your home to go back to," Anna had said as if there was something wrong with that.

But, Paula thought, do I? How can I go back?

Anna, Abby, the two became one in her mind.

Those summer months after that first night with Abby had been heaven, but then came school. They were seen kissing, holding hands. The talk started. Her parents found out.

The memory and trauma had never left her. The huge white cross, the Kingdom Hall that had once been a car dealership, the faint smell of gasoline. A long, narrow space, distorted in memory, with pews stepping up from the aisle in tiers and the congregants leaning out, looking down on her as her parents walked her the length of the aisle. It all came back to her. Tears filled her eyes.

A movement on the side of the road, a flash of yellow.

Then, in an explosion of light, the cougar was in the middle of the road, its red eyes staring at her. Time stopped. She slammed on the brakes. In a single leap, it was gone. The car skidded left then right—she couldn't control it—and she was off the road. Branches scraped, metal screamed, weeds and mud splattered the windshield, and the air bag slammed her in the face.

The car came to rest angled sharply down an embankment. She was stunned, suspended by the seatbelt across her chest, looking down at the almost dry creek bed of Shaker Brook, the only sounds the ticking of cooling metal. She couldn't move. She drifted on the edge of consciousness. How had her life come to this? It was Anna's fault, it was Abby's fault, it was her parents' fault. Would the memory of that Sunday never let her be?

She had tried to leave, but her parents grabbed her arms as the Elder, thin with a cadaverous face, railed against sin and the disciples of Satan that were corrupting the youth of America, and he put his hands on her head, and the entire congregation prayed for her deliverance, for the Lord to forgive her for giving a place in her heart to lust, and chanted, "Repent. Submit therefore to God," over and over and her parents held her there and she couldn't stop crying and sobbing and wanted to die and be no more.

She never went back to that church, and her parents had cast her out, and she had moved to Hemlock Flat to live with the Marsden family, and had run into the arms of George Baker and he had been simply too good, too sincere, too safe, not to marry.

Chapter Fifteen

Paula Baker slumped at the kitchen table staring at her empty coffee mug. She had barely slept, and the early morning light seemed to her harsh and accusing. There were dark bruises under her eyes. Her chest hurt. She heard tires crunch on the gravel driveway, a car door slam, steps in the front hall. George, back early from Manchester, walked to the counter, poured himself a cup, and sat across from her at the table. His face was hard and unyielding.

"Jesus Christ, Paula. What the hell were you thinking? We're goddamn lucky it was Arnold found you. Some of the other deputies might not of been so understanding."

Paul Arnold had been driving home from the station after a late shift, had seen the car pointed down into the ditch, and had found her in the front seat, held up by the seat belt, sobbing. He'd been kind, didn't ask where she'd been, what she was doing. He could tell, she was sure, that she'd been drinking, but didn't say a thing. Used his personal cell to call a friend who had a wrecker, kept it quiet, the way small-town folks do who've known each other for decades.

"I'm buried with this case, the state is breathing down my neck, and you do this to me?"

To you? Paula thought.

Last night, the kiss she had been dreaming of, and then . . . what had happened? She couldn't make sense of it, but what she did remember was that Anna had walked away from her, and in the kitchen her expression changed, became clouded, and she wouldn't look at her, and then she told her to go home, and the pain of that rejection.

George had yet to ask if she was okay.

"Where were you?"

"I went to a bar. Had a glass of wine," Paula said in the voice of someone who did not have the energy to care.

When had the lying, the deception started, she wondered, was it the swimming hole? That stupid earring? Was that little thing the wedge that had pushed in between them? Becoming wider and wider as each white lie required another?

"What? You? A bar? Alone at eleven o'clock at night? Women don't do that."

"Yes they do. It's boring here alone. You're working so much."

"Now it's my fault you were out driving drunk. Thank god Arnold had the sense not to test you. If he had, he would have had to report it, and then what? Christ. Think what people would say."

Yes, George, think what people would say.

"I saw it." Paula said.

"What?"

"The cougar. It was so big. It's eyes were red. It looked at me. That's why I crashed."

"You were drunk."

"I was not drunk. Aren't you going to ask if I'm okay?"

Suck it up, George Baker told himself. Get it together. They were waiting for him in the briefing room. The station's men's room was disgusting. The sink was laced with thin cracks. The mirror had dark patches where the coating had started to corrode that made his face look splotchy, like he, himself, was corroding. You, he said to the face in the mirror, look like shit.

It could have been his father staring back at him: bleary eyes, dark circles, fleshy jowls. George Baker Sr. had been a local contractor of some prominence, and a local drinker of considerable repute. Dead at fifty-eight.

Christ, that was only ten years off.

George Sr. had wanted his son to join him in the business, take over. Baker & Sons he called the company, though George was still in school and the man only had one son to begin with, but George went to the Police Academy in Concord right out of high school, became a state trooper. He had loved being on highway patrol, driving, watching the countryside scroll past his windows, but Paula had hated how much he was gone, them being newlyweds, and so he started as a deputy in the county sheriff's office, and one thing led to another and now he had to decide if he wanted two more years. Of course he did—what else would he do?—but everything seemed so overwhelming at the moment, he worried that he didn't have the energy for another election. Paula had been a big part of every campaign in the past. What if word gets out about last night? He wanted to understand what was going on with her, but a boy had been murdered and the sixteen-year-old girl who was probably the killer had disappeared. That's what he needed to focus on. He would deal with Paula later, when things settled down.

Another goddamn day, another goddamn meeting.

He splashed cold water on his face, dried himself, and threw the damp paper towels into the trash.

"It's been almost a week." George said. "Since Ritchie Kelley was killed and where are we? Nowhere." He'd assembled Korsak, Arnold, Gaetz, and all but four of the department's force of twelve deputies, and was walking back and forth in front of a wall that held everything they had relating to the murder of Ritchie Kelley: photos, notes, report summaries. Under the heading of Suspects, there was a single photo and name, Eliza Johnson.

George stopped pacing, saw Wagner leaning against the back wall, turned to Anna, said, "Fill everyone in."

She had been distant this morning, had looked tired, and different in some way. Her hair, not pulled back lacquer tight in her usual ponytail, hung loose around her face. While she summarized what they knew for the additional deputies assigned to the case, George was lost in his thoughts and realized that he didn't care all that much what Paula did.

"Sheriff?" Anna said. She'd finished and everyone was looking at him.

George saw Wagner look up from where he'd been studying his feet. Wagner was tall, almost movie star handsome, with broad shoulders that stretched his suit jacket. George found his presence intimidating, so too, it seemed, did the others. Gaetz kept glancing in his direction, and several of the other deputies stared straight ahead, rigid, as if afraid to see who was behind them. Only Anna seemed comfortable with Wagner, but then George had never known her to be intimidated by anyone or anything.

He forced his attention back to the room. "As Deputy Korsak explained, Eliza Johnson is no longer solely a missing person, she is a suspect in the murder of Ritchie Kelley. We have interviewed her family, her friends, and the only documented incident of her being violent is a minor altercation with her brother, but several people have described her as hot-tempered, intense, scary, possibly threatening. Notes on these interviews are in your packets.

"We've got two main lines to pursue. It's likely Eliza Johnson has left the area, but we can't assume anything. Gaetz, get back in touch with area police departments, follow up with the state on the APB, talk to her friends one more time.

"Korsak, you're in charge of learning everything we can about Ritchie Kelley. What was his relationship with Eliza? Interview more of his friends, try to find out what the hell he was doing wandering around in the woods. Bobby, you and I are going to follow up with Martin Kelley about a recent break-in he reported at his cabin, maybe there's a connection"—he held up a red folder—"assignments are in your packets. Let's get going."

George extricated himself from the driver's side of the cruiser and looked across the valley to where lumpy white clouds assembled above the western horizon. The air was hot and still, with the over-heated smell of scorched pine and hemlock. The storm four days ago had done nothing to break the grip of the heat wave. He walked to the cabin, climbed the stairs, and stepped across the porch, taking care not to disturb the dirty footprints. The lock had been jimmied; he wouldn't need the key Kelley had given him.

Inside, there were more of the same wide, squarish prints on the polished wood floor, probably work boots of some sort. The couch had been moved, its cushions strewn on the floor. Someone had been searching for something. The open kitchen shelves were empty as was the refrigerator. George followed the footprints into the bedroom. The bed had been stripped. The closet was open, clothes were strewn on the bare mattress, bedding on the floor.

He turned to Bobby Jenkins. "We need photos of everything. Especially the footprints, see if we can determine the make of the boot."

Deputy Macklin arrived with Martin Kelley.

"I want to know if anything was taken." George watched Kelley look through the kitchen, then followed him into the bedroom. He seemed a haunted, broken man.

"Food, maybe, but I don't remember how much was here. I had a framed photograph of Eliza on the bedside table that's not there."

"See if the photo's here anywhere," George said to Bobby Jenkins, then to Kelley. "Anything missing from the closet?"

Kelley looked into the closet, at the clothes everywhere.

"Maybe some of her clothing, but I'm not sure."

Back in the main room, George replaced the cushions on the sofa and sat down. Kelley lowered himself into a wood rocking chair on the other side of the gas heater, said, "I think I'm going to sell this place."

Jenkins returned from his search, shook his head.

Kelley rocked back and forth in the chair as if he couldn't stop, as if the motion would keep from him the knowledge that his son was dead, and his teen-age lover was suspected of killing him.

"I can't believe she would kill him," Kelley said. "He was a good kid . . ."

"Deputy Macklin will take you home. You should be with your wife."

"She left me. Ritchie's funeral is tomorrow. Will you come?"

George couldn't stop wondering how Kelley could have thought it was okay to have sex with a sixteen-year-old girl. His life was in ruins because he couldn't keep his pants zipped.

"How could you?" George said.

"She came to the house with Ritchie. I couldn't take my eyes off her. She flirted with me when no one else was around. She was amazing, made me feel alive . . ." He looked up, pleading for under-standing. "Haven't you ever felt that way?"

"Frankly, no. Was it worth it?"

Kelley rocked in his chair and George wondered briefly what the man was thinking, but his thoughts kept returning to what had come over Paula—driving drunk in the middle of the night, crash-ing the car—but if he thought about it, it wasn't just last night, she'd been moody, distant for months. When had it started, this change? He thought back and it was suddenly obvious. Not long after he'd hired Anna Korsak. How can I have been so stupid?

After the meeting broke up, Anna looked for Gaetz, to ask why he had decided to investigate the break-ins when George had specifically assigned her to, and why he hadn't filed a report, but he was nowhere to be found. She left messages on both his desk phone and his cell, then walked outside the station to grab a moment alone. Sun glinted off the chrome and glass of the parked cars, the glare hurt her eyes, and she felt a headache coming on. The hopeless, oppressive heat matched the way she felt.

Last night, after Paula had left, sleep would not come for Anna. She had climbed out of bed and wandered into the living room. Before she had opened the door, Anna had somehow known who was there, and then, before she could speak, Paula had kissed her, and her hands on Anna's face had been calloused and strong and it was hard to breathe and time had seemed to stop. She'd put her hands on Paula's shoulders and gently eased back. The apartment was in semi-darkness. The kettle that Anna had put on the stove for her bed-time cup of tea started to whistle. Anna felt rooted in place, but soon the kettle would be at full scream. She went to turn it off. Steam plumed up into the already saturated air, a mug with a tag for chamomile tea waited on the counter, underwear hung from a drying rack, a deputy's uniform was draped over the back of a chair. Paula stood in the doorway to the kitchen, and Anna saw her examine the room, and in that moment she saw Paula's eyes change, her lips tremble, as if the uniform reminded her of her husband, as if it told her she should get back in her car and go back to her life, and Paula stood in the doorway as if she was afraid to enter the kitchen. What had happened? What she did remember was Paula turning around and leaving her there, heart pounding.

The loud blare of a truck engine-braking down the hill into Newport, and the tang of diesel and sulphur in the air pulled her back to the present.

Why do I do this to myself? Fall for women who can't make up their mind?

God, Anna thought, I need to get laid. It was an ache that filled her entire body, but it was more than sex, it was this desperate loneliness she lived with day after day. How long had it been? Not since Boston, since Jess. Their love had been like nothing Anna had known, sometimes wild and rough, sometimes gentle and tender. Jess's small, lean body was strong and supple. Oh, the memories of those nights, but walking the streets of Brookline, Jess would not hold hands, would not walk close, would not touch. She was afraid that someone would see them and tell her family.

"You don't understand," she'd said. "How traditional and conservative my family is."

Anna had agreed, she didn't understand. All she wanted was for Jess, in front of total strangers, to hold her, to kiss her. Anna came to feel that Jess was ashamed of her, ashamed of their love.

Last night, Anna had gone to her empty bedroom, and retrieved the necklace Paula had given her for Christmas from a tangle of jewelry on the top of her dresser, and held it in the palm of her hand, and gazed into the deep blue of the lapis, and thought again of the swimming hole.

I should never have accepted it ... I should have left the woman alone. Why was Paula Baker so irresistible? What was so goddamn special about her?

Anna had thought moving here would give her the chance to work her way back after the mess in Boston, but now everything seemed to be coming apart. How could she stay here? Where so many things, so many places, reminded her of Paula? When every day she had to work with George Baker, and every night she would wonder what Paula was doing, if she was in his arms.

Even after more than a year, Anna still felt herself a stranger in a strange land. There was something about the emptiness of these mountains, the loneliness she felt when she looked at their bleak heights, that scared her, and she lived in a constant state of low-level anxiety that made it hard to focus, to concentrate, and she felt an almost overwhelming desire to get in her car and drive to her apartment and pack her things and go where the air was fresh and cool and she could think and somehow know what to do. Instead, she went back inside, back to work. Her desk phone rang. It was Gaetz.

"It's about time," Anna said.

"Hello to you too."

"Why did you look into those break-ins up in the hills?"

"Just trying to help out."

Trying to help out? Since when does Gaetz do anything he doesn't have to?

"Did you talk to the sheriff before you made those calls?"

"Um . . . didn't get the chance, didn't want to bother him."

"Did you file a report? I can't find anything in the log books."

"Nah, didn't seem important. Not much was taken, food, clothing. Probably just kids."

"Still, you should—"

"What's going on? Any sign of the girl?"

"Nothing."

He hung up without a word.

"Asshole," Anna said to the dead line.

Department policy was clear, when you investigated something, no matter how trivial, you filed a report. Gaetz knew that. Why would he not file?

She pulled up a chair and sat next to Paul Arnold at his desk.

"You okay?" His questioning gaze lingered.

"It's brutal outside. What did Ritchie's friends have to say?"

He looked at the yellow pad on his desk. "I talked to Bob Tryon, good kid, total nerd, into video games and these weird card games, Dungeons and Dragons, that kind of stuff. Not at all into the outdoors, and it's clear Ritchie wasn't either, and he had no idea why he was out there, or had anything nice to say about Eliza Johnson. Might of been jealous of all the time Ritchie spent with her.

"Also, I finally tracked down Kyle Hernandez. The day before he was killed, Ritchie told Hernandez that he knew where Eliza was, and that he was going to 'save her.' His words."

"Hernandez have any idea where that is?"

"Nope. I talked to Sheriff Baker, he talked to Martin Kelley. No help there."

"What do you think about these minor break-ins?" Anna said.

"Probably just kids."

"But, what if it isn't? What if it's connected to everything?" Anna wanted to explain her mystery man theory, but worried he would think that she was questioning the sheriff's leadership.

"I asked about that. The sheriff told me to stay focused on Ritchie's friends."

It was a little odd, she thought, how Arnold never seemed to refer to George by his first name. It was always the sheriff or Sheriff Baker.

"How long have you known George?"

"He was a year ahead of me in school . . . you heard about the accident?"

"What accident?"

"Paula went off the road last night. I found her in her car. She was in shock, said the cougar ran across the road in front of her, and she lost control."

"Is she okay?"

"Just banged up. In shock. She'll be fine. Sheriff Baker said to keep it quiet, but I thought you should know."

"Why?"

"Other thing she said to me when I helped her out of the car was your name."

Paul Arnold was a hard man to get to know, quiet to a fault, unassuming, and in the long silence that followed she wondered what he was thinking. He turned away, looked down at his notes, said, "I still haven't talked to Timmy Marks."

Anna took the hint and went to her desk and sat, lost in thought. What happened last night? It was so confusing, but what she did remember was that Paula had left in a rush, and then had crashed on the way home.

I shouldn't have told her to go when she was so upset.

Anna took out her cell, texted, "hrd about accident. you ok?" and wondered if Paula would reply.

❖

Routines were important to Paula Baker, they helped keep things in order, in place, helped her fill her days, and Wednesday was Paula's day to clean the upstairs bedrooms, so that's what she would do. She had her hair up, but strands of it had escaped and stuck to her damp neck and face. It was the ninth of August, and the same miserable weather, and she was tired of being hot and sweaty, of sodden clothing plastered to her skin. She ached all over. Her neck was so stiff she couldn't turn her head; her breasts and chest were bruised and it hurt to breathe, but she had to keep busy, had to avoid thinking about last night, even though every movement brought a painful reminder.

The furniture in the bedroom was filmed with dust that billowed up from the roadsides and drifted in through the screens every time a car drove past. It coated the clutter on the top of her dresser: jewelry, random shopping lists, notes, reminders for errands long since accomplished or forgotten, jars of skin cream, a dried up lipstick. She started to put the jewelry in her jewelry box, picked up a single silver and emerald earring. Did it miss it's other half that was in an evidence bag at the sheriff's department? She thought to throw it away, but then came the memory of Anna standing at the edge of the swimming hole in what seemed a different lifetime, and instead she tossed it into the tray with the others, all in pairs, all complete.

The vacuum cleaner glowered at her from the middle of the room. It was too hot to continue; she was so tired she felt faint. She went into the bathroom and splashed cold water on her face and neck. This house is too big, she thought. It's simply too big. She couldn't face doing the children's bedrooms (can she still call them children?). Nobody had used them in ages. How dirty could they be? She carried the vacuum into the hall, put it in the closet, and decided she should at least open up the rooms, air them out.

Each looked as if its former occupant had not grown up and moved away, and might return that evening, back from school, sports, or visiting friends. Charley's: his yellow Tonka truck from when he was four, scabbed with rust; a baseball in a clear plastic cube signed by a Red Sox player (she couldn't remember who), a souvenir from a father-son trip to Fenway Park. Patricia's: stuffed animals and dolls arranged on the pink bedspread; posters of an actor that she'd had a crush on (another name Paula had forgotten); the handmade dollhouse that had been George's mother's with all the furniture in it carefully arranged. Tracy's: cluttered with art, sketchbooks, paintings begun but never finished; a backpack; her first guitar.

Paula sat on Tracy's bed, stunned by the wonder of her children—each so different, each so completely who they are—and by how each of them had come into the world ready to be who they would become. How could she regret her life's choices? She had tried to be a good mother to them, but now they were off leading lives of their own while she felt her world crumbling around her.

Later, Paula stood with her hands on the kitchen counter as if her legs were unwilling to support her weight. George had come home and gone into his den without so much as a word. The walls moved in. This house, this home that she had created, had made a place where children could grow up safe and loved, this house, her world, seemed to shrink around her. She felt trapped.

Her phone pinged.

She read the text from Anna, put the phone aside, then picked it up, read it again. Someone had finally asked if she was alright. She tapped, "Im fine. Thx."

She found George in his study, crime scene photos and work papers spread out on the floor, the TV muted. She felt as if her heart was about to come out of her chest. She stood in front of the television. The big screen's light cast her flickering shadow on George's work papers.

"What are you doing?"

"I need to talk to you."

"Not now."

"Why not?"

"Jesus Christ, not now! Do you have any idea what I'm dealing with? Do you?"

He held up a photo, almost shook it in her face. She couldn't look at it: the blood, the ravaged body.

"I had to tell two parents that their son had been murdered and his body mangled by a goddamn mountain lion. That's what!"

"I can't do this anymore."

"Do what?"

"This!" She waved her arms. "This house, this life … everything."

"Not. Now."

"Fine."

"Maybe when this is all over—"

"I said fine."

But, it wasn't fine. The man didn't get it. Had they grown so entrenched, each in their own world, that they had lost the ability to talk to each other, to listen to each other? George, she thought, is himself, always himself. How does he manage, every day, every hour to be exactly the same? He tossed the photo onto the floor, picked up a sheet of paper, started reading. She watched him there, absorbed in his work, oblivious to her distress. She had spent all these years supporting him, and now when she most needed understanding, he wasn't there. He didn't have it in him.

He doesn't care. He doesn't care if I stay or if I go.

She turned and walked out of the room and climbed the stairs to the bedroom and took down the roller suitcase she had purchased for a vacation in the Bahamas that never happened. The tags were still on it. She barely saw what she pulled out of her dresser, took down from the closet, and stuffed into the case. The room swam. She thought she would faint. What was happening to her? In an instant everything had changed. How could all that she thought she was, vanish, and leave her alone like this? Where could she go? She didn't know, knew only that she needed get out of this house, needed space, room to breathe.

She was a stranger in her own home.

The earth exhaled and the evening air thickened into mist which flowed down from the meadow and encircled the house, and Jimmy Baker, alone on his front porch, felt himself at sea, lost in the fog off a dangerous coast and could almost hear surf crashing against distant rocks. He held a glass in both hands, cradling it as one might hold a warm mug of coffee on a cold morning. Sweat beaded on the back of his neck and trickled down between his shoulder blades. He'd run out of margarita mix, the freezer in Tooney's ancient fridge had quit, and he was forced to drink straight tequila, warm from the glass.

Starlight strung webs of silver on the dark.

A car came up Gap Road, headlights piercing the mist, wavering and pulsing as the car bumped its way up the rough dirt. Who came up here this time of night? Tires crunched on gravel, a car turned into his driveway, and for an instant he was pinioned by a blinding light. The car stopped, the headlights dimmed, then went off. Bright sparks and strange, orange circles spiraled on the edges of his vision. A figure got out of the car and walked slowly toward him dragging a wheeled piece of luggage, and when he saw her standing at the foot of the steps in the weak yellow light from the porch lamp, he almost didn't recognize his aunt.

"Whose car is that?"

"Loaner. Don't ask." Paula struggled to lift the suitcase. "Can you help me?"

He stepped down beside her, picked up the heavy case, and put it next to the front door.

"Can I have something to drink?"

When he returned he found her slumped in a chair. He handed her a glass, she drank, spluttered, coughed.

"Tequila. It's all I have."

"Ice?

He shook his head, pulled a chair over, sat next to her, saw the dark bruises around her eyes.

"Holy shit, Paula, what happened? Did George—"

"God, no! He would never. I crashed the car last night ..."

The moon behind the mountains edged nearer the crest, and the night moved around them and a hot breeze rustled the leaves of the oak trees. The staccato crack of an acorn on the roof of his car. Then another.

"I've been driving around forever. I couldn't keep going. I'm so tired. I'm sorry, I didn't know where else to go ... I ... I've left George."

Jimmy had turned twelve when his parents divorced and what he mostly remembered was thinking, finally. His aunt and uncle had been more his parents than his own. Why now, after all these years? He should be surprised, but realized he wasn't. He should say something, but what?

"I just couldn't anymore"—she took another sip of tequila, shuddered—"every day the same, one after the other." She brought the glass to her lips but didn't drink. "Do you think a place, a land-scape, can shape how people think, how they live? I mean the way these hills surround us, the dark narrow valleys, and how we're always going up and down, to get anywhere, and the mountains block the sunrise and how we so seldom see the horizon ..."

She drained her glass.

"Is that why I can't see ahead, see where to go, what to do?"

The porch was a yellow-lit island; the rocking chairs creaked; the night whispered.

"Do you remember what you said about that summer with Harriet that you thought would last forever, that was everything, and then nothing, and how you asked if I could know what that was like? Well … yes … I do. I had a friend once— No, a lover. We could talk and talk and never run out of things to say to each other, and I thought … but I hurt her …" She held the empty glass in her lap with both hands, looked down as if wondering how it came to be there. "Now I wake up every morning with this lump of a man snoring next to me. He barely speaks at breakfast and he's gone all day and comes home and still has nothing to say."

Jimmy rocked back and forth in his chair.

"Driving home from Anna's I saw the cougar. It looked straight at me like it was trying to tell me to go back, but I panicked, lost control …"

She slurred her words, and then, like a wind-up doll as its spring ran down, went silent.

Jimmy put his aunt, small, like a child in her parents' bed, in Tooney's vast four-poster. He descended the stairs, paused at the door to the dining room. He had taped together four topographic maps. They covered almost half of the dining room table. He flipped a switch, the huge chandelier with its countless crystals cast a strange, splintered light on the map, and he could see the entire area, the village, the hills and woods, the mountains, as if he was a red-tailed hawk, looking down, sharp-eyed, on the strange doings of humans.

Somewhere was a daughter he'd never known, and now they thought she was a killer. He imagined Eliza's picture on wanted posters in post offices. He had to find her before they did. He had to talk to her one time before he could leave. His eyes started to hurt from staring at the thin contour lines, the minuscule print.

He returned to the porch and his tequila.

He thought back to the night he'd slept outside, the cougar, and how he felt the sound of its rumbling growl in his chest, and how he hadn't been frightened, and how he'd felt it was trying to tell him something. And now, his aunt had seen it, and she had felt the same, and in his addled mind this beast, this magnificent cat long thought to be absent from these parts, became a messenger from somewhere far away where people lived the lives they were meant to live.

Why had it come all this way? What was it looking for?

The rim of the flat-black mountains glowed with the light of the moon below it to the east. A tiny sliver of bright silver appeared over the crest of Croydon Peak.

In between having a drink and being drunk was a place where, for Jimmy, the patterns of things became more distinct, more visible, but it was slippery, that place, and this understanding, this perspective, was brief, impossible to hold onto. He sipped the last of the tequila and thought of his aunt, the woman who had never stopped caring about him, upstairs asleep in his bed, then searched for memories of his mother, tried to remember the feel of her arms around him, of the touch of her hand, but couldn't. Had she ever held him? Touched him? He looked for her face, tried to see again what she looked like, her smile, her hair, but there was nothing, and it was as if she had never been there at all.

He watched dew settle on the grass and the trees and the two automobiles until everything glistened and shimmered in the golden light from the porch and the silver light from the rising moon, and the world shone like the inside of a liquor bottle backlit on a mirrored shelf in a bar somewhere in his memory. Here he was, loaded again, and he didn't know what to do. The tequila bottle was empty and the night was simmering and the air was restless and a breeze like a forgotten promise whispered in the leaves of the oak trees, and a sense of failure sat in the back of his throat like the aftertaste of warm tequila.

Chapter Sixteen

PALE, HAZY LIGHT SLANTED in through gauze-like curtains, and when Paula Baker woke she didn't know where she was. It was already hot and the sheets were damp and clingy and the first thing she thought was could she go back in time and undo what was done? Her life lay out before her, a life she had never expected, never planned for, and the unknowns of it made it hard to breathe. She found Jimmy sitting in a kitchen bleached by the harsh glare of another sun blasted day. He was hunched over, staring at the table, an empty coffee cup nearby.

"What are you doing?" she said.

"Watching this bug."

Paula moved closer and saw a small caterpillar in the middle of the table. It was injured, its back-end squashed, and it was writhing and twitching, and trying to crawl across the table.

"I stepped on it," Jimmy said. "Didn't mean to." He poked at it with the tine of a fork. "Look at it, still fighting. Do you think it knows it's going to die? Where do you think it's going? Why does everything try so hard to stay alive? What's the point?"

There was a strange glint in his eyes. He kept poking at the bug.

"Jimmy, stop torturing the poor thing."

Paula took the fork from his hand and used it to gently urge the creature toward the edge of the table. She could see that its back legs weren't working, but maybe it was one of those insects that can grow new legs. (Some can, can't they?) She carefully pushed it into her cupped hand and held it close to her face. It had beautiful eyes with long, curling green lashes. She had never known a caterpillar could have eyes like that. She carried it outside and put it on the broad leaf of a bush near the back door, and returned to find that Jimmy hadn't moved.

"What's going on?"

"How could you do this to me?"

"To you? Listen to me, Jimmy Baker, not everything in the world is about you."

"But, you and Uncle George were—"

"I think I'm in love with somebody else."

She saw surprise then recognition come slowly to his face.

"Anna?" he said. "Why aren't you there?"

"I went to her, but— I don't know. Something wasn't right. She told me to leave. What do I do?"

"You're asking me?"

The parking lot at the elementary school was empty, and Paula felt as if she was alone in the world. Where was everyone? Why am I the only one out in this heat? The only person with nowhere to be? The Fish and Game command module was gone and the searchers were gone, but Eliza was still missing, and was now a murder suspect. How could that be?

She looked at the school, a low brick building unchanged since she herself had gone there. In the weeks to come the parking lot will fill with the cars of teachers and custodians and staff preparing the school for the return of the students. She remembered dropping each of her children off for their first day of kindergarten: Patricia looking at her, resigned, quiet; Charley marching right into the place without looking back, ready to take on the world; Tracy clinging to her as if she was being left to some horrible fate.

The morning sun glared at her from a hard blue sky. She didn't know where to go, what to do. Jimmy wanted her to stay with him, but she felt that it was wrong somehow, her being there. She had never had a home of her own, never her place. The house in Hemlock Flat had been in the Baker family for generations, and when she and George married and moved into that house, she was pulled into that family, and whoever she might have been before was erased, and it seemed to her, looking back, that she had lived her life trying to fulfill everyone else's expectations.

A place of her own. The thought terrified her. A place that would be hers only. What would it be? She didn't know. What would it look like, this place of hers. Where would it be? How could she begin? She thought of going to Anna, but wouldn't that, in a way, be the same as when she married George?

Why can't I make my own way in this world?

Jimmy Baker slouched by the juice bar of the Fitness Spa in a sweaty grey t-shirt and faded climbing shorts, feeling decidedly out of place in the sleek, mauve and grey lobby. He saw Anna walking toward him, still in her workout gear.

"What are you doing here?" she said.

"Guest pass. Checking it out." What he was really doing was pretending to study the menu on the wall while waiting for her to get out of her morning Pilates class. "What the hell is Kombucha?"

"It's Korean, supposed to be good for you."

"What I want is a beer."

"At ten o'clock?"

"But, I'll settle for a coffee."

Rosey Jeke's was a trendy cafe in the college town of Hanover complete with seventeen varieties of coffee. Twelve stainless steel hot water taps of the optimum temperature for brewing individual pour-over servings lined the wall opposite the coffee bar. Anna ordered Ethiopian; Jimmy, High Altitude Kenyan. She seemed subdued, maybe blissed out after Pilates, but Jimmy sensed in her a disappointment that had not been there before.

"Shouldn't you be out catching criminals or something?"

"Even superheroes get a morning off once in awhile."

"What's going on?" Jimmy said.

"There's an APB out for Eliza. I'm sorry, Jimmy, but she's our number one suspect."

"Paula left George. She's staying at my place," Jimmy said.

There was a long silence.

She has nothing to say?

He looked at her acting like it was none of her concern. Maybe, it was none of his. He'd come to talk about Paula, but all he could think about was Eliza. He sipped his coffee, then looked at it like it tasted bad. He waved the barista over, ordered a glass of water, downed most of it, said, "I can't believe Eliza would kill Ritchie Kelley." Finished his water. "But then, I can't believe she would shack up with Martin Kelley."

"Someone broke into his cabin. Left big, clunky footprints all over the floor. How did you find the place?"

"I was there once when I was a kid. Some farmer owned it. I forget his name."

"Caleb Pierson. Kelley bought the cabin three years ago. The lawyer who handled the transaction would only confirm that the seller was Pierson's son, Alonzo."

Jimmy went quiet. Alonzo. Lonnie. The cabin. Eliza.

Anna's phoned chirped.

"I have to get to work."

Jimmy opened his mouth, then stopped.

"What?" Anna said.

"This weird guy comes by the house looking for Tooney, calls himself Lonnie."

Jimmy paced back and forth on the front porch of Casa Tooney drinking from a water bottle that was covered in stickers—Alta, Jackson Hole, Valdez Heli-Ski—places in his memory when life seemed pure and simple, when an untracked slope of snow falling away beneath his feet was all that mattered. He wondered where his aunt was. He searched for images of who she had been, and what he saw was Paula taking care of other people—of him, the way his mother never had. Had she ever taken care of herself?

He pushed those thoughts aside.

Lonnie had been by the house a few times now, and Jimmy had begun to feel sorry for him, but had stopped paying attention to his rambling words. The time when Jimmy had said, Tooney was upstairs, resting. Lonnie said, she's sick. What if it wasn't Tooney he was talking about, but Eliza? Jimmy went to the kitchen, took the photo of Lonnie and Eliza walking on Gap Road off the wall, held it up to better light, and Lonnie's expression seemed to change, become intense, covetous, and in that moment Jimmy was certain, despite any actual evidence, that Lonnie had Eliza. But, what about Ritchie Kelley? Did Lonnie kill him? Why would he? Was it all about Eliza?

Lonnie seemed harmless, but there was a look of cunning in the corner of his eyes that would disappear as soon as he noticed Jimmy looking at him, and with his size could be dangerous. Did Tooney have a gun? She must have, everyone from Texas had a gun. Where would she have kept it? He went to the walk-in closet, opened drawers, searched through underwear, stockings, linens until, under folded pillow cases, he found an unopened box of .380 ammunition, went through more drawers, and there it was, a cute pearl and robin's-egg blue pistol.

Everything with his great-aunt was a fashion statement.

He took the gun and ammunition out behind the house, loaded it, took aim at a tree about twenty yards away. The small gun was the first thing of Tooney's that didn't fit him. His hands were too big, but he managed to work his finger into the trigger guard, fired.

Then again. He had trouble extricating his finger. Jimmy figured he could handle Lonnie, but he would take it with him. Just in case.

He came on the Pierson farmhouse from the back. The place looked as deserted as it had the first time—siding falling off in places, window panes filled with tape and cardboard. He stayed in the woods until he came to what had been the farm's Christmas trees, now almost twenty feet high. A hot breeze hissed through the pines. There was something sad about these trees that had never been chosen, never surrounded by a family on Christmas morning, never heard the laughter of children. He moved from tree to tree until he was about twenty yards from the side of the house. The back door of the house opened and Lonnie stepped out carrying a canvas sack. He looked around furtively, then scuttled away. Jimmy waited before following him into the shadowed forest. Lonnie, despite his bulk, moved quickly up the steep grade. The trail leveled off. Jimmy held back, staying out of sight. He knew where Lonnie was headed.

The grey rocks of the giant's workshop were visible through the trees. Jimmy hid behind the trunk of a huge oak. He saw Lonnie stop, look left, right, then slip into the cleft between the two largest boulders. Jimmy waited a few minutes before entering the dark passage. When he stepped into the courtyard he saw Lonnie stuffing cooking pots, utensils, and a small hatchet into his canvas gunny sack. Lonnie, startled by Jimmy's abrupt entrance, fell, hit his head on a rock, cut his hand, got up muttering, then cowered in the corner on a flat rock next to the primitive shelter.

Jimmy felt like he was a kid playing at some make-believe game holding the little blue and pearl gun, but Lonnie seemed to know the thing was real.

"Don't. Please," Lonnie said.

"Where is she?" Jimmy shouted. His words bounced off the rock walls.

"It's not my fault. I didn't—"

Lonnie started to stand. Jimmy waved the gun.

Lonnie dropped back onto the stone bench. Jimmy felt the three strange manikins watching, held the gun in front of Lonnie's face. Lonnie started to whimper and Jimmy felt his resolve weaken. He sat down on a small boulder, pointing the gun away. Lonnie watched blood drip from the cut on his hand onto the sandy floor with a strangely detached expression.

"Tell me," Jimmy said.

"No. Where's Tooney? She's the only one."

"If I take you to her, will you tell her? She can help you."

"I'll come to the house."

"I'll take you to her now."

"No . . . tell Tooney I'll come tonight."

Jimmy left Lonnie in the grotto. Outside, he waited for Lonnie behind the trunk of a huge pine, planning to follow him. Time passed. Still, no Lonnie.

Jimmy returned to the grotto. Lonnie wasn't there. How had he slipped away?

❖

George Baker opened the driver side door, stood, stretched his back and looked at the old farmhouse. It was a shame the way the place had deteriorated. He remembered when Caleb Pierson and the little girl were killed. Folks in the village tried to help. Hell, everyone bought their Christmas tree from Maxine even though most of them could walk out their back door and cut their own. It was the least they could do.

Anna walked around the cruiser, stood next to him. "Could somebody actually live here?"

"Watch where you step," George said.

The patchy grass and weeds were littered with broken farm machinery, an old TV with a shattered screen, miscellaneous hunks of metal, rusting fuel cans. They came to generations of refrigerators: a fairly new one on its side, door hanging open, then one a bit older, then older still, the white enamel almost completely rusted away.

"How can someone leave all this junk lying around?" Anna said.

"Got to put it someplace."

One of the shaped posts on the front porch had been replaced by the trunk of a pine stripped of branches. The roof sagged, the trim fell away in places, the floor was missing several boards.

"I'll check it out," Anna said.

He watched her carefully work her way up the rotted front steps. He wanted to say, no, I'll do it, but then he thought, maybe she'll fall through, break a leg. Better her than me. A porch floorboard broke, her foot went through but she pulled back without losing her balance. She stepped across the resulting gap, went to the one window that wasn't boarded over, peered in.

"Can't see a thing. Too dirty."

She tried the door, put her shoulder into it, but it wouldn't move, jammed shut by the settling of the old house.

"There's nobody here," George said. "Waste of time. What do you think we'll find?"

"Let's try the back. Won't know unless we look."

They skirted around a jumble of old furniture piled against the side of the house, weeds and vines growing all through and over the pile. There was a back door with a small porch and steps, and leading away from the steps a well-worn path angled uphill across the overgrown fields toward the dark wall of the forest.

George tried the door—it opened smoothly—shouted, "Hello?" Then again, louder.

The kitchen floors were swept, the plaster walls intact. A table held a bowl with dried bits of oatmeal, the sink a pot, still warm. The dining room was now a bedroom with a single cot and a small table. What had once been a china cabinet displayed a strange collection of objects: old wristwatches, beaded necklaces, rocks of different colors. On another shelf was a line-up of soda cans, some old, faded, others newer, bright red. There was a child's reading primer patched with mold, several pairs of old eyeglasses, old-fashioned women's shoes, black with clunky heels, children's shoes.

The rest of the first floor was in bad shape, the rooms looked like no one had entered them in years. They went back outside. There was a blocky footprint near the back door.

"Looks like the prints at Kelley's cabin," George said.

"Where do you think this path goes?"

"Anywhere, everywhere."

She knelt, examined a different footprint, said, "Jimmy."

"What?"

"Jimmy. I told you what he said about Lonnie. He's gone after him."

Anna called the house. No answer. George drove, Anna next to him. He had to find his nephew before it was too late, before Jimmy did something even he, as sheriff, couldn't clean up. They skidded to a stop next to the silver rental car. Jimmy was sitting in a rocking chair on the porch holding a little blue and silver gun.

"Mind if I take that?" Anna said.

Jimmy passed it to her, handle first. She sniffed the barrel, said, "It's been fired." She wrapped it in a handkerchief, put it in her pocket, said, "Where's Lonnie?"

Jimmy's shoes were covered in dirt, there were dark stains on his shirt, a distant far-away expression on his face.

"What have you done?" George said, turned to Anna. "Take him inside, get him to put on clean clothes. Bag what he's wearing."

Anna led Paul Arnold in from the north, two other deputies approached from the south, each team with a copy of the map Jimmy had drawn showing the location of Lonnie's boulders. Jimmy had offered to guide them, but George had ordered him to stay in the house.

There was no sign of Lonnie, just the cold remains of a fire in a makeshift stone fireplace. Anna kept glancing back at the three mannikins as she took samples of blood -stained sand from the floor. She felt as if their makeshift eyes of red stones bore into her, as if they knew her thoughts.

Fish and Game was called in. Search parties combed the nearby woods. No trace of Lonnie.

Dick Gaetz put Jimmy in the back seat of a cruiser, brought him to the station. Captain Wagner from State Police was there to handle the questioning. Anna watched from the side. Jimmy declined a lawyer. Wagner came at him hard. Jimmy was flat, distant, gave the same answers over and over. Lonnie fell when he'd surprised him, hit his head, cut his hand on a sharp rock, bled all over the place. They talked and Jimmy left him there and went back to the house.

"Where'd you get the gun?" Wagner held up the pistol between his thumb and forefinger delicately, as if it might break. "Sigg 238. Good choice. But, me? I would've gone with the pink."

"I found it in her closet."

"Let me get this straight. You find the gun, load it, go out back, make sure it works, then go looking for the man you believe kidnapped Eliza Johnson."

"That's about it."

Wagner read from Jimmy's written statement. "I found the bullets in a drawer, filled the magazine. That's what you wrote. Filled. Went out back, fired it at a tree. How many times did you shoot during your little target session?"

"I don't remember. Two, maybe three?"

"The magazine holds eight shells." Wagner held up a cartridge. "Nasty things, three-eighties." He removed the magazine from an evidence bag, laid it on the table. "Can you explain why there's only three bullets in the magazine? Where'd the other two or three go?"

"What?"

"Did you fire the gun in that place. What'd you call it? Not a cave—"

"A grotto."

"Right. Grotto. Good word, that. So, did you?"

"Did I what?"

"Don't play stupid with me. Did you fire the gun in the grotto?"

"No."

"So, if we were to find a casing. a three-eighty perhaps, or a chip in one of those rocks that looks like it was made by a bullet, that wouldn't have been you?"

Jimmy started to squirm, and for the first time Anna started to doubt his version of events. What had really happened? What had he done?

They waited, but Jimmy stayed silent.

Wagner walked around the interview table, pulled out a chair, sat down next to Jimmy, and put his arm around Jimmy's shoulders. Jimmy tried to pull away. Wagner, now the consoling friend, softened his voice. "Look, I wouldn't blame you. If it was my daughter. I have two you know. They mean the world to me. If this jerk had one of my girls—"

"What was I supposed to do?"

"You left the man you think kidnapped your daughter in peace, and went back to that house of yours. Why didn't you call the sheriff?"

"I was going to, but they showed up before I got the chance."

There was a gap of an hour, Wagner pointed out. What had he been doing? —Sitting, thinking. —Not off burying a body in the woods? —No.

"Helluva a lot of blood for a cut hand. Want to bet the stains on your shirt match?"

"If I shot him, I'd never find Eliza."

"I think you're trying to distract us." Wagner waved a few sheets of paper. "Crime scene report. Want to know what we found? Shoe prints that match Eliza Johnson's near Ritchie Kelley's body. She was there. What makes you think you know her? You didn't even know she existed until a week ago."

He handed a printed sheet to Jimmy, who barely looked at it before tossing it on the table.

"I'll tell you what it says. Footprints all over the fucking place. Some of the first responders got a little too close"—he glared at George Baker—"but here, off to the side, we've identified four clear sets of prints—yours, Ritchie's, Eliza's, Lonnie's—layered over each other. You know what that tells us? Who was there, when. Ritchie's are on the bottom, Eliza's next. She was there, Jimmy, after Ritchie. She came up behind him, killed him."

"No!"

"Here's where it gets interesting. These other prints, Lonnie's, were off to the side in the woods."

Jimmy didn't seem to be listening.

"You with me? I think you found out Lonnie was there, maybe something he said, and were afraid he was a witness to your little girl killing Kelley, so later you tracked him to his hideaway and killed him."

"This is bullshit. Eliza and Ritchie wore the same shoes, the same size. How the hell do you know which is which?"

"We've got motive, Ritchie was going to blow the whistle on her plan to run away, and we know she was at the scene."

"You think she was there. You don't know shit."

"Where is she, Jimmy?"

"If I knew, I wouldn't tell you. You have to let me go."

"Oh yeah? Got a hot date? Someone else to terrorize with your little gun, which I'm keeping by the way. We'll let you go for now, but you're not to leave the area. Understand? Go back to that house of yours and stay there, and don't cause any more trouble."

Paul Arnold left to drive Jimmy home. Anna watched as George and Wagner talked quietly off to the side of the office, but couldn't hear what they said.

George came back to her, said, "Take a seat."

Anna opened her mouth to speak. He held up his hand.

"This is a goddamn mess. I warned you about Jimmy. You heard what Wagner thinks. He's ready to arrest Jimmy for killing Lonnie. Only thing missing is a body. He's bringing in dogs and CSS."

Anna prepared to stand.

"Another thing. You didn't actually think you could keep this business between you and my wife secret?"

"There's nothing between us."

"Give me a break. I'm not blind. The night she wrecked the car? Tell me she wasn't coming from your place. And now she's moved out."

"I—"

"Spare me. You think you know her, that she cares for you?"

How could she explain that, yes, Paula had come to her place, but no, nothing was going on when she wished, more than anything, that something was?

"Paula's always had a thing for the girls. Did she tell you about the little fling she had in high school? Led some poor kid on, then dumped her. Broke her heart. And 4-H? All those cute young things?"

"You want my resignation?"

"Who said anything about you resigning? Just do your job. You girls have your fun. Paula will come to her senses like she did before."

Anna crossed the station parking lot under a sun without mercy, George's words became somehow dark, threatening. What was that about high school? And, what was he trying to imply? Paula and young girls? She didn't believe it. Anna wondered if she should have tried to explain, but then thought, no. George needed her now, but she had no doubt that once this investigation was cleared up, she was screwed.

She felt so confused. Everything had been so intense, hectic that she'd not had time to think. Paula has left George. Is she okay? Anna, in that moment, wanted to talk to her, to find out what was going on. Should she call her? Should she text? She didn't know what to do.

She walked toward downtown Newport. Friday in August. Main Street was backed up with traffic heading for the lake. Tourists—hot, sunburned, and frazzled—filled the sidewalks in search of food or a place to sit down and escape the heat. A man and his wife argued about where to eat while their two kids watched. There was a line out the front door of Beantown, the only decent coffee in Newport, more hot, impatient vacationers. Are they having fun? Certainly didn't look like it.

She headed back to the station barely aware of her surroundings. Something about Wagner's reading of the crime scene didn't make sense. How would Jimmy come to the conclusion that Lonnie witnessed Ritchie's murder? And why would Jimmy kill him if he believed Lonnie was holding Eliza? What if you turn things around? Lonnie is the killer and Eliza the witness? Didn't that make more sense?

And, what if Jimmy is right and there's no way to tell which prints are Ritchie's? Which are Eliza's? The question remains, where the hell is Eliza?

George stopped her on her way into the station, stood in front of her.

Now what? Anna thought.

"You still on the clock?"

"No."

"Clock back in, relieve Gaetz on 12A. He's down where Townhouse comes in. Nasty two-car. EMTs aren't done."

Anna saw two ambulances speeding north, sirens wailing, lights flashing, as she drove south. Her radio crackled with updates. Four teenagers, three in serious condition were on their way to DHMC in Lebanon, one might need to be helicoptered to Boston.

Damn, she thought, kids.

Hemlock Flat volunteer firemen had blocked the road off, flares everywhere. Debris littered the pavement. A flatbed wrecker from Jones Body Shop in Claremont drove off with a Honda Civic that had a crushed front end, and a second wrecker was loading a small Ford SUV with a stove-in side and a flattened roof.

Anna exited her vehicle, saw Bob Wilson sweeping broken glass and shards of red plastic with a big push broom.

"Where's Gaetz? He was supposed to be here."

"Never showed up."

Anna looked at the glass scattered over the entire width of the roadway. "Bad?" she said.

Wilson shook his head slowly. "The worst."

"Local kids?"

"Claremont. The two in the Honda, a boy and a girl, came down Townhouse, must have been doing sixty, didn't even slow down, T-boned the Ford, rolled it down the bank."

"They going to make it?"

Bob Wilson shrugged.

Anna knew you shouldn't see connections where none existed, but somehow this tragedy seemed to her of a piece with everything else that was going so wrong. She felt lost in the harsh orange light of the flares, the pulsing blue of her light bar. An aura flickered on the edges of her vision. She heard the wrecker start up, felt the rumble of its diesel engine in her chest.

"Got another broom?" she said. "I'll give you a hand."

Many times in the past George Baker had come home from work to an empty house—Paula at one of her exercise classes or visiting friends—and even though nothing on the surface had changed, there was something different about this emptiness. Was it that he knew she had taken a suitcase, that she wasn't coming back this night, maybe ever?

Women. Paula and Korsak. Christ, here we go again.

George was not the sort of man who spent a lot of time looking back, re-hashing things. It seemed to him that memory was like muscle—had to be exercised to work well—and it had never seemed worth the effort, but he remembered the O'Neal girl.

He and Paula had been part of the gang of Hemlock Flat kids who rode the bus to Lebanon High School: Paul Arnold and Bea Marsden and Bobbie Trax and he couldn't remember who else. He and Paula used to sit together on the school bus, and he'd thought Paula was his girl. Then her family moved to Lebanon and she started hanging out with Abby O'Neal and didn't have time for him. As soon as school started, it was obvious the two were an item. He was so embarrassed. Losing his girl to a girl! The shit he took from the guys on the football team was the worst. But, one Monday in November he found Paula out back of the school crying, out and out miserable—she never did say what had happened—and then she moved back to Hemlock Flat to live with the Marsdens, and they started spending time together again, and one thing led to another, and he got her back.

They'd had a good life, great kids, a wonderful home. She came back to him then, she would again, but he didn't need this now. He had a murdered kid and the most likely killer nowhere to be found, and Jimmy running around with a gun. He needed Korsak to keep this investigation moving—if they didn't make some progress soon the state would take over and he'd never live down the failure—but after this was over, the woman was looking at late-night highway duty for the rest of her life.

He went to the refrigerator. There was beer, some cold cuts, vegetables. What the hell was he supposed to do with vegetables? He checked the freezer. There was a frozen pizza that had been there a long time. Must be good. How the hell do you cook the thing? It was when he realized he didn't even know how to turn on the oven in the fancy restaurant style range he'd bought for Paula that he really knew she was gone.

❖

Summer night comes on slowly in the north, twilight lingers. Jimmy Baker, wearing a gauzy, floral print dress with a scarf covering his hair, sat in Tooney's rocking chair on the porch, and watched the sky turn from pale-white to pink to orange to a deep, troubling red and then go flat-grey.

Waiting for Lonnie.

What do we bequeath our children? What had his father given him when, as far as Jimmy could remember, the man had been barely if at all aware of his son's existence. But if he was honest with himself, how much effort had he put into knowing his father?

Jimmy had risen to the top of the extreme ski world not because he was technically better, but because he was flat-out crazier, took greater risks. Had he been trying to prove himself to be more of a man than his father? To be what he thought a man was supposed to be?

What had Eliza inherited from him, the father that, as far as anyone knew, she had been unaware of? What of her wild, rebellious spirit came from him? Evenings like this, when a hot wind moved through the canopy of oaks and the leaves trembled and quivered like insecure souls there was, he felt, something moving in the world that could answer those questions if only he could slow its passage. The breeze ruffled the dress around his knees and he felt in that moment as if he was no longer James Spenser Baker, but some unknown creature and at the same time he felt at home, almost at peace.

Still, Lonnie did not come.

He dozed. A voice woke him.

"Help me, Tooney. Why did that man come to my place?"

Jimmy peered into the dark, but couldn't see Lonnie.

"He was mean. You have to help me."

"Of course, Lonnie." Jimmy tried to pitch his voice higher, softer. "What's the matter?"

"She's sick."

"Who is, Lonnie?"

"I don't want her to be sick."

Lonnie said, "her," and Jimmy was certain that could only mean Eliza.

"Where is she?" Jimmy tried to sound casual, just a nice, harmless old woman trying to help, but his heart was pounding. He pulled back into the shadows. He had to make Lonnie think he was Tooney.

"Take me to her, Lonnie," Jimmy said. How, he wondered, do you make your voice sound kind? "I can help you."

"Come," Lonnie said.

"Let me change, get ready."

"No, now."

Jimmy, in Tooney's sandals, struggled to keep up as Lonnie, , quickly weaved his way through the trees occasionally glancing back over his shoulder. The summit ridge of the mountains above them glimmered with the light of a moon still well below the eastern horizon, and the faint grey light was barely enough to see the way. The bulk of the giant's workshop reared up in front of them. Lonnie slipped into the opening. Jimmy followed. They crossed the open space of the grotto. The strange figures turned to watch them pass. Jimmy heard the screech of metal on metal. His dress pulled at his legs as he followed Lonnie through an opening in the fence into Corbin Park.

Chapter Seventeen

THE DAY CAME ON bleak and grey, the border between dark and light, night and day, barely noticed, as Jimmy followed Lonnie up slabs of rock dotted with boulders scattered like the remnants of some giant's game of marbles. Precipitous planes of stone fell away to his right, tilting at dizzying angles. The climb up through the forest had been brutal: the sandals had cut into his skin and were slippery with blood. He was desperate to stop, tend to his feet, but there was no time, soon it would be light, and Lonnie would see he had been tricked.

Above him, dark clouds built into threatening towers and the air was dense and humid. He could feel the tension building, a storm coming.

Lonnie led Jimmy across the summit of Croydon Peak. The Sugar River Valley far below was shrouded in stagnant fog. All was bare stone, shattered granite laced with cracks, some only inches wide, others a foot, or more. Jimmy heard a faint rumble of thunder, and a sound like the grinding and groaning of rock as if the mountain moved. They came to a wide fissure that was shallow at first, but deepened into a ravine that angled down out of sight.

There were dark stains on the opening's edge.

He followed Lonnie into the fissure. A trail wove its way down the floor of gravel and sand into a deepening ravine of grey and pink granite studded with crystals. They were inside the mountain itself. Walls of stone rose above them to a stripe of a darkening sky. Heat radiated off the rocks.

Lonnie turned a corner and disappeared from sight. The ravine opened up. Rocks arranged as crude steps led down into an amphitheater perhaps twenty feet across with a level floor of cracked granite, rubble, and sand, enclosed by walls of stone some fifteen feet high. Another secret place, open to the sky, where Jimmy could see storm clouds gathering.

Where was Lonnie? He'd made a shelter here, more elaborate than the grotto. There was crude, hand-built furniture, a table, stools, a rack held bits of dried meat, shelves rusted cans of food. Next to a fire pit were two blackened, battered pots.

Under a jutting overhang of rock a slim figure in yellow lay on a bed made of twisting, interlocked branches.

Eliza.

There was a dirty bandage around her leg, her hair was crusted with blood, and a pool of blood had dried on the gravel beneath her. Flies buzzed. She didn't move.

Was she dead?

Jimmy knelt in front of her, heard her breathing, shallow, but steady. She opened her eyes, struggled to speak, mumbled something that might have been, "where is he," might have been, "help."

"Hush, lie still," Jimmy said.

He looked around, no sign of Lonnie.

He found an empty burlap sack, folded it into a makeshift pillow, placed it under her head.

"Water." Her lips were cracked, flecked with dry crust. Again, "Water." Her voice barely a whisper.

Lonnie had cobbled together a shelf from random pieces of wood and filled it with supplies, canned goods, a sack of rice.

There was a plastic jug of water next to the shelf. Jimmy filled a tin cup, cradled her head in one hand, and held the cup to her lips. Water dribbled out of the corner of her mouth as she drank. She closed her eyes.

Still no Lonnie.

Jimmy did not have his cell phone. How could he have been so stupid? He'd found her, but now what? He would have to go for help, but did he have the strength? His right leg was cramping, His feet were torn and blistered. Yes, he could, he would, but he didn't want to leave her here. Lonnie might return at any moment.

In the early morning quiet of the station, Anna stared at the wall displaying everything they'd accumulated in the days since Eliza Johnson was first reported missing: interviews with her family, her friends, search maps, crime scene reports, each patiently followed up. It was all there and none of it, not one thing, answered the questions that circled: Where was Eliza? What was she? A victim? A murderer? A runaway? A fugitive?

Anna returned to her desk, opened the file for Ritchie Kelley. They still didn't know what he was doing on that trail. He'd not said a word to anyone to indicate he knew about his father's thing with Eliza, but the working assumption was that either he'd found out and went looking for her, or that he learned of her plans to run away and had tried to change her mind, to stop her.

She pawed through papers, found the crime scene report. George had told her about Wagner's complaint of murder scene contamination, and as she looked at the footprint analysis, she realized Wagner had been kind with his comments. It was a mess. Deputy's boot prints everywhere. Had they really been that sloppy?

She spread out the detailed CSS report, and looked at the footprint diagram. And, of course there was Jimmy. How was it, she wondered, that whenever the shit hit the proverbial fan, Jimmy was somehow involved? She'd taken an archeology class in college, had briefly thought she might pursue it as a career, and this was like an archaeological dig: going back in time by working down through the layers. Had anyone looked closely at this? Why hadn't she? Some of the duty boot prints appeared to be on the bottom, underneath Ritchie's and Eliza's. How was that possible? She took a marker, circled the area, made a quick note, then heard the National Weather Service's Emergency Alert blaring in the outer squad room. She rushed to Dispatch.

"What's going on?"

"Severe thunderstorm alert," Connie said. "A cell is heading this way from Vermont. Possible micro-burst. Multiple lightning ground strikes, heavy rain, high winds, hail. The sheriff's on his way, wants us out on the road. McCarthy needs you in Lebanon."

At her desk, she pushed the murder scene diagram aside—she'd deal with this later—took a moment to open the file from the grotto. The report from CSS was incomplete. Where were the DNA results?

She grabbed a red marker, wrote a quick note, left it and the report on George's desk, and exited the station to drive to Lebanon.

As Paula drove up the road toward Jimmy's house, she told herself it would only be for a couple of days, until she figured things out. One day and already she realized that the impulsive act of leaving was the easy part, learning how to live on her own would be the hard part. She had sat in a rental agent's office looking at the lease application for a studio apartment in White River Junction, and it had been all she could do to not cry. She didn't have her own bank account, her own money, her own income, any rental history. She had nothing to put in those blank spaces on that form, and that realization had made her furious, but she didn't know who to be angry at. George? The world? Herself? How could she have reached this point in life? It was as if she wasn't a real person. She'd done so much—created a home, raised three children, volunteered—yet none of it mattered, none of it counted in this world of forms and credit scores and references.

The rental agent, Ms. Loretta Wilkins, a professional woman about Paula's age wearing a navy blue skirt and a white blouse with a lighter blue scarf around her neck, had sat across the desk from her with an expression on her face that Paula couldn't read. Did she understand? Or, was it pity?

Paula slid the form back to her, said, "I've changed my mind."

"Come back," Ms. Wilkins said, "if you change your mind again."

She'd spent the night at the Comfort Inn—at least she had a credit card—and now here she was going back to Jimmy's, defeated. She parked next to his car and dragged her suitcase up the gravel walk. The house was empty. She carried her things upstairs, put them in one of the guest rooms, and ripped off her sweat sodden clothes. Naked, she walked down the hall to Jimmy's room, barely noticing that it had become his room in her mind, but when she looked at the clothes, all carefully hung in the closet, she felt her eyes fill, and a single tear on her cheek. It had seemed to her that Tooney had known how to live life, how to pick herself up after the death of her husband and create the life that she wanted, but Paula wondered now, was this really the life Tooney had wanted? What did this big house, all these beautiful clothes matter when Tooney had been alone? And in that moment something about all this finery seemed achingly sad to Paula.

Again, that deep sound, as though the house shifted under her.

Paula chose a dress without really looking at it. She went back down the staircase, almost tripping on the hem, and paused to look in the mirror. Looking back was a little girl in a much-too-big dress, and Paula remembered raiding her mother's closet when she was little, and how her mother had laughed and they had been happy together, but then came the memory of her mother choosing her church over her daughter, and the pain of thirty years of not a word, and the tears came, and she felt completely alone, and felt that there was no one in the world she could confide in, could talk to.

She thought of Jimmy on these stairs in a blue dress, it seemed a lifetime ago, and wondered if it was seeing Jimmy as a new and different person that had started her falling out of her life?

She walked out to the porch, saw Jimmy's running shoes there by the rocking chair, and wondered where he could have gone without his shoes.

We've fallen, each of us, Paula thought, and somehow landed in this house, and she felt at that moment the house hold and comfort her, and thought that Jimmy would understand.

The humidity grew, the mountains moved closer, and she saw dark clouds form and tumble over their summits. She walked down off the porch and out into the front yard, the too-big pale-blue dress trailing in the grass, and watched clouds stream in from the west and collide with the clouds that had formed above the mountains. The air turned violent.

Lightning split the sky and struck the heights somewhere with a sizzling crack, and a powerful rumble of thunder rolled down the mountain and squeezed her heart in her chest and shook the windows of the house. The first drops of rain, big and fat, hit her face like slaps, and she stood there and waited for the rain to wash away the old Paula Baker, and wondered who would be left after it did.

Jimmy watched black clouds bruise the sky. The light dimmed. Thunder boomed in the distance, then closer, rolling and echoing off the mountains, hammering his chest. A bolt of lightning struck the summit above him. Another bolt, closer, and then it was all around. The air crackled. The current rose up through his feet. The hair on the back of his neck stood.

They had to get away from the rock walls, from the electricity.

He lifted Eliza to her feet and carried her into the open. The rain fell in sheets. A sudden torrent poured out of the ravine he'd descended, flowed around his ankles. He braced himself and held her in his arms and looked up into a malevolent sky and waited for the storm to take them. The scarf was torn from his head by the wind. He watched it lift and fly away, fluttering and tumbling.

Thunder shook the ground. Lightning laced the sky.

Lonnie materialized next to him. "You're not Tooney!"

Lonnie slammed into Jimmy before he could react. Jimmy lost hold of Eliza, his leg caught in a crevice, twisted. Searing pain. He fell. His head slammed against a boulder and white light exploded behind his eyes and then everything went black.

Anna had to pull over. She couldn't see. The rain was so heavy the wipers couldn't keep up. Water streaked the windows. Lightning flashed. It was like being inside a strobe light. Rain pounded the roof of the cruiser. Her radio crackled. Nine-one-one calls were coming in to headquarters from across the county. A motorist was stranded in the middle of Stage Road where the Meriden Brook had overflowed its banks. Trees were down all over the area. Live power lines lay across Townhouse Road near the Hemlock Flat Town Office.

She turned her wipers on high, lit the light bar, u-turned, and groped her way toward Hemlock Flat. Wind pushed the car around like a child's toy. Branches and leaves littered the road. She came to where a tree, suspended by a tangle of telephone wires and power lines, leaned out over the highway. She parked the cruiser, climbed out, and was instantly soaked to the skin. She lit flares up and down the road, called it in, and returned to the safety of her SUV.

The deafening racket made it impossible to think. Branches and leaves flew through the air, a large tree limb crashed across the hood of her car. She could do nothing but wait and hope that everyone was safe. She strained to hear the radio as deputies called the station.

She felt a shift in the air, the wind lessened, the rain slowed, and almost as quickly as it had come, the storm cell moved on. The sky brightened and an eerie calm settled around her car. She cautiously opened the door and stepped out, unable to trust her senses, to believe that the storm could have passed so quickly. All around her downed trees, broken, ragged branches littered the ground. Power lines sparked on the wet pavement. Above her, clouds, like tattered and torn cloth, flew away to the east.

A single bird called nearby.

George Baker paced the office. The storm had been violent, fast moving, localized to Sullivan County and parts of Cheshire County. Lorraine was on Dispatch, backed up by Deputies Marks and Williams at their desks taking calls ranging from important: Route 120 was blocked by downed trees, a family of four was stranded in their car in the middle of Route 12A after trying to drive through what had looked like shallow water, to not so important: lost power, broken windows, missing cats, lost dogs.

He was energized by the constantly ringing telephones, the chattering radios, and felt himself at the center of things. He coordinated the efforts of fire departments and utility crews throughout the county, sent deputies where they were needed to handle traffic or get people whose homes were damaged to nearby shelters.

Almost forgotten was the note on his desk from Anna Korsak.

As afternoon wore on, it became apparent that the situation was somewhat under control, and he sent the early shift of deputies home to rest. He went to his desk to close things up before going home, saw Anna's note—CALL THE STATE—with the CSS report attached, the blank space where DNA results from the grotto should be circled in red. He checked his watch. Not yet five. Grabbed the desk phone.

No one picked up at the state lab, so he left an urgent message.

He passed by her desk on his way out, saw papers covering the desktop. She had the diagram of the Kelley murder scene spread out next to Wagner's analysis, had made notes on the diagram, circled a section with a red marker. Written, 'WHO?' in the same glaring red.

What was she up to?

He folded the papers and slotted them into his briefcase—something to do during the empty evening ahead of him—and left the station.

Anna had stayed by the downed power lines until relieved by Bobby Jenkins and was off duty until the next morning. She peeled off her wet uniform and left it in a soggy pile on the bathroom floor, and walked naked into her bedroom. A cool breeze whispered through the open window. She pulled on jeans, a t-shirt. Went back to the bathroom to dry her hair.

She was accustomed to living alone in this place, used to the meager furnishings, the bare, un-lived-in feel, but wondered now why she hadn't done more to create a home here. Was this her way of protecting herself? So she could, if things didn't work out, tell herself she never meant to stay in the first place?

Was Paula staying at Jimmy's? An intense desire to see her hit Anna, and grew until it was not merely a desire, but a need without which she felt she could not go on. She had to explain. She had to know why Paula had turned away.

Driving she became filled with doubt. Would Paula tell her to go home? Was she mistaken thinking that Paula felt for her as she did for Paula? The roads were littered with debris from the storm; roadside piles of tangled tree limbs reached out as if to block her passage.

The big house was a dark monolith against the pale sky of what had become a gorgeous evening. The storm had blown away the humidity, the air was cooling fast, and a gentle breeze stirred the oaks and maples surrounding the house, and in that moment Anna felt that the storm had blown away something in her as well, and felt as if she was coming alive, waking from the long torpor of the unrelenting heat.

Anna stepped up onto the porch, saw Paula sitting in a rocking chair. She wasn't sure, didn't know what to do, how to be. Paula reached out to her. Anna took her hand. They moved to the love seat at the other end of the porch and sat side-by-side.

"Is Jimmy home?"

"No, he's off somewhere."

"In the storm?"

"Of course. That boy has always looked for trouble wherever he can find it. I remember one time, we were having lunch in the garden with his parents. Jimmy, no more than six, had climbed up into the apple tree in the garden, spying on the grown-ups, got too far out on a branch, the thing broke and he came crashing down, landed flat on his back and lay there gasping like a fish pulled out of water. Knocked the breath right out of him."

Paula was tense. Anna sensed it in the way she sat, and if talking about anything other than the two of them, together, hips touching, helped her relax, Anna was happy to listen, to sit in the wavering light of a candle, to feel the warmth of the body next to her. Anna placed her hand on Paula's leg. Paula responded. They held hands.

"Do you think he's alright?" Anna said.

"I wouldn't worry about him."

"The other night …" Anna hesitated. "I'm sorry— I …"

Paula put her finger to Anna's lips.

The storm passed so quickly that when Jimmy came to and opened his eyes it was as if it had not happened at all. He lay on his back on jagged rocks and looked up as a breeze healed the sky. He watched clouds tear apart and drift away, and saw the failing of the light as night crept up behind him from the east. An airplane, lit by the last up-slanted rays of the sun, made a bright arrow across the sky. He wondered where it was going, then the pain in his head overwhelmed him, and he drifted again into darkness.

He woke on the makeshift bed with Eliza leaning against his shoulder.

The pain in his leg ebbed and throbbed, and a white-hot band encircled his head, squeezing thought out of him. He felt Eliza stir.

"Ritchie …" Eliza said weakly. "What happened to him? Is he … ?"

How had they come to be here, side-by-side?

Eliza was wan, feverish. She slipped in and out of consciousness. The ugly red gash on her head was crusted with black, dried blood.

"I thought I was dead and you were Tooney, and I felt okay knowing that I wasn't alone."

The night had turned cold. Above them, stars pierced the dome of the bright-black sky and seemed so close it was as if they were marooned on a barren planet somewhere in space.

A single candle held back the darkness. Anna leaned close, her scent was the air Paula breathed. Anna kissed her gently on one cheek, then the other, held her face in both hands. Anna smiled.

Her eyes, Paula thought, her grey eyes are flecked with green. How have I not noticed? She wasn't sure what to do. How do you tell someone that you're no longer afraid, tell that someone that you love her?

"It's okay," Anna said.

She reached across the candlelight to touch Paula's cheek. Kissed her again. A moment's pause, a tiny holding back, then Paula returned the kiss, and felt herself falling, but knew, this time, where she would land. Anna stood and reached down to her and took her hand and together they walked into the shadow-filled house as a breeze stirred the trees and the stars moved in the sky and somewhere along the tree-line a hoot owl called, and from deep in the forest another answered.

Chapter Eighteen

THE HORIZON WAS PINK tinged with green, and light overtook the heavens. The mountain night had been cold, and Jimmy, in his half-awake moments, had tried to shield Eliza from the bitter chill. The first yellow sunlight touched the rim of the rock walls surrounding them. His mind went with the small clouds that drifted across the pale-blue sky.

Eliza leaned her head against his shoulder; he put his arm around her, felt her body against his. His mind wandered back through the years. What had she been doing when he had been so busy playing the hero? He had missed so much.

Eliza perked up, became aware of him in the tattered print dress. She giggled.

"Tooney used to talk about my mother. What was she like, my mother?"

"I loved her."

Eliza was quiet, and Jimmy thought she had fallen asleep.

"You mean . . . you and she?"

"Yes."

"Really? . . . Are you? . . . Tooney showed me the pictures in her scrapbooks and we look so much alike that I thought that's my real father and I waited for you to come and get me"—she started coughing, couldn't stop, but summoned the strength to continue—"Without her, and my fantasy of you, I would have run away sooner. Did Tooney know? Why didn't she tell me? Why didn't you come back for me?"

He struggled to speak, finally said, "I didn't know. I'm here, now."

"A little late, don't you think."

Again, he wondered how had they come to be sitting like this?

"Where is he?" she said. "He's looking for me. Don't let him find me." She closed her eyes, slumped against him.

"Rest. He's gone."

Soon, he told himself, he will get up, take her hand, help her to her feet, and lead her down the mountain.

Morning came too soon. Anna's presence, the heat of her body, the musky, mysterious smell of her sex had kept Paula awake most of the night. She had finally drifted off to sleep, and woke from a dream of a beach with Anna, in some peaceful, faraway paradise where no one could find them. She lay on her back, looking up at the white lace canopy as the first light of morning lingered at the open windows and cool air drifted into the room. She reached over, put her hand on Anna's hip, turned to look at her. Anna was on her side, arms curled in front of her bare breasts, hair half covering her face. She moaned softly, little bits of white crud flecked the corners of her mouth. The little bow to her lips. She seemed to be smiling even in her sleep.

A brash jangling shattered the morning quiet.

Anna stirred, said, "What was that?" Her voice was husky, filled with sleep.

"The phone, downstairs."

"Crap. It could be for me. I had to give the station the number. Everyone's on call."

The phone continued to ring.

"Does the phone have voicemail?"

"No."

Anna groaned, rose, and walked across the room, naked like she had been in Paula's dream. She picked up a random t-shirt of Jimmy's from the floor. Paula pulled on the dress from yesterday and followed her downstairs.

"I'll make coffee," Paula said.

Anna slouched against the kitchen wall staring at the phone as it continued to ring. She looked half asleep, her hair was tangled and twisted. She pushed it away from her face, lifted the old-fashioned handset reluctantly.

"Yes?" Anna said, listened … then said, "What?"

Paula could hear a man's voice. It was George. She felt exposed, and wanted to run from the kitchen.

Anna twisted a strand of her hair, released it, squared her shoulders, said, louder, "You're sure?" Hung up the phone. She looked stunned.

"Holy shit."

"What is it?"

"DNA came back from the lab. The blood at the grotto, some of it was Eliza's."

On the porch, in shorts and Jimmy's t-shirt, Anna looked at her feet in gold-braided sandals, noticed Jimmy's running shoes by the rocking chair, turned to Paula.

"Where's Jimmy? Why would he go off with no shoes?"

George put his cell phone down on the kitchen table, looked at his open laptop with the DNA test results that had been sent overnight. Why hadn't we received these sooner? He had told Anna to wait for back-up, said he would get Arnold and Jensen to meet her, but if he knew anything about her, it was that she wouldn't wait, she'd go charging off.

Was Paula nearby, listening? Could she hear his voice in the telephone? He looked around the kitchen and saw signs of her everywhere. A wave of fatigue came over him. How was he supposed to do his job when his wife was shacked up with his deputy and that deputy was a goddamn woman? Maybe he should let Anna play the hero, maybe something would happen, he'd be rid of her. Who was he kidding? In his more honest with himself moments he knew Paula was gone, Anna or no Anna, and in many ways had been gone for a long time. After Tracy left for college, the house had been so quiet. Why had he thought that Paula would be content alone in an empty house?

His job, the oath he'd taken to serve and protect, that was what was important. Whatever happened with him and Paula, at least he would have his pride, at least he would do his goddamn job.

The kitchen table was covered with the diagrams and papers that he had taken from Anna's desk. He had started to take a look last night, but after a beer and a few sips of whiskey hadn't been able to concentrate, and had ended up watching another meaningless baseball game. He couldn't even remember who was playing. He picked up his coffee mug. It left a brown ring on the tabletop. He replaced it without drinking, pulled the murder scene map closer, stared at the area Anna had circled in red.

Why didn't I see this before? It was obvious when you looked closely. A deputy's boot prints underneath Ritchie Kelley's, underneath Eliza's. An image came to him of Dick Gaetz, first on the scene at the Kelley murder site, walking around the body, much too close, compromising the evidence.

Maybe it wasn't sloppy. Maybe it was deliberate. What the hell is going on?

He thought about the strange way Gaetz had been acting lately, the way he denied his connection to the Johnsons when Bill

Johnson said they were close.

He called the station. Connie answered. What would he do without Connie Armstrong? Did she ever go home?

"Who's on duty?"

"Gaetz is supposed to be here, but I haven't seen him. Arnold and Jenkins are in."

"Tell them to wait for me. I'll be there as soon as I can, and call State Police Headquarters, have them start emergency real-time tracking on Korsak's and Gaetz's cells."

The tormented manikins seemed to follow her every move as Anna searched the grotto, for what, she wasn't sure. Clots of sand tainted with dried blood were scattered on the floor—Lonnie's, and they now knew, Eliza's. Anna squeezed into a crevice between two of the larger boulders, found some pieces of burlap and a battered tin cup. The space was so tight she scraped her forehead on the rough stone when she turned around, felt a trickle of blood on her cheek. Looking up, she saw only a tiny sliver of sky and felt a wave of claustrophobia. She inched her way sideways and finally emerged into the central area, panting like she'd finished a long run.

She sat on a square block of stone. Calmed herself.

A shaft of early sun slanted in through the boulders; bits of quartz on the floor glittered silver. A yellow spark caught her eye. She went down on her knees. It was a tiny golden ski. Eliza's.

There were two more openings to search. The first was shallow, dead-ending in a blank granite face. The next was narrow, threatening. She hesitated, then forced herself to enter and was surprised to find it quickly opened up into a larger space, backed by a section of the park fence in the middle of which Lonnie had cut a panel out of the chain-link and hinged it with twisted wire to make a door into Corbin Park. A tattered bit of floral-print fabric hung from the jagged edge of the opening.

She returned to the grotto. She knew she should wait for backup, but saw the three manikins staring at her, their bones draped with rotting flesh, the skull with its protruding red eyes, and was hit by an overwhelming sense of urgency, and the feeling that every second mattered.

She ducked through the opening in the fence and followed a faint trail steeply uphill through a grasping forest, pushing herself hard, almost running at times. She came on a scrap of the same fabric tangled in the branches of a bush. Further on, another.

Was Jimmy following Lonnie? Where were they going?

The forest finally thinned and she came to bare slabs of rock studded with jumbled boulders.

She stopped, gasping for breath, and looked past angled planes of rock toward the mountain summit under a limitless sky. Everything was too big for her to grasp. There were no edges, nothing to anchor herself to. The world seemed to drop away in all directions. She felt dizzy. She didn't belong here. She was exhausted, didn't know which way to go. She'd lost the way.

A spasm gripped her side, she bent over, hands on her knees, and saw spots of blood on the granite slab. She followed them up the polished granite, came on another bit of fabric tangled in the branches of a gnarled juniper bush.

She felt a growing sense of panic. She didn't know why, but knew there was no time.

She pushed herself up the rock slabs, lungs burning, legs throbbing. The angle finally eased as she neared the summit.

"You will let us in, one way or the other," George held the phone to his ear while he drove. "With you and the rest of the park staff in handcuffs and on your way to county lock-up, or you can open the damn gate and help us find them."

"I need to make a call."

"Make it quick."

George skidded to a stop at the gate to Corbin Park, Arnold and Jenkins in a car behind him. He waited, called up the state tracking system on the cruiser's laptop. Anna was high on the upper western slope of the mountains. Where was she going? No sign of Gaetz.

It was only about five minutes, but it seemed like hours, before he heard a hum and the rusty gates, that only looked old and abandoned, started to open.

George accelerated up the drive, came to an abrupt stop in front of the building. A man in his forties, wearing khaki trousers and a dark green polo shirt, stood on the front porch, arms crossed.

"You Jones?" George said.

"This is highly unusual, sheriff,"

"I don't give a damn what it is. You got four-wheelers here?"

"Of course. I'll need permission—"

"Cut the crap. I don't have time for it. I need them, and I need them now."

There was a brief standoff. George could see Mr. Robert Jones, which was definitely a bullshit name, looking at the three of them in full uniform, Jenkins cradling a shotgun (overkill, but it looked intimidating), and could see the realization dawning that resistance was pointless.

"Come this way. Concord will hear about this."

"Bet your ass they will."

Jones led them past rustic-styled furniture, animal heads, ghastly oil paintings of overdone western scenes on the walls. They passed a room paneled in dark walnut that smelled of cigars and leather into an open space with a high beamed ceiling and tall windows with a wide, unobstructed view of the mountains, then out through massive double glass doors into bright sunshine.

George looked at Jones. "You know these mountains?"

A young man appeared wearing work pants and a dark green t-shirt. "I do. I'm Mark." He extended his hand.

George ignored the hand, held up his cell phone with a map showing Anna nearing the summit of Croydon Peak. "Know how to get here?"

They crossed an open courtyard to a metal building. Mark pulled open a roll-up door to reveal two dark green side-by-sides.

"Fire 'em up," George said.

Mark jumped in the driver's side of one, George climbed in next to him, Jenkins and Arnold followed in the other, and as they roared across the open fields toward the mountains, the image came again to George of Dick Gaetz, first on the scene at the Kelley murder site, leaning over the mangled body of Ritchie Kelley.

"Step on it!" George shouted over the whine of the engines.

The sun came up over the rim of the amphitheater, warming them as it made its ascent into the sky. Jimmy leaned back with his eyes closed, sensed Eliza next to him, felt himself drifting. A shadow crossed his eyelids, a pungent animal smell surrounded him. He opened his eyes to see the cougar no more than three feet away staring at him. I'm hallucinating, he thought.

He closed his eyes, the smell stayed. He opened them, the cougar was still there. It moved closer. A red mouth with huge white fangs gaped, dripped saliva. The smell of blood, rotting meat. The cat sniffed and Jimmy looked into its black-rimmed, yellow eyes with their bottomless black centers and felt himself face-to-face with some profound, elemental truth that he was too small and too insignificant to understand. He waited and hoped Eliza would not wake. The cat continued to stare at him, its face no more than two feet from his, then turned and with a flick of its tail, walked away.

In a single bound, it jumped to the rim of the amphitheater, and he saw a final image of the cougar, tail curved up, silhouetted against a glowing sky.

Jimmy looked at the amphitheater littered with bits of wood, sticks, shreds of paper. Most of the furniture was wrecked, shattered by the storm. Lonnie was gone. His supplies were gone. The cat was gone.

A second shadow covered him. He looked up and saw silver-white rays of light streaming out from a crown on an angel.

"Am I dead?"

"Not yet," a voice answered. It was Anna.

"You're wearing my shoes," he said, then passed out.

Anna checked Jimmy quickly, his breath was steady, his pulse was strong. Eliza was in worse shape, her breathing was shallow, erratic, her pulse weak and irregular. Her head and leg were caked in dried blood.

Dick Gaetz stumbled up to her. "Got here as quick as I could. Is she alive?"

"We need a helicopter!" Anna said. "Call the station."

"We should make her more comfortable," Gaetz said. "Take her feet. Let's get her lying down."

They gently carried her to a flat shelf of stone. Gaetz looked agitated, panicky.

"I'll find something to put under her head, make sure she's okay," Gaetz said. "You should go help Baker." She returned to Jimmy, but something bothered her. Why was Gaetz so jumpy? She looked back at him. He had his back turned to her, was bending over Eliza.

She heard motors coming closer, then voices from the rim of the amphitheater, called up, "Down here!"

Jimmy was mumbling something. Anna leaned close. "She said . . . deputy."

And then it was as if a veil fell away and things clicked into place and she knew what she should have known all along. Gaetz!

She turned, saw him pressing a wadded up cloth down over Eliza's face.

"Stop!" She screamed, charged toward him

He pulled away from Eliza. "I was just trying to help her."

George appeared at the rim of the amphitheater as if out of nowhere, raised his sidearm, shouted, "Get down! Now!"

The shouting roused Eliza and she saw Gaetz and tried to scream, but uttered only a weak, strangled cry. Gaetz looked at the rock walls surrounding him, dropped to his knees.

Chapter Nineteen

POWER HAD BEEN OUT over much of the area for two days. The National Weather Service confirmed that a micro-burst had occurred in the Hemlock Flat area of Sullivan County. If not for the mountainous terrain, it could have developed into a full-blown tornado.

George Baker stood at the corner of Front and Main streets in downtown Lebanon watching a crew from McHenry's Tree Service clean up the debris from a massive maple tree that, uprooted by the storm, had fallen across Front Street. The final sections of the trunk were almost three feet across; the thing must have been a hundred and fifty years old. The corner looked barren, bereft. He turned away, walked toward his car, stopped to look at a tattered and faded poster on a telephone pole— Have You Seen this Girl?—with a picture of Eliza in her running clothes smiling at the camera. Why hadn't someone taken it down? He looked at her, so happy, so innocent. Would she ever feel that way again?

What has happened to me that I so easily thought her a murderer?

The last two days had been brutal. The Sheriff's Department had worked double shifts, directing traffic for the utility crews that worked around the clock to restore power to thousands.

George had yet to check on Jimmy and Eliza in the hospital.

New Hampshire State Police had taken over the case, and were being close-mouthed. Hard to blame them. He knew the questions and recriminations were coming. How could he have hired Gaetz?

He tore down the poster with Eliza's picture, folded it into quarters, returned to his cruiser, and drove to the station.

"Chief, you seen this?" Lorraine said as he walked past the Dispatch window. She held up the red logbook.

"What?"

"Bigfoot calls."

"Christ, people are crazy."

"And, two break-ins. Reports are on your desk."

He spread a map out on his desk, and marked the locations of the break-ins with a blue X: May Turnbull on Turnpike Road reported clothing taken from her line, and the Smiths on Leavitt Hill, food. He marked the recent Bigfoot sightings with a red X. When he finished there was a line of five marks from north to south paralleling the fence. Lonnie? Everything they knew about Lonnie Pierson suggested that he lacked the ability to make it far in the real world. That left thousands of acres of forest and hills and mountains. There was little doubt that Lonnie was a skilled hunter. Could he survive out there on his own? Could he have another secret place, be there now, living off the land? What will he do come winter?

About twelve years ago, Corbin Park held an open house for the neighbors. George saw wild boar and elk and bighorn sheep in breeding pens. The park manager had extolled the features of the now complete fence and how it was built to protect the surrounding area, to prevent animals from escaping.

"That's a load of crap," Everett James, a local farmer, said. "We ain't that stupid. It's really to keep us out."

Since then the park had been sealed and a good portion of the county in which he had been elected to enforce the law was, by state decree, beyond his jurisdiction. Was Lonnie hiding there? Fish and Game had flown a chopper over the park but was ordered to stop. Somebody called somebody in Concord. The noise was disturbing the animals.

He folded the map, put it with the rest of the file. He wondered if they would ever find Lonnie Pierson.

The clock on the wall told him it was not yet three o'clock. He remembered when that ugly thing —big and white—had been installed. It had faded to a sort of sickly yellowish brown and now looked like it belonged. He was exhausted. Everything seemed to have come unglued all at once. What had started the collapse of his entire world? His marriage over, his job on a knife edge. The calls for his resignation had already started, Margaret Wilson, a Lebanon City Councilor, leading the charge, and there was a group of citizens circulating a petition to have a recall election.

Maybe they were right, maybe it was time.

He wanted to go home, get some rest, but Wagner from State Police was due at three to meet with him and Anna. That, he was not looking forward to.

A knock on the door frame and there was Anna. Wagner, in full dress uniform, followed her into the office.

❖

Anna watched Wagner settle himself at George's desk. It was clear he was now in charge.

"Gaetz is being held in the jail at state headquarters," Wagner said. "He has refused to say anything. We've interviewed Eliza. Gaetz had been hanging around the farm lately. It's clear he was stalking her. He knew her parents were away, and accosted her in the barn, groped her, put his hand between her legs, slammed her against a wall when she resisted, but stopped when he heard the farm manager drive up. He threatened her, told her nobody would believe her, to keep quiet or else. When she saw him at the reception it scared her so much she decided to run away."

"Why didn't she tell someone?" George said.

"Who?" Anna said. "Who could she turn to? Attacked by a sheriff's deputy, a close friend of her so-called father? Who in her life could she trust? She's so tall it's easy to forget she's a kid."

"We're still not completely sure how Gaetz found her," Wagner said. "Or how Ritchie Kelley came to be there at that moment. What we do know from Eliza is Kelley tried to protect her. Gaetz killed him. During the struggle Eliza was injured, but managed to get away. She later collapsed in the woods where Pierson found her."

Anna couldn't stop herself from second guessing everything she'd done or thought during the search and investigation. No wonder Gaetz looked for Eliza so diligently. He needed to get to her before anyone else.

Wagner continued, "There's going to be a press conference in Concord tomorrow—"

"Great," Anna said.

"Let me finish. We're not going to hang either of you, or the Sullivan County Sheriff's Department, out to dry. The focus is going to be on Manchester and the fact that Gaetz is now the primary suspect in the killing of Sally Hopkins. We will also reveal that we've been in touch with the Maricopa County Sheriff's Department in Arizona where he worked before Manchester. There's an unsolved disappearance that they are taking another look at."

There are so many kinds of silence, Anna thought, as the three of them sat, each with their own thoughts, and this one, to her, seemed to last forever. It was the silence for a murdered girl, a murdered boy, another girl assaulted and traumatized, and for all the young girls and women out there who were assaulted or killed by predatory men, and as the silence stretched out, Anna felt an anger ignite in her that she knew would never die out.

Finally, Wagner spoke directly to George. "I know you blame yourself and are facing a public shitstorm. Hang in there. No one else saw the man for what he is. At least, you nailed him before it was too late."

❖

George watched Wagner leave. Anna stayed behind. They sat across the desk from each other; neither seemed to know what to say. It was the first time the two of them had been alone together in several days. He looked at her and wanted to be angry, wanted to shout, to accuse her of stealing his wife, but didn't have the energy.

"I'm thinking about quitting," he said at last.

"Don't."

He realized that, despite himself, he still respected her as a cop, and in a way envied her strength, her certainty, how she never seemed to doubt herself.

"How can I have been so blind?" he said.

"We all were. You heard Wagner. Sexual predators don't go around wearing a sign. Creeps like that are smart, brilliant at hiding who they are. Don't beat yourself up."

"You knew."

"No. I just thought he was an asshole."

"If only I'd listened to you and never hired him."

"Then he would have been somewhere else. We got him, that's what counts."

George started to speak, stopped himself.

"Still no sign of Lonnie?" Anna said.

"Nothing."

"Why didn't he come forward? Get help?"

"Why would he when no one had ever helped him before? He was put in a residential facility after his mother died. He ran away several times, but was sent back each time. Why would he trust us now when all we ever did was lock him up?"

Anna slid a white envelope across the desktop.

"What's that?"

"My notice."

George knew this was coming, had thought not long ago about calling for her resignation, but with all the shit that was hitting the fan right now, had hoped to put it off. This would be even more material for the recall movement.

"No need to make this public at the moment," Anna said, as if reading his mind. "But, you know it's for the best."

George saw what looked like genuine concern on her face.

"You're a good cop," she said. "Have done a good job as sheriff in this county for years. Don't let these people drive you out."

After she was gone, he sat at his desk staring vacantly at the map of Sullivan County on the wall. His county. It would be so easy to resign, to not have to face the public reckoning for hiring an alleged rapist and murderer, and then he thought about his father, something he rarely did. George Baker Sr. had been a hard man, of whom George had few good memories, but there was one.

Growing up, all George had wanted was to be a football star, to make his father proud, but he was too slow, too small, and had ended up on the third string offensive line. After George had spent the final game of his senior year on the bench, his father came up to him, took the ever-present cigarette out of his mouth, and said, "I'm proud of you, son. You don't got the talent, but you didn't quit, you stuck it out." The memory was so vivid it was as if he could feel the November cold, see the grey light fading over the empty field as his father walked away, and smell the smoke that followed his father everywhere.

Alice Peck Day Hospital purred along under emergency power. Paula Baker found Jimmy in a wheelchair in his room in the general ward, recovering from serious contusions to his right leg, and a gash in his head that had required twelve stitches to close. Eliza was in the Step Down Unit recovering from head trauma, a broken fibula, and severe dehydration.

"Have you seen her? How is she?" Jimmy said.

"She's out of the ICU, conscious, eating, drinking. She's doing fine, Jimmy. She's young, strong. What are you going to do?"

"I was on my way out of here, but now … I don't know. They won't let me talk to her, won't let me see her. How can I leave without … "

"Be patient."

Paula walked to the window. The hospital was on a hill above the town and Jimmy's room on the second floor looked to the south over the rooftops of Lebanon. Only the six-story Mascoma Bank building on the downtown pedestrian mall interrupted her view of the ridge of the Croydon Mountains.

Why didn't Eliza come to me? Paula thought. Why didn't she trust me? I would have helped her. Paula scanned back through her memories of Eliza, to when Eliza was younger, and wondered what she could have done differently that would have helped the girl trust her. She remembered again that time in the garden when Eliza had been troubled, but had closed up when Paula had snapped at her. Was that all it took to drive her away? To make her feel she was alone in this world?

"How did you find her?" Paula said.

"Lonnie thought I was Tooney. If I hadn't gone so femme, she could've died up there."

Paula hesitated, finally said, "What is that all about?"

"I love how I feel wearing her things. Isn't that enough?" He smiled that rare smile that lit up a room. There was a long pause. "Does Uncle George know?"

"How could he not? He saw what you were wearing when they brought you down off the mountain. The dress was ruined, of course."

"Too bad. I liked that dress."

Paula shook her head slowly and marveled at the strangeness of it all. Who are we really? Me? Jimmy? Do we even know? Eliza is safe, and Jimmy is well. Isn't that all that matters?

"What are your plans?" Jimmy said.

"It's happened so fast. I don't know. What do I do? Where should I live? Anna wants me to stay with her, but . . ."

"You can stay at the house as long as you want. The place is big enough. We'll figure it out."

"I'm sorry. Here I am going on about my problems and you're in the hospital. How are you doing?"

"I'm okay. Leg's getting better"—again, a smile—"and the drugs are great."

"You must think I'm awful."

"Why? For leaving George? I don't know how you stayed with him."

"Don't. He's a good man. No. I mean for Anna, for . . ."

"For what?"—he paused—"Have you told your kids?"

"Charley and Patricia want me to go back to George. But, Tracy …" Paula started to choke up. On the phone, Tracy had been wonderful, caring. And, when she said she wanted to meet Anna, Paula had been unable to speak.

"Tracy still has a terrific crush on you," she said to Jimmy.

"What does Anna think? I mean, how serious—"

"What if she tires of me?"

Anna, out of breath from carrying the rented carpet machine up the stairs, looked at the ugly stain in the middle of her living room. It had been more than a week since Jimmy had puked on the carpet, and she had been too busy to clean it properly. She'd doused it with spray cleaner, which had covered up some of the smell, and then walked around it. The stink was only really bad when she first walked in the door, then it seemed to fade, as if her nose decided to ignore it. The stain was vaguely fan shaped with spatter heading away from the couch toward the windows. You had to give the guy credit, he knew how to vomit. Couldn't he at least have made it to the bathroom?

The directions for the machine made no sense. Where do you put the cleaner?

She read the back of the box again, but couldn't concentrate, couldn't get the vision of the two of them out of her mind: Jimmy in a tattered mauve and blue dress, Eliza in bright yellow, leaning back against a wall of stone, Eliza's head on his shoulder, as if they had been posed for a photograph. And the shocking image of Gaetz leaning over Eliza, pressing a cloth down on her face.

A quiet tap on the door. Paula walked in carrying a canvas shopping bag of food. "God, it still smells."

"Do you know how to use this thing?"

Paula walked to her, reached up, brushed aside damp strands of Anna's silver hair, stood on her toes, kissed her on the mouth.

"You're cute when you're all sweaty and frustrated. Put the food away. I'll get the thing running. It's not the first time I've cleaned up that boy's mess."

They showered together, and as Anna looked at Paula, her hair still damp, little strands curling on her neck, she felt a new kind of attraction, more than passion, more than lust, dare she call it, love? Paula's presence calmed her. Her competence reassured her. She had a smile that lit her face, and little creases at the corner of her eyes. There was a strength to her that she'd earned by living, by caring.

Anna left to take back the machine. When she returned with a bottle of wine, Paula had dinner on the stove— poached salmon, vegetable medley, rice pilaf—and had set the table with mismatched knives and forks, lit candles. She'd fixed the place up a bit, replaced the horrible fluorescent bulbs with smaller, warm-light bulbs, hung pots above the stove, brought candles from the house in Hemlock Flat.

With the windows open and the fans on, the chemical fumes of the rug cleaner almost, but not quite, masked the residual tang of vomit, but also obscured the delicious smells of dinner. They sat at the small kitchen table. Anna poured the wine.

"How're they doing?" Anna said.

"Good. Jimmy will be released tomorrow. Eliza not for another couple of days. However did you find them?"

"Bits and pieces of Jimmy's dress on bushes, low hanging branches."

Paula put dinner on the table.

"Have you talked to George?" Anna said.

"Once. I'm worried about him. He's upset, talked about resigning. Why is everyone blaming him?"

"He's a good man, a good sheriff. Nobody else saw, why should he take the fall?"

Anna passed her hand over the dark green tablecloth. "This is nice, and the candles are wonderful."

"Why hadn't you done more with the place? It barely looked like anyone lived here. What was your apartment like in Boston?"

"It really was Jess's. Asian, beautiful, spare, modern."

"Did you love her?"

"I thought I did."

"What happened?"

"One night, we were going out for dinner in Brookline to this basement Italian place, and I'd spiked my hair and was wearing my favorite Tomboy t-shirt and these killer leather pants, feeling proud and strong, and Jess asked me to change my clothes, to not be who I am. She was afraid to be seen with me."

A silence intruded and the two women sipped their wine and watched each other across the table.

"What about you?" Anna said. "Would you be afraid to be seen with me?"

Paula's lips trembled, she wetted them with her tongue, said, "Never," but Anna noticed the brief hesitation.

❖

Leaving George, Eliza's rescue, the storm, had all happened so fast, it sometimes seemed to Paula to have been a dream, and she would wake in her bed with George snoring next to her, and none of this would have been real, and she would still be in her previous life, trapped in the same routines.

They took the last of the wine into the living room, sat on the couch which Paula had covered with a large piece of batik with rust-colored swirls.

"I gave George notice," Anna said. "There's an opening in Boston PD's sexual violence unit. It seems I've been reinstated. The sergeant who harassed me, did it again, has been fired."

Paula looked at the scenic photos of New Hampshire she'd hung on the walls—she'd asked Anna for some personal photos to frame and hang, but had finally given up—and wondered if Anna even noticed these things. She looked more beautiful than ever, happier, as if a weight had been lifted, and Paula knew Anna was waiting for her to say something.

"Come with me," Anna said.

Paula had known this moment would come. What would it be like living together? Her heart raced. Her breath came in shallow gasps.

"Boston?" Paula said.

A vision came to her of an apartment in a city where she knew no one. Anna would be working and she would be alone. She'd never lived in the city. What would she do?

"You can do this,"—Anna turned to Paula, took her hand—"People do it all the time. Move, start a new life, find a job. I love you. What's wrong? Isn't that what you want?"

"I've lived in this valley all my life. This is the only home I've ever known. How can I leave my garden?"

"I thought you loved me."

"I do . . ."

"I can't stay here, you must see that. The job I was meant to do is in Boston."

Was her job so very important that Anna could not see? Paula thought. The seconds ticked by and she saw Anna's eyes turn opaque, as if a screen came down over them.

"Think about it, please. We'd be together," Anna said.

✂

Anna watched through the open window as Paula opened her car door and slid into the front seat without looking up. The headlights came on. She drove away, and the street was dark and empty.

I should have known, she thought. Why would a woman with such a full life—family, community— leave it all for a risky gamble for happiness? Anna remembered the night that she came to her apartment in Lebanon. Paula had kissed her with such hunger and passion, but then had backed away.

Why can't the woman make up her mind?

Anna now saw these few days together as brief as they actually were. She didn't understand, perhaps she never would. She felt loved, surely Paula felt the same?

Was it unreasonable, expecting Paula to come with her?

Anna was angry, hurt, but all she could think about was Paula, and couldn't help but think of her as a prisoner held against her will, like some damsel imprisoned by an evil king, but knew that was ridiculous, defense against facing the painful reality that Paula had had chosen life here over a life with her in Boston.

Perhaps putting her job above what Paula wanted was selfish, but it was too late, what was done, was done. Anna looked back at her apartment. It had become a home—Paula had made it so in just these few days—but soon she would leave it, would go back to Boston as she had arrived here, alone, and face again the deep feeling of not belonging, of being in the sense that counted most, homeless.

❖

Late at night was the hardest, boredom set in, and the shock of all he had been through seemed to rise up and push Jimmy down into his hospital chair. It was still so unreal: the nightmarish climb in the dark, the storm, falling, waking by Eliza's side. Had Lonnie put him there? He doubted he could have moved himself, and the cougar had come close and had looked at him as if it wanted to tell him something. Ridiculous, he thought, wild animals don't think like that, but perhaps he had imagined the cougar, and if he had, he could attribute to it whatever he wanted. He must have imagined it, mustn't he?

There was a light tap on the door. A nurse came in pushing an empty wheelchair. "Mr. Baker? There's another scan we'd like to do."

"Now?"

"I'm afraid so."

She wheeled him down a long hallway, their progress punctuated by a succession of bright fluorescent lights. He was disoriented from the pain meds, from the purple auras around each fixture. It was other-worldly quiet, the hospital sunk deep in late-night slumber. They turned into a different hallway, then yet another. He heard murmurs from behind closed doors. He craned his neck. Her face was angular, outlined by deep shadows. He'd not seen her before.

"Where are you taking me?"

"Shhh."

They stopped at a door. She pushed it open and backed him into a softly lit room. She swiveled the chair and there was Eliza, propped up in her bed, smiling. The nurse wheeled him over.

"Thank you, Maddie," Eliza said.

"I'll be back to see how you're doing."

Eliza's color had returned; her eyes were bright. He felt his heart would explode.

"They wouldn't let me see you."

"I know."

He wheeled himself closer. She reached out. He took her hand. They stared at each other for a long time, finally Jimmy looked away.

"I win," Eliza said. "Nobody can out stare me." She started coughing, finally stopped, said, "I feel so tired."

Jimmy found it hard to speak, said at last, "You remind me so much of your mother."

He felt again, the heartbreak, then looked at Eliza. His and Harriett's daughter. The wonder of it.

"Where were you going?"

"I know a girl at Middlebury from skiing, she was going to let me stay with her until I figured things out."

"How did Gaetz find you?'

"He knew about Martin's cabin. The police were here. They thought I was asleep. I heard them talking. They think Gaetz raped and killed that poor girl in Manchester. Is that what he was going to do to me?"

She closed her eyes.

"If it hadn't been for Ritchie . . ." She stifled a sob. "Gaetz was choking me when Ritchie tried to stop him. He fought so hard. I ran into the woods and kept running and running. I was so scared. I was bleeding and my head hurt and my foot caught in some rocks. I fell, couldn't get up, and crawled under some bushes and passed out. I woke up and Lonnie was there and those horrible creatures were staring at me. I thought he was going to turn me into one of them.

"Lonnie thought he was saving me. I told him to get help, that he wasn't in trouble, but he didn't believe me. He carried me up the mountain, said we were going to live there forever."

She started to cry softly, and looked in that moment so young and vulnerable Jimmy wanted to pull her close, but he felt awkward, held back. She closed her eyes. For a moment Jimmy thought she had fallen asleep.

"Poor Lonnie," she said softly. "He tried to take care of me … does anyone know where he is?"

Jimmy shook his head. In the silence that followed, he could hear muffled sounds from the hallway, a door open and close nearby.

"Are you going back to live at the farm?"

"What choice do I have?"

The door opened. Maddie came into the room.

"That's enough for now," she said. "This girl is strong, but she needs to rest."

The rubber wheels of the wheelchair whispered on the grey linoleum as Maddie, silent, pushed him through the endless corridors. Jimmy was exhausted. He drifted in and out, lost in jumbled thoughts and memories, while around him in the hospital night machines whirred and beeped and pulsed as people lay motionless in their beds; others, restless, turned in their sleep, groaned in pain; people died; babies were born; nurses walked the corridors silent in their rubber-soled shoes, sat at their stations, bleary-eyed, drinking bad coffee.

Chapter Twenty

A FEW YELLOW AND RED leaves littered the trail, harbingers of the season to come, and the light was a deep filtered green tinged with orange. The end of August and already there was a new sharpness and the smell of dying vegetation in the air. Paula, surrounded by the tall, dark trunks of the old-growth forest, was spinning slowly, arms spread wide as if trying to fly, looking up at the forest canopy far above her, an expression of wonderment on her face. She stopped, dropped her arms, looked at Jimmy, and smiled.

"My god, these woods are beautiful, aren't they?"

"We should head back. My leg hurts."

"No, I want to see it."

They walked on, came to a rotting log almost three feet in diameter covered with dark green moss and bulbous yellow fungi, and sat down to rest.

"What are you going to do?" Jimmy said.

"Anna's two weeks are almost up, and I still don't know. How can I leave all this?"

"You can always come back. What are you afraid of?"

"You never knew my parents. They haven't spoken to me in almost thirty years, but I still hear their voices in my head, telling me it's a sin to love a woman. Forty-seven-years-old, and I still hear them."

"How can they—"

"Let's get going," Paula said.

They came to the giant's workshop. She walked through the entry tunnel into the grotto, thought about Lonnie, the big, timid soul she'd once seen outside the Corner Store with his soda and cupcakes, and thought about him living with that house falling down around him, surrounded by its terrible memories. She crossed the courtyard and sat on the rough bed. Perhaps he was happier here? She looked at his creations that had been damaged by the storm and were starting to deteriorate. They looked back at her.

Jimmy gingerly lowered himself to sit next to her, flexed his leg.

"That poor, lonely boy," Paula said. "We failed him, all of us."

"Why would he make these horrible things?"

"Don't you see? It's his family. The father in the middle, his mother with her layered skirts of feathers, and him with bulging eyes. George told you what happened?"

"Yes."

"Did he tell you that some suspected it was Lonnie's fault? That it was he who put the wheel back on, didn't tighten the bolts properly. There was even gossip he did it on purpose, that he was jealous of his little sister, but I never believed it. That broken figure on the ground must be her."

Jimmy stepped out of the forest and watched Paula walk to the house. He'd lingered behind on the way back from the grotto, thinking about Lonnie. What if it was true? He couldn't imagine the guilt. He looked past his aunt, down across the fields to the house and past the house to the valley, and west to the distant hills of Vermont. Something had changed in the appearance of the house in the weeks since he'd left the hospital—it didn't look quite so out of place—though he knew the change was really within himself.

These past days he had wandered the woods to strengthen his leg and to find moments of peace, time to think. He looked for signs of Lonnie. Nothing. He purchased a field guide to North American mammals, studied how to identify animal scat, and searched for traces of the cougar. Nothing.

At night, he heard the calls of a hoot owl, the yap of coyotes, and once or twice, the howl of a bobcat.

He wondered where Eliza was. She went to school a week after being released from the hospital. Prevented by a restraining order obtained by Bill Johnson from speaking to her, he had watched from the other side of the road as she'd turned and waved, before being swept through the double doors of the high school by a torrent of laughing, talking teenagers, as if nothing had changed.

He followed a worn path in the field to the front porch, slowly climbed the steps, limped past a wheeled suitcase to the kitchen for a glass of water. Paula had been living in the house for two weeks, and he had grown used to her presence. The house seemed not so much a place of the past, but one with a present, and a possible future. He looked for her, found her in the dining room looking through some of Tooney's papers.

"I saw the bag. You don't have to leave."

"Yes, I do. I need my own place." She held up an official looking document. "Have you read this? It's a coda to her will that she specified remain private."

"What's it say?"

"She left quite a sum of money to a woman in Dallas, Christina Garcia."

"Who?"

"The will says she was their 'faithful housekeeper.'"

"These are from Christina." Paula pointed to letters on plain white stationary scattered on the table, each with an envelope. "I never knew. I don't think anyone did. Tooney wanted Christina to come here, to live with her, but Christina wouldn't leave, her family."

"Couldn't she have found a housekeeper here?"

Paula gathered the letters, returned them to their envelopes one at a time.

"The letters from Christina are love letters."

She tied the envelopes into a bundle with a blue ribbon.

"It's so sad . . . Tooney loved her, but Christina wouldn't come. Why is everything so hard?"

Yes, Jimmy thought, why is living so hard? He had stopped wearing Tooney's clothes after leaving the hospital, but the pull was too strong, and he was wearing a grey skirt and a loose red sweater, and felt more himself than in his own clothes. Paula seemed to no longer notice, as if this, to her, was who he is and that's just fine, but in his quiet moments, when he let himself be still, Jimmy wondered who he was, and what was he going to do?

He drove into Lebanon, turned left onto Dulac Street, and continued past Storrs Hill, the small town-owned ski area. He parked on the street, crossed the road, looked across the Mascoma River, and watched the water, swollen and brown after another late summer storm, surge against the foundation of a four-story brick building. It had been a mill once, textiles of some sort, but had been converted to offices. Looking at that building brought to him thoughts of his mother. She'd worked for a law firm that occupied the entire top floor. She moved to California shortly after leaving him with his aunt and uncle, and there had been little communication since, and he has tried to live as if he didn't have a mother, and has pretended that the woman was nothing to him, but of course, despite his best efforts, that was not true, and now, there was an empty place in his memories where she should be, a place he rarely visited for the pain that lived there.

He re-crossed the street, stepped around a padlocked gate of elaborate cast-iron scroll-work, and walked underneath the high arched sign for Mount Calvary Cemetery. He left the paved entrance road and walked slowly up the grassy, terraced hill stopping to look at the names on the old headstones: Dumas, Painchaud, Coutermarsh. French-Canadian families that had come here to work the mills along the river.

He reached the height of land where the cemetery leveled off and turned back to look out over the town. Small, lonely clouds drifted lazily across the deep blue sky. In the distance he could see the golden tip of the Dartmouth College Library bell tower.

It took almost an hour wandering the broad expanse for him to find her grave, a slightly raised rectangle of turf in front of a simple slab of polished pale granite. Altoona Lindsay Baker, no dates, was etched into a raised panel with scalloped edges.

He felt like he should say something, but what could he say to a woman who had, from her grave, changed his life? Did anyone else come here? Paula? Eliza?

He thought of that granite amphitheater high on the summit of Croydon Peak under an indifferent sky, and wondered if Lonnie was alive somewhere, or if the stone of the mountain was his grave marker.

He heard footsteps, turned to see Anna walking toward him. She was wearing jeans, and a chartreuse and white checked blouse. As gorgeous as ever. She stood next to him.

"Nice hair," she said after awhile.

They'd shaved almost half his head at the hospital.

"It's growing back."

"You should keep it. Very cool."

"Any sign of Lonnie?" Jimmy said.

"Nothing. I don't get it. All along, people knew he was alone, struggling, living with that house falling down around him, scavenging in the woods. Everybody knew—George, Paula, Arnold, all of them—and no one did anything. He'd been pilfering stuff for years. Nobody cared enough to make the connection? Tooney and Eliza were the only ones who cared. Did you know Eliza went to Social Services in Lebanon about Lonnie and was ignored? What is up with that? If he doesn't exist, they don't have to help him?"

"Sounds about right."

Anna turned away and stared down at the memorial. Jimmy felt ashamed of his flip remark. Why wasn't he as outraged as she?

"What are you going to do?" Anna said.

"I'm not allowed to talk to Eliza. My emails have been blocked. I can't text. They've changed her cell number."

"Don't you have rights as the biological father?"

"I've filed with something called the Putative Father Registry, but Johnson's lawyers are better than mine. He's seeking to block it, claiming that wearing women's clothing makes me a pervert. Fucking pisses me off. If I could get my hands on that creep. And, what the hell is a putative father anyway?"

"Eliza has filed for emancipation," Anna said. "Don't do anything stupid that'll screw it up. Be patient."

"Let's walk," Jimmy said.

Anna took his arm and they strolled down the gradual slope toward the road like some genteel couple on a boulevard somewhere. Jimmy stopped and looked at a small gravestone—Robert Raymond Allard, 06 November, 1906 -15 March 1907.

"So young," Anna said. "So sad."

The leaves of a nearby maple lifted. Quiet voices from a far off service drifted on the breeze.

"What're your plans?" Jimmy said.

"My notice is almost up. I'm going back to Boston."

"Have you talked with Paula?"

"Not for a few days. She's not coming with me."

He looked at her and saw hurt and sadness in her eyes, but also, anger, determination. All along, he had been worried about Paula, but perhaps it was Anna for whom he should have been worried. There was, he now realized, a fragile person beneath the uniformed shell she presented to the world.

"Talk to her, she's confused, scared."

Anna walked away, stood in front of a tall tower-like gravestone with a winged angel on its top, returned.

"She made her choice. If she doesn't want me, she doesn't want me."

"The job is that important to you?"

Jimmy turned and walked downhill, conscious of Anna's eyes on him.

George Baker had been so busy he hadn't had a lot of time to think about Paula, but in the few hours he spent at the house every night her absence became more and more obvious. There were dirty dishes piled in the sink. He was almost out of food, down to his last frozen meal. Hadn't had a clean uniform in two days.

The woman should be here, helping me, he thought. Hadn't she promised to love and obey or something like that? She'd had her fling. Time to come home. she couldn't possibly believe that this thing will last. Korsak will dump her for some hot young item, and then where will she be?

Old, alone in a city where she knows no one.

George had the TV on but barely looked at it. It was strange, when he stopped thinking about this as a contest with Paula as the prize, he would begin to realize living alone wasn't so bad. He could do what he wanted, when he wanted. He could hire a woman to clean, take care of the place. Is that what Paula had become to him?

He turned the TV off, went into the kitchen, opened the fridge. At least there was beer. He carried the bottle out to the deck and stood looking across the flats. What would it be like, living alone after all these years?

The land-line rang. He went back into the kitchen.

"Yes?"

It was Charley.

"Don't worry, I'm fine . . . Yes, I talked to her."

The call continued, Charley finally calmed down.

"My best to Deborah and the kids . . . soon . . . definitely."

George put the handset back in its cradle and looked at the wall phone. He hated that their kids seemed to be taking sides. Why is Charley so mad at her? She was still his mother, and George knew, still loved him. And Patricia, telling him he could move in with them as if he can't take care of himself. What had Paula ever done but love and care for them? Only Tracy had any sense. I love you both she'd said, whether you're together or separate, and then she'd said, be good to each other, that's all I ask. Go figure. The one he'd never understood, had always thought flaky.

He heard someone at the front door, opened it to see Jimmy standing there holding a bottle of Jameson's by the neck.

Jimmy looked at his uncle; he seemed tired and lost, and Jimmy felt a sudden wave of compassion for the man who had been so hard on him, and who, Jimmy thought, had hated him.

"You gonna let me in or do I have to drink this by myself?"

Jimmy limped as they walked down the hall. In the kitchen, he found two glasses, poured a generous portion of whiskey in each, handed one to his uncle, said, "Cheers".

His uncle was staring at him, and Jimmy, who was wearing jeans and an old t-shirt, felt uncomfortable, and wondered what his uncle was thinking, was he imagining him in women's clothes?

"Gotta hand it to you," George broke the silence. "Disguising yourself, pretending to be Tooney to get Lonnie to lead you to Eliza. Smart."

Jimmy wanted to explain how it wasn't a disguise, but didn't know how to begin, instead said, "Any sign of Lonnie?"

"Nothing. We need to find him, winter's coming."

George picked up the bottle and studied the label, said, "Eighteen year, the good stuff." He carried it out to the deck, watched Jimmy lower himself slowly into a chair.

"How's the leg?"

"Getting better," Jimmy said. "How're you doing?"

"Hanging in there. Recall's going to happen. November."

"What're you going to do?"

"Fight it." He poured for both of them. "Helluva thing." George sipped his whiskey. "When I need her the most, she's not here. Why the hell she marry me in the first place? Almost thirty years we been together. How does that end?"

"She still cares for you, you know she'll help you. Maybe it hasn't ended, maybe it's changed is all." Jimmy drank, hesitated before speaking. "I've been here a month, haven't seen you touch, smile at each other, or do anything together."

Silence descended on the two of them after the second shot of whiskey, Crickets called to each other as the evening cooled, mist formed over the flats, and dew settled on the grass.

"I remember the two of them together," George said. "I hated that O'Neal girl because Paula never looked at me the way she looked at her, never laughed with me the way she did with her." George picked up the bottle. "One more." He missed the glass with half of the pour, laughed. "Shit, did you come here to get me drunk?"

"I came over because—hell, I don't know—because you were there for me."

"Hah! All we ever did was fight. You hated me."

"Never did. And I'm not taking sides now."

"What're your plans?" George said.

"Eliza's filed for emancipation. I've petitioned to be declared her father. I want her to come live with me." Jimmy lifted his glass but didn't drink. "What's it like, being a father? How do you do it?"

There was a long silence as both men drank.

"Damned if I know. You just do."

"You were more my father than that asshole, Matthew," Jimmy said.

"I never understood what my sister saw in him." George stared down at the brown liquid that swirled in the glass held in his gently trembling hands. "I was too hard on you."

"At least you cared."

George was unsteady when he stood. They stumbled, arms around each other into the kitchen.

"You better sleep here," George said. "Take Charley's old room."

Paula paced the kitchen, waiting for George to come home from the station. She had called him earlier and said they needed to talk. He'd grunted, then agreed to come home, and now she was here and her stomach churned and her hands trembled and the speech she'd rehearsed had vanished into a fog of anxiety.

The place was a mess. Couldn't the man take care of himself? The least he could have done was clean the kitchen. She heard a car pull into the driveway, footsteps on the walk, the screen door slam, and there he was, in uniform, smaller somehow than she remembered. Had he lost weight? There were dark circles under his eyes. His uniform was wrinkled. She tried to sense what he was feeling, but his face was blank, unreadable as always.

He tossed a manila envelope onto the table, it landed with a slap that made her flinch, said, "Paula."

She thought for a moment he would come to her, would take her in his arms, tell her all was forgiven, and if he did, what would she do? But he didn't. He walked slowly across the kitchen, turned to face her, and leaned back against the counter with his arms crossed.

"God, what a week. You said you wanted to talk, so talk."

She came to tell him their life together had been good, was not a waste, that she still loved him in a way, but that she had to go, needed to grow, to be her true self. She couldn't think of what to say, where to begin.

"After all this time?" George said. "Where did this come from? How could you just leave?"

"Oh, George. You know it's been over for a long time. We've just been holding on. When was the last time we made love?"

Silence.

"Right. You can't remember either."

"We were happy once, weren't we? What happened?" George said.

"People change. I still care for you, it's just that—"

"Do you have any idea what everyone is saying? What about the kids? Did you think of them at all?"

"I think about them all the time, but they're grown. They have their own lives. This isn't about them."

"I know, I know . . . but Charley and Patricia are very upset."

"They'll get over it."

"Are you going to Boston?"

She'd promised herself. No tears. Be strong. But she felt herself weaken. It would be so easy to go back, to be forgiven, to live in this house and hide from the uncertain world out there.

"I don't know."

It was hard to breath, her face was hot, her eyes stung. She felt her heart fluttering like a trapped bird.

"Come back. I need you," he said softly, stood facing her. "Come back right now, and it'll be alright. I'll make everything good again."

She moved toward him; he took her in his arms.

"I can't . . ." She stepped away, walked over to the table. "But, I want us to be friends. Can we do that?" She picked up the envelope, saw the county seal. "The recall."

"I thought about resigning, but the one thing I remember my father saying was, 'Never quit.' Figure I'll let the voters decide." He looked away. "Will you help me?"

"Of course I will."

She looked at the half empty bottle of whiskey on the counter.

"Jimmy was here," George said. "Stayed over. He said something last night that made a lot of sense."

"What?"

"I forget." They looked at each other. "It was good once, wasn't it?" he said.

"Yes, it was, but it's not what I need now."

George returned to work.

Paula stood in the middle of the kitchen. Here had been the center of her world since they'd first moved into this house. Here had been her life. She remembered the chaos of getting three kids off to school, homework papers strewn across the breakfast counter, stained with jam, orange juice. God, how she had loved those mornings filled with the chatter of her children.

This house had such a powerful hold on her, it seemed as if gravity was stronger here, and would hold her down, and keep her from drifting away. For a moment, just one moment, she had thought she could go back, that history would repeat, and she would again run from the arms of a woman to George's protection, but no, she couldn't, she wouldn't.

She stepped onto the back deck. Evening comes on early at the end of August, the sun is lower, the shadows are longer. Small pools of mist were already forming over Emerson's fields, and the cows were strange ephemeral beings, somehow insubstantial as the mist gathered and drifted around them.

The time with Anna now seemed to her so brief as to have been the blink of an eye, the flutter of a hummingbird's wing, but those nights with her had seemed to last forever. Never before had Paula felt so alive, or so frightened. She was safe here surrounded by the familiar accumulations of a life. Here she felt solid, there with Anna she had felt fragile, as if a single word could shatter her like a crystal vase dropped onto a tile floor.

Anna would be leaving soon. They should say goodbye, but Paula was afraid to see her, didn't think she could stand it. Paula had thought that beneath the hard exterior Anna showed to the world was a caring, loving person, but felt now that Anna wore a uniform whether she was on duty or not.

Paula's luggage was in the car. She wanted to be on her own, and was going to stay in White River Junction for awhile.

A cool wind came down off the mountains, worried at the corner of the house behind her. Fall was coming, that most beautiful of seasons and the trees will turn yellow and red and orange and the world will be bathed in a golden light, and the days will be cool, and the nights cold, and frost will sparkle on the fields in the early morning sun, and Anna will be gone.

Chapter Twenty-One

Saturday, September 9th. Cars were parked up and down both sides of Gap Road and several white panel vans, the largest of which had, "Rogers and Sons, Estate Auctions," in an elaborate script on the side, filled the driveway to Jimmy's house. Paula parked on the road and walked slowly up the drive, skirting the vans, dragging her roller bag behind her. The sky was that clean, pierced blue that autumn brings to New Hampshire, that makes the damp buggy spring, the hot, dreary days of summer worth enduring. The air had a cool freshness that made it a delight to breathe.

This was a day that brought an ache to her heart because she knew that this beauty was fleeting, that soon would come the dark, barren days of November, and then the long, cold winter.

There was a tent, as if for a wedding, set up on the lawn. In it rows of chairs faced a stage, and on the stage a man called out, "Lot Number 12." Two men carried a large armoire onto the stage and the bidding began. There were people everywhere, milling about on the lawn, standing on the porch holding plastic glasses of wine. She went inside and elbowed her way along the crowded hallway searching for Jimmy. The kitchen was empty. She looked out the window toward the back fields and saw him standing in the meadow staring up at the mountain ridge.

"Where have you been?" he said when she approached.

"A motel in White River Junction. It was awful. You're selling everything?"

"Just some of the furniture, some of the jewelry. I need the money."

"The house?"

"There's been interst, but I've decided to wait."

"Can I come back, Jimmy. Stay here?"

"Of course. I've been waiting for you."

"Anna is leaving for Boston."

"Why?"

"I don't know. I was willing to give up almost everything for her, but when I asked her to stay here, she said no. That job means more to her than I do."

She looked at him; he moved to her and held her. He knew that Paula was strong, that she was brave, that she would cope with the pain, that she would move on, and he hoped that one day she would find the love she deserved. They parted, and Jimmy looked across the meadow to the wall of dark hemlocks and spruce, toward where the fence hid in the shadows, toward Croydon Peak, and then higher as if he was looking for answers in the small white clouds that drifted across the sky from the west.

Paula wondered what he was thinking, what was there in those heights that called to him, that drew him so.

They climbed the back steps, passed through the kitchen. People wandered the rooms holding a printed color catalog, looking at the furniture, touching the polished wood, examining the jewelry under the watchful eyes of an armed guard.

"Doesn't this make you sad? Selling her life like this?"

"They're only things. I don't think Tooney would have cared. She must have known, leaving it all to me, that this might happen."

They went out to the front porch. A white SUV came barreling up Gap Road, turned into the drive and skidded to a stop. Anna got out and stood there with her feet apart, as if afraid to move.

She's come to stay goodbye, thought Paula. Couldn't she just leave? Must she make it so hard? Paula stiffened, prepared herself.

Anna stood for a long time at the bottom of the steps looking up at the two of them.

I shouldn't have come back, she thought; she won't have me; I've hurt her too deeply.

The patter of the auctioneer drifted on the breeze. The oak trees listened. Somewhere a wind chime.

Anna was up the steps. She faced Paula and then reached for her and they came together and Jimmy watched the two women hold each other close, and he felt a small, bright, glimmer of hope.

Anna stepped away from Paula.

"Can I stay with you, Jimmy?" Anna said.

"You can stay here . . . with both of us."

Anna pulled Jimmy to her and held him tight and whispered in his ear, "Eliza will come, Jimmy, as soon as she can."

Epilogue

OUTSIDE THE HOUSE, THE trees are naked, their bare branches grasp at the grey November sky.

Jimmy comes into the kitchen where Paula is beginning dinner preparations; he's shaved, his hair is wet. The gash on his head has healed, the limp is gone. He looks good, Paula thinks. She never knows who will come down those stairs. It's kind of fun, exciting. She has come to think of Jimmy as brave, not because (as he might claim) he has skied down mountains where to fall would be to die, but because each day he comes down those stairs as who he wants to be, as who he is, as only who he is. This evening, Jimmy is wearing wide-leg jeans and a pretty orange and muted-purple blouse, gold trimmed flats, a necklace, earrings.

"Those jeans can't be Tooney's, can they?"

"Nope, bought them in town." Jimmy turns to the side. "What do you think?"

He goes to the refrigerator, takes out a bottle of beer, twists the cap off, plops down at the table, takes a long drink.

"What time is it? Friday traffic can be brutal."

"Jimmy, stop worrying. They'll get here."

"How's the store?"

"Slow." Paula manages a small bookstore, The Reading Room, in White River Junction. "If it wasn't for the used section—"

"The holidays are coming, things'll pick up." Jimmy drinks from his beer. "I still can't believe it, Anna working for the state."

Anna turned down the job in Boston and is training for a position with the new major crimes unit in Concord.

"Plainclothes. What's she going to do without her uniform?" Jimmy says.

"Find another."

Jimmy wanders out to the porch, gazes down the driveway at the empty road. November afternoons are quiet, gone are the creatures of summer, tucked away safely in their burrows, or flown away south.

Friday night, the traffic is terrible. Anna longs for the department cruiser, the siren, the light-bar. She is late, and worries that by being late, she will somehow screw it up, that Eliza won't be there, that Bill Johnson will not let her leave, that there's a deadline, that if Eliza's not gone by a certain time, she will be trapped forever.

She turns off Route 120 and drives up Turnpike Road, blasts into the Johnsons' driveway, and screeches to a halt behind a sheriff's department cruiser.

What's going on?

She walks up to the door, sees George Baker in uniform talking to Bill Johnson, who stands with his arms crossed, scowling, simmering like he's ready to boil over.

"George," she says.

"Anna," George says. "How's the state treating you?"

"I'm still training, but it's going well."

George looks good, she thinks.

"What are you doing here?"

A thin smile flickers on George's face. "Can't a guy stop by to see his great-niece?"

Anna is again confused by the inter-relatedness of the families. Is he really her great-uncle? But, she thinks, does it matter? Eliza appears at the door, a pack on her back, pulling a wheeled suitcase. Bill Johnson begins to move forward. George steps in front of him, grabs the suitcase, says, "Let me take that," then looks at Johnson who has still not spoken.

"How's Paula?" George says as he loads the suitcase into the back of Anna's car.

"Good. She misses you."

"Tell her I'm doin' okay."

"I'm glad you beat the recall." Anna reaches out, touches him on the arm. "Thank you for being here."

Eliza steps up to him; she's taller than as he is; they hug. She whispers in his ear. He smiles.

Anna gets behind the wheel. Eliza hesitates, looks back at the house. Bill Johnson turns away, shuts the door behind him.

"You ready?" Anna says.

"You have no idea."

"It's not my birthday," Eliza says. "This is crazy."

"It's a different kind of birthday," Jimmy says.

The kitchen glows with the light of candles, not those wimpy things that usually go on top of a cake, but sixteen tall pillar candles, some on the table, others arrayed around the kitchen. The remains of a dinner eaten with gusto and laughter and not a few tears are everywhere: dirty plates on the counter, empty wine bottles; half-full glasses, and a cake that looks like it was attacked by bears on the table.

"When are you going back?" Paula says.

"Tomorrow," Anna says.

"So soon?"

"Something's up. I may be sent north, could be gone for a few days."

Paul tries to hide her disappointment.

"I'm going to change my name," Eliza says.

Jimmy gags, spews crumbs of cake across the table, says, "What's the matter with Eliza?"

"Not Eliza, silly. Johnson."

"What's it going to be?" Anna says.

The three of them wait.

"Baker."

In the warmth of the kitchen, Jimmy sits in the yellow light of the candles. In this moment he knows he will stay, he will do his best to be this girl's father, he will be a friend to these two women.

He stands, goes out to the porch, steps down to the front lawn.

The house is alight, the golden glow of the windows casts geometric patterns of light on the frost tinged grass. The voices and laughter of the women rise and fall, filling the house, but behind the warmth and love, there lurks in Jimmy a dark corner of regret: where were we, all of us, when Eliza needed someone she could trust? Could turn to?

November nights are cold, his breath curls up into a sky that circles above him. Jimmy looks toward the mountains, black in the darkness, for something that cannot be found there. A long, graceful shadow leaps and bounds across the field and disappears into the deep frozen forest, and the brittle quiet of a crystalline night is shattered by a scream, not human, but a scream nonetheless, a lonely, questioning sound. How, Jimmy imagines the cougar wondering, have I come to be thousands of miles from my home, the only one of my kind? You should go, Jimmy says. I will stay, but you should go. Again, a scream. It echoes off the mountain where bare rock is veined and patched with ice, and rises up into the star-filled sky.

Jimmy thinks to go back inside to the light, to the warmth, but stays outside, waiting, hoping to hear that call again.